The Ivy House

LAURA-ELISE BISHOP

This book is dedicated to all those who are brave enough to love, despite the risks.

Contents

Chapter One

August 2012, Brighton, Sussex, England

When Kate opened her eyes and sat up in bed, she was still wearing her denim dress from the night before and, for some reason, only one of her Converse high tops. Downing the glass of water on her bedside table, she staggered out of her bedroom, along the hall and into Hannah's bedroom.

Hannah stared open-mouthed at Kate. 'You don't look so good.'

'I don't feel so good.' Kate sat on the floor next to Hannah, who was methodically folding t-shirts into a suitcase. She ran her eyes over Hannah's shiny dark brown hair and her glowing olive skin. 'How do you do this? Why do I always look like I've been dug up after a night out, and you look like you've just done a cover shoot?'

'I hardly drink,' Hannah said. 'And you drink like it's your last night on Earth. How bad do you feel?'

'It's bad. The last cocktail was a mistake.' Kate sighed. 'I'm clearly not dealing with leaving you very well.'

'Saying goodbye to each other sucks, doesn't it?' Hannah said softly. 'We should be used to it by now.'

'I know,' Kate replied. 'As soon as I get used to having you around, it's time to say goodbye again.'

She and Hannah had been best friends since they were born. When Hannah and her family moved to London just before she and Kate started secondary school, Kate had been sure she would never see her again, but they'd stayed just as close. Now, three years later, they were leaving Brighton for good.

'True,' Hannah said. 'The last three years have gone so fast. How can we have graduated already? It feels like we only just got here.'

'I know,' Kate replied. 'I'm not ready for this.' Her stomach lurched as she thought about storming out of her house six months ago. Going back there was going to be painful.

'You can do this. Last night was the perfect goodbye.' Hannah paused, a smirk creeping over her face. 'Do you remember anything about last night?'

Kate stared at Hannah. 'I kissed Tom!' A hazy memory slowly became clearer. They had met their friends Tom and Sophia, in a beachfront bar, where they'd drank Prosecco, and watched the sunset. After a few cocktails, she'd started dancing on the bar, then she'd slipped and fallen into Tom's arms, and thanked him by kissing him like he'd saved her life.

The sound of Hannah's laugh brought her back into the room, and she glared at her. 'It's not funny!' she retorted. 'What the hell am I going to say to him?'

Hannah stopped laughing. 'Kate. He kissed you back. And drunk hook ups are pretty on brand for you, anyway, aren't they?'

'Yes, but I don't usually have to see them again,' Kate replied. 'This is Tom. He's my friend.'

Hannah stood up. 'Have a shower. I'll make you some toast. I can't help you with Tom, though.'

'I know. I can't face talking to him right now.' Kate stood up and walked down the hall to the bathroom, her cheeks burning with embarrassment.

When she got back to her room after a shower, she smoothed some curl cream through her mass of strawberry blonde curls. They were difficult enough to deal with when she was sober, but hungover, they were a nightmare. She tied them into a messy bun, then let out a huge sigh of relief as she saw her rings sitting on the shell-shaped dish on her bedside table.

The ruby cocktail ring was a gift from her eccentric grandmother, and the hammered gold band was the first ring she had ever made. They were irreplaceable. After she had put them on, she added her favourite necklaces, one with a gold star pendant, and the other a heart shaped rose quartz.

She slid on a plain white t-shirt, and skinny jeans, the only style that fit her petite frame. Her eyes lit up as she saw Hannah walking into the room with a mug of tea and a plate of toast. 'Thanks, love.'

'You're welcome.' Hannah handed Kate the mug and put the plate down on the bedside table. 'How do you feel?'

'Better. I think I'm ready to face today now.' Kate picked up a piece of toast and took a bite, her empty stomach growling.

'Do you need a hand?' Hannah asked, looking around Kate's room, which was a mess of half packed suitcases.

Kate shook her head, her mouth full of toast. 'No, thanks. It's not as bad as it looks.'

'Right.' Hannah cast her eyes across the clothes strewn across the floor. 'I'll let you get on then.'

After she'd eaten her toast, Kate steeled herself, cautiously picking up her phone. She wrinkled her nose as she scrolled through the photos she'd been tagged in, shaking her head at the one of her and Tom kissing. He'd sent her a message.

> Hey Barton, WHAT THE HELL?? I know it was our last night together but I didn't expect that! Please come back and do that again sometime X

Kate burst out laughing and typed a reply.

> I'm so sorry! I was very drunk. You know I love you, but you're my friend. Are we good? X

> Of course we are! If you change your mind you know where I am ;)

She put her phone down, then looked around her room. Why hadn't she packed last night like Hannah had? Right now, she hated past-Kate. She was a selfish, disorganised mess. Grabbing the nearest suitcase, she started stuffing clothes into it.

A couple of hours later, Hannah slid her arm around Kate as they stood together in the empty living room. 'I'm going to miss you.'

'I'll miss you too.' Kate rested her head on Hannah's shoulder. 'Just think, in a few months, you'll be an actual teacher, with an actual class. You'll be an awesome teacher, I know it.'

'Thanks, love,' Hannah said, her face softening. 'You're an awesome friend.'

'I'm always cheering you on,' Kate replied. 'Plus, you know way too much about me, I need to keep you on side.'

Hannah laughed. 'Same!' She let go of Kate and picked up her bag. 'We should go.'

Kate nodded, and followed her out to their cars, which were packed with the stuff that they'd collected over the last three years.

'Until next time,' she said to Hannah, giving her a hug, knowing it was easier for Hannah to say, than goodbye.

'Until next time,' Hannah replied, her eyes teary. 'Love you, dude.'

'Love you too,' Kate called as she walked to her car and climbed in.

Three hours later, the silver-grey spires of the cathedral welcomed her back to Canterbury. She drove through the city, before she joined the narrow road that led out to her home, tucked in a village on the outskirts of the city.

It wasn't long before she turned onto the long gravel drive and her house swung into view. In the bright sunshine it looked welcoming, but the gargoyles positioned on the corners of the pointed roof indicated that it had a darker side. It was a large, Gothic pile, with crumbling bricks and cracked roof tiles. It had been in her family for hundreds of years, and whilst its official name was Barton Hall, the thick ivy vines curling around the upper windows gave the house its nickname, the Ivy House.

She parked her car on the drive and walked along the path through the immaculate front garden, passing the ornately shaped hedges and colourful flower beds. As she walked up to the front door, she remembered storming out of it six months ago.Taking a deep breath, she unlocked the door, and pushed it open. The vast entrance hall was quiet, and empty.

'Mama, are you home?' There was no response, and her trainers squeaked across the tiled floors as she walked through the hall into the kitchen.

Spread out across the table were sheets of paper, covered in notes and proofreading symbols indicating that Amelie, Kate's mum, was in the middle of another manuscript. While Kate was creative, Amelie was academic, and that had been the root of their furious row six months ago.

As Kate stood in the kitchen, she could hear the dogs barking in the garden, so she pushed open the back door and walked outside, towards a figure in gloved hands, carefully trimming the plants in the flower beds. Bella and Tia, her beloved King Charles Cavalier spaniels, hurled themselves at Kate excitedly, and she bent down to stroke them.

'Hello, girls! You've missed me, huh?' She pulled herself to her feet, just as Amelie did the same. 'Hi Mama,' she said tentatively. 'I'm back.'

She felt both angry and sad at the same time and studied her mother's face, trying to work out how she was feeling.

Amelie peeled off your gloves, and smiled at her. 'How was your journey? I've been thinking about you. The traffic is always hideous in Brighton in the summer.'

Kate knew Amelie well enough to know that she was trying to make polite conversation rather than address the elephant in the room. With only twenty years between them, sometimes Amelie was more like an older sister than a mother. They were so alike, right down to their strawberry-blonde hair and green eyes. The fact that they hadn't hugged each other felt weird. They'd always been close, but right now there was an ocean between them.

'I didn't notice. I guessed I'm used to it.' Kate laughed nervously.

'I bet you are.' Amelie nodded at the flower bed. 'I'm finished here. Do you want a cup of tea? You look a little pale.'

'I'd love one,' Kate said, and followed Amelie and the dogs into the kitchen. 'I had a late night.'

Amelie filled the kettle and opened one of the cupboards on the wall, sorting through a collection of metal tins of tea bags, before choosing one. 'I think we'll go for something herbal and restorative today, darling. I bet you're hungover, and I'll admit I had a little bit too much wine last night. I was so nervous about you coming back. Christmas was such a disaster, wasn't it?'

'It was a total disaster,' Kate said. There was no other way to describe it.

Amelie brought the mugs over to the table, passing one to Kate and sitting down next to her. 'I need to apologise to you. When you told me that you wanted to stay in Brighton after you graduated, I just lost it.'

'I noticed.' Kate took a sip of her tea. 'I said I was thinking about it. Brighton has so many jewellery shops. It would have made sense to stay there.'

'So what made you change your mind?' Amelie asked.

'Everything and everyone I love is here,' Kate replied. She was going to hold onto her trump card until later on. 'I know you think I've wasted the last three years of my life, but I promise you, that's not the case.'

Amelie shook her head. 'I don't think that at all. When I saw your portfolio, and how hard you've worked, I was blown away.'

Kate smiled. 'Thank you, Mama, that means a lot. I'm going to prove to you that I can make a career out of this.'

'You never have to prove yourself to me,' Amelie said firmly. 'I believe in you. I see how determined you are. I know you're going to do amazing things, and I can't wait to see them.'

Kate felt a lump in her throat and she swallowed hard. 'I've waited so long to hear you say that, Mama.' She gulped down her tea, afraid she would burst into tears.

'I know.' Amelie took a sip of her tea. 'It's long overdue. This is your life, and these are your decisions to make, not mine.'

'I'm sorry for what I said to you,' Kate said. 'You didn't deserve it. You aren't selfish. You work so hard to keep this place afloat.'

'We were both the worst versions of ourselves,' Amelie replied. 'Can we put it behind us? I hate falling out with you.'

Kate nodded. 'Of course we can, I hate falling out with you too. It's been so weird not speaking to you. I'm so used to telling you everything.'

'I can tell there's so many things you're hiding. Are you sure we're OK? I've felt sick all day thinking about you coming back and hating me.' Amelie's eyes filled with tears.

'We're OK. You should be used to dramatic rows, you have enough of them with Marie.' Kate smiled, thinking about the heated exchanges that she'd seen over the years between her mum and her aunt. 'I feel bad about walking out on you though, that's what Dad did, and I still hate him for it.'

Amelie sighed. 'I'd hoped we could all live here happily, but it wasn't to be.'

'I'll always forgive you, but I'm not ready to forgive him yet,' Kate said.

'Maybe in time. Everything heals with time,' Amelie replied.

'Wise words, Mama.' Kate smiled. 'You sound like you're speaking from experience.'

'I have a *lot* of experience at holding grudges, and it just is not worth the time or energy. The important thing is that you and I can move on from this, *and* enjoy the summer together. How long are you staying for?' Amelie asked.

'I don't know,' Kate said. 'Maybe a few months?'

Amelie's eyes lit up. 'Stay as long as you like, darling. I've had the rewiring done, so you can make toast without the fear of getting electrocuted. My electrician is happy to come over whenever I need him.'

'I bet he is.' They both laughed, and Kate rolled her eyes. Amelie had a way of charming every man that she met.

'I've got so much to tell you, but I need to go and get my car unpacked first.' Kate stood up and rummaged in her bag for her keys.

'Do you want a hand?' Amelie asked.

Kate smirked at Amelie. 'We both know you're not cut out for physical labour unless it's gardening.'

'You might have a point there,' Amelie said, 'and I do need to get this manuscript finished. Perhaps we can catch up over dinner.'

'Sure. Sounds good.' Kate nodded to the messy table. 'Good luck with that.'

'I've got the easy job, darling.' Amelie raised an eyebrow. 'I saw your flat. I can only imagine how much stuff is in your car.'

Kate laughed as she walked down the hall, and out into the bright sunshine. She emptied her car, taking her suitcases up to her bedroom, and pushing open the sash windows. Flakes of white paint from the crumbling wooden frames scattered across the wooden floor. She unzipped the first suitcase and opened the door of her wardrobe, a relic from one of the guest rooms in the house and started hanging up her clothes. Her phone ringing interrupted her, and she darted across the room to answer it.

'Are you back?' It was Hannah. 'What's fallen off the house since last time? Have you spoken to your mum yet?'

'So many questions.' Kate laughed. 'I'm back, nothing has fallen off. In fact, Mama's had the house rewired. We apologised to each other, and she told me that she's proud of me. It was pretty intense.'

'Wow, that's a lot. You've only been home a couple of hours. Did you tell her about your job?' Hannah asked.

'Not yet. I can't wait to see the look on her face.' Kate smiled. 'How's your new flat? Have you met your housemates yet?'

'The new place is amazing,' Hannah said. 'You know how anxious I get about meeting new people, but I've met Matty and Scarlet, and they're great. Are you seeing Mia and Lucy tonight?'

'No. I'll see them tomorrow,' Kate replied. 'I'm going to spend tonight with Mama, so we can catch up.'

'Don't get pressured into living in that haunted house forever,' Hannah said.

Kate rolled her eyes. 'There are far worse places to live.'

'We'll have this conversation again in six months once winter's started and you're freezing,' Hannah quipped.

'I see you've already perfected your teacher voice,' Kate said, grinning.

Hannah groaned. 'Hilarious. Look after yourself. Say hi to Amelie for me.'

After they hung up, Kate put away the rest of her clothes, and once the suitcases were empty, she went back downstairs to the kitchen.

Amelie was chopping tomatoes and tossing them into a bowl. 'Hello, darling, you're just in time. Dinner's almost ready. Would you like a drink? There's a bottle of rosé in the fridge.'

'Sounds good to me.' Kate poured them both a glass of wine, and put the glasses on the table, noticing that the papers had gone, replaced with pale green votive candles. 'Can I do anything to help?'

'Can you put the salad on the table? I'm just dishing up the pasta now.' Amelie took a large pan off the stove and set it on a trivet on the counter. 'I might have made too much, as usual.'

Kate opened the cutlery drawer and found the salad servers, put them in the bowl and put it on the table.

Amelie followed with the dish of pasta and sat down. 'Help yourself. It's amatriciana, just like we had on holiday in Tuscany, remember?'

Kate inhaled the scent of tomatoes and pancetta and her eyes lit up as she recalled the tiny trattoria her mother had taken her and her brother to. The owners had plied them with homemade bread, pasta and tiramisu, and they'd spent all evening talking. 'I do! This smells delicious.' She helped herself to the pasta, then added some salad to her plate. 'Thank you, Mama. The table looks beautiful.'

'I might have made a special effort. I grew the salad leaves myself, so they're not perfect.' Amelie filled her own plate, then picked up her cutlery.

'That makes them even *more* perfect.' Kate bit her lip. 'The only things I can grow are cacti.'

'Well, they are still living things, aren't they?' Amelie smiled. 'Are you all unpacked now?'

'Sort of. Hannah rang and I got distracted,' Kate said. 'She loves her new place and she's going out with her housemates tonight.'

'Wonderful,' Amelie replied. 'I know how difficult she finds it to make new friends.'

'You would too, if you were bullied like she was,' Kate said through a mouthful of pasta. Hannah's high school experience had been traumatic and she didn't trust many people.

'I can't imagine it, darling. People can be so mean. I'm so glad you two are such good friends.' Amelie wiped her mouth with her napkin. 'Are you going out tonight?'

'No, I thought we could have a catch up tonight. I'm seeing Mia and Lucy tomorrow night, but it won't be a late one because...' Kate paused, her eyes lighting up. 'I start my new job on Monday. At Correll's.'

Amelie's cutlery clattered onto her plate. 'Really? Oh, that's wonderful! I'm so proud of you. When you started doing work experience there, I hoped it would lead to something, and it has.'

'Thank you, Mama. That means a lot,' Kate said, feeling a huge swell of pride. 'I'm covering Rebecca's maternity leave. It's only a short term contract, but it could lead to something else. Emmett is so well connected.'

This was Kate's trump card. She had got a job at Amelie's favourite jeweller, a tiny independent one in the city.

'You never know where these things might lead, Kate,' Amelie replied, picking up her cutlery. 'This could change your life.

'I hope it does. It's a dream come true, but I'm so nervous. Rebecca and I swapped a few emails before she left last week, and David will show me the ropes.' Kate wrinkled her nose. 'At least I hope he will.'

Amelie laughed. 'He's a man of very few words, but the ones he does say are either sarcastic, or clever.'

'I know,' Kate said. 'I was terrified of him the first time I met him, but he's actually really lovely.'

'He did a wonderful job with my ring.' Amelie twisted it around on her finger. 'He's very handsome as well, isn't he?' She raised her eyebrow.

'Oh, Mama,' Kate said, shaking her head. 'He's married and he's got kids.'

'I know. But he's still handsome.' Amelie shrugged. 'So's Emmett. You've really landed on your feet there.'

'Emmett is wonderful. I can't wait to start. I can pay you rent too.' Kate knew what response this would elicit, but she wanted to at least offer.

Amelie shook her head. 'I don't want your money. Save it for your own place.'

'Are you sure?' Kate frowned. 'Last time I was here, there was a massive list of things that needed mending. The window frames in my room are literally falling apart.'

'It's all in hand,' Amelie said firmly, standing up and taking their plates to the sink. 'Do you want another glass of wine?'

'Of course. We've got a lot to celebrate.' Kate walked over to the fridge and pulled the bottle of wine out. 'I know you won't say no to another glass.'

'Maybe a small one.' Amelie sat back down at the table. 'Then you can fill me in. I need all the gossip.'

Kate poured the wine, taking the glasses back to the table, and raising her glass. 'Santé, Mama.'

Amelie clinked her glass against Kate's. 'Santé, my darling.'

Chapter Two

August 2012, Canterbury, Kent, England

The following evening, Kate pulled open her front door to greet Mia. Blunt, methodical and tidy, Mia was the complete opposite of Kate, but they clicked on their first day of high school over a shared dislike of PE lessons and had been inseparable since then.

'Hello, love. How are you?' Mia put her arms around Kate and pulled her in for a hug, her long dark hair shining in the evening sun.

'I'm good. So much better now I've seen you.' Kate said as Mia came into the hall. 'How are you?'

'I'm fine,' Mia replied, 'I'm excited for tonight, it's been so long since we've all been together.'

'It has, and I can't wait, but I am *not* drinking tonight.' Kate grimaced. 'Mama and I bonded over a bottle of wine last night, and I was already hungover, so today I feel even worse.'

Mia shook her head. 'Have you called a truce?' She looked around. 'Is she here?'

'She's in the study working. We talked last night, and it's all good. I'll fill you in on the way.' Kate grabbed her keys. 'Do you want me to drive?'

'Absolutely not. Your driving is terrifying, and you've just told me how hungover you are.' Mia pulled her car keys out of her pocket. 'I'm a mother. I can't afford to take any risks. Come on, let's go.'

'How's Lilly?' Kate asked as she shut the front door behind them.

'Adorable as usual,' Mia said, unlocking her car. 'But she's so bossy. She gives me such a hard time.'

'I wonder who she gets that from?' Kate smirked at Mia. 'You are the bossiest person I know.'

Mia glanced at Kate as she started the engine. 'Kate, I am a nurse. I have to be firm. It's part of my job.'

'Very true. How's Pete?' Kate adored Mia's boyfriend, even though her relationship with him consisted of sarcastic comments and bickering.

'Wonderful as always,' Mia said as they drove into the city. 'I've barely seen him this week, as we keep working opposite shifts. He always makes us something to eat together before one of us goes to work though.'

Kate glanced at Mia. 'He's a sweetheart, and a pain in the ass. It's a good combination.'

'I'll tell him you said that,' Mia said as she pulled into the car park.

'Are we going to Lucy's first?' Kate asked Mia as they got out of the car. Lucy was Mia's friend first, but she and Kate had bonded quickly in high school and had been close ever since.

Mia shook her head. 'No, Lucy's going to meet us at Mimosa.'

'Ooh, we're going to Mimosa! Brilliant!' Kate exclaimed.

Mimosa was her favourite cocktail bar, and one of the busiest, liveliest bars in Canterbury. Kate knew she was guaranteed a good night there.

When they walked into the bar, Lucy threw her arms around Kate. 'You're back!'

Kate's voice was muffled as Lucy's grip on her tightened. 'I'm back for good this time!'

'I know!' Lucy's bright blue eyes lit up as she let go of Kate. 'We've missed you loads.'

'I've missed you guys too,' Kate said, feeling guilty. She hadn't seen them since Easter when they'd come to Brighton.

'It's so good to have you back, but I'm going to miss my trips to Brighton to see you,' Lucy said, tossing a blonde curl over her shoulder. The overenthusiastic hug that she had given Kate had disrupted her perfectly styled hair.

'We can still go,' Kate replied, although she'd decided that steering clear of Tom for a while was probably a good idea.

Despite her lingering hangover, Kate ordered a mojito, then squashed onto a sofa in the window with Lucy and Mia, telling them about her last night in Brighton.

'I literally landed right in Tom's arms and kissed him. Not a friendly kiss, more like a 'get a room' style kiss.' Kate snorted with laughter.

Mia looked horrified. 'What happens now? Do you want to kiss him again?'

'No, of course not,' Kate scoffed. 'He's not my type at all, and he's my friend.'

'Does he feel the same way?' Lucy asked.

'Kind of,' Kate paused, remembering his text. 'I think he was hoping for more, but I made it clear that it wasn't happening.'

Mia shook her head. 'You're a liability when you're drunk.'

'Mia, she's just enjoying herself,' Lucy said. 'Now you're back, we can reinstate Friday night drinks. I've been waiting for this.'

'Me too,' Kate replied. 'In Brighton it wasn't just Friday nights. Once a week is probably more sensible.'

'Is it weird being back at your mum's house?' Lucy asked. 'Have you guys made up?'

Kate nodded. 'It's weird knowing I'm not going away again, but I'm so happy to be back here, and even happier to have made up with Mama. I'll stay with her for a while until I find somewhere else.'

'It's going to be hard to live anywhere else, isn't it? I know it's a bit spooky, but it's like nothing else,' Lucy said, her eyes widening with awe.

'I know. I feel the same way.' Kate felt a familiar tug at her heart. 'Some grotty flat, which is all I'll be able to afford, is going to suck after living there.' She drained the rest of her cocktail and put her empty glass on the table in front of her.

'I wish I could help, but I've got a new housemate.' Lucy replied.

'Don't worry, I'm fine in my haunted house for now. Anyway, what's happening with the hot doctor?' Kate asked. 'I'm surprised you've not mentioned her already. I've had so many photos, so many messages, all about Rachel.'

'It's going well,' Lucy said. 'I was hoping she could come tonight, but she had to work. She's finishing medical school in May, so it's really full on for her right now.'

'I can't even imagine what it must be like.' Kate turned to Mia. 'Although I bet you can.'

'I didn't do medical school, that's a whole other level of hard.' Mia shuddered. 'My nursing degree was hard enough.' She put her empty glass on the table. 'Another round?'

'Yeah, but I'll have a virgin mojito this time.' Kate looked at her empty glass. 'This is my third night in a row drinking.'

'Probably wise. You might end up kissing one of us,' Lucy quipped.

After they finished their drinks, Kate and Mia walked Lucy back to her house, then Mia drove Kate home.

Fumbling in her handbag in the dark, Kate located her keys and let herself in, stepping into the dark hall. At this time of night, the house had its own language of creaks, bangs and bumps, which to her were comforting and familiar. For first time visitors to the house, they were terrifying.

Kate woke up the following morning with a clear head, thanks to the virgin mojito. After she'd showered and dressed, she went down into the kitchen, where her mum was sitting at the table, drinking a cup of tea.

Amelie took a look at Kate's face. 'You look much better than I expected you to.'

'I didn't drink that much.' Kate shrugged. 'I was still recovering from Friday night.'

'Brilliant.' Amelie shook her head. 'You can make the pancakes then.'

Kate opened the cupboards and pulled out a bag of flour, gathering eggs and milk and making a batter. Amelie disappeared out into the garden and returned with a bowl of strawberries and raspberries, still damp from the morning dew.

After they'd eaten, Amelie cleared her throat theatrically and put down her mug. 'I'm worried about your drinking. I see these stories on the news about girls getting attacked while they're drunk and I worry it's going to be you. Mia worries too.'

'I'm careful, Mama. I've always got my friends with me, and I keep an eye on my glass.' Kate said. Secretly, she was always relieved when she woke up safely in her own bed. 'And I don't want you and Mia gossiping about me behind my back.'

'We won't have to now. We can say it to your face.' Amelie paused. 'You're my daughter, my only daughter, and I worry about you. It's more dangerous for women to binge drink than men, and you seem to be doing this more since you split up with Will.'

Kate raised her eyebrow. 'You weren't worried about my drinking when I was with Will.'

'I was, but I knew he would protect you. He was sturdier than this house.' Amelie paused. 'I'm not saying you should have stayed with him. I just worry about you.'

Kate looked down at the table. It had been a year since she'd handed him back the engagement ring. A shiver went down her spine as she remembered the heartbroken look on his face as she told him that she couldn't give up her life in Brighton to move to Plymouth with him. The Navy had been his dream, not hers.

'It was the right decision.' Kate swallowed hard. 'I still feel bad about it though.'

'You made the right choice,' Amelie said gently. 'You don't need another man. You just need to cut down on the amount you drink.'

'I will.' Kate stifled a giggle. 'I kissed Tom while I was drunk the other night.'

'Whoops,' Amelie said, smirking. 'He's cute though, isn't he?'

'Don't start that,' Kate warned. 'I'm not looking for another relationship right now. I need to figure out what I want.'

'That's great.' Amelie stood up and picked up her gardening gloves from the worktop. 'Just try not to get trashed every weekend. I'll be in the greenhouse if you need me.'

Kate thought again about Will as she walked upstairs to her bedroom. She'd been sure that he'd loved her for who she was, but she had been wrong. Falling for someone who tried to change her was out of the question. It was the summer, and she was here to have fun.

As she opened her wardrobe she was hit by a wall of nerves, and her mind started racing. Would Emmett be a nightmare to work for?

Would she lose one of their rare diamonds and spend the rest of her life paying Emmett back? She shook her head. '*what if*' was a dangerous game to start playing. Flicking through her clothes, she settled on an all-black outfit for tomorrow. It would hide the dust. As she set aside the t-shirt and jeans, her phone buzzed with a message from Mia.

How are you feeling after last night? I've booked Forno for dinner tomorrow so we can celebrate your first day at work! X

Terrified/hungover/excited. Forno sounds good. Love pizza almost as much as I love you X

She put her phone into her pocket, and went downstairs into the living room, her favourite room in the house. It was just the right mixture of grand, old and cosy. The wooden floors felt cold under her bare feet, and she felt the breeze from the open bay window on her skin. She looked around the room, trying to figure out what had changed since she had been there last. Definitely not the comfy cream sofas, or the huge brick fireplace. The walls seemed a lighter colour, and the crystal chandelier above her head had been cleaned, the rays of sunlight making the tiny droplets sparkle. Sliding past the large coffee table, she sat on the sofa and rummaged in the basket of books next to it, picking one at random. She and Amelie had the same taste in books, so if Amelie liked it, Kate knew that she would too. Book in hand, she walked along the cool tiles of the corridor.

At the end of the corridor, opening out onto the garden, was the sunroom, a wooden framed conservatory. Kate pushed open the door, watching the sunlight stream across the huge glass panes onto the flagstone floor. She walked over to the bamboo shelving unit that housed her collection of cacti. She sank into the soft cushions of one of the sun loungers which faced the door, listening to the chirping of the birds as she read her book.

Amelie joined her a while later, gesturing to the book that she was reading. 'Good choice.'

'It's so good,' Kate said. 'I can't put it down.'

'I've got the sequel to it once you finish that one.' Amelie looked around the room. 'Isn't it stunning in here now? Don't ask how much the new glass cost.' She rolled her eyes.

'It's lush, Mama. The new sun loungers are so comfy too.' She looked over at the old wicker table and chairs on the other side of the room. 'I'm glad you kept that furniture, though. Nanna and Papa would be so proud of you for keeping this place alive.'

'I hope so. It's a constant battle, but I'm doing the best I can.' Amelie looked thoughtful. 'Have you let your dad know that you're home?'

'No. I'll wait until Rob's back.' Kate wished she was like her brother, who didn't hold grudges.

'He'll be back this afternoon, so you'll need to find another excuse.' Amelie looked at her watch. 'I came in see if you wanted to go to the nursery with me. I need some more shrubs, that patch near the gate is rather bare.'

'Sure.' Kate put her book down. 'Let's go.'

Kate spent a long time deliberating over the succulents at the nursery, eventually deciding on two small, spiky cacti. Putting the plants into her basket, she looked around for Amelie. As she walked out of the large polytunnel, she stopped, her eyes widening. In front of her stood Amelie, with James, who had been the Ivy House's gardener. Amelie had fallen in love with him after her divorce, but they'd split up, and he'd moved abroad. But here he was, chatting to Amelie, running a hand through his messy blond hair. When he kissed Amelie on the cheek and walked away, Kate shot over to her.

'Mama, you didn't tell me that James was back on the scene,' she said under her breath. 'How long has that been going on? Talk about dark horses.'

'It's not like that. I didn't know he was back.' Amelie lowered her voice as they walked to the till.

'He's still hot. How long is he back for? Is he single?' Kate put her plants onto the counter.

'Are you in heat?' Amelie hissed. 'You can't talk about him like that.'

'I see you didn't ask the important questions. Disappointing,' Kate whispered as she paid for her cacti.

Amelie put her lavender plants onto the counter. 'I've not seen him for three years; I was too shocked to do anything more than stare at him. We did swap phone numbers, though.'

As they drove back home, Kate looked at Amelie, seeing a flicker of vulnerability in her eyes. 'Are you alright, Mama?' she asked cautiously.

Amelie nodded. 'Sort of.' She took a deep breath. 'I can't stop thinking about him.'

'What actually happened between you two? Why did you break up?' Kate asked.

'I broke it off when it started getting serious,' Amelie said. 'He was younger than me, and I was divorced with two teenage children. I felt guilty about...well about all kinds of things, but he's back and the feelings are still there.'

'Why don't you go out for a drink with him?' Kate asked.

'One drink wouldn't be enough,' Amelie replied. 'I know it wouldn't. But I can't imagine never seeing him again.' She pulled onto the drive and a smile spread across her face. 'Oh look, Rob's here already.'

Kate smiled as she watched her brother getting out of his car. Her mother flew out of the car to greet him, almost knocking him off his feet. Giggling, Kate walked over to them.

'Hey, sis!' Rob let go of Amelie, and turned to Kate, lifting her off her feet and squeezing her tightly. 'Have you missed me?'

'No!' Kate shrieked and slapped him until he put her down .'It's been so peaceful here without you.

'Lies,' he replied. 'It's never peaceful

Chapter Three

Kate was full of nervous energy the following morning. She'd showered, dressed in her all-black outfit, and pulled her hair into a messy bun, tying a floral bandana around it. The studio had a whole bunch of dangerous tools, and equipment and having loose hair could be disastrous, so she'd removed most of her jewellery, apart from her tiny stud earrings. Before she left her room, she applied a coat of cerise lipstick and hurtled down the stairs.

Her nerves increased as she ate her breakfast. The toast seemed to be sharper than usual and she forced it down, her throat dry as a thousand what ifs about her new job whirled around her head. She listened to Amelie and Rob bickering with each other as she finished her tea. 'I'll see you guys later,' she said, taking her plate and cup to the sink.

Amelie stood up, giving Kate a hug. 'Have the best day, darling. Just be yourself. They will love you.'

'See, I was going to say don't be yourself,' Rob mumbled through a mouthful of toast.

Kate shook her head. 'Thanks. See you later.' She picked up her bag and keys. 'Have fun!'

Having arrived in the city earlier than expected, Kate sat in her car and took a few deep breaths, before climbing out of the car and walking along the King's Mile to Correll's. The street, full of independent boutiques, was so familiar, and it eased her nerves. The heady scent of Papillon, the handmade chocolate shop enveloped her, and she peered into the window of the boutiques she couldn't afford to shop in. Further along was the board games shop, and the crockery shop where Amelie bought her thick earthenware mugs. Before she reached Correll's, she walked past a café that she hadn't seen before. Through the large, orange framed windows, she could see scrubbed wooden tables, and a counter full of cakes. It looked inviting, but she carried on to Correll's, pausing outside.

The frames around the large windows matched the sage green door, and the letters on the sign above them were painted in a swirl of gold. Today it felt like she was seeing it for the first time, even though she'd been there many times before. In the bay window, bright spotlights illuminated the velvet pads of jewellery. As she pushed the door open, she thought to herself that, soon, her work would be sitting on them. Her boots clattered across the battered wooden floors.

'Hi Emmett!' she said excitedly, spotting him sitting behind the desk at the back of the shop. 'I had no idea what the traffic would be like, and I'll be honest, I'm usually late for everything so I wanted to make sure I was on time.'

Emmett laughed. 'Honesty. I like it. Seeing as you're here, we can get started on the paperwork. Have a seat.' He gestured to the chairs in front of the desk.

'I've been dreaming about this since I was little,' she said as she sat down. 'I still can't believe I'm officially here.' She studied Emmett, who was in his usual sharp suit, today a pale grey, which contrasted with his hazel eyes. His curly, light blond hair faded into grey at the temples.

'We're glad you're here.' Emmett pulled out some forms from a folder on his desk. 'We'll get the paperwork filled in, then you can get started.'

The front door opened and Kate looked up as Lisa, the sales assistant, came in. Her freckle covered face broke out into a smile. 'Morning Kate! How are you doing?'

'So excited I might burst, but also slightly terrified.' Kate wasn't usually this open, but the words flew out of her before she could stop them.

Lisa laughed. 'Don't be scared. We don't bite.' She glanced at Emmett who was filling out a form. 'I'll catch up with you once you're settled in.'

'Thank you,' Kate whispered and turned back to Emmett.

After the forms were filled in, Emmett led Kate to the spiral staircase at the back of the shop. 'These stairs are a nightmare, as you know.' He nodded at her lace-up black boots. 'Perfect choice of footwear.'

Kate nodded, remembering how she'd almost slipped on them last year. She followed him up the stairs and down the narrow corridor to the studio.

Pushing the door open, dramatically, Emmett turned to Kate. 'Here's your new home.'

'Kate! How are you?' David stood up and came over to greet her. 'We're looking forward to having you on board.'

His Scottish lilt contrasted with Emmett's plummy tones. Kate winced as he gripped her tiny hand in his shovel-sized one. He had fiery red hair which looped in tight curls around his hairline, the rest scooped into a bun on the top of his head. His beard and eyebrows were the same colour. He was broad too, with large, muscly shoulders barely contained by his t-shirt. A battered, dirty, leather apron covered most of the rest of his body.

Kate had to tilt her head back to even make eye contact with him. 'Thank you. I'm so excited to be here for real, not just for a few days.' She let go of his hand, and looked at the tools scattered across the benches, feeling the urge to get started immediately.

David laughed. 'I thought you'd be keen.' He turned to Emmett. 'I'll get Kate up to speed.'

'Wonderful.' Emmett looked at his watch. 'I'll catch up with you at lunchtime.' He smiled at David and Kate and left the room.

Kate walked over to the window. From this elevated position, she could see the shoppers and tourists on the street below. She flicked her eyes over to the wall, and the tools hanging neatly on the racks.

'Ready to get to work?' David asked, following her gaze.

'Sure.' Kate pulled out the stool from under the bench opposite David and sat down, running her hands across the smooth wood. 'Where do I start?'

'Let me fill you in,' he replied, opening a large notebook.

When the clock hit one, David put down his tools and took off his apron. 'Come on. Tools down. You need to scrub up.'

Kate put down her hammer. 'Wow, I was right. I knew you'd be bossy.' She clapped a hand over her mouth. 'I'm so sorry, I always blurt things out when I'm nervous.'

David chuckled. 'Me, bossy? No, I'm a pussycat. I live in a house full of women, Kate. I'm not the one doing the bossing around.' He stood up. 'Emmett always takes new employees out to lunch on their first day and you need to get a shift on because they won't hold the table for us.'

'Aren't you coming?' Kate asked.

David shook his head. 'No, Lisa and I will stay and man the shop. I'll come downstairs with you, though, as I'm going to nip out to the café for a sandwich.'

'Do you mean the café with the orange windows? That looks amazing,' Kate asked.

'Aye, that's the one, it's called Blossoms. I spend far more time and money than I should in there,' he said with a laugh. 'I'll take you there tomorrow if you like?'

'Sure, I'd love that,' she said, before washing her hands, which were covered in a thick, grey dust.

Once David had washed his hands, he slung a canvas satchel over one shoulder, and gestured to the narrow stairwell. 'After you.'

'Thanks,' Kate walked down the stairs and frowned at a large white box on the wall at the bottom of the staircase that she hadn't noticed before. She looked up at David. 'What's that?'

'Ah, that's the control panel for the security system,' David said. 'Emmett has a friend who sorts out all the cameras, door locks and safes and he showed us all how it works.'

'It sounds complicated.' Kate wrinkled her nose.

David shook his head. 'You'll get the hang of it. Emmett will show you how it works, I'm sure.'

She hadn't really thought too much about the level of security required to protect a shop that was full of precious metals and gems. It *had* to be very high tech. And anything to do with technology was not her forte.

As she walked onto the shop floor, Emmett shut his laptop and stood up. 'So, how was the first morning? You're still smiling. That's a good sign.'

'I loved it.' Kate grinned. 'David is a very good teacher.'

David shrugged. 'I do my best. You've definitely earnt a break.'

'Well come on then, let's go. Patricia is a stickler for timekeeping and she *will* give our table away.' Emmett opened the front door and gestured for Kate to follow him.

'This place is new,' Kate said as they walked into the Italian restaurant around the corner from Corrells. 'It smells heavenly in here.'

'It's been open for two months, and you cannot get a reservation for six weeks,' Emmett replied. 'Luckily, I know the owner.' He greeted the tall, dark haired woman behind the bar. 'Patricia, hello darling. This is Kate, my new jewellery designer.'

'Lovely to meet you. Your table is ready for you, come with me.' Patricia spoke with a strong Italian accent, and gave Kate a warm smile. She led them to a table in the window.

Kate sat down opposite Emmett and glanced around for a menu.

Emmett smiled. 'There is no menu at lunchtime. Patricia makes sharing platters of meats, cheeses and whatever produce she has.'

'Oh my goodness, that sounds incredible. I love the sound of that.' Kate smiled.

'Wonderful. What would you like to drink?' Patricia asked.

'Something soft, please' Kate replied. 'A lemonade would be great.' Getting drunk on her first lunch break was not a good idea.

'Same for me please, Patricia,' Emmett added.

'Two Sicilian lemonades, and a platter of my favourite things.' Patricia nodded. 'I'll be right back.'

In no time, a large wooden board filled with focaccia, grilled vegetables, salami, and cheese arrived on the table, and Kate's stomach rumbled appreciatively. Her earlier nerves dissipated as she and Emmett dived into it.

'Why did you decide to come back here, rather than staying in Brighton?' Emmett asked.

'It is, but there's something about Canterbury that I couldn't leave behind,' Kate said. 'I love the history, and I couldn't get the idea of working here out of my head. It's what I've been dreaming of for years. I still can't believe you took me on. I don't have that much experience.'

'The experience will come,' Emmett replied. 'You already have the passion, and in our line of work, that is the most important thing.'

'That's how I feel too, but it's intimidating trying to follow in David and Rebecca's footsteps,' she admitted.

'Rebecca is only six years older than you,' he said. 'She came to us from London, and she was a graduate too. And, like you she was full of creativity and ideas. I gave her the freedom to be creative, and she flourished. And so will you.'

She cocked her head to the side. Rebecca had always seemed much older than her, but the knowledge that she had started out just like she had was comforting. 'You think I could be as good as Rebecca?'

'Of course. I wouldn't have hired you otherwise,' he said. 'If your portfolio is just a snapshot of what you are capable of then I feel very fortunate indeed. Brighton's loss is our gain.'

'That's very kind of you to say.' She blushed, feeling self-conscious.

He smiled. 'It's true, but I don't want you to feel pressured or overwhelmed. I remember my first day at Corrells, almost forty years ago. I was a bag of nerves. David and I are here to support you, but we are also here to help you grow and learn.'

'I appreciate that.' She smiled back.

He took a sip of his drink. 'I see my employees as my family. In this business, it is the only way. Creativity, trust and kindness are the foundations of whar we do.'

She considered this. 'I like that ethos. And I'm honoured to be part of the family.'

'Then welcome aboard.' He lifted his glass and clinked it against hers.

The house was empty when Kate got home. She put on her favourite pale blue summer dress, and hastily chucked her make-up bag, and spare underwear into a bag before running down the stairs and throwing her bag into her car. Ten minutes later, she arrived outside Mia's cottage and rang her doorbell.

Mia opened the door and nodded approvingly at Kate's outfit. 'Looking cute as usual.'

'A compliment? That's unexpected.' Kate laughed as Mia left the house, shutting the door behind her.

'I can be nice sometimes.' Mia smirked. 'How did it go today? I was thinking of you.'

'It was brilliant. I feel energised *and* exhausted which is a good sign, I think,' Kate said, then climbed into her car, waiting for Mia to get in. 'How come you agreed to let me drive?'

'There is no way you'd be hungover today, so I figured it was a safe bet.' Mia smirked as she put her seat belt on.

'Very funny,' Kate said, as she started the car. 'I hardly did any driving while I was in Brighton. I'm out of practice.'

'Was that because you were drinking most of the time?' Mia asked.

'No, I was studying most of the time.' Kate retorted. 'What have you been telling my mum?' She entered the crawling city traffic and tapped her hands on the steering wheel.

Mia raised an eyebrow. 'The truth. You drink too much and then you end up making bad decisions.'

'I overdid it in Brighton,' Kate said, turning into the car park, 'but I'm going to cut down and I'm not drinking tonight. I need to be on the ball tomorrow.'

Mia nodded approvingly. 'See, this is better. The old Kate wouldn't have cared.'

'This is the new sensible Kate.' Kate parked the car, and climbed out, then followed Mia into the city.

The cobbled streets were busy, every restaurant and bar had tables outside full of people drinking, eating and talking, their voices floating through the warm breeze towards her. Although she had loved Brighton, Canterbury was home. In the summer it felt like you were in any cosmopolitan European city, with the diverse range of cuisine and inhabitants.

Forno was an upmarket pizza restaurant housed in a traditional flint building in the middle of the city centre. The low ceilings gave it a cosy feel, as did the candles flickering on the tables. Kate spotted Lucy immediately, and the auburn haired woman next to her, and flew over to greet them.

'Evening, babes. How are you?' Lucy asked. 'Kate, Mia, this is Rachel.'

'Lovely to meet you,' Rachel said, her hazel eyes sparkling. 'I've heard so much about you guys.' She turned to Kate. 'It was your first day at your job, right? How did it go?'

'Oh, I loved every minute of it,' Kate replied. 'It's my dream job, I feel so lucky to work there.'

'That's amazing,' Rachel said. 'And Mia, you're a nurse, is that right?'

As Mia and Rachel swapped hospital stories, Lucy and Kate opened their menus.

When the pizzas arrived, Kate smiled as she watched Lucy and Rachel immediately cut their pizzas in half, swapping one of the halves with each other.

'We can never decide,' Rachel said. 'So we just order both choices and share.'

'Such a good idea,' Kate replied. She turned to Mia. 'Why didn't we think of that?'

'I have to share my food with a toddler every day. This pizza is mine,' Mia quipped.

Everyone laughed, before Lucy cleared her throat dramatically. 'Who's in for City Sound Project next month?' she asked, beaming. 'You can thank me now, if you like.'

'No way!' Kate shrieked.

She loved City Sound Project, an annual city-wide takeover of bars, restaurants and clubs, and this year, she was even more excited as Bastille, one of her favourite bands, were playing.

'How did you get the tickets?' Mia asked.

Lucy shrugged. 'I only had to refresh the page every thirty seconds. No big deal.'

'She spent the entire evening on the edge of the sofa.' Rachel laughed.

'That might be true.' Lucy nudged Rachel playfully. 'My house-mate is away for the weekend then, so if you guys want to stay, I've got room.'

'Yes, please,' Kate and Mia said at the same time, then burst out laughing.

Lucy turned to Kate. 'It's only two weeks away. Do not forget and disappear off to Brighton for the weekend or something. We know what you're like.'

'I'm putting it in my phone now. I've not even got any plans to go to Brighton.' Kate's face flushed, as the memory of her kiss with Tom flooded back.

After they left the restaurant, Mia slid an arm around Kate's shoulders as they walked back to her car. 'Tonight was fun. Aren't they the cutest couple ever?'

'Absolutely.' Kate smiled. 'Did you see the way Lucy looked at Rachel? So cute.'

'Does it make you want the same thing for yourself?' Mia asked as they arrived at Kate's car.

'A relationship? No.' Kate wrinkled her nose. 'Someone who looks at me longingly, yes. I want someone I can share my bed with, but not my life.'

'You're hilarious.' Mia said, laughing. 'Be careful what you wish for.'

Kate drove them back to Mia's cottage, with the radio on full volume, and both of them singing at the top of their lungs.

'Do you want a cup of tea?' Mia asked as she took off her shoes, tucking them into the rack in her hallway.

'Of course.' Kate put her shoes next to Mia's and followed her into the kitchen.

'I got some Bourbon biscuits, just for you,' Mia said, handing Kate the biscuit jar and putting the kettle on.

'Thanks, love. Forget Lucy and Rachel, you and I are the cutest couple.' Kate took a biscuit from the jar and leant against the counter as she ate it, while Mia made their tea.

'I missed you.' Mia shrugged. 'I made you a toiletries bag as well. I figured that way you could just stay over whenever you feel like it.' She handed Kate a cup of tea.

'You are too good to me,' Kate said, feeling guilty. 'I didn't think about you and Lucy when I decided not to come back here. I was angry with Mama, not you, and I let that stop me coming back.'

'I knew that.' Mia took a biscuit out of the jar and dipped it in her tea before taking a bite. 'I'll be honest though, it did hurt.'

'I'm sorry, I never meant to hurt you.' Kate gave Mia a hug.

'You're forgiven,' Mia replied. 'Life's too short to hold grudges.'

Kate woke up in the morning before Mia, just as the sun was coming up. She crept out of the bed and showered, wrapping herself in one of the luxury bath towels from Mia's linen cupboard. She got dressed in her black t-shirt and jeans and went down into the pristine kitchen.

Mia was not only very organised, but obsessively tidy and definitely wouldn't let Kate in there unsupervised. But Mia was still asleep, so Kate decided to make a batch of pancakes, knowing that when her friend did wake up, she would be hungry.

She had just finished making the pancakes, when Mia walked in, rubbing her eyes.

'Are you alright, love?' Kate asked her. Mia's face was pale, and her eyes were red-rimmed.

'I'm fine. I just slept badly,' Mia said, looking at the kitchen worktop, which was covered in flour and eggshells. 'What happened in here?'

'I made pancakes.' She followed Mia's gaze. 'Don't worry, I'll clear up.'

Mia scoffed. 'No you won't. That's my favourite part.'

'I'm hoping that the pancakes will be your favourite part.' Ka took three plates out of the cupboard and handed one to Mia. 'You first.' She gestured to the pile of pancakes stacked onto a serving plate, then got some cutlery out of the drawer, putting it onto the cleanest part of the worktop.

'These look great.' Mia put a couple of pancakes onto her plate.

Kate handed her a knife and fork. 'Go and sit down, I'll bring the syrup. I made a fruit salad. I'll go and grab that too.'

'Wow,' Mia picked up her plate. 'Thank you, love.'

They had just started eating when they heard the front door open. 'Uh oh,' Mia said. 'I hope you made extra.'

Pete walked into the dining room wearing a crumpled set of blue scrubs and running a hand through his messy brown curls. His eyes lit up as he spotted the plate of pancakes on the table. 'It smells good in here.'

'You're right on time,' Mia said as he came over to kiss her on the cheek. 'How was your shift?'

'Long. Complicated,' he replied. 'How was last night?'

'It was great. That pizza place is amazing. We have to go there,' Mia said through a mouthful of pancake.

'It's a date.' Pete looked at Kate. 'I might have known you'd be here this morning.'

'You know what? I just can't tell if you're pleased to see me or not.' Kate smiled at him and gestured to the extra plate. 'I made extra pancakes for you, and I fetched you a plate.'

'Now you're talking,' Pete said, then frowned at her. 'Wait. Are you still drunk? Do you need a lift home, or can I have a shower?'

Kate rolled her eyes. 'I have to leave for work in half an hour, and no, I'm not drunk. Hangover taxi not required.'

'You're not drunk, and you've made breakfast? Who are you? This is not the Kate that I know.' He grinned at her.

'This is the new improved version.' Kate gave him a smug smile.

'We'll see.' He nodded to the door. 'I'll just go wash my hands.'

'Ignore him. He loves you just as much as I do,' Mia said to Kate.

'I'm the annoying sister he never wanted. When he met you, he didn't realise I came as part of the package. Poor guy,' Kate quipped.

'He knew what he was getting into.' Mia laughed. 'He takes his big brother role very seriously.'

'A little too seriously,' Kate whispered, afraid he would hear her. 'I can look after myself.'

The doorbell ringing interrupted them again.

'I bet that's Dawn with Lilly.' Mia stood up. 'I'll be right back. So much for our nice, peaceful breakfast.' She returned with a chattering Lilly in her arms. 'Lilly, Auntie Kate's home.'

Lilly eyed Kate suspiciously for a moment, then held out her arms to her. 'Auntie Tate!'

'Marvellous.' Mia deposited Lilly onto Kate's lap and sat back down. 'You can look after her for a minute.'

Kate smiled at Lilly. 'Hello, darling. Did you have a good time with Nanny?'

Lilly nodded and looked at Kate's plate hopefully. 'Pantates for me?'

'Of course, sweetie.' Kate cut one of her pancakes into small pieces for Lilly and helped herself to another one, nodding to Mia. 'Just as well I made a large batch, wasn't it?

Pete reappeared, walking over to Lilly, and planting a kiss on her forehead. 'Morning, sweetie.' He sat down next to Kate, smiling at her, as he picked up his plate, helping himself to the pancakes. 'Thanks for this, Kate. I appreciate it.'

'Oh you're welcome!' Kate glanced up. She was trying to cut her pancake one-handed with the side of her fork. 'I have no idea how you do this.' She turned to Mia. 'I'm sorry. I've dropped blueberries all over your floor.'

Mia waved a hand. 'It'll get cleared up. Don't worry about it. Shall I take Lilly?'

'No, I'm good.' Having mastered eating her breakfast one handed, while feeding Lilly with the other, Kate felt accomplished. She would ignore the maple syrup smear on her t-shirt. It was going to get dusty before long anyway.

Chapter Four

SEPTEMBER 2012, CANTERBURY, KENT, England

Kate left the studio on Friday evening, the breeze blowing her hair as she walked through the busy streets. The city's population had swelled with the students who had arrived to start their new term at university. She pushed her way through the crowded streets to the Marlowe, a tiny pub in the Buttermarket, where Lucy was waiting for her.

'Hello, love.' Lucy got up from her stool and gave Kate a hug. 'Can you believe it's the weekend already?'

'It kind of snuck up on me,' Kate said, untangling herself from Lucy and taking the bar stool next to hers. 'What are you drinking?'

'Rhubarb gin and tonic. Want one?' Lucy nodded to the barman, who came over to them, brushing his floppy blonde hair out of his eyes.

'Hey, Callum.' Kate gave him a high-five. 'The same as Luce, please.'

'Sure. I'll be right back.' Callum winked at Kate and pulled two empty glasses down from the rack.

Lucy gave Kate a knowing look. 'He doesn't see you for months at a time, but he always remembers you, doesn't he?'

'He remembers all of us because we went to school with him,' Kate said, laughing. 'I know what you're getting at, but he's not my type.'

'He was.' Lucy smirked. 'But that was just a one-off, right?'

'It was a kiss, that's all,' Kate hissed as he came over with her drink. 'Thank you, Callum. Good to see you.'

'Same.' Callum winked at her. 'Enjoy your night, ladies.'

'Kate, quick, that sofa's free!' Lucy pulled Kate away from the bar, and over to a sofa in the corner, where they sank into the soft cushions.

Kate took a sip of her drink, remembering her conversation with Mia. 'Luce, I'm sorry for being away for so long.'

'You don't need to apologise.' Lucy put her hand on Kate's. 'You needed to be away from here for a while and that's fine. We still saw each other.'

'So we're cool?' When Lucy nodded, Kate continued. 'Mia told me that she was hurt that I hadn't come back. I'm Auntie Kate to Lilly, and I'm Pete's unofficial younger sister. I have responsibilities with them that I don't have with you.'

'I guess you do. How did you leave it with Mia? Are you guys cool?' Lucy asked.

'We're good.' Kate smiled. 'We talked, and when I saw the toiletry bag she'd put together for me I figured I was forgiven.'

'Mia loves you, and she doesn't hold grudges. She says what's on her mind and she moves on. So that's what I think you need to do now,' Lucy suggested.

'Moving on is *not* my forte. Holding grudges and overthinking is more my kind of thing,' Kate confessed.

As she took a sip of her drink, her eyes met the piercing blue eyes of a tall, dark haired man on the other side of the room. His hair had a hint of grey running through it and his dark eyebrows gave him an intense expression which softened as he smiled at her. Her heart started racing as he held her gaze. She had never seen him before, and she couldn't take her eyes off him. One of the friends he was with caught his attention, and he looked away, but she didn't. She was strangely drawn to him.

'I'll get the next round in if you tell me which one of those guys you've got your eye on,' Lucy whispered, pulling a note out of her purse and handing it to Kate.

'Not very subtle, huh?' Kate laughed and lowered her voice. 'Linen shirt, dark hair, blue eyes I would happily drown in.'

Lucy leant towards Kate. 'Bit old for you?'

'*Experienced*,' Kate corrected her. 'He could teach me all kinds of things.' She ran her eyes over him again, drinking him in.

'I'm sure he could.' Lucy handed her empty glass to Kate. 'But you'd have to talk to him, and we both know that's not your strong suit. Want me to come and be your wing woman?'

'No. He might fall in love with you,' Kate hissed playfully.

'It wouldn't matter, would it? I'm not changing teams.' Lucy sniggered. 'Not even for him.'

'Fine.' Kate wiped her sweaty palms on her dress and walked up to the bar, smiling at Callum. 'Two more gin and tonics please, Callum.'

'Coming right up,' he replied with a wink.

As she waited for her drinks, she discreetly ran her eyes over the handsome stranger at the end of the bar, admiring the way that his tight black jeans clung to him. As her eyes flicked up to his face, she noticed who he was talking to, and quickly looked away. Callum returned with her drinks, and she paid him, quickly returning to Lucy.

'What happened?' Lucy asked with a puzzled face.

'He's over there with Pete's brother.' Kate sat down and handed Lucy her drink. 'So he's off limits.'

'Why? He might not be my type, but I'm not blind. He's stunning.' Lucy took a sip of her drink. 'What's the issue with him knowing Dan? Everyone knows everyone in this city.'

Kate clutched her glass tightly. 'That's half the problem. If I sleep with one of Pete's friends, I will never hear the end of it from him and Mia. They're so overprotective.'

Lucy nodded. 'I'm with you.' She snuck another look at the bar. 'You're really going to pass him up?'

'I am.' Kate turned away from the bar. 'Maybe if I don't look directly at him, I won't fall under his spell.'

After another drink, Kate and Lucy left the bar to walk back to Lucy's flat. Still thinking about the guy in the bar, Kate put her hand into her pocket, where her phone should have been, and her heart sank. 'Shit. I can't find my phone. I must have dropped it in the bar.

Lucy rolled her eyes. 'Why am I not surprised?' She turned around. 'Come on.'

Kate walked back to the bar with Lucy, and, leaving her outside, pushed the door open, making her way over to the sofa that they'd been sitting on. She spotted her phone peeking out from under it and knelt down to pick it up. As she got back up, she banged her head on the corner of the coffee table and squealed as the sharp pain shot through her.

'Are you alright?'

Kate whipped her head around, but she had a feeling she knew who would be there. The hot guy from the other side of the bar. Obviously. 'Hi.' Her breath caught in her throat. 'I'm fine.' *Smooth*, she thought to herself.

His brow furrowed with concern, and his deep blue eyes locked onto hers. 'Really? It sounded like you hit your head hard.'

'Uh, yes, but I'm alright.' She stood up and her pulse raced as she studied the deep blue of his eyes.

'Can I get you a drink? It might help with the headache,' he asked, his face softening.

'I'm sorry, I can't. My friend's waiting for me. I just came back here to get this.' She held up her phone.

'Sure,' he said. 'Maybe another time.'

'Maybe.' Kate couldn't stop the smile from creeping across her face. 'I'm Kate, by the way.'

He gave her a thousand watt smile, his blue eyes crinkling. 'Alex.' He pulled his phone out of his pocket and handed it to her. 'Can I get your phone number?'

'Sure.' Kate put her number into his phone and handed it back to him. 'I'll see you soon.'

She couldn't take her eyes off him. Everything about him was perfection, from his chiselled cheekbones to the way that his shirt clung to his muscular arms.

'I hope so.' Alex raised his eyebrow at her. 'Have a good night, Kate.'

Kate walked out of the bar, her body on fire. With a huge smile on her face, she walked up to Lucy. 'I spoke to him.' She slipped her arm through Lucy's as they turned back down the road.

'No!' Lucy shrieked. 'What happened?'

'I smashed my head on the table while picking up my phone. When I stood up, he was just... there,' Kate said. 'He offered to buy me a drink, and I gave him my number. His name's Alex.' She smirked at Lucy. 'If I was as ballsy as you I'd be going home with him.'

'Are you suggesting I'm a slut?' Lucy giggled. 'Kind of ironic to call a lesbian ballsy isn't it? Balls really aren't my thing. I thought he was a hard pass?'

'Well, up close he's even hotter, and anyway, he might never call me. I bet he gets all the girls.' Kate laughed.

'I'm impressed that you didn't launch yourself at him,' Lucy said. 'How's your head? We could take you to see Mia.'

'Mia works in the gynaecology ward. There's nothing wrong in that department.' Kate snorted. 'It's been shut for a while.'

Lucy grinned. 'I think Alex might be the one to open your doors again if you're willing.' She wiggled her eyebrows at Kate.

Kate had to stop walking; she was laughing so hard. She gripped onto Lucy. 'Oh, I'm willing.'

When they arrived back at Lucy's house, Kate pulled off her heels and coat, unable to wipe the smile off her face.

'I don't even need to ask what you're thinking about,' Lucy said.

'I'm still going to tell you,' Kare replied. 'I'd love to know what's hidden under that posh linen shirt.' A shiver of excitement ran through her.

Lucy snorted. 'Go get it, girl.'

Chapter Five

October 2012, Canterbury, Kent, England

When Kate got home from Lucy's the following afternoon, the house was strangely silent. 'Hello? Is anyone home?' she called. The dogs came to greet her and she patted them until they lost interest and went back to their beds. A muffled voice came from upstairs and Kate followed the sound to Rob's bedroom.

'Are you alright?' she asked, pausing by his bedroom door. Judging by the frown on his face and the hurried way that he was packing, she thought probably not.

'It's just hit me that I'm actually going. Did you feel like this too?' Rob looked up at her from the floor, where he was sitting, surrounded by piles of clothes.

'I couldn't wait to leave and I didn't want to go.' She sat down next to him.

'It took me a while to settle in, then before I knew it, it was time to come back here again. I know it's scary, but I know you're going to love it there.'

Rob nodded and carried on folding his clothes. 'Will you still be here when I come back at Christmas? I don't like the idea of Mama being on her own.'

Kate carefully put the folded t-shirts into a suitcase. 'I don't know, Rob. I don't like the idea of her being on her own either, but she told me that she wants us to live our own lives, so that's what we need to do.'

'You're right. It's hard, though.' He passed her a pile of neatly folded clothes.

She realised that he'd been used to being the man of the house, and that stepping away from that role, into the unknown, was difficult for him. 'You're doing the right thing.' Having filled the suitcase, she zipped it up. 'You can always call me if you need me, you know that.'

'Same,' he replied, frowning at her. 'You were out last night, weren't you? How come you're not hungover?'

'I've cut down on my drinking. Starting the morning without feeling like I've been dug up is pretty good.' She heard the front door bang. 'Ah, something wicked this way comes.'

He laughed. 'Go and say hello to her. Thanks for the pep talk. I needed it.'

'I've always got time for you,' she said as she left his room, heading for the stairs.

As she got to the bottom, she saw her mother, who was taking off her coat in the hall. 'Evening, mother dearest. How was your trip?' she asked.

'It was good.' Amelie took off her boots. 'I met my new client. Her work is breathtaking. Then Vyvienne and I had dinner together. We got in so late last night.' She shook her head.

'Quelle surprise.' Kate followed Amelie into the kitchen. 'You guys always don't know when to quit. How's my lovely godmother?' Hannah's mum, Vyvienne, was a carbon copy of Amelie. Strong, independent, and unpredictable.

'Busy as usual.' Amelie said as she filled the kettle. 'Not too busy to do my eyebrows, though. What do you think?'

'They look gorgeous, Mama.' Kate nodded approvingly. 'When I go up to London to see Hannah, I'll have to see if she can do mine.'

Vyvienne's salon in the heart of Chiswick had an extensive waiting list, but she always managed to squeeze Kate in.

'Hannah came over for breakfast.' Amelie continued as she made them both a cup of tea.

'How is she?' Kate replied, remembering their tearful goodbye. 'I've not spoken to her this week. I know she's finding the job a bit overwhelming.'

'She's alright. I think she's starting to settle in.' Amelie passed Kate a mug of tea. 'How was last night?'

'Good.' Kate didn't meet her mum's eyes. Alex and his deep blue eyes were her little secret. 'Mia was working, so it was just Lucy and me. We didn't drink much and went back to hers and fell asleep watching a film.'

'I'm pleased you're cutting down on your drinking, darling.' Amelie gave Kate's arm a squeeze and lowered her voice. 'How's Rob?'

Kate paused, torn between telling Amelie the truth, and protecting Rob. She made her decision. 'He'll be just fine. I'll make us some dinner, shall I?'

A couple of hours and a bottle of wine later, Amelie, Kate and Rob were full of pasta, and playing cards in the kitchen.

'Kate, she's cheating. I swear I saw a card fall off her lap,' Rob complained to his sister.

'Mama, can you at least try to play fair? Just for once? It's his last night here.' Kate rolled her eyes. Amelie had yet again had too much to drink.

'Don't remind me.' Amelie took a gulp of her wine and looked at Rob. 'I'm so excited for you. I know you'll come back with so many stories to tell.'

'Thanks, Mama. I won't be telling you any of them, though.' He pushed a hand through his messy hair. 'I'm gonna call it a night. I need to get going early tomorrow morning.' He smiled at Kate and Amelie. 'Thank you both for being you. I'll see you in the morning.'

'Sleep well, darling.' Amelie's voice cracked as she spoke, and she busied herself with collecting the cards and shuffling them.

Kate picked up the hand that Amelie had dealt for her. 'He's going to be alright. He's way smarter than I was at his age.'

'That's not true,' Amelie said. 'I remember thinking how grown up you were the night before you left for Brighton.'

'Really?' Kate asked as she lay her card.

'Yes.' Amelie narrowed her eyes as she looked at Kate's card, then laid one of her own. 'You've always known exactly what you want, and how to get it. I admire that.'

'Rob's the same,' Kate replied. 'We have you to thank for that. You showed us what was possible if we worked hard.'

'Darling, I've discovered that everything is possible if you try hard enough,' Amelie said mysteriously.

'Are you going to expand on that, Mama?' Kate put down another card.

'No.' Amelie picked up another card, not meeting Kate's gaze.

The following morning, Rob left in a flurry of tears and hugs. Without him, the house felt quieter and smaller somehow. Kate closed the front door and turned to face her mother who was sat on the bottom stair, sobbing.

'How can he have *gone?* He's still a baby, Kate,' she wailed.

'He's eighteen, Mama.' Kate sat down next to her and put her arm around her shoulders. 'He's definitely not a baby. He's six feet tall and wears size eleven shoes.'

'He is very tall.' Amelie wiped her eyes. 'I will always see him as my baby though. However old he gets. You too.'

'Mama, you were my age when you had me,' Kate pointed out.

'Yes and I was still a baby then!' Amelie stood up. 'I thought I knew everything and I knew *nothing.*'

'Why don't I make you a cup of tea?' Kate suggested. 'You haven't had any breakfast yet and it might make you feel better.'

Her mother was always far more dramatic when her blood sugar was low.

'Good idea.' Amelie sighed. 'I'm so glad you're here. The house feels so big and empty when I'm alone.'

After tea, and jam slathered toast, Amelie's face brightened as she regaled Kate with stories from her night out with Vyvienne.

'Mama, what did you mean last night when you said that everything was possible if you try hard enough?' Kate asked.

A smile crept over Amelie's face. 'I meant James. I took your advice and called him. We're meeting next week for a drink.'

'Really?' Kate's eyes lit up. 'Mama, that's amazing.'

Amelie wrinkled her nose. 'I've got that proper teenage crush thing going on. My stomach's full of butterflies.'

'It's the best, isn't it?' Kate's eyes widened. 'But also the worst.'

Every time she thought about Alex, she felt the same thing. She had no idea if he would call, but she had a feeling that last night wasn't the last time she'd see him. Was it wishful thinking? Maybe. Was he older than her and out of her league? Possibly, but it had been a long time since anyone had turned her head like him.

'You've summed it up pretty well.' Amelie looked intently at Kate. 'Why are you blushing? Are *you* crushing on someone too?'

'Me? Of course not,' Kate said, hoping her expression didn't betray her.

On Monday, the soft sunshine of the morning turned into a grey, dark storm by the afternoon, the crackles of thunder punctuating Kate's careful work on an engraved bangle. She looked out of the studio window nervously, thinking about her home. In stormy weather, the Ivy House always lost.

'You alright, mate?' David looked over at her, his thick brows furrowed.

Kate put down the bangle. 'Sort of. My brother left for university at the weekend and,' she gestured out of the window, 'the bad weather's starting now, which means we'll spend the next six months fighting to keep the house in one piece.'

'That's a lot.' David frowned. 'Your brother... He'll find his feet, eh? And the house, well, we're only ever guardians of these buildings. We're not in control of them.'

Kate was used to his bluntness. He'd told her about his tough upbringing on one of the most remote Scottish islands. 'You're right. Mama and I, we want to be able to pass the house down through the generations, like it always has been. It makes me feel sad to think we might not be able to do that.'

'Aye, it would be a shame, but it's more of a shame to spend your time worrying about the what ifs.' He rested his chin on his hand. 'The Kate that I first met wasn't thinking about the future. What's changed?'

'I don't know.' Her voice was soft as she looked down at the bangle. 'I think I'm just seeing things as they really are. It's good advice to focus on the present, though.'

'And at present it's absolutely pissing it down. Good thing we're staying late. It might stop by the time we leave, no?' He stood up. 'Another cup of tea? Might help you concentrate.'

'Sure, thank you.' When David left the room, Kate could feel the hairs on the back of her neck rise. She hated being in the studio on her own.

'What's up?' She was still in a daze when he returned, plonking the cups of tea on the table, before sliding on his apron. 'You've gone pale.'

'Thank you.' She picked up her mug, taking a sip. 'For some reason, I hate being here on my own in the dark. It just unsettles me.'

He sat down opposite her. 'It's an old building. I've heard things before when I've been up here on my own. Sometimes my tools seem to have moved from where I left them.'

Her jaw dropped. 'So I'm not imagining it?'

'Ah, no, I don't think so,' he said. 'Some people are just more in tune with it, aren't they?'

She nodded. 'I think I'm in tune with it. I have been for a while.'

'That house you live in, that's hundreds of years old. Don't you get spooked there sometimes?' he asked.

'There's one room that no one ever goes into,' she replied. 'It's got a strange atmosphere, but for the most part, I think if there are ghosts there, I think they're benevolent. I think they're there to protect us. I don't like being there on my own though, and I don't think I'd like being here on my own.'

'Good thing you aren't then, isn't it?' He smiled at her. 'I've only been here on my own once, and I didn't like it.'

At that moment, the wind rattled the window and she jumped, dropping her pliers. 'Oh my goodness! I'm never staying here alone! I nearly jumped off my stool and that's with you here!'

His soft chuckle made her heart rate slow and she picked up her pliers, giggling.

Chapter Six

October 2012, Canterbury, Kent, England

Kate applied a coat of deep red lipstick and turned to Mia. 'Is it too much?'

She was sat on Mia's bed, surrounded by make up and clothes as they both got ready for the City Sound Project.

'Nope,' Mia said. 'You look gorgeous.'

'Thanks,' Kate replied. 'So do you. Leon got it spot on, didn't he?'

'It fits like a glove.' Mia smoothed out the plum fabric of her skater dress. 'I have the most talented friends. He dresses me, and you make my jewellery. Although he was your friend first.'

'I'm more than happy to share him with you. We annoy the hell out of each other.' Kate put her make-up away. 'Are you ready?'

'Hold on.' Mia carefully put her mascara on. 'Now I'm ready.'

'Are you sure you don't want me to drive?' Kate asked. 'You're always the sober one.'

'I like being the sober mum,' Mia replied, 'besides hangovers are so much more painful when you have children. You can't get away with hiding in bed all day.'

'Good point.' Kate couldn't imagine sacrificing her sleep for anyone, but she and Mia were very different people. She followed Mia down the stairs and put her boots on.

Mia's eyes widened. 'Woah! They're new. Where did you get those boots?'

Kate twirled on the wooden floor. The gold studs covering her black ankle boots twinkled in the light. 'Brighton. I've not worn them out yet. They're so high. I'm not even going to think about those bloody cobbles right now.'

'Just as well you're not driving tonight,' Mia said with a smirk.

Kate rolled her eyes. 'Come on. For once I'm not late. Let's go.'

It was still raining when they pulled into the car park a few streets away from Lucy's house, tucked away in the back streets of the city. She counted to three, then climbed out of the car, and linked her arm through Mia's, prayed that she wouldn't slip over on the wet pavement.

A few minutes later, they arrived at Lucy's front door, and Kate hammered on it, ducking under the porch out of the rain.

Lucy opened the door. 'Give me a second, will you?'

'Have you *seen* this weather?' Kate grumbled and followed Mia into the house. 'Love your outfit.' She gave Lucy a hug, admiring her tight black dress. 'And the necklace I made you.'

'What else would I wear?' Lucy ran her fingers over the tiny silver heart pendant. 'Come on, we've got time for a quick drink before we go.'

In the kitchen, Rachel was getting some glasses out of the cupboard. 'Hey, guys. What do you want to drink?'

'Something soft for me. A Coke if you've got one,' Mia said. 'I'm on nights tomorrow.'

Lucy turned to Kate. 'I know you won't say no to a drink.'

'You know it. I'll have a Coke, and a teensy bit of rum, please,' Kate said to Rachel. 'I need to pace myself tonight. Last year I drank way too much before we even left the house.'

'Last year we had to ask that guy you'd hooked up with to carry you to the taxi because you couldn't stand up.' Lucy snorted with laughter.

Kate shook her head. 'That's why I'm pacing myself. I can't believe we're going to see Bastille. Tonight I'm not getting drunk and I'm not hooking up with anyone.'

'Cheers to that,' Rachel said, handing Kate her glass.

'Cheers,' Kate replied, clinking her glass against Rachel's.

After another round of drinks, they left the house. The rain had stopped, but the damp air penetrated the city. Crowds of people huddled outside every bar, drinking, talking, and laughing. The scent of grilled meats, herbs and spices wafted from the restaurants, along with the clinking sounds of cutlery and glass.

Kate heaved open the heavy wooden door of the Penny Theatre, which had been a theatre since the 1700's and was now a pub. It was packed, the low ceilings making it feel smaller. She shouted over the noise of what seemed like a hundred people talking all at once to the barman and slid him a note in return for their drinks. She passed Lucy and Rachel their beers, then handed Mia a Coke, before picking up her own rum and Coke. She followed them away from the bar, into the corridor, and the large room opposite which had once been a theatre. A heavy duty lighting rig was set into the beams on the ceiling, and a stage, cloaked by a black curtain, took up one side of the room. The lights beamed down onto the stage, and the curtains swept back, revealing a band that Kate hadn't seen before.

'Who are these guys?' Kate asked Mia. 'I thought we were seeing Bastille?'

'They're on later.' Lucy looked down at the ticket in her hand. 'This is Future Proof.' She shrugged. 'Never heard of them.'

'I have,' Mia said. 'I think you're going to like them. Dan's friends with the lead singer.'

'Hello, you gorgeous people,' the lead singer yelled into the audience. 'We're Future Proof!'

As they started playing, a shiver spread up Kate's spine. It was a sound like she'd never heard before, guitars with a kind of 80's synth background. The lead singer winked, his long dark hair falling over his eye as he sang. Kate slid her arm around Mia, sipping from her beer as she moved to the music.

Their hour-long slot wasn't long enough, and the crowd cheered loudly until the lead singer walked back to the front of the stage.

'Thank you! We love you all!' He blew kisses into the crowd. 'But this is definitely our last song. It's called Never Hurt You Again.'

It was a slow, sexy love song, which made the most of the lead singer's incredible voice that sank so low it vibrated through the room, then soared up high again. As they reached the chorus, Kate spotted a figure, dressed in black at the side of the stage. His piercing blue eyes met hers, but as the band played the last note, he disappeared.

'Luce!' Kate grabbed Lucy, shouting in her ear. 'I saw him! On the stage. That guy from the bar. Alex! It was him!'

'No way! Did he see you?' Lucy asked.

'Yes! He must know the band.' Kate gestured to the door. 'I'll be right back.'

'You can't leave! Bastille will be on soon,' Lucy hissed.

'I need to see him again.' Kate walked away from the stage and down the corridor, the spotlights in the ceiling guiding her way. A door flew open, almost hitting her in the face, and a familiar dark-haired man came out from behind it.

Kate's heart rate sped up. 'Alex!'

'I thought it was you,' Alex said, his voice gravelly, his eyes burning into hers.

She took a moment to study him, from the flecks of grey running through his dark hair, to the long eyelashes that framed his glacial blue eyes. He was wearing a black leather biker jacket with a tight black t-shirt underneath. A silver chain was just visible around his neck. As he moved closer, her eyes focused on his lips.

Alex's eyes locked onto hers. 'I'm sorry I haven't called you. Things have been kind of chaotic. I'd offer to buy you a drink, but you're with your friends, right?'

'Again. Yes. Sorry.' She moved towards him in the narrow corridor, his lips now temptingly close to hers.

'I think you were shorter the last time I saw you.' He looked down at her boots. 'You definitely weren't wearing those.'

'I wasn't.' She slid one of her feet towards him, the gold studs on her boots catching in the light above their heads.

'I like them.' A smirk pulled at the corner of his lips. 'They're hot.'

'I like you. You're hot.' She ignored the voice in her head telling her to shut up.

'Really?' He raised his eyebrow. He was close now, so close that the woodsy scent of his aftershave enveloped her.

She nodded, trying to control the rush of lust pulsing through her body. His hand rested on her waist as he kissed her cheek, and she turned her head, her lips meeting his. He deepened the kiss and she pressed him against the wall.

As he pulled away from her, he brushed her hair away from her face, rendering her unable to focus on anything else but him. 'I guess I should let you get back to your friends,' he whispered.

'I guess so.' Before she could say anything else, he had disappeared.

She walked, dazed, back into the bar. Every fibre of her body wanted more of him, and as she breathed in, his scent flooded her senses.

'Where did you go?' Lucy's brow was furrowed with concern.

'Uh, I went to the ladies.' Kate flicked her eyes at Mia, indicating that she didn't want to say anything else in front of her.

Lucy gave her a knowing smile and turned back to the stage. 'Looks like we're just in time.'

Bastille's set was phenomenal, as Kate knew it would be. Yet she kept peeking to the side of the stage, where she could see Alex and his friends, his eyes moving between the band and her. He didn't smile much, she noticed. His face stayed serious, while his friends laughed and joked with each other.

❧ ❧

When Bastille finished their set, Lucy slid her arm into Kate's, and led her into the bathroom. 'Alright, spill it. Where did you actually go?'

'Remember how I said that I wasn't getting drunk and hooking up with anyone tonight?' Kate replied as she looked at her matte lip paint in the mirror. It hadn't budged, despite the heavy action it had seen. 'I only stuck to one of those promises. Alex and I had the most intense kiss I've ever had in my life.'

Lucy's eyes lit up. 'Yes! I love this for you. Then what happened?'

'Oh he vanished. This man likes disappearing.' Kate studied her flushed cheeks in the mirror. 'We have to somehow get out of here without Alex realising I know Mia, or Mia realising that I know Alex.'

As she walked into the bar, Kate grabbed Lucy, holding her back. 'Shit! He's there, look, with Mia.'

Lucy followed Kate's gaze across the bar, where Mia and Rachel were talking to Pete's brother, Dan, and Alex. 'Things just got complicated.' She sniggered. 'He *is* one of Pete's friends. Just what you didn't want.'

Kate was in the middle of trying to come up with a plan, when Alex gave Dan a hug, kissed Mia on the cheek, and disappeared out of the front door of the pub. 'Phew,' she said to Lucy. 'Looks like he's gone. Don't say anything to Mia, alright?'

'I got you,' Lucy replied as they walked over to Mia.

'Hey!' Dan gave Kate a hug. 'Long time, no see. Did you enjoy the gig?'

'I did'I loved Future Proof,' Kate said. 'Mia said you know them.'

'Kind of,' Dan replied. 'My friend Alex is friends with their lead singer. He's just moved back here, too. His brother Ben was Pete's friend in high school. It's weird, this city, isn't it? Everyone knows everyone.'

'They do,' Kate replied. *And that's half the problem, she thought to herself.*

Chapter Seven

Alex, and that kiss didn't leave Kate's mind for the entire week after the Bastille. The intensity of her feelings for him, unlike anything she had ever experienced before, had thrown her completely.

As she sat working in the studio, on Friday evening, the bright lamp next to her illuminating the delicate gold band she was working on, she remembered his strong grip, the way that he'd looked at her, almost right into her soul. A loud, male voice downstairs pulled her out of her thoughts and she clattered down the spiral staircase into the shop.

'Hey Leon,' she said, smiling at him. 'I thought I heard your voice. I just need to clear up, I'll be with you in a minute.'

'Sure,' he replied, his brown eyes meeting hers.

He'd been her friend since her A-Level art classes, and as usual, he was dressed head to toe in his own clothes, from the wool coat he'd made himself, to his embroidered sneakers. He sat down on one of the chairs, unbuttoning his coat.

Kate paused by the staircase, getting the feeling that she'd just interrupted something as she saw Lisa's bright red face, and the way that Leon's gaze settled on her. Biting her lip, she walked back up the stairs. Her tools were scattered messily across her bench and she picked them up, quickly slotting them onto the rack.

'You alright, mate?' David asked her. 'You've got a funny look on your face.'

'I lost track of time and Leon's here already,' Kate replied. 'He's downstairs, probably flirting with Lisa.'

'Oh aye, he's got a crush on her, has he?' David raised an eyebrow. 'Keep me posted. I need to know how this plays out.'

'You're such a gossip.' Kate laughed. 'He thinks he's trying to be subtle about it, but he's about as subtle as a sledgehammer.' She slipped off her apron and picked up her bag. 'I'll see you later.'

In the restaurant, Kate and Leon devoured burgers, chips, and fruity cocktails as they caught up. Kate toyed with the idea of telling him about Alex. He was detached enough from Mia, so he was probably a safe bet.

'Are you just going to spit it out already?' Leon asked, raising an eyebrow. 'What or who are you hiding from me?'

'Am I that obvious?' Kate laughed.

'Uh, yeah.' Leon rolled his eyes. 'You might as well have a neon sign over your head that says, "I'm hiding something and it's really juicy." So, spill it.'

Kate took a deep breath. 'I keep bumping into this guy and he is...' she kissed her fingers. 'Aside from his name, and the fact that he knows Pete, I don't know anything else about him. But he's so hot, I nearly collapsed when he kissed me.'

'Noice!' Leon nodded approvingly. 'Lemme guess, it was a drunken snog and you'll never see him again.'

Kate raised an eyebrow. 'I wasn't that drunk and I want to see him again. Like really want to see him. Ideally... naked.' She raised her eyebrow.

'I enjoy this side of you. Thirsty Kate. I love it.' Leon picked up his burger with both hands and took a huge bite.

'He's something else.' A smirk crept across her face. 'Only snag is that he's got my phone number and I haven't got his.'

'What do you want to happen?' He looked quizzically at her. 'I thought you didn't want a relationship right now.'

'I don't. But I want him.' She took a sip of her drink. 'I love the way he just appears, knocks me off my feet, and disappears into the night again, like some kind of superhero.'

He looked pointedly at her drink. 'No more cocktails for you.'

'I've only had one!' she squealed. 'I'm drunk on lust.'

He laughed. 'Good for you!'

'Anyway.' She pushed her empty plate away and raised an eyebrow. 'Did you hear back from the college?'

'I missed out on a place this year, but they loved my portfolio and told me to apply for a place in January.' His eyes lit up. 'So now, I can stop worrying about whether I can afford it and start worrying about whether I'm good enough to be a student at,' he lowered his voice, 'the London College of Fashion.'

She gestured to the denim skater dress she was wearing. 'You've made half of my wardrobe, and you've worked your arse off in that skate shop to save the money for this. You're definitely good enough.'

'Thanks, mate.' He smiled and carried on eating his chips. 'It does mean moving to London,' he said with a thoughtful look. 'I'm going to miss you, but I promise I'll put you on the VIP list for my show at Fashion Week.'

'I'll hold you to that. Does this mean you'll get a new muse?' She looked at him sadly.

'Probably,' he replied. 'I'll still make your wedding dress, though.' He finished his burger and wiped his hands on the paper napkin.

She snorted. 'That is a long way off, my friend. What about you? You've not been on a date in months.'

'Awell, I've got one lined up. I'll tell you more another time.' He tapped his nose.

'Is it who I think it is?' she asked.

'I'm saying nothing.' He picked up the cocktail menu. 'Another drink? I'll regret it tomorrow, but why not?'

'No.' She shook her head. 'I'll have a lime soda please.'

'Not a bad idea. I'll join you. I've had too many hangovers already this month.' He stood up and walked over to the bar, returning with two sodas, handing one to Kate.

'Cheers, friend. This time in a few years, you won't be Leon Bergen, skate shop sales assistant; you'll be Leon Bergen, fashion designer.' She clinked her glass against his.

'I won't forget my humble beginnings, I promise,' he said.

She rolled her eyes. 'There's nothing humble about your beginnings. Your parents are both lawyers, and they're minted.'

In the studio the following morning, Kate had her head down, working on an engagement ring. It was an unusual custom order, with pink sapphires set into a white gold band. David wasn't in, and the studio was quiet without his booming Scottish voice. When Emmett shot into the studio, his face white, he startled her.

'Kate, darling, I've got to go. My father's had a heart attack.' He clutched his car keys tightly in his hand.

Kate's tools clattered to the bench. 'Oh, no. Emmett, I'm so sorry. Yes, just go. Let me know what's going on when you can.'

'I will. Lisa's downstairs. I'll let her know on my way out. You two will need to lock up tonight. Can you manage that?' He looked concerned.

'We'll be fine. Just go.' Kate followed him down the stairs.

'I'll be in touch, ladies.' Emmett nodded to Kate and Lisa as he left.

'What a shock, right?' Kate shook her head. 'I hope Emmett's dad is OK.'

'I know.' Lisa nodded furiously. 'The idea of something happening to my parents is my worst nightmare.'

'Same,' Kate said, wrinkling her nose. 'You alright down here?' She looked out of the window at the heavy grey clouds. 'This ring is taking a lot longer than I thought it would, and if the weather's like this, I don't want to be staying late.'

As the afternoon went on, the skies got darker. Flashes of lightning illuminated the tiny studio, casting shadows across the wall, and rain lashed the thin windowpanes. Cracks of thunder overhead made Kate jump, and she dropped her chisel onto the floor more than once. She focused on her breathing, trying to stay calm. The violent weather outside and the creaking wooden floors of the studio gave her the feeling of being at sea, trapped in a galleon in the middle of a storm. Shivers ran down her spine as the last vestiges of daylight disappeared, and the city was plunged into darkness.

She pulled her phone out of her bag and unlocked it, scrolling through her playlists, searching for something noisy and distracting. Finding the right one, she clicked onto it. The soaring strings of Nero's *Promises* came blaring out of her phone. It was a remix that she'd stumbled across, and one she'd played many times already. It echoed around the bare brick walls of the studio, masking the noises of the storm, allowing her to focus on the engagement ring.

Lisa came up the stairs and poked her head into the studio. 'I need to go, Kate. Are you ready?'

Kate gestured to the ring, clasped carefully in her fingers. 'I can't leave this right now. I need to stay a bit longer.'

'Do you need me to stay too?' Lisa asked, frowning.

'Don't you have a date tonight?' Kate asked and stopped at that. She'd already decided not to interrogate Lisa or Leon. 'I have no idea how long I'll be.'

Lisa blushed. 'I do, yes, but if you need me to stay, I can cancel.'

Kate shook her head. 'No, I'll be fine. I know the alarm code. I've seen David do it enough times. Have you got the keys? I'll come downstairs with you and lock myself in.'

Lisa pulled a ring of keys out of her bag and handed them to Kate. 'Good idea.'

They both walked carefully down the stairs and into the front of the shop, where Lisa gave Kate a serious look. 'I don't feel happy about leaving you here on your own.'

'I'll be fine. I'll only be an hour or two.' Kate opened the door and poked her head out, before retreating back in and shutting it quickly. 'Go enjoy this lovely weather.' She grinned as the rain lashed the panes of glass. 'And fill me in on Monday.'

'Sure,' Lisa said, blushing as she pulled on her coat and put her hood up. 'Can you just text me when you leave tonight so I know you're safe?'

'Of course. Now go, so I can get back to work. I'll text you as soon as I'm out of the door, I promise.' Kate locked the door behind Lisa and went back into the studio.

She turning the volume up on her phone and sang at the top of her voice to get through the next hour, wishing that David was sitting opposite her. Storms didn't bother him. Once she finished, she carefully put the ring and her tools away. When the studio was tidy, she scrubbed her hands and unlocked her phone, turning off the music. Now, she could hear every creak, every rattle of the thin panes of glass in the windows. She felt a draught creeping in from the window, and she shivered. Lightning illuminated the studio once again, and her heart rate sped up. With her trembling fingers fighting with the laces, she took off her clumpy work boots and slipped on the stud-encrusted stiletto ankle boots from under her desk. The clatter of her heels on the wooden floor reverberated around the empty room, as she walked over to the door. When she switched off the ceiling lights, the moonlight shone through the window, casting strange shadows across the floor of the studio.

As she walked down the corridor, the dim light from the shop guided her way to the staircase. At the top of the stairs, a crack of thunder made her jump and her heel slipped on the uneven floorboard. She frantically clutched at the bannister as she slipped, but missed, her gasp echoing around the darkened stairwell.

Chapter Eight

OCTOBER 2012, CANTERBURY, KENT, England

When she opened her eyes, Kate wasn't immediately sure where she was. As her eyes adjusted to the darkness above her, she could make out the staircase. Her legs were above her and her head was hanging off the bottom step. Something warm was running down her forehead and into her left eye. Shaking, she tentatively put her hand up to her face, gasping as her fingers came back bright red. She pulled the sleeve of her jumper over her hand, and put it to her forehead, before sliding onto the floor. When she tried to pull herself to her feet, a stab of pain shot through her right knee and she collapsed. Tears sprung from her eyes, and she wiped her other sleeve across her face. Spurred on by pain and fear, she forced a deep breath and used the post at the bottom of the stairs to pull herself to standing, putting her weight onto her left side.

She glanced at the alarm panel. If she could get the alarm set, she could hobble to the taxi rank and get herself to the hospital. With trembling fingers, she punched the numbers in. An error message came up. Her second attempt at entering the alarm code brought up another error. She took another deep breath, knowing that she only had one more attempt before she was locked out. As she carefully put the code in, the siren rang out across the deserted shop floor.

'Shit,' she shouted, pulling her phone out of her pocket, calling David, Lisa, and Emmett, but there was no answer. She called the alarm company, whose number was on the alarm panel, her heart still pounding. 'Hi, my name's Kate. I work at Correll's. The alarm system won't set.'

A male voice responded calmly. 'Can you please give me your passcode and your full name?'

'Sure, it's 0610 and it's Kate Barton,' she said.

'Thank you,' he replied. 'I can see that you've been locked out of your system. Please hold while I speak to an engineer.'

'Sure.' Kate focused on her breathing, which was still ragged.

'Hello, is that Kate Barton?'

It was a different voice from the previous one and it sounded like he was outside. She could hear sirens in the background.

'Yes,' Kate replied. 'Can you help me reset the alarm?'

'I'm on my way. I'll be with you in five minutes,'

'Thank you.' She hung up and lowered herself back onto the bottom step of the staircase, putting her hands over her ears to block the sound of the siren out. Remembering the tissues in her bag, she grabbed the packet and took one out, pressing it onto her forehead. The pain in her knee intensified as she pulled off her boots, throwing them onto the floor. Under her skirt, she had thick black tights on and she slid them off, gasping as she saw her right knee, which was now a red, swollen mess.

A face appeared at the door, startling her, and she dragged herself to her feet, then hobbled over to it. Through the glass pane, she could make out a male face. He held an ID badge up to the door, which she recognised from the alarm panel, and she fumbled with the keys in the lock, swinging the door open.

'Alex?' He looked just as confused as she felt. He stepped in, carrying a bag of tools.

'Kate?' His eyebrows shot up. Grabbing a chair, he guided her into it. 'Wait right there, let me sort the alarm out.' He ran straight past her to the panel on the alarm system, silencing the siren. Then, he disappeared up the stairs only to return a moment later.

He crouched down next to Kate. 'What happened to you?' His brow crumpled as his eyes met hers.

'I slipped at the top of the stairs.' She grabbed his hand, needing to feel something solid to prove to herself that she wasn't dreaming. 'Then the alarm wouldn't set.' Her head was pounding and every part of her body hurt.

'It's all sorted. The window in Emmett's office was open. That's why the alarm wouldn't set.' His eyes trailed from the cut on her forehead, down to her leg. 'I need to get you to the hospital.'

'No, I can't ask you to do that. I'll get a taxi.' Her phone started ringing, and she picked it up. 'Emmett, hi. Don't worry, everything's fine.'

'I got a notification on my phone that the alarm was going off. What's going on?' Emmett asked.

'I um...' Kate closed her eyes, a combination of the pain and the awkwardness of explaining to Emmett that she'd been alone in the shop sweeping through her.

Before she could carry on, Alex had taken the phone out of her hand. 'Emmett, it's Alex. Everything's fine. Kate locked herself out of the alarm system, but I've reset it. She's fallen down the stairs, but don't worry, I'll take her to the hospital now.'

Kate pulled herself to her feet and pressed against Alex so that she could hear Emmett's response. 'Thank you, Alex.' Emmett's voice sounded thin through the phone. 'Are you sure you'll be alright to take her? I know hospitals are...'

Alex cut him off. 'She needs help. The shop's secure and Kate's my next priority.' He ran a hand through his hair.

She noticed his brow furrow even further. What had Emmett meant? Why were hospitals an issue for him?

He hung up and handed the phone back to Kate. 'I'm sorry I intervened. I'm worried about you.'

'I wasn't going to tell him about the fall,' she said, letting out a long exhale. 'He's with his dad who's had a heart attack.'

He shook his head. 'I'm so sorry, I didn't know. I was just trying to help. Emmett's a friend of mine. I've done all the door locks, cameras and security system in here, so I know this shop like the back of my hand. It's lucky I was on call tonight.'

'You're telling me,' she replied. 'I have no idea what I would have done if you hadn't come.'

'Let's not think about that.' His eyes flicked from the cut on her forehead to her knee again. 'You couldn't have kept this to yourself anyway. You're hurt and you need help. Can you walk?'

She shook her head. 'Not really. It hurts if I put any weight on it.'

He sat her back down in the chair and looked at the boots sat by the staircase. 'You can't wear those, either.'

'My work boots are under my desk,' she said.

'I'll get them.'

He moved carefully past her and went upstairs, returning with her dusty boots. He knelt down and gently slid them on. His fingers brushed softly against her bare legs and she looked down at him, feeling a rush of lust and nerves, fear and excitement, just like she'd felt at the Penny Theatre when he'd kissed her. *Woah*, she thought to herself, even battered and bruised, I want him. She smiled at the precise and gentle way he tied the laces of her boots.

'I'll go and get my car and then I'll take you to the hospital,' he said, standing.

'What was Emmett saying to you about hospitals?' She looked up at him and saw his face cloud over.

'It's nothing.' He shook his head. 'Bad memories.' He pulled his car keys out of his pocket and picked up his bag of tools.

She nodded, feeling conflicted about letting him take her to the hospital. Hospitals were clearly an issue for him, and, while he had links to various areas of her life, he was still a stranger.

Studying her worried face, he knelt down in front of her, clasping her hands in his. 'You can trust me. You weren't afraid to kiss me, were you?'

Laughing and crying at the same time, she nodded. 'I wasn't.'

And I can't stop thinking about it, she thought to herself.

'I'll be right back.' He took the keys out of the front door and locked it behind him as he left, running down the road through the rain.

After he left, the tears that she had been holding back flooded out as the pain from the fall spread through her body. She grabbed another tissue from her bag and her compact mirror, wiping the smeared mascara and half-dried blood from her face. She'd just cleaned her face, when he walked back in, and crouched down next to her.

'It's going to be alright. We'll get you to the hospital and they'll sort you out.'

She stuffed the tissue back into her bag and nodded. 'Thank you for being here. Sorry I'm such a mess.'

He put his hand on hers. 'You're not a mess, alright? You've had an accident and I want to help you, but you need to let me. How do you feel about me carrying you into the car?'

'I would like that,' she mumbled, her throat dry.

In fact, she couldn't think of anything she'd like more than that.

'Let me know if this hurts your knee,' he said. 'I'll be as careful as I can.' He bent down and lifted her onto her feet, then picked her up, one hand splayed across her back, the other gripping her bare thighs. She put her arms around his neck, holding tightly as he carried her out into the pouring rain.

A black Land Rover Defender was parked on the double yellow lines outside the shop, the hazard lights flashing. One of his hands gripped tighter around her legs as the other pulled open the passenger door. He carefully lowered her onto the seat.

'Thank you. Can you lock the door? You need the two large ones.' She handed him the ring of keys.

'I know.' He smiled.

'Of course. Sorry.'

He went back into the shop to set the alarm and lock the door, before climbing into the car. His brow was furrowed and his face was tight. There was a hard clunk as he clipped his seatbelt in, and his knuckles were white as he gripped the steering wheel. The storm above them was playing out across his face, and she felt that there was more to it than concern for her.

At the traffic lights, he fiddled with the display on the dashboard and the first few bars of Pompeii burst out of the speakers. 'I don't know much about you, but I know you like Bastille.' He kept his eyes on the road, but a smile crept across his face.

'I do. They were so good, weren't they?' She smiled.

'They were great.' His eyes flicked between hers and his rearview mirror as he battled through the city traffic. 'They weren't what I remember most about that night, though.' He paused. 'And this isn't how I imagined us meeting again.'

'Me neither. I swear I'm not the damsel in distress type.' She paused. 'I'm sorry for taking you away from your work.'

'It doesn't matter. Let's focus on getting you checked out. Did you go down the stairs in those high-heeled boots?' he asked.

She winced, then nodded. 'I wasn't thinking straight. Being alone in the studio in the storm scared me. All I could think about was getting out of there.'

Remembering that she was supposed to have met Lucy, she got her phone out and sent her a message.

> Not going to make it out tonight. Am fine. Will explain later. Love you x

She typed another message to Lisa, deciding not to tell her what was going on. She could fill her in later.

> Shop all locked up. Enjoy your date. X

Putting her phone into her bag, she chucked it onto the back seat, before wrestling her blood-stained jumper off, revealing her faded black t-shirt. She rubbed her bare arms, thinking about her coat, which was in the shop in the cupboard under the stairs.

'We're here.' Alex parked outside the hospital, jumping out of the car and running round to the passenger side. 'I'll carry you in, got it? I don't want you trying to walk on it.'

Kate nodded. She rarely let anyone tell her what to do, but as she felt his strong arms sliding under her thighs, she was powerless to argue. Clinging to his damp jacket, she put her arms around his neck.

When they reached the reception desk, Alex bent down, lowering her to the floor, and gave her his arm so she could lean on him.

The receptionist smiled at Kate under the glare of the fluorescent lights. 'Hello, my love. I'm Beverley. I need to take some details from you. Can I take your name, date of birth and address?'

Kate held onto Alex tightly. 'Kate Barton, twenty-first of July 1991, Barton Hall. Glade Lane, Canterbury, CT3 1HN

'OK, I've found you on the system.' Beverley smiled at Kate. 'Name and phone number of next of kin, please.'

Kate's face fell. 'I'm sorry, I don't have her number on me, I left my bag in the car.'

'You can take my number,' Alex whispered into her ear.

'Are you sure?' she whispered back.

He nodded. 'My name is Alex Compson, my number is 0789654231.'

'Thank you Mr. Compson,' Beverley replied, then turned to Kate. 'Can you describe your injury or illness briefly please?'

'I fell down the stairs at work and I've damaged my right knee,' Kate said.

'Alright, I've got your details onto our system. Have a seat in the waiting area. You'll be called in soon.' She smiled at Kate and Alex.

Alex helped Kate hobble over to the two empty seats in the waiting area.

'Thank you,' Kate said as she sat down. 'That's the second time you've bailed me out tonight.'

'I'm not counting.' Alex studied her face. 'You're very pale. Are you nauseous?'

'What makes you say that?' she asked as she shifted in the uncomfortable plastic chair.

'First aid training. Instinct.' He shrugged. 'You didn't answer the question.'

'I do feel sick. And embarrassed.' She turned to look at him. 'I shouldn't have been wearing those boots on the stairs and I've pulled you away from your job. You don't have to stay.'

'Let me guess, you'll be fine.' He raised an eyebrow at her.

'I'm your next of kin now, though, so I'm staying put.' He took off his wet jacket, his tight black t-shirt revealing toned, muscly forearms.

She could see a scar running up his left forearm, almost to his elbow. He'd said he had bad memories of hospitals. Was this scar anything to do with it? The scar looked nasty. Had he been in an accident? She shivered.

'You're cold. Come here,' Alex lifted his arm and slid it around her, tucking her into the warmth of his body.

Under the bright lights of the waiting room, she rested her head against his shoulder. She breathed in the scent of his aftershave, imagining that they were anywhere else but here.

They were quiet for a moment before he spoke. 'I didn't know you worked at Correll's. You must be Rebecca's maternity cover.'

'That's right.' She sat up, and his arm slipped to her waist, holding her tightly. 'I've been in Brighton for the last three years, and I came back in the summer to work at Correll's.'

'That might explain why we'd never met before,' he said.

We are connected though, Kate thought to herself.

'If I remember correctly, you'd injured yourself the first time we met.' A smile played across his lips.

She shook her head. 'Oh my God, I'd forgotten about that. I'd love to tell you that I'm not usually this chaotic, but it wouldn't be true.'

He paused as if contemplating something. 'Don't you think it's weird that we keep meeting?'

'Kismet. Do you believe in fate?' She thought about what Amelie had said about James.

He nodded. 'I do, and you're right. Fate has literally thrown you into my path.'

She smiled at him. 'I think fate wants us to see each other again, and I don't think we should argue with it.'

'I agree,' he replied, and at that moment his mobile started ringing. He groaned as he looked at it and stood up. 'I'm so sorry. I'll be right back.' He walked out of the front doors, into the darkness.

As the doors slid shut behind him, a nurse appeared in the waiting room, holding a clipboard. 'Kate Barton?'

Chapter Nine

OCTOBER 2012, CANTERBURY, KENT, England

After an examination and an x-ray, Kate hobbled back into the waiting room. She scanned the room for Alex, smiling as he walked over to her. 'You stayed,' she said.

'Of course I did. I'm technically still on call, so I just had to sort out someone to cover for me, but I'm here, and I'll make sure you get home.' He pulled his car keys out of his pocket and looked down at her knee. 'How bad is it?'

'It's only a sprain. I'm glad it's not broken. That would have been a nightmare,' she said, trying to pretend that even the tiniest step on her foot was excruciatingly painful.

'It would, but a sprain will still take a while to recover,' he said.

'I'll be doing all I can to speed it up,' she replied as he opened the passenger door.

He helped her into the car, and she caught sight of her face in the side mirror. The nurse had cleaned the blood off her face, along with most of her makeup, and put a waterproof dressing onto the cut on her eyebrow. As he climbed back into the driver seat, she smiled at him. Over the last month, she'd fantasised about seeing him again, but it involved high heels and scarlet lipstick, leather jackets, and tight jeans. Not this.

'Thank you for tonight. I know I said I would be fine on my own, but I needed you.'

'Why do I feel like you don't say that very often?' he asked. 'I needed to know you were safe.'

Every time he opened his mouth, he made Kate like him even more. She was tempted to tell him as much, but she wasn't going to give away how into him she actually was.

'That's really sweet of you.'

'It's nothing.' He put her postcode into the sat nav.

She pulled her phone out of her bag and sent Lucy a message.

> OK, I lied earlier. Not totally fine. I fell down the stairs at work. Am on my way home with a sprained knee, and a bumped head… in ALEX'S CAR! Will call tomorrow. X

When he turned into the lane that led to her house, her heart sank. The journey had gone too quickly, and she wanted to stay in the car longer, watching his strong hands grip the wheel as the rain lashed the windscreen.

He sucked in a breath as the house loomed up in front of them. 'Wow. This is your house?'

The full moon above them illuminated the curling ivy on the side of the house and the gargoyles that glared menacingly down at them.

'It's a beast, isn't it? It's been in my family for centuries,' she said, not mentioning the costly upkeep, or the constant fear of it falling apart.

His eyes widened as he took it in. 'A beast is right. I've never seen anything like it. It must be such a cool place to live.'

'It is pretty cool,' she replied. 'There's nowhere else like it.'

He stopped the car on the drive and opened the door for her, offering her his hand. They both looked at the drive. 'I'll need to carry you, just over the gravel. Is that alright?'

Inside her head, she was screaming yes, I need to be pressed against your body again, but she responded with, 'Good idea.'

She rested her head against his chest as he lifted her out of the car, his heart beating right underneath her cheek.

He put her down right outside the front door, and she fumbled in her bag for her keys. 'Do you want to come in?'

'I would love to, but I should get back to work. Are you going to be on your own?' His brow furrowed.

'I won't be alone,' she said. 'Can you imagine being in this house on your own?'

He shook his head. 'I can't. I need to go, but... I can't stop thinking about that kiss.'

'Me neither,' she whispered, pulling him closer to her. 'I was starting to think I'd imagined it.'

His lips found hers in the darkness. She murmured with pleasure as he pulled her towards him, holding her steady.

'I didn't imagine it,' she whispered. 'It was that good.'

A smile pulled at the corners of his lips, and he kissed her cheek. 'Look after yourself, alright? I'll be in touch.'

She unlocked her front door and watched him walk back to his car. As he drove off, she smiled. He was still a mystery to her, but she could live with it, especially if he kept kissing her like that. She walked cautiously through the door, and closed it, leaning against it. The whole evening had been a whirlwind, but at least it had ended well.

'Darling, what on earth happened to you?' Amelie appeared in front of her, her brow furrowed with concern.

'I had a little accident in the studio tonight,' Kate said, as her mind raced, lurching between flashbacks of the fall, and the kiss. She walked into the living room, collapsing onto the sofa.

'What do you mean?' Amelie asked as she sat down next to Kate.

'I got spooked and fell down the stairs.' Kate took a deep breath. 'That place gives me the creeps at night.' She shivered, not wanting to let on that she'd been on her own there. 'I've sprained my knee, bruised my ribs and cut my face, but nothing's broken.'

Amelie shook her head. 'I knew something bad had happened. I came down with the most awful headache, and I was so tempted to call you, but I thought you'd be cross. I wish I had now.'

'Maybe you're psychic,' Kate said. 'There was nothing you could have done though. I locked myself out of the alarm system, so I had to call the security company and their engineer took me to the hospital.' She felt the heat rising in her cheeks as she spoke.

'What a gentleman.' Amelie studied Kate. 'Why do I feel like that's not the end of the story?'

'It is for now.' Kate loved her mum, but for now, she wanted to keep Alex to herself.

'Point taken,' Amelie looked down at Kate's boots. 'Do you want some help taking those off?'

Kate hadn't even realised she was still wearing her boots. 'Oh. Yes, that would be great, thank you.'

Amelie undid Kate's boots and slipped them off. 'I'll make you a cup of tea.'

Unable to protest or insist that she would do it herself, Kate nodded. 'Thank you, Mama.'

When Amelie left the room, Kate settled her head back on the sofa and closed her eyes. The scent of Alex's aftershave, which was still lingering on her clothes, wafted up to her, and she breathed in deep, memories of him taking her mind off the pain from the fall. The dogs clambered onto her lap, and settled down next to her, somehow knowing she needed them.

Amelie reappeared, handing Kate a mug of tea. 'How on earth are you going to manage the stairs?'

'Thank you so much.' Kate took the mug from her and sipped her tea. 'I hadn't thought that far ahead. I think I'll just sleep here.'

Amelie nodded. 'Good idea, but if you need me I won't be able to hear you.'

'Would you be able to hear me from your room if I was in mine? Last time I checked, you weren't a bat.' Kate pulled the blanket from the back of the sofa around her. 'I'll be alright here. I've got the kitchen and the cloakroom within hobbling distance, and if I can't sleep, I'll just find a trashy film to watch.'

'If you're sure.' Amelie stood up.

Kate nodded. 'I'm sure. Take your phone up to bed with you. If I really need you, I'll call you.'

'Good idea.' Amelie picked her phone up and tucked it into the pocket of her dress. 'Sleep well, darling.'

'And you, love you.' Kate smiled at her mother.

'Love you too.' Amelie blew her a kiss, then left the room. Kate's phone started ringing, and she answered it.

'Did you fall or were you pushed? Has someone got it in for my best bitch?' Lucy's voice made Kate smile.

'No, I fell.' Kate grinned. 'I got spooked, and I tripped. I'm an idiot.'

'What happened and why was Alex there?'

Kate explained what had happened to Lucy.

'Wow. That's a lot. Are you alright?' Lucy asked.

Kate wrinkled her nose. 'I think so? I'm still processing it.'

'You need to rest up, binge watch some crap and eat all the snacks. I've not found anything that advice doesn't apply to.' Lucy paused before she continued. 'You know where I am if you need me, but I'm not sure I'm much use in my current half-drunk state.'

'Thank you. That's really sweet of you. I'll let you know if I need anything.' Kate paused. 'What did you tell Mia?'

'Very basic details,' Lucy said. 'She's working nights all weekend, so you've got a couple of days to decide what you want to tell her.'

'Thank you! I appreciate it,' Kate replied. 'I'll speak to you soon.'

She hung up and sipped her tea, her thoughts turning to Alex, remembering his horrified face when he'd seen her, covered in blood. Emmett had said something to him about hospitals being hard for him, but he'd still taken her there.

She was scared to get involved with someone who was linked to every part of her life, but she couldn't forget that kiss. For another kiss like that, she'd fall down a thousand staircases.

'How are you feeling, sweetheart?' Amelie sat on the sofa, as Kate groggily stared at her the following morning.

Kate sat up. 'I don't feel brilliant. I took some painkillers a minute ago.'

Amelie nodded. 'Would you like some toast?'

'That would be great. Thanks, Mama.' As Amelie left the room, Kate tried to stand up, crying out in pain. Frustrated, she sat back down again.

When Amelie brought her a plate of toast, and a mug of tea, she took them gratefully. She wolfed down the toast, and sipped her tea, and once she'd finished, she felt a whole lot better. 'Is there anything that tea and toast can't cure?'

Amelie shook her head. 'It's like magic. Hungover? Tea and toast. Broken heart? Tea and toast. Sick? Tea and toast.'

Kate smiled. 'It's helped me through all of the above.'

'Me too.' Amelie put her empty mug down on the coffee table, then held her hand out to take Kate's.

Kate handed her plate and mug to her mother. 'I need a shower or a bath or something. Can you help me up the stairs?'

'Wow,' Amelie said, clutching her chest dramatically. 'Is this you asking me for help? You must really be in pain.'

'I really am, and I do really need your help,' Kate admitted.

'Then let's go.' Amelie stood up, then offered Kate her hand, pulling her to her feet. She held onto Kate's arm all the way up the stairs, along the corridor, and into the bathroom.

'Right, this is where you leave me.' Kate sat down on the small armchair in the corner of the room. 'I can manage it from here.'

'Give me a shout if you need me,' Amelie said, pulling the door closed behind her.

'Thanks, Mama.' Kate peeled off her t-shirt, inhaling another waft of Alex. Sliding her skirt and underwear off, she carefully hobbled over to the claw foot bath in the middle of the room.

She'd helped Amelie to redecorate the bathroom when Papa died. They had ripped out the old suite and painted a huge mural across the walls, filled with exotic flowers, palm trees, and brightly coloured birds. It was one of her favourite rooms, somewhere you could imagine you were in a luxury hotel instead of a crumbling relic.

The bath relaxed her and after climbing out carefully, she stared at her reflection in the ornate, gold mirror above the sink. Her forehead and cheek were bruised, as well as the left side of her body, a swirl of purple and red stretching from her rib cage down to her hip. She went back to her room and pulled on her bathrobe, then reapplied the bandage on her knee.

Instead of getting dressed, which felt like hard work, she called Emmett.

'Morning, Kate. How are you feeling?' He sounded brighter than he had last night.

'Very minor damage.' She didn't tell him how much pain she was in. 'A few cuts, bruised ribs, and a sprained knee.'

'Doesn't sound minor to me. Alex called me after he'd dropped you off last night.'

'I'll rest over the weekend and I'll be good as new on Monday,' Kate said brightly, trying to ease Emmett's concern.

'And how are you planning on getting up those stairs?'

'I don't know, but there's too much to do for me not to be there.' She felt embarrassed for being a burden on him.

'You can handle the social media accounts. I don't have time to do it and you can do it at home. With your feet up.' He paused. ' I'll speak to David and we'll sort out some assembly work you can do at home, am I clear?'

'Very clear. I'm so sorry to give you more work,' she said apologetically. 'How's your dad?'

His voice cracked slightly as he spoke. 'He's improving. We're waiting to see the consultant today to see what their plan is. I'm hoping to be back next week. Thanks for asking. Look after yourself.'

She hung up and closed her eyes, letting out a long exhale. Maybe resting wouldn't be such a bad idea. She was in pain, and she felt like she would burst into tears at any moment.

Amelie appeared at her bedroom door. 'Do you feel better after your bath? Can I get you anything?'

Kate shook her head. 'I just spoke to Emmett, and I've got to stay here this week. I can't go into work until I can get up the stairs.' A tear fell onto her bathrobe.

'Oh, sweetheart,' Amelie said. 'You had such a shock last night. Do you want me to help you downstairs, or do you need some time alone?'

'I think I need some time alone,' Kate replied, her voice shaky.

Amelie nodded. 'Of course. Let me know if you need me. I'll keep the bat ears open.'

'Thank you, Mama.' Kate smiled at her through blurring eyes, but waited until the door was closed before she burst into tears.

She had just struggled into her clothes when her phone rang. It was an unknown number, and she answered it cautiously. 'Hello? Who is this?'

'It's Alex. How are you feeling this morning?'

Her heart started beating a little faster as she thought about their kiss. 'Hey! I didn't expect to hear from you.'

'I like surprises,' Alex said. 'But you didn't tell me how you are.'

'I feel like I fell down a flight of stairs last night,' she quipped. 'I've been instructed to rest. I've just spoken to Emmett. Someone told him what happened at the hospital last night.' She smiled, waiting for his reply.

'I was worried about you,' he said. 'I was sure you'd just shrug it off and go straight back to work.'

'I don't work Saturdays. I've got the whole weekend to rest,' she replied. 'I plan on spending it in my sweatpants watching Netflix.'

'Sounds perfect,' he said.

'Come and join me if you like,' she replied quickly.

'I have to work, but I'd much rather spend the day with you.'

'You have to work on the weekend too? Now I feel even worse about letting you take me to the hospital, it was *late* when we got back last night.' She chewed her lip.

'You didn't know I had to work today. I did and I still chose to take you, so don't feel bad.' He paused. 'Things are kind of complicated right now, but I'd like to see you again. When you've recovered, would you want to meet for a drink?'

'Absolutely,' she replied, a rush of excitement flooding through her. 'I'd love that.'

'Great. I'll be in touch,' he said then hung up.

Was a date with Alex a good idea? He was tall, dark and ridiculously handsome, but she knew nothing about him. Could she trust him with her heart, or trust herself not to break his?

Chapter Ten

October 2012, Canterbury, Kent, England

On Monday morning, Kate watched her mum's eyes flicking to the clock every few minutes as they ate their breakfast. 'Relax, Mama. You've got loads of time.'

'I have *half an hour* until I need to leave,' Amelie said. 'and I always get nervous about meeting new authors. I don't know why. They always tell me they're nervous about meeting me!' She laughed. 'I'm meeting Vyvienne for a drink but I won't stay in London tonight. I don't want to leave you alone.'

'Do I need to remind you that I'm twenty-two and I can look after myself?' Kate huffed.

'Do I need to remind *you* that you can barely get up the stairs by yourself?' Amelie retorted. 'I'm not treating you like a child, I'm treating you like an adult with a sprained knee.'

'Stay at Vyvienne's. I will be fine,' Kate said firmly. 'If I need anything I can call Mia or Leon.'

'Of course you *can*,' Amelie said, 'but it doesn't mean you *will*. I know all too well how stubborn you are.'

'I learnt from the best.' Kate finished her tea and put her empty mug down on the table. 'You and Marie are the most stubborn people I know. I have all the time in the world to argue with you, but you have a train to catch.'

Amelie let out a long exhale, then stood up, picking up their empty plates. 'Fine. Just promise me that you will rest today.'

'I will rest today,' Kate said sincerely. 'I need this knee to heal *tout de suite* so I can go back to work.'

That was only part of the reason she needed her knee to heal. The quicker it did, the quicker she could have a date with Alex.

'Marvellous. In that case, I'll stay in London tonight and I'll be back tomorrow.' Amelie stood up. 'I'd better go, the traffic is *so* unpredictable.'

'See you tomorrow.' Kate blew her mum a kiss as she walked out of the kitchen.

As Amelie was leaving the house, Mia, bearing a large bunch of flowers, arrived. 'Oh, love, how are you feeling?'

'I've been better,' Kate said as Mia stepped inside and took off her coat and shoes. She nodded to the flowers. 'They're beautiful, thank you.'

Mia followed Kate into the kitchen, still clutching the flowers. 'Are you going to tell me how you're really feeling?'

'Put the kettle on,' Kate replied with a grin. 'Then maybe I'll talk.' She sat back down at the table.

'Tea? I need a coffee. I've barely slept.' Mia filled the kettle and took two mugs out of the cupboard.

'Were the weekend shifts awful?' Kate wrinkled her nose.

'Not awful, just really busy, and I couldn't get to sleep during the day yesterday so I feel so gross today.' Mia opened the cupboard under the sink and took out a vase. Grabbing a pair of scissors from the cutlery drawer, she expertly trimmed the stems of the flowers and arranged them neatly.

'It's very sweet of you to come and see me, when you could be sleeping right now,' Kate said.

'My best friend has an accident and I'm supposed to ignore it to take a *nap?* I don't think so.' Mia put the vase of flowers on the table in front of Kate. 'I can catch up on my sleep tonight.' She washed her hands in the sink, then made a tea for Kate and a coffee for herself. Once she had delivered t the mugs to the table, she sat down opposite Kate. 'Now, tell me everything.'

'Thanks for the tea, and the flowers.' Kate picked up the mug and took a sip. 'So. Emmett's dad was sick, and I had to stay late, and there was a storm, so I got spooked because I was on my own. I had those boots on, the high heeled ones and I just slipped at the top of the stairs and fell.'

Mia gasped. 'Oh, Kate! That's so scary! You could have seriously hurt yourself.'

'I know.' Kate winced. 'The boots were a bad idea, being on my own there was a bad idea, but I was trying to finish an order. Lesson learned.'

'What happened next? How did you get home?' Mia asked.

'Well, I managed to set the alarm off when I was trying to set it,' Kate said. 'They had to send an engineer out to reset it, and he took me to the hospital.'

'What a nice guy.' Mia raised her eyebrow. 'Why are you blushing? Was he hot?'

Kate bit her lip. She wasn't ready to tell Mia any more yet.

Mia didn't miss this. 'Oh, I see. There's more to this story.'

'Something like that.' Kate winced. 'I'm sorry. It's just that you and Pete... you can both be a little bit too involved. He wants to be my big brother and protect me and you want to marry me off. Sometimes it's hard.'

'I didn't realise that.' Mia looked down at her coffee. 'Why haven't you ever said anything?'

'I didn't want to hurt your feelings.' Kate swallowed. Falling out with Mia was not on the cards for today.

'I watched you and Will break each other's hearts and I would do anything to prevent you getting hurt again,' Mia said.

'You don't need to prevent anything.' Kate took another sip of her tea. 'Just be my friend. That goes for Pete too.'

Mia nodded. 'Of course. And as for this guy, I'll back off. You tell me when you're ready.'

'When there's something to tell, I'll tell you.' Kate wasn't sure if this was the truth. Alex was a delicious secret, and one she intended to keep to herself for as long as she could.

'Morning, my wee klutz. How are we doing?' David asked as he sat down next to Kate at her kitchen table the following day.

'Morning, David. I know I'm an idiot.' She put her head in her hands.

He nodded. 'Aye. I was so worried about you. You look alright, though. It's a shame you can't walk. I want to have a snoop about this place. It doesn't look so spooky in the daytime, but I bet it's terrifying at night.'

'You're not wrong,' she said. 'It's my home though, and I love it. Even if it is a little spooky.'

'I'd love a tour another time.' He opened his large canvas bag. 'I brought you some bits. Can you put some earring wires onto these?' He handed her a small clear plastic bag.

'Of course. No problems.' She took the bag and opened it, tipping out some small pearls with tiny holes drilled in them. 'These are gorgeous. Did you bring some pliers?'

'Yep.' He handed her two sets of pliers. 'Oh, I have a little treat for you. From all of us.' He took a box of chocolates from his bag and handed it to her. 'Figured it might cheer you up.'

'Oh, thank you so much! These look incredible!' The pale pink box was from Papillon, the shop she walked past every day on her way to work. Their chocolate was the best she had ever tasted, but the price tag made it a rare luxury.

'Ah, you're welcome. The wee lass in the shop let me have a sample.' He smiled. 'I picked you all the best ones.'

'I'll text Lisa and Emmett and thank them too,' she said, admiring the box. 'Has it been busy? I'm so sorry for leaving you in the lurch.'

'It can't be helped, and it's been manageable.' He paused. 'Your sapphire ring's been a bit of a hit, eh?'

The ring that she had stayed late to finish had been collected by the customer, and he had filmed his proposal. The video, which Corrells had been tagged in, had been shared thousands of times, and the previous day, Kate had responded to countless messages from potential customers, asking for similar rings.

'I know!' she squealed. 'It was my first consultation and design, and I was so nervous, that was why I was working late, to get it finished. I'm so bummed that I wasn't there when the customer collected it.'

She had sent him a message to congratulate him, but she would have much rather been there to give him the ring.

'He's going to come back to us for his wedding rings.' She smiled. 'So even though I'm injured, it was worth the extra hours to see the smile on his wife-to-be's face.'

'I do admire your ability to put a positive spin on everything,' he said, 'and I knew that ring would be a hit.'

Amelie swept into the kitchen. 'Oh, hello, David. Did you want a cup of tea?'

'Don't worry about a cuppa. I need to head back. I've just dropped off some work for Kate. Something to keep her out of trouble, you know?' He grinned at Amelie. 'Great house you've got here, by the way.'

'Thank you.' Amelie leant against the worktop and smiled back at him. 'Good to see you again.'

'And you,' David replied, then turned to Kate. 'I better get back. When are you planning on coming back in?'

'Next week,' she said firmly. 'I'll see you on Monday.'

'Will ye be able to get your boots on by then?' He gave her bandaged foot a doubtful look.

'Absolutely.' A week of being on her own at home was long enough. She missed the studio, and was certain that with some painkillers, her foot would tolerate the boot. 'Thanks for coming over, I appreciate it. Send my love to Emmett and Lisa.'

'Of course.'

'Thanks for coming over, David,' she said, 'and for the chocolates which I'm going to inhale once you've left.'

He laughed. 'See you next week.'

Amelie led him to the front door, then came back into the kitchen, and sat down next to Kate. 'He is gorgeous isn't he? I could listen to him talk all day.'

Kate shook her head. 'Don't you have work to do?' She picked up her phone as Amelie swished out of the room, smiling at the message from Hannah.

> How's the knee? Are you resting? I know we said we'd meet up at half-term, but I'm going to Jordan with Norina. So sorry! X

Her heart sank as she read the message. She missed Hannah, but travelling was a way of life for her.

> I'm fine! Resting and bored... Have a great time, I'll see you when you get back. X

She opened the box of chocolates and picked out a small circular one, biting into it, savouring the smooth hazelnut paste. She had the house to herself, some jewellery to make, and a box of chocolates. It was shaping up to be a good day.

By Friday, the chocolates had almost gone, and Kate had settled into a routine, juggling jewellery making and designing, the social media accounts, and the exercises that Mia had sent her. She was determined that she would be back in the shop on Monday, and once she had a goal in mind, nothing would stop her from achieving it.

She'd just set out the last few pearls on the table with her pliers when the doorbell rang. Slowly, she made her way to the door. When she opened it, she instantly regretted her outfit of leggings and an oversize hoodie.

'Alex! Hi! Come in.'

She smiled but inside she was cringing. Why hadn't she at least put some makeup on? He looked perfectly put together as usual in a linen shirt and black jeans, and was holding an enormous bunch of roses. Her hair was scooped into a messy bun on the top of her head, and her t-shirt was crumpled. Hot mess was probably a step up from where she was.

'How are you doing? You don't look quite so...'

'Nauseous? Terrified,' she interjected. 'No, I'm good.'

He smiled. 'I'm glad to hear it.' He held out the flowers. 'These are for you. I've been thinking about you a lot this week.'

She nestled the flowers in her arm. 'Thank you, they're beautiful. Can you stay for a minute or are you working?'

'I am working, but I can stay,' he replied.

Delighted, she led him into the kitchen. 'Can I get you a tea or a coffee?'

'You're injured,' he said. 'How about I make *you* a tea or coffee?'

'That is very sweet, but I can manage.' She smiled and gestured to the table. 'Have a seat.'

'I should have known better than to offer to help you.' He smiled back at her. 'A black coffee would be great, thank you.'

She made him a coffee, and herself a tea, then sat down next to him. 'I wondered how long it would be before you came back. I could tell that the house intrigued you.'

His eyes met hers. 'It wasn't just the house I wanted to see.'

'Smooth.' She nodded approvingly.

'It wasn't a line,' he protested. 'I meant it. I wanted to see you. I've thought about you a lot this week. I've never met anyone like you before.' He took a sip of his coffee, still holding her gaze.

'Is that a good thing? I seem to attract chaos wherever I go, in case you hadn't noticed.' She clutched her mug tightly. He somehow managed to excite and unnerve her at the same time.

'I like chaos.'

Her breath caught in her throat. 'We're a good match then.'

'Seems that way.' His eyes flicked to the vase of flowers next to him. 'I see I've been beaten to it.'

'They're from my best friend,' she said quickly, keen to ensure that he knew she was single. 'And the chocolates are from Emmett, David and Lisa.' She opened the box. 'Can we just pretend that I saved you one because I somehow knew you were coming over?'

'We can.' He glanced at the chocolates. 'Which one do you recommend?'

'Either the square one which has a pistachio cream inside, or the oval one, which is dark chocolate with a raspberry mousse.' She studied him. 'I feel like you're a dark chocolate kind of guy.'

'You'd be right.' He picked up the oval chocolate and took a bite. 'Wow, this is good. They're from Papillon, right? I do their alarm systems too, and it smells so good in there.'

'Do they pay you in chocolate?' she asked.

'I wish.' He put the other half of the chocolate into his mouth.

Picking up the pistachio chocolate, she bit it in half, still processing the fact that Alex was here, in her house. He'd barely left her mind all week, distracting her from the pain in her knee.

He took a sip of his coffee. 'Thanks for this, and the chocolate. Are you going to tell me how you're actually doing, or are you going to insist that you're fine?'

She smiled. 'I'll be honest. It hurts. A lot. I'm bruised all over, and my knee is still painful, but honestly, I am fine. I can walk on it a little more and by Monday I'll be ready to face the stairs again. Just not in those boots.'

He laughed. 'They're still in my car. I'll get them before I go.'

'I think I'm better off without them.' She shuddered.

'I don't know.' He cocked his head to the side. 'The first time we kissed, you were wearing them.'

'Would you accept a kiss from me in my fluffy socks instead?' she asked.

He moved closer to her. 'I'd like that.'

When his lips met hers, it wasn't the desperate, urgent kiss of Friday night. It was gentle, almost tentative, and it left her longing for more, which, she decided, was exactly what he wanted to achieve.

'So if you're going back to work on Monday, does that mean I can take you on a date next week?' he asked.

'You can,' she said. 'I have no plans. I'm all yours.'

Literally. Figuratively. However he wanted her.

'Glad to hear it.' His lips curved into a smile, but he didn't reply to suggest that he was hers. This made her want him even more. 'I should go but I'll be in touch to arrange that date.'

He finished his coffee and stood up, and she followed him into the hall. Before he left, he kissed her again, this time with a ferocity that almost knocked her off her feet. She watched him leave, unsure of exactly *how* she had fallen for him, but certain that she had. Whether he felt the same way remained to be seen.

Kate was still sat at the kitchen table when Amelie got in that evening. 'Hi, Mama, how was your day?' she called out to her.

'Oh busy as usual.' Amelie sat down opposite Kate. 'Your new boots are back in the hall. How did they get there? You didn't drive anywhere today, did you?'

'No, Alex, the engineer who came to my rescue at Corrells, brought them over.' Kate tried to sound as nonchalant as possible.

'Oh really?' Amelie rested her chin on her hands, her attention piqued. 'Did he bring you these gorgeous roses too?' She ran her fingers over one of the petals.

'He did,' Kate said. 'And he asked me out.'

'So why do you sound hesitant?' Amelie asked.

'My last relationship went down in flames, and I don't know anything about Alex, other than the fact that he knows Mia, and Pete, and all I can think about is that this could all get so messy,' Kate blurted out.

Amelie shrugged. 'Does all that matter if you really want him?'

Kate let out a long exhale. 'Fate keeps throwing us together. In my case, literally, down a flight of stairs. I've not felt like this about anyone in a really long time, possibly ever, but something is stopping me from jumping in, probably the fear of getting burnt again.'

'Would it be so bad to go on a date with Alex, and just see where it goes?' Amelie suggested. 'Just one date.'

'I already know that one date wouldn't be enough,' Kate said. 'I've only spent a few hours with him and I always want *more.*'

Amelie nodded. 'I know this feeling very well. It's how I've always felt about James. Fate threw us back together at the right time and I couldn't fight it.'

'Oh my God!' Kate squealed. 'You're seeing James again?'

'It turns out one date wasn't enough for me, either.' Amelie gave Kate a sheepish smile.

'Nice.' Kate nodded approvingly. 'I'm happy for you.'

'Thanks, but be happy for yourself,' Amelie said. 'Let yourself fall and see if he catches you.'

Kate considered Amelie's words. The fall down the stairs was nothing compared with the potential pain of falling for Alex and it all going wrong. She thought of him sitting next to her in the hospital, holding her tightly, and it made her chest tighten. Was she brave enough to let herself fall? And if she did, would he catch her?

Chapter Eleven

When the doorbell rang on Sunday evening, Kate hurried to the door as fast as she could, hoping it was Alex. Ignoring the stabbing pain in her knee, she flung the door open. 'Oh, it's you.'

Leon rolled his eyes. 'Well, that's a nice welcome.'

'I'm so sorry, Leon. I was expecting...never mind. Come in.'

He peeled off his coat and scarf, and Kate draped them over the radiator. 'I was in the city having a drink with Matt, and it started raining on the way to my car.' He groaned and ran his hand through his sopping hair. 'I'm sorry it's taken all week to come over. Am I the worst friend ever?'

'Of course not. You're here now, aren't you?' She glanced at his dripping wet hair, and jeans, which were dripping all over the wooden floors. Then she noticed that he was shivering. 'Why don't you take a shower and borrow some of Rob's clothes?' she suggested.

'Might be an idea. I'll be right back,' he said.

'I'll make us a cup of tea.' She started towards the kitchen, but he stopped her.

'You're supposed to be resting. I'll do it once I've had a shower.'

She huffed dramatically. 'I've spent all week resting. Mama's been watching me like a hawk.'

He paused at the bottom of the staircase. 'Speaking of your gorgeous mother, where is she?'

She glared at him. 'Out. With her lover. You've missed your chance.'

She rolled her eyes. Leon never passed up the opportunity to flirt with Amelie.

'Never mind, maybe next time.' He smirked, then went up the stairs.

She rolled her eyes, then went into the kitchen, making the milky tea that he loved, and one for herself.

When he returned from his shower, he squashed himself right next to her on the sofa, running his eyes over her. 'Your face looks a lot better than that grim photo you sent me.'

'Yeah, it's healed well, but look at this.' She lifted one side of her t-shirt and he winced at her bruises.

'Ouch. What's your excuse for the state of your hair, though?' He grinned.

'Oof. That was mean. I've not had the energy to sort my hair out. Your tea's over there.' She gestured to the coffee table. 'Can you pass me the biscuit jar?'

She picked up her own cup of tea and took a biscuit from the jar that he offered to her.

'How did it go with your mystery date?' she asked, dipping the biscuit into the tea.

He grabbed a chocolate biscuit for himself, and put the whole thing into his mouth. When he eventually swallowed, he replied. 'It was awesome. I really like her. We just clicked and I can't wait to see her again.

'What does she do?' She had a good feeling she knew exactly what the answer was.

'She, um, works in a jewellery shop.' He took a sip of his tea, avoiding her gaze.

'I knew it! Leon, I *work* with her.' She sighed. 'I'm stuck right in the middle of this.'

'Hence the mystery.' He smiled. 'I really like her.'

'In that case, I'm happy for you,' she said, 'but I like her, too, so please don't break her heart.'

'What if she breaks my heart? What then?' he asked.

'Then I will be there for you, like I always am,' she replied.

'How about you?' he asked. 'Have you heard from your superhero since he came over?'

'He might have sent me a couple of cute texts,' she said. 'He's taking me out next Friday.'

He sipped his tea, studying her. 'Why do I feel like this guy's a bit different? You're into him, aren't you?'

'I am,' she admitted. 'He's ridiculously good looking, he literally saved me, and when he kisses me, it's so intense that I practically forget my own name.'

'So *that's* who thought was at the door,' he said triumphantly. 'I'm so sorry to disappoint you.'

'I wasn't disappointed, honestly. And I'm not even expecting to see him until Friday, I just thought...'

He interrupted her. 'You were *hoping* it was him. There's nothing wrong with that. Should I go, so you can invite him over?'

She shook her head. 'No. Stay. I'm not inviting him over. I don't want him to *know* that I can't stop thinking about him. I need to play it super cool.'

He laughed. 'You don't do playing it cool. He's gonna find that out sooner or later.'

'Later is good with me,' she said. 'You can stay over if you like. I know you hate driving in the rain, which is why I was kind of surprised to see you.'

'Uh, no.' His eyes widened and his face turned pale. 'I can't sleep in the blue room again.'

'We told you not to sleep in there, but you didn't listen.' She gave him what she hoped was a sympathetic smile. 'It creeps me out in there.'

He shuddered. 'I should have listened. I will never forget that door slamming shut. I nearly wet myself.'

'We've stopped using it as a guest room,' she said, managing to contain her laughter. 'You can stay in the floral room instead.'

'Oh I like the floral room.' He nodded approvingly. 'And it isn't *rain* out there, it is practically a flood.'

'So dramatic.' She gave him a playful nudge. 'If you are staying, would you give me a lift into work tomorrow?'

He shook his head. 'You're not supposed to be at work, remember?'

'I'm bored at home.' She fluttered her eyelashes at him. 'I need to go back to work. Please?'

'You know I will. Now, can I go to bed? I've had to watch the others downing pints all night while I stayed sober so I could come over to see you.' He yawned. 'It's so much easier to stay awake when you're trashed.'

'It is, but it's not much fun the next morning and you're snarky enough when you're *not* hungover,' she quipped.

He stood up and held out a hand, pulling her to her feet. 'Less of your cheek, Barton.'

She followed him out to the hall, and he scooped her up, throwing her over his shoulder.

'Hey!' she squealed. 'I can manage the stairs.'

'I'm not taking any chances,' he retorted.

In the morning, Leon made them both tea and toast, and Kate fought the rising tide of nausea in her stomach, as she thought about how she'd left the shop, crying and covered in blood. Her knee support was tight and uncomfortable, hidden under her denim dress and black leggings. She looked at Leon. 'I'm scared about going back.'

'You're bound to be.' His eyes met hers, and he gave her a reassuring smile

'I'm sure that by the end of the day, you'll feel fine. And if you don't, call me and I'll come and get you.'

'Thank you.' She looked at the clock and downed the rest of her tea. 'We'd better go.'

When she arrived at the shop, Kate took a deep breath. She thought about Alex's kiss, focusing on it so hard, that the memory of her fall left her mind. Swallowing hard, she pushed the front door open.

'Kate!' Emmett slid out of his chair and gave her a hug. 'How are you? How's the knee?'

'It's wrapped up so tightly, I can't even feel it. I don't love the knee support, but it's doing its job.' She turned to David and Lisa, who were leant on the glass counter, arranging one of the pads of jewellery. 'Hey guys, did you miss me?'

'Oh, aye, I've definitely missed your out-of-tune singing.' David raised an eyebrow and smirked. 'I'm glad you're back.'

Lisa gave Kate a gentle hug. 'I'm so pleased to see you, your accident sounded so awful, I was so worried about you.'

'Ah, I'm tougher than I look,' Kate replied, feeling a stab of anxiety as she looked at the staircase. 'I have no idea how I'm going to get up there, though.'

'I've got an idea,' David said, turning to Emmett. 'Close your eyes. You'll not like this.' He bent down and lifted Kate over his shoulder.

Emmett turned his back. 'If I didn't see it, it didn't happen.'

'Why does everyone do this to me?' Kate squealed.

David held onto the handrail with one hand, gripping Kate tightly with the other as he carried her up the stairs. When they reached the top and he put her down onto the wooden floorboards, she was laughing so hard, she'd practically forgotten about the fall.

'It was a good idea, eh?' David smiled at her. 'You looked like you'd seen a ghost when you looked at the staircase. I thought you could do with a laugh.'

'It worked! Thank you.' In the daylight, it wasn't so scary. She walked into the studio and sat at her bench, letting out a sigh of relief.

David sat down next to her. 'You're walking a lot better. Has it really healed, or have you just forced yourself to come back?'

'A little of the former, a little of the latter.' The painkillers she was taking were helping, as were the exercises that Mia had given her.

'Fair enough.' He lowered his voice. 'Let me know if you're in pain, or if you need a break. It might take you a while to find your feet again if you'll excuse the pun.'

'Hilarious. I think the stairs are going to terrify me for a while, but it's so good to be back in here again.' Her apron was laid on her bench and she stood up, slipping it on. 'I feel like I've come back home.'

'Well, I'm glad to have you back,' he said. 'How about a cup of tea?'

'I would love one,' she said. 'I can make them though, you don't need to wait on me.'

'Oh I know. You can make the next one.' He gave her a reassuring smile, then left the room.

She glanced around. Her tools were all stacked neatly on her bench where she'd left them. The sun streamed through the window, landing on the tiny emerald studs that David was working on. Her earlier nerves began to dissipate and she picked up her sketch book. Last week she'd had two video calls with clients who'd requested pink sapphire engagement rings, and now she could get to work on them.

Chapter Twelve

November 2012, Canterbury, Kent, England

The following evening, Kate watched her mother pacing the kitchen nervously.

'Is it too cold in here?' Amelie asked. 'She always complains about it being cold.'

'It's *tropical* in here, Mama,' Kate replied. 'Relax. It's going to be fine.'

She wasn't entirely sure that this was the case. Her aunt Marie was due to arrive at any minute, and Marie and Amelie's relationship was like a house of cards teetering on the verge of collapse.

'She'll complain about my cooking, or that the wine isn't as good as the French wine that she's used to.' Amelie bit her lip. 'She can't come for Christmas this year so I invited her over this week, but now I'm regretting it.'

'You always get like this before she arrives, and then you have a great time together,' Kate reminded her. 'Take a deep breath. It's gonna be fine, and if she's mean, I'll step in.'

Amelie smiled. 'Thank you, darling. You always know just what to say.'

'Not really. I've just seen you like this a hundred times already.' The doorbell rang and Kate glanced at the door. 'It's go time.'

'Right.' Amelie took a deep breath. 'Here we go.'

Kate followed her to the front door.

Her aunt's bronzed skin and candy floss pink hair seemed so out of place in the stormy Kent countryside. 'Bonsoir my darlings!' Amelie breezed in, her coconut perfume trailing behind her. She gave Amelie a hug. 'You're looking good. Is it James that's put the sparkle back in your eyes?'

'Perhaps,' Amelie replied, taking one of Marie's suitcases and shutting the door. 'How was your flight?'

'Like clockwork, unlike the collection of the hire car. I had to wait half an hour...' Marie trailed off, spotting Kate. 'It's my favourite niece!'

'Your *only* niece,' Kate reminded her.

'Still my favourite.' Marie gave her a hug. 'How is your knee? Your accident sounded so terrifying.'

'It's healing. It'll take a few weeks, but I'm doing all I can to speed it up,' Kate said.

'You're impatient, like your mother,' Marie replied.

Amelie snorted. 'You're no better!'

Marie ignored her sister and turned back to Kate. 'I hope it gets better soon. You must rest it properly.'

Kate laughed. 'You two are so alike! I have been resting it.'

She followed Amelie and Marie into the kitchen.

'It's so warm in here,' Marie said. 'Makes a change.'

Kate flicked her eyes to Amelie, waiting for an outburst at Marie's snarky tone.

'It's always warm in here,' Amelie said. 'It's just the rest of the house that's freezing. Dinner is almost ready. We'll eat in here, as it takes an age to heat up the dining room as you know.'

'It's so *formal* in there.' Marie wrinkled her nose. 'I've always preferred the kitchen. It's so cosy. Whatever you're cooking smells wonderful.'

'It's a lamb tagine,' Amelie replied, as she lifted the dish out of the oven.

Kate lit the candles on the table, and fetched some cutlery, while Marie washed her hands. 'See, it's all going well,' she whispered to her mother.

'So far so good,' Amelie whispered back.

Over dinner, the conversation remained good natured, with the occasional snarky remark from Marie.

'Are you still enjoying working at Correll's?' Marie asked Kate.

'I am,' Kate said. 'I love it. I feel like I've been there forever, but it's only been a few months.'

'What are you going to do when Rebecca comes back?' Marie asked.

'I'm not sure, but I've got almost six months left there, so I'm not thinking about it yet.' Kate smiled. 'You know me, I don't like to plan too far ahead.'

'What if *I* had an offer for you?' A smile crept across Marie's face. 'My friend Lucien owns a studio in Nice. I showed him a photo of that pink sapphire engagement ring you made, and he wants you to come and work for him next summer.'

Kate was stunned. 'Really? Are you serious?'

Marie nodded. 'Very serious. I explained that you were under contract here until next year, but he asked me to try and persuade you to join us for the summer.'

'Us?' Amelie looked puzzled. 'I thought Lucien was just a friend. That's what you've been telling me for the last six months.'

Marie glared at Amelie. 'And why do you think that is? You've never liked any of my boyfriends. I wanted to keep Lucien for myself, but now it's kind of serious between us.'

Amelie put her hand on Marie's arm and looked up at her. 'I'm sorry. If I'm being completely honest, none of your previous boyfriends were good enough for you. That's why I never liked them.'

'And yours were?' Marie raised a perfectly groomed eyebrow. 'That guy you were seeing at university, Greg, he cheated on you with your roommate!'

Amelie glared at her. 'Don't do this in front of Kate.'

'I think it's lovely that you two are *so* protective of each other.' Kate decided to try diplomacy.

'She's my younger sister, so of *course* I'm protective of her,' Amelie said to Kate, then looked at Marie. 'I'm sorry if I ever upset you. I never meant to. I'm not exactly a brilliant example of someone who knows how to have a healthy relationship. I'm divorced and dating the man I had an affair with while I was married.'

Marie frowned. 'It was more than an affair. You were in love.' She glanced at Kate, then put her hand over her mouth.

'Kate knows,' Amelie said. 'And yes, we were in love, but it wouldn't have worked between us then.'

'And now?' Marie asked. 'Do you feel like it might work now?'

'I do. How about you? Is it love?' Amelie asked.

'I think it is.' Marie smiled. 'I'm very happy.'

'Then I'm happy for you,' Amelie said. 'Is Lucien the reason you won't be coming over for Christmas?' Amelie asked.

'Yes, he's taking me to meet his parents in Normandy.' Marie blushed. 'He's a little older than me, but he's so wonderful.'

'How much older are we talking? Old enough to be your dad?' Kate paused. 'Grandad?'

Marie laughed. 'He's eight years older than me, so he's just turned fifty.' She took her phone out of her pocket and showed Kate a photo of him.

Kate took the phone from Marie. 'Oooh Marie, he's a silver fox! Why are French men so much more stylish than English men?' She handed the phone to Amelie. 'Check him out!'

'Marie, he's gorgeous. When can we meet him?'

'Why not come out with Kate next year?' Amelie suggested. 'Then you can both meet him. He's moving in with me in after Christmas. His bachelor pad in the city is way too small for all my stuff.'

Kate smiled as she thought about Marie's eclectic hilltop villa. 'That's awesome, I'm so happy for you both.'

Amelie handed Marie her phone. 'I'd love to meet him. Count me in.'

'Wonderful.' Marie turned to Kate. 'I'll send you over the details of Lucien's studio. Take a look at it and let me know what you think. There's a ton of paperwork to sort out, so the sooner we can get started on it, the better. And it would only be a short term offer, Lucien suggested from April until September.'

'That suits me,' Kate said. 'The South of France is *the* place to spend the summer.'

'I couldn't agree more.' Marie smiled. 'I was only supposed to be there for a year, but I never came back here. How could I? If I can get the renovations to the bar finished by the time you come over, we will have a perfect summer.'

'How's it going?' Kate asked.

Her aunt owned a bar in the Old Quarter of Nice. It was smalll, chic and always full of locals, all of whom Marie knew. After a water leak in the tiny kitchen, last month, Marie had closed the bar and embarked on a full renovation.

'They're still sorting the plumbing out.' Marie sighed. 'I've hired the best contractor in the area, but if it is open again by the time you come over, it will be a miracle.'

'Last summer we were drinking cocktails in the sunshine.' Kate smiled. 'Then we went to that music festival, do you remember?'

'I do! We crawled into bed at five am. The sun was already coming out.' Marie laughed. 'We can do it all again next year.'

Kate noticed the smile disappearing from her mother's face, and she wondered what it must have been like for her when Marie moved to France. She and Rob had never been apart for very long, and she knew she'd miss him if he lived in another country.

'You can come too, Mama. You'd love the music festival,' Kate said, trying to include her mother, who was now chewing her lip.

'I'm sure I would. I adore Nice, but I couldn't live there. My roots are, and always have been, here.' Amelie glanced at Marie, then back at Kate. 'Am I to be the only Barton left at Barton Hall?'

'I'm not going forever, Mama.' Kate put her hand on Amelie's and squeezed it. 'I'll only be gone for the summer.'

'Not all of us want to hang around in this crumbling old house for the rest of our lives, Amelie,' Marie interjected.

'And not all of us want to walk away from our pasts, *Marie,*' Amelie snapped.

'I didn't walk away. I went to explore the world. And what I found was more desirable than my life here.' Marie held Amelie's gaze, almost daring her to respond.

Kate let out a long exhale. 'I don't understand you two. You don't see each other for months, and when you do, you don't waste any opportunity to tear each other down. I don't get it.' She stood up. 'I'm going to bed.'

'Wait.' Marie turned to Amelie. 'I'm sorry. I was unkind. Again.'

'You were.' Amelie glared at her. 'Again.'

Kate sat back down, torn between walking away from the conflict, and staying to referee it.

'This house has always felt so overwhelming,' Marie said, 'and I love Canterbury, but when I graduated, I couldn't wait to escape. I think there's a part of me that feels jealous that you're so able to feel at home here, when all I can see is how much work it is to maintain it.'

'It's work I'm happy to do,' Amelie replied, her tone gentle.

Marie seemed to consider this for a second before she replied. 'And that's why I'm glad Papa left you the house, because you're a much better custodian of it than I ever would be.'

'Was there a part of you that felt resentful that he did?' Amelie asked, her tone cautious.

Marie's response was immediate. 'No. You left your own house and moved in here, and you cared for him in his last few years, even though your marriage was collapsing, and so was the house. You made this house your own and so it *should* be yours. I still feel guilty that I didn't do the same thing.'

'Your whole life was in another country,' Amelie said. 'You couldn't have dropped everything whereas I could. You were here as much as you could have been. And now, you can come over whenever you like. I know we fall out a lot, but I do love seeing you, and especially love seeing you here, where we grew up.'

Marie smiled. 'I love seeing you too. I'm sorry I've been such a bitch. I think all of the guilt and resentment has been clattering around my head for years. You were the perfect, dutiful daughter, with two amazing children, a husband, and I didn't even have a home or a boyfriend until I was in my thirties.'

Amelie shook her head. 'We're very different people. I admired your bravery, and ability to make your home wherever the wind took you.' She turned to Kate. 'I think you're a mix of both of us. You like to spread your wings, but you know where your roots are too.'

'That's very poetic, Mama.' Kate smiled. 'I love you *both*, and hearing you both being honest with each other rather than flicking barbed comments at each other is amazing. Please keep it up. I don't plan on moving to France, but I'm young and opportunities like the one that Lucien is offering don't come around very often, so I'm going to take it.'

'As you *should*.'

Kate noticed that Amelie's eyes were filling with tears. 'Mama, it's going to be fine. Remember that when I go, Rob will be back from university for the summer.'

'Good point. The two of you are like ships in the night and I am delighted that you're spreading your wings.' Amelie wiped her eyes with her napkin. 'I need to get over myself. I knew this day would come. I can't just expect to keep you both here.'

'We might go, but we'll always come back.' Kate stood up. 'I'm going to go to bed so that you guys can talk properly. I think there's a lot you need to talk about and it's not necessarily for me to hear.'

'I don't want to push you away,' Marie said, her brow furrowing.

'You're not,' Kate assured her. 'I'll see you both in the morning.'

She left Amelie and Marie talking, and went upstairs to her room, praying that it wouldn't descend into chaos without her to intervene. Tonight had been a mixture of the usual, predictable conflict, and a few surprises. Including the offer of a job next summer in Nice, a place that felt like her second home. Her aunt had always felt more like an older sister than an aunt. Working and living there for a few months would be an experience that she would never forget. As she read her book, she imagined herself laying on a sun lounger around Marie's pool, sipping a cocktail and watching the sunset. It was a world away from the dark, cold corridors of Barton Hall, and she wondered who she was more like, her free spirited aunt, or her cautious, family orientated mother. She couldn't imagine trying to maintain a house like this, while working full time and raising two children. But she also couldn't imagine walking away from everything she'd grown up with and embracing the unknown. Next summer, she would get the opportunity to do just that, and she was excited to see where it would lead her.

Chapter Thirteen

When Kate got home on Friday evening, she found Amelie sat at the kitchen table, surrounded by old photos.

'Hello, darling.' Amelie looked up. 'Marie and I got this box of photos out. Look at this one.'

Kate sat down next to her and took the photo that Amelie handed her. 'Mama, you look just like me!' The photo had been taken in the back garden of the house she'd grown up in, before they moved to Barton Hall. Amelie was smiling at the camera and cradling her large baby bump.

'I know. I was just about to have you. Marie took that photo. It was the last one she took before you arrived. I will never forget that drive to the hospital.' Amelie shuddered. 'She was an incredible birth partner though.'

Kate knew this story well. Her dad had been at work in London, and Marie had ended up being Amelie's birth partner while they waited for him to arrive.

'Have you enjoyed this week with her?' Kate asked. 'Something's changed between you two, hasn't it?'

'It has.' Amelie paused. 'There's still a lot we need to talk about, but the tension between us seems to have lifted. I don't want to question it or overanalyse it too much.'

'Good idea. So does this mean you guys will see more of each other now?' Kate asked.

'I hope so,' Amelie said. 'I've wanted a real relationship with her for so long, and I assumed she didn't want that. She thought the same thing, and it's taken us probably ten years to even *have* this conversation so it's going to take some time to figure that out. This week has been incredible, and I genuinely can't wait to see her again.'

That wasn't how the end of Marie's visits always went. Sometimes there were arguments, sometimes she and Amelie were in tears because they didn't want to say goodbye to each other. Their relationship was a rollercoaster ride.

'I'm so pleased for you, Mama. This year's ending on such a high note for you. You have a hot new boyfriend, you've fixed your relationship with Marie, *and* you have a little French girls trip with me next year to look forward to!' Kate smiled. 'I am so intrigued about Lucien. I spoke to him earlier, and his voice is so dreamy. I could listen to him talk forever. He explained the job offer a little more, and I just about managed to keep up with his French. I need to talk to Emmett and give him an answer in the next few weeks.'

'Do you think he's a little too old for her?' Amelie lowered her voice even though there wasn't anyone else in the room. 'She's always been a lot...*younger* than her age. He's her first proper boyfriend in years, and he's *fifty*.'

'He's only eight years older than her, and if I'm right, you're five years older than James,' Kate pointed out.

'So I am.' Amelie raised an eyebrow. 'Does that make me a cougar?'

Kate laughed. 'Probably.'

'I've started using a slightly more intensive moisturiser.' Amelie prodded her cheeks. 'I can't have people thinking I'm his mother when we go out.'

'Highly unlikely, considering they don't even believe you're *my* mother,' Kate said. 'I hope I've inherited your age-defying genes.'

'It's more than genes.' Amelie held up a hand. 'It's proper hydration, a good SPF and a quality moisturiser.' She ticked each item off on her fingers. 'When you go to France for the summer, you'll have to keep all of those things in mind.'

'I will, and now I'm working I can actually afford decent skincare,' Kate said. 'Are you OK with me going?'

They hadn't discussed the job offer in Nice without Marie around, and Kate wanted to know what Amelie actually thought about it.

'Of course.' Amelie put the lid on the box of photos. 'It's a wonderful opportunity, and if I was your age I would jump at it. It's only my own selfishness that wants to feel put out about it, as I love this house so much more when it's full of people. When I'm alone it feels twice the size.'

'It is a massive house, and I totally understand that, but you can invite James over, and you can have fancy dinner parties every weekend like Nanna and Papa used to do,' Kate suggested.

'That sounds kind of fun.' Amelie looked thoughtful. 'I *do* like a dinner party.'

'Well, there you go.' Kate looked at her watch. 'I need to get ready for my date with Alex.'

'Where's he taking you?' Amelie asked.

'We're going for a drink in the city,' Kate replied. 'I met Leon for an early dinner after work as I knew I'd be too nervous to eat tonight.'

'The first date is always the worst. It'll get easier, I promise.' Amelie smiled.

'It had better get easier,' Kate said. 'The butterflies in my stomach must be so tired, they do not stop fluttering every time I speak to him. I can't figure him out. He asks a lot of questions but he doesn't answer many.'

'Tell me you're not attracted to the mystery?' Amelie raised an eyebrow. 'It's just your kind of thing, being teased with the bare minimum of information. If he'd told you his life story the first time you met, you'd have never spoken to him again.'

Kate smiled. 'True, but he knows way too much about me. I need to even things up.'

Leaving Amelie with her photos, Kate went up to her room and changed into a black jumpsuit, adding her thin gold chain, and a couple of pendants, one with her birthstone, and another a gold star. She slid on her thin gold bangles, then walked carefully down the stairs.

She sat on the bottom stair and put on the ankle boots she'd bought yesterday. The heel was neither as high, or as sharp as her studded boots, and she hoped her knee would tolerate her walking in them because going on a date in her trainers or her work boots was not an option.

As she took a few tentative steps, the doorbell rang. Her heart starting beating faster, and she checked her reflection in the mirror before she opened it.

'Hi Alex' she said, her heart rate sky rocketing as she ran her eyes over him.

He wore a navy blue, silk bomber jacket, with a black t-shirt underneath and a silver chain peeking out of the collar. His black jeans clung tightly to his toned body. His shoes were suede, a navy-blue desert boot, with not a scratch or scuff on them.

'Hello, beautiful.' He stepped forward and kissing her cheek. 'How's the knee? Can you walk, or shall I carry you to the car?'

She smiled. 'As much as I'd love to be pressed right up against you, I can walk just fine.'

'The offer is always there,' he said. 'Are you ready to go?'

'I am.' She nodded and pulled on her coat. She had no idea where her mother was, and getting Alex out of the house before she appeared was vital.

She followed him out of the house and shut the door behind her, slipping her arm into his as she walked tentatively over the gravel.

As he drove into the city, Alex turned to Kate. 'Where do you want to go? I was planning on drinks in the Marlowe. It's small...' His eyes flicked to hers. 'Intimate.'

Kate nodded. Somewhere small and intimate was just what she wanted. 'That sounds perfect.'

The rain beat down on the roof of his car as they reached the city. With his arm in hers, he led her to the Buttermarket, a small square with shops and a couple of pubs. The statue of Jesus looked down from his position at the top of the Christgate, one of the entrances to the cathedral that loomed over the city.

Alex opened the door to the Marlowe, a blast of hot air, and a hundred voices flooding out. 'After you,' he said.

'Thank you.' She walked up to the bar and smiled at a familiar face. 'Hey, Callum, busy tonight, isn't it?' She turned to Alex. 'Alex, this is Callum. He's a friend of mine.' She prayed that Callum wouldn't let on that they'd had a drunk kiss. Or maybe two. 'Callum, this is Alex. I fell down the stairs at work and he came to my rescue.'

Callum's eyebrows shot up. 'Oh, my God, are you alright?'

'I'm a little battered, but fine,' Kate said. 'I was just lucky Alex was nearby.'

Callum held out a hand to Alex. 'Great to meet you, mate. What are you drinking? Your drinks are on the house. Sounds like you're the hero of the hour.'

'Thanks. I think hero's a bit of an exaggeration, but I'll take it.' Alex gave Callum a wry smile. 'An Everleaf and Coke please.'

'Coming up. Kraken and Coke for you, Kate?' he asked and she nodded. 'Be right with you.'

'So I'm a hero, am I?' Alex asked, raising an eyebrow.

'You are to me,' Kate said. 'I don't know what I would have done if you hadn't been there.'

Alex's eyes burnt into hers. 'You would have figured it out. I have no doubt about that.'

Callum returned with their drinks and refused Kate's offer to pay for hers.

'Thanks, Callum.' She took her glass from him, then followed Alex to the back of the bar, and slid onto a stool at one of the empty tables which were made from oak barrels. Tealights flickered in small glass votive jars, and she admired the reflection of the light in Alex's eyes as he sat down next to her, so close she could smell his aftershave. Everyone else ceased to exist in the dimly lit bar. Tonight it was just her and him.

She clinked her glass against Alex's. 'Sante.' She took a sip, the spiced rum warming her throat as she swallowed.

'Santé? You speak French?' His eyebrow quirked.

She nodded. 'My aunt lives in Nice, and she's just been staying with us. I kind of lapse into French when she's around.'

'I wish I could speak another language,' he said. 'Languages weren't my thing at school.'

'What was your thing?' she asked.

'Maths and science,' he replied, 'and engineering, which is kind of how I ended up doing the job I do now. How about you? I'm guessing you were into art?'

'I was.' She smiled. 'I've always been obsessed with jewellery, and when I realised you could actually make jewellery for a living I decided that was what I wanted to do.'

'So there are people out there who are doing their dream jobs.' He shook his head, laughing. 'You're a unicorn.'

'Don't you love your job?' she asked.

'Kind of, but I wanted to be a DJ.' He looked down at his glass, then back up at her. 'I still do. I played City Sound Project a few years back with my mate, George.'

'Really?' She moved closer to him. 'What kind of stuff do you play?'

'Mainly drum and bass, although I'll remix anything I can get my hands on,' he said.

'What's your DJ name?' She was even more intrigued now.

Alex lowered his voice. 'Celestial.'

A thought popped into her head, and she pulled her phone out of her pocket, scrolling through her playlists until she found the right track. 'I've got your remix of Nero's Promises. I've listened to it about a thousand times. It's *so* good!'

He smiled. 'I love that one too.'

'How do you juggle being a DJ and working for Guardia?' she asked.

'I only started working for Guardia a few months ago, and I've not had time for anything other than work, but I'll get back to it soon.' He lowered his voice. 'Music is my life, but until I have the time to devote to making it happen full time, I have to fit it in around everything else and right now I don't have time.'

She nodded. 'Maybe you could give me a private performance.'

'I'd like that,' he replied. 'Trust me, I'll make it happen.'

'How did you decide on the name Celestial? Is it because of your heavenly body?' she quipped.

'I love that, but it's actually because of my dad. He and I used to love looking at the stars when I was a kid,' he said.

'Oh my goodness, that's lovely, and I made it smutty. I'm so sorry.' She cringed, wishing the floor would swallow her up.

'Don't be,' he said, smiling. 'I thought it was funny.'

She breathed a sigh of relief. 'Good. I'm sorry, I make jokes when I'm nervous.'

'You don't need to be nervous.' He put his hand on top of hers, his palm warm on the back of her hand. 'You know me. We aren't strangers.'

'I don't know much about you,' she said, but I think you like it that way.'

'You would be right.' His eyes burnt into hers. 'I know you want to know more about me, but I need to trust someone before I let them in.'

'So do I.' She held his gaze. 'I feel like I can trust you though. You've seen me at my most vulnerable and you protected me.'

His eyebrows furrowed. 'There was no way I was going to leave you alone and injured in the shop.'

'But you could have left me at the hospital,' she pointed out.

'There's no way I could have left you. I couldn't have slept until I knew you were safe,' he said.

'And that's how I know I can trust you. What you did went above and beyond the callout service.' She paused. 'Especially the kiss. The kiss was my favourite part.'

'It's not a service I plan on offering to anyone else.' His eyes moved from hers, down to her lips, then back to her eyes again.

'Good to know.' She felt herself moving closer to him, until his lips met hers.

The kiss was so intense, so perfect, and so *brief.* He had pulled away from her before she realised it. She fought the urge to throw her arms around him, and instead, raised an eyebrow. 'Is that your game plan, to leave me wanting more?'

'Is it working?' he asked.

'It is,' she said.

'In that case, yes.' He took a sip of his drink. 'Are you less nervous now?'

'I am. I'm not sure if it's the rum, or the kiss, or both.' She smiled. Her glass was already empty.

'Can I get you another one?' he asked, picking up her empty glass.

'I'll get these.' She jumped off her stool. 'Same again?'

'Sure, thank you.'

When she returned with their drinks, he thanked her, and she watched his Adam's apple bob as he took a sip. He was a mystery, but he was a hot one.

'How do you know Mia?' he asked. 'I saw you with her at the Penny Theatre.'

'I went to high school with her,' she said. 'And you know Pete, through your brother, is that right?'

He nodded. 'My brother, Ben, was Pete's best friend at school.'

'Mia and Pete are amazing, and I love them, but they're also quite overprotective of me, so I haven't told them I'm seeing you tonight. I wanted to keep you for myself,' she admitted.

'I get it. I was like Pete's older brother when we were at school. I've not told a soul about you. I want to keep you for myself too.' A smile crept across his face.

She took a sip of her drink. 'I understand that you take a while to trust people, but you know so much about me already, and I don't really know anything about you.' She moved closer to him, so close that his scent enveloped her.

He rubbed a hand over his chin. 'That's a good point. You want to even things up, right? I'm Alex Compson. I'm a client systems manager at Guardia, and your boss Emmett is a client, and a friend of mine.'

'How did you get into working with security systems?' she asked.

'I kind of fell into working with security systems after I finished my engineering degree. I worked for a big company in London, managing multi-million pound properties, but I left that job in the summer and moved back here.'

This was where he stopped talking, and Kate watched as his eyebrows furrowed. Was this a touchy subject 'Do you miss it? London, I mean?' she asked tentatively, wondering how much he would disclose.

'Oh, definitely, but I've got a lot going on here, so...' He shrugged. 'I don't know if I would move back there now.'

She was itching to ask more questions, but she had no idea if he would answer them.

'Where did you go to university?' he asked. 'Emmett said you'd graduated recently.'

'I went to Brighton. It was amazing, it's like Canterbury but by the sea,' she said.

'The Lanes are full of jewellery shops. What brought you back here?' he asked.

'My family, my friends, and Corrells. I'd done some work experience there and knew it was the place I wanted to work. When Rebecca announced her pregnancy I pretty much begged Emmett to take me on.' She bit her lip. 'Now I've got what I wanted and I have to prove myself to him.'

'You don't have to prove yourself to anyone. Be yourself, that's enough,' he said, putting his hand on hers again.

'Good advice.' She took another sip of her drink, and slipped her fingers between his. The butterflies in her stomach were still fluttering, but they seemed slightly calmer. 'What else do you do apart from working and making music?'

'I run,' he said. 'Where I live there's a lot of woodland and I can go for miles without seeing another person.'

'Impressive. I would only ever run for the bus, or an ice cream van.' She smiled.

'And I guess you can't run very far at all right now,' he said.

'No, but I'm working on it.'

His easy smile and gravelly voice were addictive. She could listen to him talk all night.

'What are you thinking about?' she asked.

'That I've never, ever wanted anyone as much as I want you,' he said.

Heat rose in her cheeks and, for a moment, she couldn't breathe. 'The feeling is mutual.' Her head was swimming. Had he really just said that? It didn't feel real. She glanced down at their intertwined fingers. 'I can't let go of you.'

He cupped her face in his hands. 'Then don't.' He kissed her, and she sank into him.

'Are you satisfied? Did you get what you came for?' he whispered as he pulled away from her.

'Yes,' she whispered back, still breathless after the kiss that she knew she'd spend all night thinking about. She gazed at him, willing him to kiss her again.

'If you keep looking at me like that, I'm not going to sleep tonight.' He tipped her chin up, brushing her lips with his.

'I know I won't,' She whispered against his lips. Tonight felt like a dream. One that she was worried she would wake up from.

He finished his drink. 'Shall we get out of here?'

'Sure,' she replied. Right now she'd go wherever he asked her, as long as he kissed her like that again. She stood up and grabbed his hand. 'Let's go.'

He led her out of the bar, into the cold darkness of the night. He didn't let go as they walked through the streets, past the crowds of people outside the bars. She felt like he was protecting her but also claiming her as his, and she liked it.

'Tonight was worth the wait,' she said as they walked under the Christmas lights strung up between the shops.

'You were definitely worth the wait,' he replied, sliding his arm around her waist. His phone started ringing and he groaned, pulling it out of his pocket. His eyebrows drew into a frown when he looked at the screen, then he sighed, answering it.

'Hey, what do you need?' He listened, nodding, and his brow furrowed. 'I'll be right there.'

They arrived at the car park and he hung up. 'I'm really sorry, but something's come up. I didn't want this to be the end of tonight.'

'It's alright. I understand. I have a feeling I'll be seeing you again.' She opened the door and climbed in.

'Was that your attempt at playing it cool?' He laughed as he put on his seatbelt. '*I get the feeling I'll be seeing you again.* You know what effect you have on me.'

He shook his head. 'Later tonight, when we both can't sleep, we'll sort out another date, OK?'

She smiled softly. 'I look forward to it.'

Back at her house, Kate climbed out of Alex's car and followed him to the shelter of her front porch. 'Please tell me you're going to kiss me again like you did last time we were here,' she said, sliding her hands inside his bomber jacket.

'Seeing as you asked so nicely.' He looked down at her, his eyes twinkling. 'This was easier when you had your heels on. Hold on.' He bent down and scooped her up, gripping her thighs, so that her face was level with his as she draped her arms around his neck. 'Much better.'

He pressed her body against the wall, and his lips met hers. Her fingers slid to the back of his neck, and she murmured with pleasure as he deepened the kiss. Her senses flooded with the scent of his aftershave and the herbal taste of the Everleaf.

When he pulled away from her, and she opened her eyes, his gaze was locked on hers. She took in his dilated pupils, the usual stormy blue replaced by a dark desire. Her breath caught in her throat as he gently lowered her to the ground. 'I should let you go. I'll be thinking about that private performance though.'

'Really?' His voice was rough as his lips brushed her cheek. 'You're not the only one. How about next weekend?'

'Perfect. I'll see you then.'

She watched him walk back to his car, the gravel crunching underneath his feet. Tonight had been everything she'd wanted. He had given her just enough of himself to keep her hooked, and she was already desperate for more.

Chapter Fourteen

November 2012, Canterbury, Kent, England

On Monday morning, Kate walked into Corrells, smiling as she saw Lisa behind the counter. 'Morning, love!'

Lisa grinned. 'Morning! Looks like you had a good weekend. Are you going to fill me in?'

Kate paused by the staircase. 'I had a date and it went pretty well. That's all I'm saying.'

Lisa opened her mouth to reply but was interrupted by the door swinging open.

'Rebecca!' Kate and Lisa shouted at the same time.

'It's me! And I'm not alone. Meet Luca.' Rebecca turned her body, and Kate could see a tiny head, with tightly shut eyes and a couple of dark curls peeping out out of the fabric wrapped around Rebecca's waist.

'He's adorable, Rebecca,' Kate said. 'How are you? You look incredible, motherhood suits you!'

Her skin was glowing, and her dark curls were scooped up into a messy bun, which looked way more stylish than Kate's haphazard attempts. She took off her coat, revealing several gold chains clustered around her neck, and the star sign pendant that Rebecca had made when Luca was born, studded with tiny diamonds.

'Thank you, love.' Rebecca smiled. 'I'm doing really well, thanks. Motherhood is a wild ride, but so far totally awesome. I credit my looks entirely to the good weather in Italy, and a very expensive concealer. How's it going here?'

'We're super busy.' Lisa was talking to Rebecca, but her eyes were on Luca. 'As you know, this time of year is wild.'

'Oh yes. It doesn't stop,' Rebecca said, then turned to Kate. 'How are you getting on, love? I've been keeping an eye on the website and I'm loving your designs. Emmett made a good choice with you.'

'Wow, that's a huge compliment,' Kate replied, her heart about to burst with pride. Having Rebecca's approval meant everything to her. 'You're a hard act to follow.'

Rebecca laughed. 'I don't think so. I started out here at the same age as you, and that wasn't so long ago. When I started I was so intimidated by David, but he told me to just stay true to myself so that's what I did, and that's what I see in your designs. I see *you*.'

'Thank you.' Kate smiled. 'David is so great to work with and he's forever walking me through my overthinking.'

'He did the same with me.' Rebecca smiled back at her, then looked down at Luca. 'Hello, sweetie, you're awake now, are you?' She lifted him carefully out of the fabric wrap, and turned him to face Kate and Lisa. 'This is Kate, and this is Lisa. And this is the shop that I worked in before you arrived.'

'How did you manage the stairs while you were pregnant?' Kate asked.

'With difficulty.' Rebecca settled Luca in her arms. 'That's why I went on maternity leave a little earlier than planned.'

'Kate fell down them last month,' Lisa said. 'She was so lucky she didn't break anything.'

Rebecca gasped. 'Oh, Kate! How awful. What happened?'

'I was working here late on my own, got spooked at the top of the stairs and slipped,' Kate said. 'Then I set the alarm off. It was an evening I won't forget in a hurry.'

'She had to call Alex out to come rescue her,' Lisa added.

Rebecca's eyes widened. 'The lovely Alex. Did he swoop in and save you?'

'Uh, yes. I guess he did.' Kate felt her cheeks flush, and avoided Lisa's gaze.

'Is there more to this story?' Rebecca asked.

Kate glanced around the shop, even though it was empty. 'We went on a date this weekend.'

She'd planned on keeping that to herself, but she couldn't trust her face not to betray her. She could feel her cheeks burning.

'I knew it!' Lisa cried. 'He *carried* her to his car, Rebecca, and he stayed with her at the hospital, then drove her home.'

Rebecca raised an eyebrow. 'Wow. He must really like you. I've been working here for five years and I can barely get him to say a word to me. He's quite mysterious, or maybe that's just what he's like with us.'

'Oh no, that's what he's actually like.' Kate smiled, remembering the teasing kiss he'd given her, knowing she wanted more. 'He doesn't give much away, but I like a mystery. I'm an oversharer, and he's like a clam that I'm trying to prise open.'

'I love that!' Rebecca exclaimed. 'You have to tell me how this plays out.'

Kate nodded. 'I will, but don't tell Emmett or David. I don't know if they'd approve.'

'I will say nothing.' Rebecca mimed zipping up her mouth.

'You know I won't say a word,' Lisa said. 'I'm so invested in this.'

Rebecca gestured to Luca, who was staring at one of the display cases. 'Do you two want a cuddle while he's awake and not crying?'

Lisa shook her head. 'He's still a bit too small.'

'I love babies. I'll have a cuddle if he's happy to leave you,' Kate said.

Kate sat down next to Rebecca, who cautiously handed Luca to her.

'He likes to be upright, where he can see what's going on.' Rebecca took a travel coffee cup out of her bag. 'Thanks, Kate. I can have a hot drink in peace.'

Kate cautiously stood up and showed Luca around the shop, pointing out the bright lights and sparkling diamonds. He gripped her shirt tightly, and she felt relieved that she hadn't had a chance to get it covered in dust yet. 'He's taking it all in,' she said to Rebecca.

'He seems very content with you,' Rebecca replied. 'He's not like that with everyone. He adores my sister, but refuses to let my mother-in-law pick him up.' She bit her lip and Kate suspected she was hiding a smile.

'What about sleep? Does he sleep?' she asked. Lilly still wasn't sleeping through the night every night and Mia was always exhausted.

'He does three or four hours at a time, and I can deal with that,' Rebecca said. 'He even slept all the way to Italy last month. Nico's mum had a huge party for her seventieth birthday, and he wanted to introduce Luca to his family. I was so nervous about taking Luca on the plane, but he was less bothered by the flight than I was.' She laughed. 'Then when we got to Tuscany we had an army of Italian aunties fighting over who got to cuddle him first.'

'He's a popular little guy,' Lisa said. 'Emmett won't be back from his meeting for another hour, can you stay that long?'

'No, we need to go for his check up, but we'll come back another day.' Rebecca turned to Kate. 'Could you hold Luca while I go and see David?'

'Sure.' Kate nodded. 'Go and catch up with him, we'll come and get you if we need you.'

'I'll hear him, trust me. I'll be back in a minute,' Rebecca said, then went up the spiral staircase to the studio.

'Why didn't we get David to come down here?' Lisa asked Kate.

'Maybe Rebecca wants to talk to David alone?' Kate suggested, then took Luca over to the display case of engagement rings. 'These are the *really* sparkly ones. What do you think of these?' she asked him.

'I would be so scared of dropping him, ' Lisa said. 'but you know just how to hold him.'

'I had some practice with my friend Mia's daughter, Lilly,' Kate replied, her eyes still on Luca. 'She's almost three now, and I'm the fun aunt. My mum had me when she was my age, and although Luca is cute, there's no way I'd want a baby now. I'll be the fun aunt for as long as I can.'

She thought about Marie, her own fun aunt, who had never wanted children. Could she see children in her future. Possibly. Was she already imagining them with dark hair and piercing blue eyes? Absolutely. There was no way she'd tell anyone else that though.

The doorbell rang, and Lisa left Kate to serve a customer, so she wandered around the shop with Luca pressed against her shoulder.

Rebecca came back down the stairs a few minutes later, and took Luca from Kate. 'It was so good to see you. Please keep in touch with me. I need all the gossip to break up the endless slog of laundry and feeds.'

'We will,' Kate assured her. 'Maybe we can meet up for lunch? Or dinner? Or whatever works for you.'

'Dinner sounds great, but I can't leave Luca yet as he won't take a bottle,' Rebecca said. 'Why don't you come over for lunch sometime? You've got my number. Let me know when you're free.'

'If you're sure? Maybe I can bring lunch over,' Kate suggested. She couldn't imagine how tough it was for Rebecca to juggle a baby and feeding herself, let alone anyone else.

'Sounds great. Drop me a message and we'll sort it out.' She gave Kate a hug, careful not to squash Luca, then waved to Lisa before she left.

Kate went back upstairs and sat down opposite David. 'Hey. Did you have a good chat with Rebecca?'

'I did,' he replied. 'She's enjoying being a mum, eh?' There was a mischievous twinkle in his eyes.

'What did she say to you?' Kate asked. 'And are you going to tell me?'

When he didn't respond, she picked up her sketchbook and started to draw a custom order. If she pretended she wasn't interested, he would tell her.

'Rebecca might not return, but you didn't hear that from me.' He remained focused on the tiny silver band gripped between his fingers. 'She may change her mind, but you never know, a longer term contract might be on the cards for you. If you want to stay, that is.'

Kate thought about Lucien's offer. He had advised her to wait until he had looked into the legalities of hiring her before she spoke to Emmett, and with six months left on her contract, she'd put Nice to the back of her mind, but what if Rebecca didn't return *and* Lucien offered her a job. What would she do then.

'Interesting,' she said. 'I love working here, but until Rebecca decides what she wants, I'm going to try not to get too attached.'

'A wise and pragmatic decision for someone so young,' he said dramatically.

She laughed. 'I think that's your influence. No one has ever called me wise.'

When Friday evening came around, Kate was so focused on a set of wedding rings, that when her phone buzzed with a message from Alex, she realised she was already late to meet him. She smiled to herself as she re-read his earlier message. He'd been sending her song lyrics every morning, leaving her to work out which song they were from. This morning's one had puzzled her. It had taken her a while to figure out which song the lyrics came from, and when she finally realised it was "Lemon Crush" from Prince's 1989 Batman soundtrack, she'd put it on, and it had been playing in the background on repeat all afternoon. She typed out a quick reply.

> Sorry, I'm running a bit late, I'll be there in 15
> K x

At lightning speed, she cleared up her bench and scrubbed her hands, before adding a coat of lipstick. With the studio to herself, she whipped off her dirty black dress and replaced it with a clean, scoop neck skater dress in a deep mossy green. She'd forgotten to bring some shoes to change into, so her clumpy black boots would have to do. She picked up her coat from the stand by the door and carefully walked down the stairs, before hurtling out of the shop, the pain in her knee now gone. Even better, the butterflies in her stomach were now under control, and she felt brave enough to eat in front of him, although she had no idea where they were going. Alex had told her that he liked surprises, and even though she didn't, she trusted him.

When she got to the Burgate, she saw Alex. He stood under the arch of the entrance to the cathedral, illuminated by the lights above him. They gave him an almost ethereal glow, framed in the centre of the ancient stone gateway.

'I'm sorry I'm so late. I lost track of time.' Feeling flustered, her words flew out.

'I've literally just got here.' Alex bent down and kissed her cheek. 'How's your knee?'

'It's much better. I pretty much ran here.' She looked down at her feet. 'I'm sorry about my boots. I forgot to bring something to change into.'

'Stop apologising,' he said, a serious look on his face. 'I'm into you, work boots and all.'

'I remember you lacing them up.' She smiled. 'You were so gentle with me.'

'I can be gentle,' he whispered, and even in the wintery twilight, she could see his eyes darkening, 'but I can also be firm. Depending on what you're into.'

'I like the sound of firm.' She looked up at him. 'This is why I can't remember anything. You keep melting my brain with the things you say.' She let out a long exhale. 'In case you hadn't realised, I don't do playing it cool, Alex.'

'What makes you think I do?' he replied, raising his eyebrow. 'Come on, let's get a drink.' He steered her into the Marlowe, and they made their way to the back of the room, where they'd sat the previous week.

He took her coat, hanging it up on the coat stand behind them. 'You look gorgeous,' he said, his eyes raking over her body. 'That dress is stunning.'

'Thank you,' she replied, smoothing down the soft fabric, as she sat down. My friend Leon made it for me. I have it in four different colours.'

'He made it?' He nodded approvingly, sitting down next to her. 'He did a good job.'

'He's going off to university next year to study fashion design. He's been saving up for years,' she said, smiling.

'Talented friends, huh? I bet you made your necklace, right?'

Her fingers slid across the heart shaped crystal pendant around her neck. 'I did. It's a bi-colour sapphire. Can you see how it changes from blue to green?'

'It's beautiful. You're talented too.' He nodded towards the bar. 'Can I get you a drink? Kraken rum and Coke, right?'

'Sure, thank you.' As he walked to the bar, she admired the way that his jeans clung to his toned body, and the buttery soft leather jacket that perfectly hugged his arms. He was a work of art, and he was here with *her*. She almost had to pinch herself. This felt like a dream.

When he returned, she thanked him for her drink, and took a sip. The nerves that had plagued her the last time they met were long gone, and tonight all she could think about was finding out more about him, and hoping that he might let her just a little further into his world.

'Would you like to see Future Proof tonight?' he asked. 'They're playing at the Penny Theatre and we'd have the best seats in the house.'

'Uh, yes. I would love that!' she said. 'When you say the best seats in the house, do you mean like where *you* were watching them last time?'

'Yeah, we'd be right at the side of the stage. Is that alright? We can go out on the floor if you want,' he said.

'No, I'd love to be right there next to them,' she replied. 'When are they on?'

He checked his watch. 'We have a couple of hours. I'll let George know we're coming.' He pulled out his phone and typed a message.

'How do you know them?' she asked.

He put his phone into his back pocket. 'George and I went to school together. He was my best mate, and he introduced me to Pete, whose brother was my brother's best friend. We all hung out until George and I moved to London when we went to university. He came back here years ago, but we stayed in touch, and when he set up the band, I helped them as I had some contacts in the industry.'

'Of course you do, and of course you helped! You're always looking out for other people,' she said.

'I try.' A hint of a smile played at his lips. 'It's great being back here with them.'

'What about your brother?' Kate asked. 'Mia said he moved away.'

'Yeah he went to university in Cornwall and never came back.'

She could tell from his guarded expression that this had been painful for him. 'I'm sorry, I didn't mean to pry...'

'You weren't.' He paused. 'It's kind of a sore spot for me.'

'I know it's hard for you to open up,' she said, 'but you can trust me. I trusted you at the hospital. You were there for me. I can be there for you if you let me.'

'Right. You did trust me.' He took a deep breath. 'We were in a car accident when I was twelve and Ben was seven. My dad didn't make it. We all found it hard, but Ben really struggled, and when he left, he didn't want to come back. There were too many memories here for him.'

'Bad memories,' she said, remembering his words at the hospital. He had been so young when his dad died. Her eyes flicked to the scar on his arm.

He followed her gaze. 'I got this in the accident. And the scar above my eyebrow, just like the one you've got now.'

'I'm so sorry. I can't imagine how hard that must have been.' She caught his eye. 'I understand why hospitals aren't your favourite places. Why did you take me there?'

'You needed me.'

If she hadn't already fallen for him, this would have been the moment that she did. She leant forward and kissed him. 'I had no idea what you were going through that night, because you put me first, but you don't have to pretend or hide with me. I can be there for you too.'

'I know that now, but that night I couldn't have told you what was actually going on.' He slipped off his jacket, revealing a tight black t-shirt and those muscular forearms that had taken centre stage in her dreams. He was wearing a thin silver cuff with a faded inscription and she squinted, trying to read it in the flickering candlelight. 'This was his. It has his date of birth and the place he was born, Hong Kong, inscribed on it. His father was in the Merchant Navy and was stationed out there.'

'It's beautiful.' She studied the faint lettering. 'I always notice everyone's jewellery, but I've never seen you wear this before.'

'I don't wear it that often. It's so old, I don't want to risk damaging it, but I put it on when I'm missing him. It makes me feel closer to him.'

She looked into his stormy blue eyes. 'Jewellery is more than just pieces of metal. It evokes memories, it brings comfort, joy and love.'

'I love that. You're so right.' He held her gaze as he twisted the cuff around.

'Your DJ name makes even more sense now,' she said, 'and I feel even worse about the smutty joke.'

'I told you, it's fine. You didn't know and I thought it was funny.' He took her hand, lacing his fingers in between hers. 'If I'm giving you the real me, I need the real you, jokes and all.'

'I can do that.' She'd give him whatever he wanted if he kept stroking the back of her hand with his thumb, and gazing into her eyes.

'Good.' He checked his watch. 'Do you want to get some dinner before we go to the Penny Theatre? We could go to the new taqueria in Butchery Lane.'

'Yes!' She beamed at him. 'I've been meaning to go there for weeks.'

It was a dark, cloudy night in the city, where the restaurants were packed and the windows were steamy. The sound of cutlery and clinking glasses floated through the air as Kate walked through the streets hand in hand with Alex, as strings of fairy lights glowed above their heads. At the taqueria, there were only two seats free, on one of the large communal benches that took up most of the restaurant, and the waitress showed Kate and Alex to it.

Kate opted for mildly spicy tacos and when they arrived, she was grateful, after taking a bite of Alex's spicy one. 'Oh wow. That's hot.' She took a gulp of her agua fresca and wiped her mouth with a napkin.

'I love spicy food,' Alex said. 'I went to Mexico a few years ago, and I loved it.'

'Oh, really?' she asked. 'Where did you go?'

'We stayed in Mexico City,' he replied, 'but we travelled around a bit. It's such a beautiful country. Have you been?'

'I went with my Hannah, my other best friend,' she said. 'I loved the food, but my mouth was on fire the whole time. I was not prepared. Hannah didn't care, though. She'll eat anything.'

'Was Hannah who you were with at the Bastille gig?' he asked.

She shook her head. 'No, that was Lucy, another high school friend. Hannah and I have been friends since we were born, and we were at university in Brighton together. She's gone back to London to teach in a secondary school.'

'She's brave. You must miss her,' he said.

'I do but we're never far apart.' She smiled. 'We always find a way to see each other.'

'George and I are the same. He went travelling after university and I didn't see him for a year.' He took a sip of his agua fresca. 'When I moved back here, we just picked up where we left off. I used some of his vocals on a track, and the band came together off the back of that.'

'That's so cool. I love their sound. It's so unique.' She took another mouthful of her taco, being careful to avoid dropping it down her top.

'They're playing a few festivals next year, and releasing an EP' he said. 'I'm remixing a couple of the tracks right now.'

'Can I hear them?' she asked.

'At your private performance?' He raised an eyebrow. 'Of course.'

She put her napkin next to her empty plate, and finished the last of her agua fresca. 'Those tacos were so good, but my lips are tingling.' She pressed them against his cheek. 'Can you feel that?'

'No.' He smirked. 'Try again.'

She kissed him again. 'How about now?'

'Nothing, but I'd let you keep trying forever,' he said.

She laughed and took another sip of his drink. 'This is good, I'm keeping this one.'

'I'll order another one,' he said. 'And some churros, I can see you eyeing them up.'

A dish of churros and chocolate sauce had arrived at the other end of the bench, and Kate smiled to herself. He missed nothing. He caught the eye of the waiter and ordered more drinks, and the churros, which arrived moments later.

Alex passed her the dish. 'You first.'

She picked one up and dropped it, wincing. 'They're really hot!'

He wrapped a napkin around one end and held it out to her. 'Here.'

She leant forward and took a bite. 'Perfect! Thanks.'

He smiled. 'I meant for you to take it.'

'Oh no! I thought you were holding it for me to take a bite from. Why do I always embarrass myself in front of you?' She shook her head.

He laughed. 'Don't be embarrassed.' He finished the churro, then wrapped another one in a napkin. 'Make things even. Take this and I'll take a bite.'

She took it and dipped it in the chocolate sauce then held it out to him. 'I'm slightly less embarrassed now.'

'Good.' His lips curved into a smile. 'You can give me another one if that helps?'

Once the churros were gone, Alex paid the bill before Kate could even get her purse out, and then held out his hand to her, helping her to her feet.

She linked her arm with his as they walked to the the Penny Theatre, and once they were inside he took her backstage, where the band were hanging out. 'Guys, this is Kate. Kate, this is George, Ed and Connor.'

'Good to meet you.' George brushed his floppy brown hair out of his eyes. 'I've seen your face before, right? You look familiar.'

Kate smiled at him. 'I saw you here in October. You guys are amazing.'

George smiled. 'You're a fan? Brilliant. I figured Alex persuaded you to come along. I had no idea he was seeing anyone. He's so secretive.'

Alex raised his eyebrow at George.

'Looks like I've said too much as usual.' George laughed. 'You guys are welcome to watch from up here.' He gestured to one of the large flight cases behind him. 'Grab a seat.'

Alex patted him on the back. 'Thanks, mate. You want a beer?'

'You know it,' George replied. 'You get these, I'll get the next ones.'

Alex nodded and walked off to the bar, while Kate sat down, and watched the band sound checking.

Alex returned with a tray of drinks. He set it down on the flight case and handed Kate a glass. 'Rum and Coke?' He picked up a bottle and clinked it against her glass. 'Sante.' He sat down next to next to her. 'You need to teach me some French.'

'I'll teach you the best words,' she whispered.

She leant her head against his shoulder as the band started playing. George's voice was as faultless as it was the last time but seeing them this close was something else. As the first few chords of "Never Hurt You Again" started, Kate led Alex down the stairs and onto the packed dance floor, where she pressed her body against his. As the music surged through them, she brushed her lips over his neck. The crowd in the dark room closed in on them, pushing them closer to each other.

'I want you,' he whispered into her ear.

She looked up at him. Even in the darkness, she could see the inky pools of his eyes, his pupils dilated, the icy blue replaced by a deep black. 'I want you too.'

He gripped her hand tightly, pulling her through the crowds and out of the bar, into the darkness outside. She pushed him against the ancient brick wall, and as his hands slid around her waist, her lips met his.

When they sprang apart, breathless, he gazed into her eyes. 'I know I said I wanted you, but we at least need to make it home.'

'I have an empty house,' she said, hearing a rumble of thunder.

'Let's go,' he replied, gripping her hand as he led her through the back streets of the city. As they reached his car and climbed in, the rain started pounding down on the car.

Chapter Fifteen

November 2012, Canterbury, Kent, England

When they got back to Kate's house, claps of thunder echoed in the sky above them. Alex parked the car and they paused for a second, listening to the rain, before running up to the porch. Kate unlocked the front door and pushed it open, a loud creak echoing through the hall.

'Oh, shit. This place is creepy in the dark,' Alex whispered as they walked into the hall.

Kate turned on the lights, flooding the hallway in a soft white glow. 'Not so scary now, huh?'

'I didn't say I was scared,' he said.

'Show me how brave you are,' she rep;ied, her words far bolder than she actually felt.

He was here, in her house, and he was all hers. She sucked in a deep breath as he studied her, a smile pulling at the corner of his lips.

His mouth was on hers in a flash, his body pressing her against the wall. His fingers moved across to the light switch and flicked it off. 'This brave enough for you?'

Now she could barely see him. She could only feel his hands on her body and his lips on her neck. 'Yes. Come with me.'

Following the moonlight streaming through the stained glass window on the staircase, she led him to her bedroom, switching on her bedside lamp, which bathed the room in a soft glow.

'So now you have me here, in your bedroom, what happens next?' he asked.

She slid her hands around his neck. 'Wait and see.'

As she kissed him, she felt conflicted. This was supposed to be a fling, but the more time she spent with him, the more time she wanted to spend with him.

He stroked her face. 'That night in the corridor at the Penny Theatre, the way you kissed me, it made me think if she kisses like that, what else is she capable of? I haven't been able to stop thinking about it since.'

'Really?' Had he been thinking about her in exactly the same way she'd been thinking about him?

'Have you ever heard me make a joke?' he asked, tipping her chin up so that her eyes met his.

She frowned. 'No, not once.'

He slid his hands to the back of her dress, slowly unzipping it, and sliding it onto the floor. 'Then trust me, I'm serious.'

A crack of thunder woke Kate up in the middle of the night and she lay still for a second, waiting for her heart rate to slow down. Alex was asleep next to her, and trying to be as quiet as she could, she slid out of bed, and put on her bathrobe. She was just about to leave the room when he sat up.

'Hey, are you alright?' he asked sleepily.

'I'm just going to grab a glass of water,' she said.

'I'll go,' he replied. 'It's dark and creepy and I don't want to risk you falling down any more stairs.'

'I'll be fine,' she insisted, but he was already pulling on his t-shirt and jeans.

She got out of the bed too, and switched on the lights in the hall, then followed him down the stairs and into the kitchen. She filled two glasses with water, handing one to him. As she picked up her glass, the house was plunged into darkness. She heard another crack of thunder above her and groaned. 'Shit.'

'What happened?' he whispered. 'Is it a blown fuse or a power cut?'

'It's just a power cut,' she said. 'We get them during storms.'

'What now?' he asked.

She felt her way along the worktop and pulled one of the drawers open, rummaging in it and pulling out a torch. 'This is not my first rodeo.' She pointed it up to the clock on the wall. 'It's three am. The power cuts usually only last a couple of hours. We'll see what the situation is in the morning.'

She shook her head. One night. That was all she wanted. Just one night with Alex without drama.

When Kate opened her eyes the following morning, she was nestled into Alex's chest. He was already awake, and he held her tightly. 'Morning beautiful.'

'Morning,' she said. 'Can I admit that for the whole of our date I was hoping that we'd end up here last night?'

'Really? Did I live up to your expectations?' he asked.

'You surpassed them,' she said. 'Although, if you're here with me, you can't send me any song lyrics. I love them.'

'Why do you think I send them to you first thing in the morning? You're the first thing I think of when I wake up.' Pulling her closer, he kissed her forehead. 'Waking up next to you is so much better though.'

Her eyes flicked to the window and the rain lashing across the thin panes of glass. She flicked the switch on her bedside lamp, and the room was flooded with light. 'The power's back. That's a good start. I need to check that everything's still standing. Do you want to come with me?'

'Of course.' Alex sat up and swung his legs over the side of the bed. He grabbed his jeans and pulled them on, then his t-shirt.

Kate pulled on her sweatpants and a hoodie, then rummaged in her wardrobe, pulling out an oversize hoodie. 'You might need this. It's going to be really cold downstairs.'

He pulled it on. 'Fits perfectly. Who did you steal this from?'

'Leon. He left it here one, and I claimed it. He's far too stylish to wear hoodies now.' She smiled. 'We'll start downstairs so we can light the fire.'

She shivered as she walked down the stairs, wondering if Alex was as cold as she was.

He studied the photo frames lined up on the table by the front door. 'Wow, this is a lot of people. Who lives here? Do all of these people live here?'

'No.' She shook her head and pointed to one of the photos. 'I live here with my mum. That's my younger brother Rob, who's at university.'

'Wow, you all really look alike.' He studied the photo. 'Your mum looks really young.'

'She was twenty when she had me, so she would have been mid-twenties there.' Kate picked up another photo. 'This is my Nanna and Papa. This was their house, but when they died, Mama inherited it and she's been slowly restoring it since. My dad did live here, but he always hated this place, and when we moved in to look after Papa, he and my mum split up.'

'I'm so sorry. Families are complicated,' he said gently. 'Do you still see your dad?'

'Not very often,' she replied. 'I haven't seen him since I've been back from Brighton.'

She thought about his dad, who had died so young, and wondered how she would feel if she never saw her dad again. A pang of guilt gnawed at her as she walked into the living room and knelt down in front of the fire.

'Do you want a hand?' he asked, kneeling down next to her.

'Nope, I've got it,' she replied, and a few minutes later, she had the fire lit. 'It should warm up in here soon. These old houses take a while to warm up. Have you ever stayed in a house like this before?'

He shook his head. 'Not one as old as this. Your mum's brave. What she's doing is not an easy task, and always more expensive than you'd think.' He studied the watercolour paintings on the walls.

She followed his gaze. 'All painted by Mama. Mainly nudes, as you can see. She loves a pair of boobs and an ass.'

'Can't blame her.' He smirked. 'Do you think she'd paint one for me?'

She laughed. 'She might.' She peered at the fire. 'I can leave this now. We can check the rest of the house.'

He stood up and offered her his hand, pulling her to her feet. 'Lead the way.'

She pushed open the door to the dining room, releasing a rush of cold air. 'We don't use this room very often, as you can probably tell.'

He ran his fingers over the wooden panelling. 'This must be hundreds of years old. It's beautiful.' He looked at the long dining table, which stretched all the way to the French doors at the other end of the room. 'I bet this table has seen some impressive banquets over the years.'

'It has. This house has been in our family for two hundred years, so it has seen *all* kinds of things. My grandparents threw the best parties too.' She smiled. 'I miss them, but we have Christmas and New Years Eve parties in here and I feel like they'd love that.'

'I'm sure they would.' He smiled. 'You're carrying on their traditions and keeping their memories alive.' He spotted the coat of armour in the corner of the room. 'Does he keep an eye on the house for you? I wouldn't want to argue with him.'

'My brother likes to move him around the house to scare us.' She rolled her eyes. 'I never know where he's going to appear.'

He laughed. 'He sounds like fun.'

'He is, but he's also really protective of Mama and I. He really jumped into the role of the man of the house when my dad left.' She imagined Rob meeting Alex. Like Rob, Alex was a helper, someone who looked out for others. 'Come on, we'll go check the library.'

She led him along the corridor and pushed open the door, which creaked loudly. The library was cold, but everything was in its place, not always a guarantee after a storm. The ceilings and windows were extremely unpredictable.

'Someone loves books.' Alex's eyes widened as he took in the floor to ceiling shelves.

'We all do,' Kate said. 'Some of these belonged to my grandfather, so they're really old. We'll go check his study now.'

She left the library and opened the door opposite. As she walked in, the familiar scent hit her; a musty smell that no amount of air freshener or open windows would shift. The mustard-coloured walls were lined with bookcases filled with leather-bound classics. While she checked the ceiling and windows, Alex studied the books, before walking over to the huge leather desk.

'This chair is incredible.' He ran a hand over the smooth wooden arms. 'Can I try it out?'

She nodded. 'Sure. It's really comfy.'

He sat down on the chair, wincing as it creaked underneath him. 'Do you use this room much?'

'I come and sketch designs in here when it's sunny.' She gestured to the window. 'The light in here is really good. My mum works in here when she's not in London. She's either in here or at the kitchen table, but if she has a book deadline, she'll shut herself away in here.'

She noticed his puzzled expression. 'She's an editor. She works for a romance imprint in London.'

'I thought she was an artist?'

'That's just her hobby,' she said.

He stood up. 'Ah, she's a creative, like you. Do you paint?'

'Not as well as her.' She closed the library door behind them. 'Drawing is my thing. I'd like to paint more but who has time?'

'Good point. Where's next?'

'The sunroom is the last room down here.' She opened the door and breathed a sigh of relief when she saw that the glass was still intact. Outside in the garden, several large branches had fallen from the conifers and lay forlorn on the grass. The sky was still dark and the clouds gathered menacingly.

'There's more books in here? And cacti?' Alex turned to Kate. 'They must be pretty cold out here.'

'They're mine. I've collected them since I was a teenager. I relate to them. I guess I can be a bit spiky sometimes too.' What she was really thinking was that sometimes she hurt people if they got too close to her.

'Can't we all?' He looked up at the large panes of glass on the ceiling. 'This place must be incredible in the summer.' He shivered. 'Maybe not right now.'

'No, right now it's freezing. We won't really use it again until Spring.' As he walked out of the room, she closed the door behind them.

As they walked down the corridor, Alex looked at the oil painting on the wall of her ancestors. 'You can feel the history in this place. It's incredible, but there's something else as well.' He paused. 'It's almost like it knows we're here.'

At that moment, a door slammed shut upstairs. Kate sucked in a breath and her stomach lurched. She knew exactly which room that noise had come from. Her palms started to sweat as they climbed the stairs. She started with Amelie's room, trying to ignore the locked door next to it, and then took her time with Rob's room, the floral room, and the bathrooms. Pausing in the corridor after they left the bathroom, she closed her eyes, sucking in a breath.

'We missed one,' Alex said, pausing outside the locked door. He looked at Kate. 'What's up?'

'This is the blue room. We don't go in there much. It has a bit of a reputation. When I was maybe six or seven, Rob and I were playing hide and seek during a storm. I came in here to look for him, and the door slammed shut behind me. I can still remember the flashing lightning and screaming for my mum.' She shuddered.

'I'm sorry, Kate. That sounds so scary.' He took her hand. 'We'll do it together.'

She nodded, unable to speak, and unlocked the door. As she walked in, ignoring the strange atmosphere that hung in the air, like fog, she looked up at the ornate, moulded coving on the ceiling, checking for water damage. The sash window, which was slightly open, caught her eye. Walking over to it, she pushed it closed, then turned around, then leaned against the piano, watching Alex inspecting one of the shrouded shapes in the middle of the room.

'What's this?' he asked, his voice echoing around the room.

'Have a look,' she replied.

He lifted the white dust sheet. Underneath was a weather-beaten, metal statue of a woman, her verdigris-covered arms stretched up, her fingers tangled in her hair. Her face was rusted, the metal bent, but the soft curves of her body were still intact.

'She needs repairing, but we can't afford to do that right now,' she said and gestured to the other dust sheets. 'These are all things that need repairing. They give me the creeps.' Her heart rate was racing. The air felt colder in here and goosebumps covered her skin.

'Can I look?' he asked. 'Or do you need to get out of here?'

She walked over to him. 'No, you can look. I'll be brave.'

'Alright, but let me know if you need to leave.' He moved to the next dust sheet, uncovering an oil painting of the house and the fields that surrounded it.

'This is beautiful.' He carefully put it back, then lifted up another dust sheet. Underneath was another metal statue, but this one was a young girl knelt down with cupped hands.

'This is actually part of a fountain that got damaged in another storm.' She crouched down next to it.

'You might think these things are creepy, but I think they're beautiful. They just... need a bit of love and care.' He turned to Kate. 'I don't know if you can relate to that, but I know I can.'

She stood up and pulled the dust sheet back over the statue. 'I can.' She thought about the way that her friends and family had helped her bounce back after her dad left, and after she broke up with Will. 'We all need a bit of love and care, right?'

He wrapped his arms around her. 'Exactly.' He kissed her forehead. 'Are you still scared?'

She shook her head. 'Not when I'm with you.' As she let him go, she nodded to a collection of portraits leaning against the wall and took his hand. 'Come and look at these. Those are my ancestors.' She sat down on the floor and sorted through them. 'They were in the dining room, but Mama took them down. She said they kept staring at her.'

He sat down next to her. 'They're great.' He pointed to a picture of a woman in a pale green dress, her eyes staring defiantly back at them. 'She looks like you.'

'That's my great-great grandmother.' She studied the picture, seeing her own features in the other woman for the first time. 'Apparently, she was like me. Small but dominant, like a Jack Russell.'

His laugh echoed around the room. 'Pretty accurate.' He carefully replaced the white sheet and stood up. 'It's not so bad in here, you know.' He offered her his hand and pulled her to her feet.

She smiled. 'Maybe I just hadn't brought the right person in here. You make me braver. You're fearless.'

He smiled back at her. 'Trust me, I get scared. I haven't opened up to anyone in a long time because I was afraid to, and you're helping me get over that. With you, it's not scary.'

Their eyes met, and Kate thought back to the night in Correll's when she had let him take care of her. It would have been so much worse without him, just as being in here right now would be so much worse without him. She wanted to keep her distance from him, but the more time they spent together and the more he showed her how much he cared about her, the harder it was getting.

She gazed up at him. 'Sometimes, when you face up to your fears, they're not so bad. Maybe we're pulling off each other's dust sheets, and what's underneath isn't as frightening as we'd thought.'

'I think you're right.' A gust of wind rattled the thin glass panes. 'Ready to get out of here?'

'Absolutely,' she said and happily locked the door behind them, shivering as they walked back to her bedroom. 'We need to warm up. Do you reckon we can both fit in the bath?'

He raised an eyebrow. 'I don't know... but I feel like we'll have fun trying.'

A few minutes later, she'd run a deep bath, filled with some luxury French bubble bath that she had brought back from Nice. The last time she was in this bath, she had been exhausted, and bruised, but unable to stop thinking about Alex. Now he was right here with her, offering her a hand as she climbed into the bath. Her knee was almost healed, but he seemed to know exactly when she needed him to help her.

He climbed in, sitting opposite her.

'Looks like we do fit,' she said and leant closer, kissing him.

Sometime later, Alex wrapped Kate in a towel and kissed her cheek, before wrapping another towel around his waist. She couldn't take her eyes off him. He was like one of her mother's works of art. Chiselled, honed, perfect. She pulled on a pair of leggings, and a long striped woollen dress with long sleeves.

'Nice dress,' he said. 'It shows off your curves.'

'I can't wear my sweatpants around you,' she replied. 'I've never seen you in anything that wasn't tailored or made from very tight black denim. Do you even *own* sweatpants? Your definition of casual wear is a lot different to mine.'

He laughed. 'You can wear whatever you like around me. And I *do* own sweatpants.'

'I bet they're tight and black,' she quipped.

'You'd be right.'

She smiled. 'Would you like some breakfast?'

'I would.'

She ignored the faint stab of pain in her knee as she walked down the stairs, and once she reached the kitchen, she cut some slices of bread for toast, while Alex made tea and coffee. It felt surprisingly natural having him in her kitchen, and she wondered whether he felt the same way. For the last couple of months, she'd been determined to keep her relationship with him casual, but after last night, and the moment they'd shared in the blue room, she found herself seeing a future with him, and that both scared and excited her.

After they'd eaten, she studied him as she sipped her tea. 'Before last night, I felt like you were a mystery, but I'm starting to figure you out.'

'Sometimes I have to be.' His eyes met hers. 'Do you like a mystery?'

'This one's got me hooked.' Her eyes moved from his, down to his lips.

'Good.' He leant forward and kissed her. 'Maybe I'll give you a few more pieces of the puzzle next time I see you.'

'Does that mean you're going?' She tried to hide her disappointment.

'I have to work today. I'm sorry,' he said. 'Last night was incredible. Next time will be even better.'

'I'll hold you to that.' She kissed him again, determined not to let on that she was already missing him, and he hadn't even left.

'I hope you do.'

Reluctantly, she walked to the front door, and kept her expression neutral as he put his jacket and shoes on. She put her arms around his neck and kissed him, keen to ensure that she stayed on his mind long after he'd left.

He gave her one of his thousand-watt smiles as he pulled away from her. 'Thank you for letting me into your castle, Kate. Next time, I'll let you into mine.'

Chapter Sixteen

Dᴇᴄᴇᴍʙᴇʀ 2012, Cᴀɴᴛᴇʀʙᴜʀʏ, Kᴇɴᴛ, England

'Where are you taking me?' Kate asked.

It was Friday night, a week after she'd last seen him. Alex had met her at Corrells, and she had no idea what he had planned, only that they were walking through the darkened city streets together. They reached the car park and Alex stopped by a black sports car, unlocking it.

'You'll see,' he said, opening the boot.

'Why do I need an overnight bag? And where's your Defender?' he asked.

'I swapped it for this for the weekend.' He held out his hand, taking her bag and putting it in the boot, before opening the passenger door for her. 'Mind your head. It's low,' he said as she climbed in. He closed the door and got into the driver's seat, turning the key in the ignition. 'You ready?'

'I think so,' Kate said hesitantly.

He nodded. 'On y va!' He raised his eyebrow at her and turned the volume up on the stereo.

She smiled. It was the same song that he'd sent her the lyrics from that morning, MJ Cole's "Sincere". She'd puzzled over the snippet he'd sent, but now, as he drove out of the city, the engine roaring, it made sense. They were taking a ride on the wild side. 'I like the car.'

'It's not actually mine, and it's not massively practical for where I live.' He looked in the rearview mirror, before turning out of the city, into the darkness.

'Where do you live?' she asked, exasperated. 'You keep your cards very close to your chest.'

'Don't worry. I'm about to reveal my hand,' he said mysteriously, steering the car down one narrow lane, then another.

The rain lashed the car and the wind blew streams of amber leaves across the windscreen. His hands gripped the steering wheel tightly. She stared at his furrowed brow, the way his eyes never left the road in front of him, wishing she knew what he was thinking.

He turned into a long driveway lined with trees, their branches swaying in the wind. Ahead of them, was a large brick building. He slowed down as they reached a gravel-lined car park.

He stopped the car and got out, coming round to the passenger side door and opening it for Kate. 'You let me into your castle. This is mine.'

Floodlights illuminated the front of the house and Kate sucked in a breath as she took it in. It loomed over her, just as her house did, although instead of crumbling bricks and ivy, there were neat wooden shutters on each window and a large wood-framed porch. As she reached the front door, she saw a metal sign next to it with swirly gold writing and frowned, puzzled at the words *Woodlands Hotel and Bar.*

Alex grabbed the wrought iron door handle and pushed it open. 'After you.'

Kate stepped into a wood-panelled hallway, her heels echoing on the grey slate floor. 'Wow, this place is fancy,' she said, turning to Alex as they walked towards a large glass door.

'I'm glad you think so,' he replied, pulling the door open for her.

She walked into the room, and gasped. 'This is the most beautiful bar I've ever seen!'

The floor was covered in black and white Victorian tiles. Glass votive candles sat on each of the wooden tables, flickering gently, and above their heads were two elegant chandeliers. Everything looked brand new. Behind the bar, a rack of lights illuminated the bottles on the shelf.

'I'm so confused,' she said. 'Is this your bar?'

'Sort of. Let's get a drink and I'll explain.' He smiled at the barmaid. 'Hey, Mel. How's it going tonight?'

'Quiet.' Mel looked at Kate. 'You must be Kate. You're just like he described you. Gorgeous.' She held out her hand. 'I'm Mel, Alex's long-suffering barmaid-slash-friend.'

Her red hair was cut short, and her sparkly green eyeshadow emphasised her bright blue eyes.

Kate took Mel's hand, marvelling at her strong grip. 'Nice to meet you.'

'Same. What can I get you to drink?' Mel asked, leaning on the counter.

'I'll have a rum and Coke please,' Kate said.

'Kraken, right? He made me get some in just for you,' Mel gestured to Alex, then took down the bottle and unscrewed it.

'That's right. Thank you.' Kate smiled at Alex. 'Thank you. That's really sweet of you.'

'It was nothing. I wanted you to have the rum you like.'

It wasn't nothing though. It meant a lot to her. When Mel handed them their drinks, Alex led Kate to a booth in the corner of the bar, waiting for her to sit down before he slid into the seat next to her.

Kate took a sip of her drink, then looked meaningfully at Alex. 'This is the part where you explain things.'

'Right.' Alex nodded. 'So, this is where I grew up. My mum decided last year that she was going to open it up as a hotel and did a complete renovation of the place, but... midway through, she had a stroke.'

Her heart leapt into her throat. 'Oh, my God. Alex, is she alright?'

'She wasn't at first.' He gripped the glass tightly. 'Mel was here with her, and got her to the hospital, and they transferred her to London, where I was living at the time. When she got better, she came back here.'

'And so did you,' she added.

'Sort of,' he said. 'I'd already decided to come back here and I'd been offered the job I'm doing now, but it didn't start right away. So when Mum was ready to come home, I moved back here to care for her full time until I started the new job.'

'Wow. That's a lot to take on. Caring for your mum, moving back here, and starting a new job.' He was no longer a mystery, he was probably the kindest person she'd ever met.

'It was a lot to juggle,' he admitted, 'and I went from working on my own to managing a team of five people in my day job, as well as overseeing the renovation here, and caring for Mum.'

'When did you sleep?' she asked, her eyes widening.

'I didn't. Or at least not very much. I just wanted to keep everything afloat. I knew things would get better, but not without me intervening.' His fingers traced a pattern in the condensation on his glass. 'I'm sorry I didn't tell you any of this.'

Her heart ached for him, and what he'd been dealing with. 'You don't need to be sorry. You told me that you take a while to trust, and to open up. I wanted to give you the space and time to do that.'

'I appreciate it. That's the reason why I've brought you here, and why I'm telling you all of this.' He smiled. 'I know I can trust you, and you're someone I want to share all of this with.'

'That means so much.' Her voice cracked as she spoke, fighting back tears. She had spent the last year trying to lock her heart away, determined not to risk falling for anyone else, but he had made it impossible for her not to 'How is your mum now?'

'Much better, and very determined to get back on her feet. She's pretty tough, just like you.' He smiled. 'She's gone away with some friends to a spa for the weekend.'

'She sounds incredible,' she said. 'And the spa weekend sounds like just what she needs.'

'It is. And that's why I've got her car. She took mine as it's more reliable for driving long distances. I offered to drive her, but she was far too stubborn to let me.' He shook his head.

'She drives that fancy sports car? Wow. I like her even more.' She smiled.

'I helped her pick it out.' He took a sip of his drink. 'My dad was a fan of sports cars. I think he'd approve.'

'I think he'd be so proud of you and everything you're doing,' she said.

'He would, but he would also tell me to stop micromanaging everything, including Mum. I told you I take a while to trust people and there's a reason for that. We did have a manager here, but he was stealing from us, so Mum and I have been sharing the role since August.'

'That's awful!' She shook her head. 'People suck sometimes, right?'

He took a deep breath. 'I felt responsible because I'd hired him, so I offered to help Mum until we found a replacement. The new guy starts next week.'

This explained a lot of things. Why he had had taken so long to arrange a date with her. Why things had been *complicated,* in his words, and why he had had to leave their first date early.

She slipped her hand into his. 'Owning your own business must be hard. You can't do it all, but not doing it all means relying on someone else.'

'Exactly. I find it really hard to trust people. ' His eyes darkened. 'And sometimes, when people see this place, they make assumptions about me, and my family, and take advantage. You must have experienced the same thing.'

'Sort of. People assume that when you live in a big house, you must be rich. We're not. We inherited it, and we're struggling to keep it alive.' She looked down at the table. 'Sorry, I didn't mean to dump that on you.'

'I get it.' As she looked up, her eyes met his. 'I see how important your house is to you, and I also feel like it's looking out for you somehow.'

'It makes or breaks relationships,' she said ruefully. 'It destroyed my mum and dad's marriage, but my Nanna and Papa were so happy there. I'm cautious about who I bring back there.'

'Well, in that case, I'm honoured,' he replied. 'What do your friends think of it?'

'Leon is terrified of it, Mia hates the cold, Lucy is just in awe of it, and Hannah is just unbothered because she's grown up with it. That's pretty much it. I have a small circle.' She shrugged.

'Ditto. George and I have been best friends since school, and Mel is actually Ben's ex-girlfriend. I can trust her implicitly.' He smiled. 'She was working in a club in the city and I persuaded her to come and work here. She's my eyes and ears when I can't be here. I told her about you because I knew she would give me some sensible advice.'

'And did she?' she whispered.

'Yeah.' He paused. 'She told me to stop being such a dick and take you out on a date.'

'I like her.' She looked around the room. 'Is it usually this quiet here?'

Only half the tables were full, and the bar was almost as big as Mimosa, which was always packed.

'Sometimes,' He followed her gaze. 'The restaurant is always full and we have six rooms upstairs, which we're starting to get bookings for, but the bar is quiet.'

'You've only been open a few months. It'll pick up.' She hoped that her words were reassuring, as she had no idea about how to run or promote a business.

'That's what we're hoping.' He handed her one of the menus on the table. 'I think you should sample the food. Stefan, the chef, is French, and it is so good that I don't mind the fact that I eat here most nights.'

'What do you recommend?' she asked, looking at the menu.

'The house burger,' he replied immediately. 'Don't ask me how often I have one. It's just as well the gym's down the road from my office.'

Shethought about the toned body under his shirt. 'I got the hint that you were a fan of the gym.' She finished the rest of her drink and looked at Alex's empty glass. 'Do you want another drink? And can I order the food at the bar?'

He stood up. 'Yes, but I'll go.'

She shook her head. 'No, you always pay. Please let me get these. What are you having?'

'An Everleaf and Coke, and a house burger. Thank you.' He sat back down.

'Sure. I'll be right back.' She picked up their empty glasses and took them back to the bar, where Mel was stacking the glass racks.

'Hello, love! Would you like a refill?' Mel asked, putting two glasses onto the counter. 'One Kraken and one Everleaf, right?'

'And two house burgers, please.' Kate pulled some money out of her purse and handed it to Mel.

'How did you manage to get him to let you pay?' Mel asked as she made their drinks. 'I've known him for years, and he's never let me buy a drink.'

'I just told him I was doing it.' Kate shrugged.

'I'm impressed.' Mel handed the glasses to Kate. 'See if you can persuade him to take some time off too.' She nodded to their table. 'I'll bring your food over in a minute.'

'Thanks, Mel.' As Kate walked back over to the table, she breathed in the familiar botanical scent of the Everleaf and realised she'd never actually seen Alex drink alcohol. She put Alex's glass down on the table and sat down opposite him.

'Can I ask you something?' He nodded and she continued, looking at his glass. 'Don't you drink?'

'No. My dad was killed by a drunk driver, so I don't drink. I never have.'

'I'm so sorry. That's awful.' Kate bit her lip. 'If I had known, I wouldn't have drunk around you.'

He waved a hand. 'Don't worry about it. I can't stop everyone around me from drinking.'

She cleared her throat, her chest feeling heavy. 'I used to drink a lot, when I was in Brighton. I don't know if you would have liked who I was back then. I'm not proud of it, but that's not who I am now, and I never drove when I'd been drinking. I wouldn't ever do that.'

'You don't need to explain, or apologise for anything at all. I went to university, I know what it's like. It was just different for me.' He paused. 'I worked in a bar when I was at university, and in a weird way it helped me to deal with what had happened to my dad. I made sure that there were free drinks for designated drivers, and I called cabs for people who'd had too much to drink.'

'You're always looking out for everyone else.' She smiled. 'Your dad would definitely be proud of you. I worked in a bar too, in Brighton. If you ever need a hand here, you just need to ask.'

Mel arrived at their table with their food and her eyes lit up. 'Did I hear you say you used to work in a bar, Kate? Fancy coming and doing a shift with me one night? You smile a lot more than he does,' she quipped, gesturing to Alex, 'and you're a lot cuter.'

Alex rolled his eyes. 'Am I that bad to work for?'

'No, you're a great boss. You just have a different vibe to Kate,' Mel said diplomatically. 'I should go before I say something else I regret.'

'Have you had a break tonight?' Alex asked.

'Ed's going to cover for me in half an hour.' Mel paused. 'If Stefan will let him.'

'If he doesn't, let me know,' Alex said firmly.

'You're off duty tonight,' Mel replied just as firmly. 'Catch you later.' She walked back to the bar.

'Wow, I like her. She puts you in your place,' Kate whispered to Alex.

'That's exactly why I made her the bar manager. I know she'll always tell me what I need to hear,' he said.

She looked at her enormous burger. 'How on earth do I eat this?'

'Like this.' He picked up his burger and took a bite.

She unfolded her napkin and laid it on her lap, then picked up her burger, taking a cautious bite, unsure if the contents of the burger were going to fall out. When she swallowed, she nodded approvingly. 'This is so good.'

'Stefan used to work in a restaurant in Paris. He makes everything from scratch. Even the croissants we serve for breakfast are handmade.' He paused. 'The restaurant is so busy, but we can't afford to employ more staff until we make more money so we all have to pitch in to cover for each other.'

'That sounds difficult,' she said. 'Are you the peacekeeper?'

'I have to be,' he replied. 'My mum is... compromised. She and Stefan are pretending that they aren't into each other, but they are.'

'How do you feel about that?' she asked, wondering how far he would let her in.

He dipped one of his fries into his ketchup and chewed it thoughtfully. 'I miss my dad, but I want her to be happy. It's something I need to work through. How about you? How would you feel if your mum was dating someone?'

'My mum *is* dating someone, and he makes her happy, so I'm totally on board. I might feel differently if my dad wasn't around anymore. I would definitely feel conflicted.'

'Conflicted is the right word. You're very perceptive. You understand me in a way no one else ever has.' He smiled at her.

A rush of excitement flooded through Kate. He'd let her inside his walls, something she knew that he didn't do very often. 'The more I get to know you, the more I understand you.'

'I feel the same way,' he replied.

'Would you like me to show you around?' Alex asked after they'd eaten. 'It seems fair. I got the guided tour of your house.'

'I'd love that.' Kate smiled. 'Tell me about this room, what did it used to be?'

'This was a living room and a smaller parlour that we knocked through to make one big room,' he said. 'We designed it keep the feel of the original Victorian building, but make it also feel modern too. This is where guests come to check in, to have a drink, and when we have events, this is where they'll be. The restaurant isn't really big enough. Come with me, I'll show you that next.'

He nodded to Mel on the way out. 'See you later. Make sure you get a break.' He laughed as she rolled her eyes at him and led Kate into the corridor, stopping at another doorway opposite the bar. 'This used to be our dining room.'

It was like a larger, less formal version of her own dining room, with cream pannelled walls, high ceilings and sparkling chandeliers. There were eight round wooden tables, which were all full. The hum of chatter and clink of cutlery floated out towards her.

'Wow, it's busy,' she whispered, not wanting to draw attention to herself. 'Having eaten Stefan's food, I can see why.'

'It's always packed. We don't advertise much. It's all word of mouth. We're full most nights, that's why we ate in the bar tonight. I can't even get a table, and it's my house.'

She moved away from the doorway, admiring the abstract artwork on the wall of the corridor. 'That doesn't seem very fair.'

He shrugged. 'If it means we're making money I don't care.' He took a card out of his pocket and put it into the card slot in the next door along. 'This is our office. It used to be my dad's study.' He pushed the door open, revealing a small room with two large desks next to each other.

'You and your mum share an office? That would *not* work for me and my mum.'

'It doesn't always work for us. She loves to chat,' he said.

She laughed. 'You two sound like me and David. I'm always distracting him.'

'I'd let you distract me.' He raised his eyebrow. 'I wouldn't get any work done if you and I shared an office.'

'Neither would I. I wouldn't be able to keep my eyes off you, and probably my hands too.' She smirked and walked out of the office. 'What's next on the tour? The gift shop?'

'No, we're going upstairs to my room.' He locked the office door behind them and led her down the hall.

'Well, that's better than a gift shop,' She followed him up the stairs at the end of the hall.

He unlocked a door at the end of the corridor and pushed it open. 'This is my room.' He turned on the light switch and gestured for her to go in first. 'This was my room when I was a kid, but it's had a major upgrade.'

The walls were painted a deep, forest green, and a chandelier hung from the ornate ceiling rose. The walls were pannelled, like the dining room. A large wooden bed took up most of the room, and an antique wardrobe stood in one corner.

'It's cosy,' she said, then ran her hand over the crisp white duvet on the large wooden bed. 'Hotel sheets are the best, aren't they?'

'One of the many perks to living here,' he said, before taking her hand and leading her to the large sash window. 'You need to see this view.' He switched off the lights, plunging the room into darkness. 'I never draw the curtains. You can see the stars so clearly here.' He stood behind her, wrapping his arms around her waist. 'I missed this when I lived in London.'

'It's so beautiful,' she said, looking up at the stars dotted across the inky sky. She turned away from the window and looked at the large photo collage on the wall next to the desk, which was obviously Alex as a child, with another boy who looked just like him. 'Is that Ben? You guys are so similar.'

'Yeah, that's us. And those are my cousins, Chris and Jake.' He pointed to another photo of four boys standing together on the beach. 'We caused absolute havoc when we got together. Chris lives in Leeds now, and Jake lives in Cornwall, so we don't see each other a huge amount, but when we do, it's chaos.' He laughed.

'I can imagine.' She looked around the room again. 'This room has your personality stamped all over it. It's dark and moody, and full of technology.' Her eyes flicked to the wardrobe. 'I bet that's full of linen, leather, and tight black jeans.' She smirked. 'Or is that where you keep your superhero costumes?'

He laughed and slid his hands around her waist. 'Possibly, but superheroes never reveal their identities, do they?'

'I don't know,' she said. 'Michael Keaton took Kim Basinger back to the Batcave, didn't he?'

'He did.' He raised an eyebrow. 'And he was way more mysterious than me.'

'I'd rather have you,' she whispered, pulling him closer.

Chapter Seventeen

With just two weeks until Christmas, the city streets were busy, and Kate pushed her way through the crowds, past the hot chestnut cart, its sweet, warm scent filling the air. She walked up to the crêpe stall, and placed her order with Florian, the owner. He smoothed his wooden paddle over the batter on the hot skillet, before drizzling Nutella onto her crêpe, and folding it up before handing it to her.

'Merci, Florian. À bientôt.' She gave him some money and returned his huge smile before she walked away.

She walked back to the shop, thinking about her weekend with Alex. He'd brought her croissants and coffee in bed on Saturday morning, and then taken her to lunch, and a show at the theatre. Their connection had gone from being purely physical, to something deeper. Having been let into his world, she now understood him better. The mystery surrounding him was disappearing like sunshine burning through the fog, and the more she learnt about him, the closer she felt to him.

She went back into the studio and looked at her phone again, smiling at Alex's text. It was yet another garage classic from the early 2000's, "Imagine" by Shola Ama, and it made her smile. The lyrics he sent her were building a picture of exactly how he felt about her. Putting her phone away, she flicked through her sketchbook, to find the design for the wedding band she was working on, then started work.

'Kate? Mia's downstairs,' Lisa appeared in the studio in front of Kate, making her jump.

Kate looked up at Lisa, then at her watch. 'Oh, no, I totally lost track of time. Thanks, Lisa.' She stood up and took her apron off before going to the bathroom to scrub her hands. Grabbing her bag and coat, she carefully went down the stairs, clinging to the rail.

'Hello, darling.' She kissed Mia on the cheek. 'You look cute.' Mia's lipstick was deep red, and her dark hair hung in loose waves.

'Thanks, love.' Mia gave Kate a hug. 'You look dusty. Are you wearing those to the pub?' She looked down at Kate's black Dr Marten boots.

'Yes, I am,' Kate retorted. 'I forgot to bring any other shoes with me. I don't keep my heels under my desk anymore, for obvious reasons.'

Lisa and Emmett were locking away the jewellery, and Kate waved as she left with Mia. Outside the shop, they linked arms, and strolled together to the pub.

At the bar, Kate squinted at the bottles lined up behind the counter. 'What are you having, Mia? I'm driving, so I can give you a lift back if you want a sloe gin? They've got your favourite.'

'Not for me.' Mia looked sheepish. 'I'm not drinking.'

Kate's hands flew to her face, as it slotted into place in her head. 'Are you pregnant?"

Mia shushed her. 'Yes. I'm five months pregnant, actually.'

A lot of things started to make sense now. Mia insisting on driving and not drinking, and her feeling sick when Kate had stayed over at her house. But why hadn't Mia told her? She squashed that thought and gave Mia a hug. 'Congratulations! That's amazing news! I'm so happy for you. How are you feeling?'

'Better now,' Mia replied. 'The last few months have been tough.' As the barman came over to take their order, she turned to Kate. 'Can we order food as well? I've got past the morning sickness, and I'm starving now.'

'Sure,' Kate said, nodding and picking up a menu, even though she already knew what she was having. 'An elderflower lemonade, and a beef pappardelle, please.'

Mia's eyes lit up. 'That sounds great, I'll have the same.'

When the barman returned with their drinks, they took a table in the window.

A few moments later, the waitress came over with their bowls of pasta, and they both thanked her at the same time.

'I should order something different, but I love this too much,' Kate said as she twirled the pasta around on her fork.

'So do I and right now I need to eat something I know,' Mia said.

Kate studied Mia's face. 'Are you really feeling better now? If I'd have known you weren't feeling great I would have come over rather than dragging you out.'

Mia shook her head. 'It's fine. I'm feeling a lot better, and I wanted to come out. I'll be honest, I've had a few weeks of living off toast and scrambled eggs, but I'm past that now.'

'Pregnancy sounds like so much fun,' Kate said dryly.

'I know, right' Mia paused. 'Are you upset at that I didn't tell you?'

'Kind of,' Kate admitted. 'Why didn't you tell me?'

'I wasn't ready to share it with you,' Mia replied. 'It hasn't been the easiest pregnancy.'

'But if you had told me, I could have been there for you,' Kate said gently.

'I didn't think you would understand.'

Kate felt hurt. She had done all she could to be there for Mia through her first pregnancy, even though she was in Brighton. 'I would have tried to understand.'

'I'm sure you would.' Mia took a sip of her drink. 'I don't like being fussed over, you know that.'

'You fuss over everyone else!' Kate exclaimed. 'Why not let other people look after you?'

'That's not my thing,' Mia said. 'You know now, and that's the main thing. I'm due in May, and I'm having a boy.'

There was an undercurrent of tension between them, and Kate didn't like it, but she didn't want to ruin Mia's news with an argument.

'How exciting! How do you feel about being a boy mum? Is Pete excited?' she asked.

'I can't wait. I love my little brother, and I bet Lilly will be a great older sister. I do wish I hadn't bought so much pink stuff for Lilly.' Mia smiled. 'Pete is over the moon, but he assured me that he would be regardless of whether we were having a boy or a girl. I was sure he was a girl, but I was wrong.'

'Little brothers are cool.' Kate thought about Rob, who still hadn't replied to her last message. 'I'll get you some more neutrally coloured baby clothes. Oh, and I can ask Rebecca. I met her for lunch last week, and she has a ton of baby clothes that Luca has grown out of.'

'How is she?' Mia asked. 'Do you know when she's coming back to Corrells?'

Kate shook her head. 'Not yet, she's going to talk to Emmett after Christmas. We're going to meet up in the New Year, she's desperate for a night out.'

'Cool. What else is new with you? II've barely seen you for weeks, and you were really cagey when I asked what you were doing this weekend.'

Kate took a deep breath. 'I've met someone.'

'I kind of gathered that,' Mia said. 'Are you going to tell me any more than that?'

'His name's Alex. I think you might know him.' Kate braced herself for Mia's response.

Mia raised her eyebrow. 'I thought so. George said to Pete that you were at his gig with Alex. Why didn't you tell me?'

Kate took a sip of her drink before she replied. 'Alex is Pete's friend and you're mine. I needed time to figure out what Alex and I were to each other before I told you.'

'So, what's going on? Are you guys in a relationship then?' Mia's brow furrowed.

'No. We've been on a couple of dates, but it's not serious.' She shrugged, trying to look more nonchalant than she felt. She was rapidly changing her mind about what she wanted from Alex.

'What's wrong with being in a relationship?' Mia asked.

'Nothing, it's just not what either of us want. I'm still finding my feet at my job, and he's juggling two jobs right now.' Kate's chest tightened as Mia looked intently at her. 'He's not got time for anything more, and neither have I.'

'I know you and Alex have both got things going on,' Mia said, 'but you're either lying to yourself, or you're lying to me about your feelings for him. I know you like him more than you're letting on.'

Kate sucked in a breath. Mia had once again seen through her. 'Can we just leave it?'

'Why can't you tell me how you actually feel?' Mia frowned.

Because I'm scared, Kate thought to herself. I'm scared of letting myself fall for someone.

'I don't want to talk about it anymore, Mia. Why can't you just leave it?'

'Because I care about you, and about your happiness,' Mia said. 'I don't think you're telling me the truth and that hurts.'

Kate wiped her mouth with her napkin. 'Maybe I don't know how I feel. Can I be allowed to figure that out on my own? You didn't tell me about your pregnancy and I respected that.'

'This is a totally different situation,' Mia retorted. 'I'm not pretending, and you are!'

'Fine.' A hot burst of anger flooded through Kate. 'I *do* like him, and I'm scared about what that means, not just for me, but for him too. Are you happy now? *This* is why I didn't tell you about him in the first place, because I knew you'd insist on asking me lots of questions about it.'

'After you broke up with Will, you spent the year getting drunk and hooking up with random guys, so when there's a new guy on the scene who you are dating, *sober,* I want to know more about him.' Red angry spots appeared on Mia's cheeks.

'And I'd prefer to keep him to myself for now,' Kate said firmly.

'Got you.' Mia stood up. 'I'm going to the ladies.'

As Mia walked out of the restaurant, Kate glanced around the room, an itchy, tense feeling pulsing through her body. She hated falling out with Mia, but there was no way she wanted Mia and Pete involved in her very new relationship with Alex. This was something she wanted for herself, and one of the reasons why life in Brighton had been so much easier.

When Mia returned, she gave Kate a tight smile, and they made pleasant, but stilted conversation over dessert. When Pete arrived to collect Mia, Kate breathed a sigh of relief. Tonight had been beyond awkward, and she felt frustrated.

As she walked back to her car, her tears fell onto the cobbled streets. Her chest felt heavy and the hurt expression on Mia's face as she walked away was lodged in her mind. Knowing that Mia had been hiding her pregnancy for so long made her question how close they actually were. She thought about Alex. The reason she'd kept him to herself was to avoid drama, but instead she'd made it worse, and then lied to Mia about not wanting more from Alex.

She took her phone out of her pocket, needing to hear his voice. 'Alex, it's me. Are you home?'

'Yeah, I am. What's up? You sound really weird.'

The sound of his voice calmed her, and she wanted to see him, to kiss him, knowing that a night with him would distract her from her fight with Mia.

'Can I come over?' She hadn't planned to invite herself over, but the sound of his voice had pulled her in.

'Sure, I'm here. Text me when you get to the car park, and I'll come and meet you.'

She hung up and switched her music back on, listening intently to the lyrics as she drove. It was another one of Alex's song choices, Kele Le Roc's "My Love", but she'd never really heard it the way that she did tonight. As she listened to the lyrics, she smiled. She wasn't running away from him. She was running towards him.

When she arrived at the hotel, she sent Alex a message, and a few minutes later, he appeared at the front door. She ran over to him, putting her arms around his neck and kissing him.

'Woah, that was some hello,' he said as he pulled away from her. 'What's going on?'

'I just wanted to see you.'

'Come in,' he said, his brow creasing as he looked at her face. 'Do you want a drink or do you want to go upstairs?'

'Upstairs, please,' she replied, afraid that she would burst into tears again.

'Of course.' He led her up to his room.

He looked down at her feet and smiled. 'Whenever I see a pair of these boots I think of you.'

'They make me think of you,' Kate said, remembering the gentle way he'd put them on after her accident. 'They're like you, reliable, and practical.'

'Thanks,' he replied. 'My dad was always someone you could depend on, and I want to be that person too.'

'You are,' she said softly. 'You've come to my rescue more times than I can count.' She looked over at his desk, which was covered in pieces of paper, and a laptop. 'Oh, no, I've stopped you working. I'm so sorry.'

'Doesn't matter.' Alex swept the papers into a pile, and shut his laptop. 'What's going on?'

She remembered why she'd come and sat down on the bed. 'I had dinner with Mia tonight, and I told her about us. I'm sorry.'

'Why are you sorry?' Alex asked, sitting down next to her.

'We said we'd keep it ourselves,' she said.

'We did, but that was never going to happen,' he said. 'We both know too many people in this city. I thought Mia already knew? Pete knew as he gave me the whole "take care of her" chat when we met for a drink the other night.'

She gasped. 'Oh no! He didn't?'

'He did.' He smiled. 'It's fine. I like that he's looking out for you.'

'I can look out for myself!' she exclaimed, 'and this is why I didn't want either of them knowing.'

'Is it so bad that they do know?' he asked.

'It is if Pete is interrogating you, and Mia is pushing me to tell her exactly what's going on between us,' she said.

He nodded. 'Why don't you tell me what happened tonight? You seem upset, and I get the feeling that there's more to this than Mia finding out about us.'

'There is, but it's fine.' She glanced at the pile of papers. 'You've got so much going on right now. I should go.'

'Wait.' He put his hand on her thigh. 'I know you don't like to need help, or advice, but you seem upset, and you chose to come here tonight, rather than going back to your haunted house. I think you want to let me in, but you're afraid to.' He paused. 'Am I right?'

'Yes,' she admitted. 'I just don't want to add to the amount of things you're already trying to juggle.'

'If I didn't have the capacity to support you, I'd say so. Trust me.' He held her gaze. 'I can be there for you, if you let me.'

She smiled. This was exactly what she'd said to him in the bar. 'It all went south so fast. Mia told me that she was pregnant, which is amazing. I asked her why she hadn't told me sooner, she told me that the pregnancy hadn't been easy, and I wouldn't understand. That hurt because I've tried *so* hard to be a good friend to her, even though I have no idea about kids. And then I told her about you, thinking she'd be happy for me, but she kept asking more and more questions, and this is so new and exciting that I don't want to have to explain it to anyone else.'

He rubbed a hand over his chin. 'Do you need advice, comfort, or for me to just listen?'

'Probably all of the above,' she said.

'Come here.' He slid an arm around her and kissed her forehead. 'You and Mia have been friends for what, ten years? This is a bump in the road. You probably need some time to cool off, and then you can talk.'

'I hope so.' She bit her lip. 'We never fight like this. I'm worried that we've grown too far apart. She was right when she said that I wouldn't understand. I have no idea what it's like to be pregnant, or to have a difficult pregnancy.'

'You don't have to know what it's like to be able to understand something,' he said gently. 'I know how caring you are, and how much you love Mia. Pete told me that it had been really rough for her in the first few months, and if she's like you, and doesn't want to ask anyone for help, then that might be even harder.'

'We're both as bad as each other.' She smiled. 'If I was having a rough pregnancy, chances are I wouldn't ask for help either.'

'Exactly. So give her some space, and then try and talk it out with her.' He paused. 'As for you and I, whatever this is, you definitely deserve to figure out how you feel in your own time.'

'The only person I want to talk about you and I with is you,' she said. 'When we first met, I wasn't ready for a relationship, and I thought you'd be the hottest summer fling I'd ever had, but the more time I spend with you the more I want you.'

'This could be more, if that's what you want,' he replied.

'What do you want?' she asked. 'I do love the mystery, but I need to know if we're on the same page.'

He smiled. 'I want a relationship with you, but I got the impression you didn't want anything serious, and right now, I don't know if I can give you the relationship you deserve.'

Her eyes filled with tears. 'Every time I think you couldn't get more perfect, you crank it up a notch. Thank you for understanding.' She kissed him. 'And I didn't want to pressure you into committing to a relationship. Can we just...figure it out as we go?'

'Of course.' He wiped the tear from her cheek. 'Just keep talking to me.'

She nodded. 'I will. You too. Can I tell you something? I tried so hard not to fall for you. Six months ago I broke my ex-boyfriend's heart, and he broke mine. That's why Mia and Pete are so overprotective. They didn't see it coming, and neither did I. He wanted me to give up my dreams of becoming a jewellery designer to become a Navy wife, and when he proposed, I realised I didn't love him enough to do that.'

'That sounds like it was a tough decision to make,' he said gently.

'It was, and I swore off relationships because I was too afraid to break someone else's heart,' she replied. 'Then I met you, and before I knew it I couldn't stop thinking about you. The fact that I'm *here* instead of hiding in the library at home, tells me that I've fallen for you. I knew that seeing you would make everything seem better.'

'I feel the same way about you.' He smiled. 'You're like a ray of sunshine, and you make the hard things seem less hard. I agonised for so long about calling you, because you were so hot, and obviously younger than me, and I thought you were out of my league.'

'I thought it was just that you were working two jobs and holding everyone else's lives together as well as your own,' she said.

'Well, that too,' he replied, 'but also all the things I just said.'

'I'm only eight years younger than you.' She paused. 'I did the maths, and if your brother is five years younger than you, and he was at school with Pete, that makes him twenty five, and you thirty. Am I right?'

'I turned thirty in September.' He smiled. 'Good detective work.'

'And I'm not out of your league. I thought you were out of *my* league!' she exclaimed.

'This is why we need to talk about this stuff,' he said. 'Does it bother you that I'm older than you?'

She shook her head. 'Not at all. When I first saw you in the bar, I realised you were older, and I made a smutty joke to my friend about all the things you could teach me.'

He laughed. 'Well, seeing as you're here, where do you want to start?'

'Here.' She cupped his face in her hands and kissed him.

Kate let herself into her house the following evening. Spending the night in Alex's bed had made her forget about her fallout with Mia. He had definitely taught her a few things, and she had returned the favour. Even better, he wanted the same thing as her, space and time to figure out what they were to each other without the pressure of everyone they knew sticking their noses in.

She'd spent her day focusing on what she could do to help promote the hotel. The empty bar was an issue, and with Alex working flat out and his mum still not back to full strength, they needed more help. She had no knowledge or skills in marketing, but she knew a girl who did, and after a call to Sophia in Brighton, she had a plan.

'Evening, darling.' Amelie raised an eyebrow as Kate walked into the kitchen. 'Walk of shame, is it?'

'I'm not ashamed of anything,' Kate said defiantly. 'I had the best night with Alex.'

Amelie frowned. 'I thought you were meeting Mia?'

'Yeah, that went very badly.' Kate sat down at the kitchen table. 'What smells so good?'

Amelie got a large dish out of the oven. 'I was cold and hungry, so I made chicken laksa. Do you want an early dinner?'

'I'd love that,' Kate said. 'Is it rude to eat and run, though? I'm going back up to Alex's tonight.'

'Of course not.' Amelie started ladling the laksa into two bowls. 'I can't stand in the way of young love.' She pressed a hand to her chest.

'Very funny.' Kate rolled her eyes. 'Tell me that you aren't seeing James tonight.'

Amelie handed Kate a bowl and a spoon. 'I can't. I'm meeting him for a drink later once I've finished these last few pages.' She gestured to a book open on the table.

Kate took her bowl to the table and sat down.

Amelie sat down opposite her. 'What are you and Alex doing tonight?'

'He doesn't know it yet, but I've got some ideas to help him promote the bar at the hotel. It's kind of quiet, and if they want to make more money they need more customers, so Sophia gave me some advice. He's really busy, and his mum's still recovering, so I figured if I could help in any way...'

Amelie nodded. 'You like this man, I can tell. Have you met his mum yet?'

Kate shook he head. 'No. We're not there yet.'

'Fair enough.' Amelie took a spoonful of the laksa.

This was why Kate loved her mum. Instead of firing questions at her, she had just accepted Kate's explanation of their relationship.

'What happened between you and Mia?' Amelie asked.

Kate filled Amelie in as they worked her way through the spicy soup, her cheeks blossoming with the heat.

Amelie listened carefully until Kate had finished talking. 'Oh, love, that sounds so painful, have you heard from her since she left the restaurant?'

'No. Alex suggested I give her some space, then talk it over, and I think that's the best idea,' Kate replied.

'You went to him for advice?' Amelie raised an eyebrow. 'You must like him. You didn't even confide in Will.'

'Will didn't like talking about feelings,' Kate said. 'I made a lot of mistakes with him and I don't want to do that with Alex.'

'Learning from our past relationships is key.' Amelie paused. 'I'm trying to do the same thing with James. I'm trying to fight the guilt, and it's hard.'

'Guilt about what?' Kate asked.

'I've not been completely honest with you.' Amelie looked down at the table, running her fingernail over one of the scratches. 'We didn't get together after your dad left.'

Kate frowned. 'So when did you get together?'

'When James started working here, I fell for him instantly. Things were pretty bad between your dad and I. We were barely speaking, and he was away a lot. James and I just found each other. I was absolutely powerless to resist him. It was a stronger feeling than I'd ever had before.' Amelie looked up at Kate. 'That feeling is back, and I'm scared.'

Kate looked into Amelie's eyes, seeing for the first time, the fear in them. 'It's okay to be scared. I'm scared about how much I like Alex.'

She laughed. 'These feelings that you have for James, they won't go away, and if he feels the same way, you have to see what this could be between you.'

'That's very good advice,' Amelie said, picking up Kate's empty bowl, stacking it with hers, and taking them to the sink. 'But I don't know how to move past the guilt over how we first got together, or the possibility that it'll end in disaster like last time.'

Kate remembered what Brene Brown's words. 'Guilt needs an audience, and no-one is judging you for wanting to be happy with James.' She stood up and gave her mum a hug. 'You told me to let myself fall, and see whether Alex caught me, and that was such good advice. I think you need to do the same.'

'Thank you, darling.' Amelie let go of Kate. 'It was rather good advice, if I do say so myself.'

Kate laughed. 'So humble. Have fun tonight. I'll see you tomorrow. I love you.'

'Love you too,' Amelie said and blew Kate a kiss as she walked out of the room.

Kate packed an overnight bag, filling it with clothes and make up, and trying to ignore the photo of her and Mia on the dresser. A few minutes later, she left her house, and drove to the hotel, already imagining herself in Alex's bedroom.

'I've been thinking, and I've got some ideas,' she said as Alex let her into his room.

'Do any of them involve you naked in my bed?' Alex asked, kissing her on the forehead and sliding his hands around her waist.

'Well, some do.' Kate raised her eyebrow, before wriggling out of his grasp and sitting down on the bed. 'But I've got some other ones, too, about marketing this place. You're not on social media. You don't have an Instagram account.'

Alex made a face but sat down next to her anyway. 'I don't use it. Isn't it just selfies? How will that help?'

'No, it's not just selfies.' Kate got her phone out of her pocket. 'My friend Sophia works in event planning and she uses Instagram a lot. She helped me when I was looking after the social media for Correll's, so I called her today, and she gave me some tips.' She opened up the shop's Instagram page and scrolled down, letting Alex see the posts and read the comments. 'This is what you need. You can use the photos from the website. It's a good way to connect with other hotel owners too.'

He looked at the screen. 'I hadn't thought of it like that.'

'This could bring in more business.' She started typing. 'You can find industry-relevant hashtags. I'll search for unique hotels and see what comes up.' She scrolled through beautifully shot photos of hotels across the world. 'Aren't they cool?'

He smiled at her. 'So cool. Look at that one there.'

She clicked on an image of a pool on a large balcony, the view across a bay dotted with boats below it. 'Hotel Palazzo, Sorrento. It's on the Italian Riviera. Isn't it gorgeous?' She clicked on the hotel's profile and scrolled through the photos. 'It's built into the cliff, so all of the rooms have a view straight out over the sea.'

He looked thoughtful. 'Can we compete with that, though? A view over the fields isn't the same, is it?'

She shook her head. 'Different audiences. You need to attract people who want cosy, countryside hotels with luxury rooms and food. I'll give you Sophia's number if you like, and she can steer you in the right direction.'

'That would be amazing, thank you.' He kissed her cheek.

'I'm not overstepping am I?' she asked. 'I just wanted to help, especially as I stopped you working last night.'

'You were so worth it,' he said, his eyes sparkling in the dim lamp light. 'It's getting late, so if you had any other ideas you wanted to discuss, I'd be open to that.'

She put her phone on the bedside table. 'I had an idea about your bed and my body.'

'I'm listening.'

Chapter Eighteen

Kate arrived home from work the following day, parking her car next to Amelie's, and noticed there was another car on the drive too. Rob's.

'Just in time. Can you come and hold the ladder?' Rob was at the top of a ladder, in a t-shirt and shorts, despite the freezing weather, and threading fairy lights through the ivy on the front of the house.

'Shit!' She ran over and grabbed the bottom of the ladder. 'Are you serious? You'll fall and break your neck.'

'Nah, I'm a pro.' He wobbled slightly as he reached Kate's windowsill.

The front door swung open and Amelie flew out, running towards the ladder. 'What are you doing up there? I told you not to do this without me, and I turn my back for a second and you're gone!' She let out an exasperated sigh, then smiled at Kate. 'Hello, darling. How did last night go? Did Alex like your suggestions?'

'He did,' she said. 'We set up an Instagram page for the hotel, and Alex is going to speak to Sophia today.'

'Good work,' Amelie said, nodding approvingly, as she gripped the other side of the ladder. 'Can I take James up there for a drink or is that too weird? I'd love to see it. It sounds beautiful.'

'Sure,' Kate replied. 'No one would know who you are, and they definitely need more customers.'

Rob made his descent from the ladder, and, once he was safely on the ground, Amelie glared at him, hand clutched to her chest. 'Every bloody year, you get up that ladder and scare the life out of me.'

'And every year you tell me how beautiful the house looks with the lights on it,' he replied, his eyes twinkling. He looked down at his bare legs. 'It is bloody freezing out here, though. Let's go indoors.' He collapsed the ladder and took it through the gate into the garden.

As Kate went into the house, her phone buzzed in her pocket, and she took a deep breath as she read the message.

> Can we meet for a drink before Christmas? Let me know when Rob's back and we'll get together. Dad x

She felt a pang of guilt as she read the message. Usually she would ignore his messages for a few days, but thinking about Alex, and his dad, she replied straight away. Christmas was the perfect opportunity to put the past behind her.

> Rob's just got back. I'll talk to him and sort out a date. See you soon x

Kate stuffed her phone back into her pocket and followed Amelie into the kitchen. Rob appeared at the back door.

'Kate, will you let him in?' Amelie said as she stood by the fridge. 'I locked the door earlier because the wind keeps blowing it open. I need to fix the handle.'

'Do I have to?' Kate said. 'It'll be more peaceful if he stays out there.'

Amelie gave her a warning look and Kate walked over to the door, unlocking it.

'She wanted to keep me out there, didn't she?' Rob asked Amelie, then glared at Kate.

'I do love it when we're all together,' Amelie said, smirking at him. 'I'm making Pad Thai for dinner. That was always our favourite at the Thai restaurant we went to before the theatre. Do you remember?'

Rob laughed. 'Yes, and Kate would always forget about the chillies and sit through the whole show with a red face.'

'I needed an interval ice cream to cool me down,' Kate said, giggling. 'Can we help with dinner?'

'No.' Amelie shook her head. 'You two go and catch up, and I'll call you when it's ready.'

Kate followed Rob into the living room, where they flopped onto the sofa. 'You know how quickly she can make Pad Thai,' she started. 'So you best spill all of the things you don't want her to know now.'

'What makes you think I want you to know them?' Rob asked, grinning. 'It's been a blast, but you know what they say, when in Rome.'

'Yeah well, you know what happened to Rome,' Kate quipped. 'To be fair, I spent a lot of my time in Brighton out on the lash, so I can't really judge you.'

Rob made a face at her. 'I don't want to think about what you get up to when you're out partying.'

She shrugged. 'Then don't.'

He rolled his eyes. 'Brilliant. What's new with you?'

'I'm kind of seeing someone but it's not serious, and I've told Dad we'll meet him for a drink before Christmas. I've not actually seen him since I've been back because we didn't get around to it before you left and I didn't want to see him without you...'

'Woah, slow down, you talk too fast!' he interjected. ' Firstly, do I get to meet Alex?' An evil smile crept across his face, and he rubbed his hands together excitedly.

'Uh, no. Mama hasn't even met him and I actually like her.' She grinned at him.

'Well, that's rude,' he huffed. 'What's new with Mama? She seems different, happier somehow.'

She opened her mouth, then shut it again. 'I'll let her tell you.'

'If she will. You two do the deep and meaningful stuff, I doubt she'd talk to me.' He frowned. 'Did you really say that you'd meet Dad?'

'I need to let go of the grudge I've been holding against him,' she said quietly.

'I've been saying this for years,' he replied, 'but I knew you needed to come round in your own time.'

She smiled. 'I did. You have to come with me and kick me under the table if I get out of line.'

'Happily.' He smiled back at her. 'You're the queen of holding grudges. I hope Alex knows what he's getting himself into. I'd love to meet him. I could tell him so many things.'

'That's exactly why you won't be meeting him,' she said.

'Who won't be meeting who?' Amelie asked as she walked in.'

'Alex,' Kate said.

'It's none of my business,' Amelie looked at Rob. 'Or yours. Are you guys ready to eat?'

'Always.' Rob stood up and followed Kate and Amelie into the kitchen.

After dinner, Kate, Amelie, and Rob carried the boxes of Christmas decorations down from the loft and into the living room. Amelie put some Christmas music on and poured them all a glass of wine. With Kate's help, Rob wrestled the Christmas tree into position in the alcove next to the fireplace, the tip grazing the high ceiling.

Kate carefully opened one of the dusty, cardboard boxes. Years worth of memories were captured in glass angels and crystal snowflakes, gaudy red and green baubles and musty smelling tinsel. Next to her, Rob had moved on to unwinding lengths of fairy lights and swearing under his breath every time he hit a tangle.

'How does that look?' Amelie asked Kate and Rob, putting down the secateurs she'd been using to trim the branches of the tree.

'Like a tree,' Rob deadpanned.

Amelie rolled her eyes. 'Put the lights on, smart arse. Then we can get the baubles on.'

Once the tree was decorated, the three of them stood back in the doorway of the living room, admiring it all.

'Christmas can finally start now,' Amelie said, smiling.

Rob smiled back at her. 'It started for me the minute I got back here.'

Kate watched the fire blazing and the lights twinkling. 'I love this time of year. It's magical.'

Amelie looked at Kate. 'Christmas has always been magical for me. More so once I had you two. I've tried to keep it that way ever since.'

'You have,' Kate said. 'The reason we love Christmas is because you make it special.'

'She's right.' Rob smiling at Amelie. 'You're the best Christmas fairy.'

Two days later, in a small pub in the city, Rob and Kate sat at a corner table. Every time the door opened, they looked at it nervously.

'He's late.' Kate took a sip of her drink.

'Relax, he'll be here,' Rob said. 'And when he does get here, remember, this is the season of goodwill.' He took a sip of his cider. 'Play nice.'

'I will.' Kate gripped her glass tightly. 'I want to move on.'

He lowered his voice. 'If Mama has, then so can you. I heard her on the phone to him in the summer. I think they've been talking again.'

'Unlikely. She would have told me.' She looked over at the door to the pub and spotted a familiar face. Her dad, Michael, walked in wearing an expensive-looking cashmere coat. His short grey hair was neatly cut, and he looked older somehow. Had it really been that long since she'd seen him? She stood up as he came over to their table. 'Evening, Dad. How are you?'

He kissed her on the cheek. 'Very good. It's so good to see you both.' He gave Rob a hug. 'Hello, mate.'

She watched him closely, observing the nervous way that he fiddled with his shirt sleeves. He wasn't his usual confident self. 'What do you want to drink?' she asked.

Michael shook his head. 'These are on me. Rob, what are you having?'

Rob held up his almost empty glass. 'Cider. Kate knows which one. I've got no idea.'

Kate grinned. 'He's had a few already. I'll come with you.' She slid out of her chair and gestured to the bar. 'It's busy, so we might have to elbow our way in.' She led him to the bar, then helped him carry their drinks back to their table.

As they sat back down at the table, Michael slid Rob's cider over to him and raised his glass of wine. 'Merry Christmas to you both. It's good to see you.'

'Merry Christmas, Dad.' Kate and Rob clinked their glasses against Michael's.

'Thanks for the cider, Dad.' Rob grinned and took a gulp. 'I can't get this in Loughborough.'

'How are you finding it there? You've made it through your first semester. That's a good start.' Michael smiled at Rob.

'I think if you can make it through Freshers week, it's a good start.' Rob shrugged and looked at Kate. 'I miss my girls, though. Although they both bombard me with messages all the time.' He shook his head.

'We just miss you, that's all,' Kate said, smiling sweetly at him.

Michael's voice trembled as he spoke. 'I feel the same. I'm missing out on your lives, both of you.'

'I'm sorry, Dad.' Kate's eyes met his. 'I've spent so long being angry and pushing you away.'

Michael nodded. 'I don't blame you. If I were in your shoes, I'd have been angry too. I know things didn't end so well between me and your mum, but I have never stopped loving either of you.'

Kate swallowed the lump in her throat as memories of her dad came flooding back. She remembered making sandcastles on the beach with him, and him taking them into the city to see the Christmas lights every year. These memories were a stark contrast to her graduation, where she'd barely said a word to him.

She looked up at him. 'I don't feel so angry anymore. I know that what happened with you and Mama wasn't all your fault, and I'm sorry I pushed you away.'

Michael's eyes widened. 'Wow. I didn't expect that.' He smiled at Kate, his eyes twinkling with tears. 'You seemed pretty set on not speaking to me, what's changed?'

'I talked to Mama about what happened between the two of you, and I understand it a bit more.' She bit her lip, remembering that Rob didn't know about Amelie and James's affair. 'Also, I've been seeing this guy, Alex. His dad was killed in a car accident when he was younger. I couldn't imagine that happening to you and never seeing you again.'

Michael put his hand on Kate's. 'That's a real tragedy,' he said softly. 'I can understand how it would make you reflect on things. I can't promise that I'll always be around, but I can promise that we'll spend more time together, alright?'

Kate nodded. 'I'd like that. Thanks, Dad.'

Michael smiled and let go of her hand. 'So, tell me about Alex.'

Kate took a sip of her Coke, feeling the familiar rush of excitement as she thought about Alex. 'He's the security system engineer at my work, but he's also a DJ, and he's like a puzzle that I'm slowly trying to work out.' A smile crept across her face.

'Is that what you want?' Michael asked, his brow furrowing.

Oh yes, Kate thought to herself. 'I like that he doesn't reveal everything about himself right away,' she said. 'It makes it more meaningful when he does tell me things. And he's always looking out for everyone around him.'

'He sounds great,' Michael replied. 'Maybe I can meet him over Christmas?'

Rob shook his head. 'Alex isn't meeting anyone. It isn't serious between them.'

'Thank you, Rob.' Kate put her hand on his arm squeezing it just tightly enough for her nails to dig into his skin. She looked at her dad. 'I'd love to see you over Christmas, but no one is meeting Alex yet.'

'That's your call. You can let me know when you're ready. I'm just glad to be seeing you. How about you, Rob? Are you seeing anyone?'

'Sort of.' Rob blushed.

Kate smirked. 'Do tell.'

'Oh, it's nothing serious.' Rob raised an eyebrow. 'Just like you and Alex.'

Michael shook his head. 'I forgot how much you two tease each other. How about we go for dinner after Christmas?'

'Perfect. I'd love to,' As the words left Kate's mouth, she realised she meant them. She was so used to pretending around her dad, but this was real.

'Can you believe it's Christmas Eve already?' Kate shook her head. 'How quickly has this year gone?'

She was sat at a long table in the Italian restaurant around the corner from Corrells, where Emmett had taken her. Patricia had made platters of porchetta, grilled potatoes and vegetables, which Kate and her colleagues were all devouring.

'I say the same thing every year,' David replied. 'This year my boys turn six. Where did that time go?'

'I bet Christmas is fun in your house,' Kate said.

'It's wonderful.' His eyes twinkled in the candlelight on the table.

'I sometimes wish we'd had children,' Emmett said wistfully. 'Julian and I didn't really talk about it until we were in our fifties, and it was a bit late then, but I have plenty of godchildren. Our Christmas probably won't be as magical as yours, but it will involve both of our families and lots of wine.' He turned to Rebecca. 'It's the first Christmas with your little one. How exciting.'

'Our families have bought so much stuff,' Rebecca said. 'My mum has been knitting for months, and I'm slightly concerned about where we'll put it all. We've only bought a few toys. Next Christmas he'll be walking and that seems wild.'

'They grow up very fast,' David said, then turned to Kate. 'What is Christmas in the haunted house like?'

'Usually like Emmett's,' Kate replied. 'Full of food and wine, but this year, I'm cutting down on my drinking, and my aunt, who is usually the one who encourages us all, is in France with her new boyfriend, so there will be less wine and it will be a lot quieter, just me, my mum and my brother.'

Emmett raised an eyebrow. 'You're definitely not inviting Alex over?'

Kate smiled. She had been unable to keep her relationship with Alex a secret for very long. Mainly because David had seen her kissing him outside the shop. 'No. It feels too soon for that. We're taking it slow.'

She wasn't even sure if that was true anymore. She'd spent so much of the last few weeks at the hotel, and when she wasn't with him, she was thinking about him far more than she'd like to admit. She wasn't just falling for him, she'd fallen, utterly, and completely.

Emmett's eyes crinkled as he smiled. 'I'm so glad you two have met. You were made for each other. I see the way that he looks at you. You're both fooling yourselves if you think this is something casual.'

David chuckled. 'Don't mince your words, Emmett.'

'She can take it,' Emmett said, nodding at Kate. 'She knows I'm always honest.'

'You are, and you're right. It's not casual. I've never felt anything like this. Alex is everything I didn't know I needed, but I'm not rushing into anything.' She felt her cheeks flush. 'I'm so happy, and I don't care who knows it!'

'Good for you.' Emmmett smiled. 'You're both so different, but you complement each other so well.'

'Opposites attract.' She turned to David, keen to take the heat off her. 'My lovely colleague is a man of few words, but I met his wife last week, and she's so chatty! I adore her.'

'One of the many things I love about her.' David smiled proudly.

Kate turned to Lisa. 'Are you excited about your parents meeting Leon tomorrow?'

'Yes, but also so nervous.' Lisa bit her lip. 'My parents are quite conservative, and he's...not.'

Kate stifled a giggle. 'That's true, but he does know how to behave in polite company.'

'It's not him I'm worried about. I'm worried about them saying something rude. When I told my dad that Leon was going to fashion college next year, he was horrified, and said that only gay men are fashion designers.' She winced. 'Please wish me luck.'

'I wish you all the luck, and if it all goes tits up, you can come and join us,' Kate assured her.

'Thanks, love,' Lisa said as their plates were cleared, and replaced with plates of tiramisu.

When the table had been cleared, Emmett clinked his glass with a knife. 'Thank you all for coming today, and for your hard work this year. Have a wonderful Christmas and an even better New Year!' He sat back down again to cheers from the others.

'Same to you, mate,' David said. 'Another year of steering the ship done right.'

'Thanks for making me feel so welcome here,' Kate said, a rush of emotion flooding her.

'Thank you for always being there for all of us.' Lisa smiled at Emmett.

'And thanks for inviting me today, I love seeing you guys,' Rebecca added.

'You are like family to me,' Emmett replied, his voice cracking. 'I will always look after my family.'

The sky darkened around Kate as she pulled away from the bistro, driving to a small cottage outside of the city, hoping she could build some bridges with Mia. She knocked on the door, shifting the heavy bag of presents on her shoulder as she waited.

'Kate,' Mia said as she opened the door, her face falling. 'Come in.' She was wearing her coat.

'Are you sure?' Kate asked cautiously. 'If it's a bad time, I'll go.'

Mia shook her head. 'No. Come in.' She slipped off her coat. 'I was going to come over to yours.'

Kate laughed and shook her head. 'Great minds think alike, huh?' She followed Mia into the living room where Pete was sprawled out on the floor, surrounded by pieces of pink plastic.

'Hey,' he said, nodding at her. 'Thought a princess castle was a brilliant idea for Lilly until I got it out of the box. I'm going to be up all night at this rate.'

Kate sat down on the sofa. 'Do you need a hand?'

He stood up. 'Probably, but you guys need to talk. I'll leave you to it.' He pulled himself to his feet and walked out of the room, closing the door behind him.

Mia sat down next to Kate. 'I'm sorry for what happened in the restaurant. I was overwhelmed, and hormonal and unkind.'

'I'm sorry too,' Kate replied. 'It's your pregnancy. You don't have to tell me anything you don't want to.'

Mia nodded. 'The reason I didn't tell you about the baby is that it's a little bit more complicated than last time. I didn't want to tell you until we'd had some more scans and knew what was going on.'

'Is everything alright?' Kate asked, her stomach lurching.

'Yeah. I've got more fluid than I should have, and he's a bit smaller than he should be,' Mia said.

'He's a he?' Kate said excitedly. 'That's amazing!'

'Oh, shit.' Mia put her head in her hands. 'I've managed not to tell anyone that.' She held out her little finger to Kate. 'Pinky swear you'll keep it to yourself.'

'I pinky swear I will keep it to myself. What about the extra fluid?' Kate wrinkled her nose. 'What does that mean?'

'It could mean nothing. It could mean I go into premature labour,' Mia said calmly.

Kate's eyes widened. 'Wow. That's a lot. The last thing you needed was your best friend being a complete arsehole to you.'

Mia smiled at Kate. 'I was an arsehole too, Kate. I worry that you won't ever let anyone get close to you the way that Will did. Sometimes I wade in when I shouldn't.'

Kate shook her head. 'You called me out, and you were right. I do have feelings for Alex, but I don't know what they are yet.'

'That's great.' Mia beamed at Kate. 'If you want to talk about it, I'm here. If you want to keep it to yourself, I understand.'

'So are we good?' Kate asked tentatively.

'Yes,' Mia said, nodding, a smile breaking out across her face. 'I've been worrying about whether you'd ever speak to me again, but I know you need time to cool off, so I wanted to give you that.'

'I appreciate that,' Kate replied. 'I did need time to cool off, and I thought you did too. I know you're only looking out for me, and I figured that if I could mend my relationship with my dad, then I could definitely fix ours.'

Mia's eyes widened. 'You made up with your dad? How? When?'

'Rob and I met him for a drink a few days ago.' Kate bent down and picked up the instructions for the castle from the floor.

'How did you get to that point, though? I thought you hadn't forgiven him for leaving?' Mia looked puzzled.

'I spoke to Mama, and I realised I didn't know the full stor about how they broke up.' Kate paused. 'I was blaming him for something that wasn't totally his fault. Then Alex told me about his dad dying, and that made me want to reconnect with my dad.'

'I'm really proud of you.' Mia's eyes filled with tears. 'I've watched you carry that hurt for so long, and you've just let it go.'

'I'm not holding grudges anymore,' Kate said. 'It's stupid.' She smiled at Mia. 'It felt amazing to give him a proper hug. I could see how much he missed us. Life's too short to hold onto the past.'

Mia nodded. 'I couldn't agree more. That's why I was on my way to see you. I hated the idea of it being Christmas and us not speaking.'

'Same,' Kate said. They had fallen out plenty of times over the years, but they always came back to each other. She looked at the instructions again. 'Seeing as I'm here...'

Mia's eyes lit up. 'Ooh, I'll get Pete. I think we definitely need another pair of hands.'

Chapter Nineteen

December 2012, Canterbury, Kent, England

When Kate woke up on Christmas morning, the sky was grey and cloudy and the house was silent. She smiled to herself as she remembered what had happened when she'd got back from Mia's house the night before. When she'd walked into the kitchen, her mum and Rob had been drunk and playing cards. She had pulled up a chair, knowing it wouldn't be long before it went sideways.

'You cheated!' Amelie had shouted at Rob, and thrown her cards down on the table, before draining the rest of her glass of wine.

Kate had dealt the next round so that she could keep the peace between them, but after Amelie had dropped her entire hand on the floor, and then nearly fallen off her chair trying to pick it up, Kate had intervened, and suggested that they have something to eat.

Having had a feast of grilled cheese and homemade tomato soup, they had headed to the living room to huddle around the fire. Amelie had wobbled over to the bookcase, selecting a book and putting her glasses on. Kate and Rob had giggled to themselves as she sat down on the sofa, cleared her throat, and slurred her way through "The Night Before Christmas." She shook her head as she remembered her mum pausing at the end of every page to push her glasses back onto her nose, and Rob, as usual, coming up with rude names for the reindeer.

She pulled herself out of bed, feeling an icy cold blast of air coming through the leaky windowpanes. After showering and dressing in thick, warm clothes, she went downstairs into the kitchen.

'Morning, Mama! Merry Christmas!' Kate said, then winced at her mum's pale face. 'How's your head?'

Amelie was putting some croissants onto a baking tray. 'A little sore. I think I might have had a little bit too much to drink last night. I'll go easy today.' She smiled at Kate. 'Croissants for breakfast?'

'Yes, please,' Kate said. 'I'll make the hot chocolate.'

Rob surfaced just as the croissants came out of the oven and the table had been laid. 'Morning, guys, Happy Christmas!' He pulled Kate in for a hug, then Amelie.

After they'd eaten, Kate, Rob and Amelie pulled on their thick coats, boots and hats and walked across the frosty fields with the dogs, with mist hanging in the air. Kate wished she had brought her gloves with her as she stuffed her hands further into her pockets. The still, silent atmosphere made her pause and reflect on the last few months. When she'd come back to Canterbury, her relationship with both of her parents had been fractured, and she and Mia had drifted apart. Now, she'd mended all of those relationships, and built a brand new one with Alex. A shiver of anticipation rushed through her as she thought about what the coming year might have in store for them.

When they got back from the walk, Kate was cold and damp and her clothes were muddy. She went upstairs to change, pulling her phone out of her pocket when she felt it buzz.

> Merry Christmas Beautiful! I'm going kind of traditional today, but with a twist… Bastille's Tuning Out. It reminds me of one of the best nights of my life. Looking forward to seeing you tomorrow A x.

She smiled, remembering the night that she'd seen him at the side of the stage, his leather jacket, and his piercing blue eyes holding her attention more than the band on the stage. It had been one of the best nights of her life too, and she would never forget that kiss.

It was one of the best nights of my life too! O Holy Night is my favourite Christmas carol. I love Dan's vocals on this version. Can't wait for tomorrow K x

She sat down on the bed, her head reeling. He got her. They were so similar in some ways.

They both took time to open up, to trust. He was quiet, introverted, and methodical, a contrast to her noisy disorganisation. She knew now that she was ready for a relationship with him, even though it was scary. Even though it was hard to forget what had happened before. She peeled off her damp clothes, showered, then raided her mum's wardrobe.

'Is that my dress?' Amelie asked Kate as she walked back into the kitchen. 'It looks wonderful on you. You must keep it. I never wear it anymore.'

Kate smiled, smoothing her hands over the forest green velvet. 'Thanks, Mama. I was only going to borrow it.'

'You're welcome,' Amelie said with a smile. 'Can you and Rob get the fire lit in the dining room?'

'Sure,' Kate replied, nodding to Rob, who'd walked in and was helping himself to a bag of pretzels. 'Come on, Christmas elf, we've got work to do.'

'You ever seen a six foot elf? If anyone's the elf, it's you.' Rob burst out laughing and walked out of the kitchen.

Kate let out a sigh, and followed him. Once the fire was lit, Kate laid the table with a tablecloth, placemats, and cutlery, while Rob took the silver candlesticks out of the mahogany dresser and polished them. Amelie rummaged in one of the drawers of the dresser and found the long cream tapered candles that slotted into the candlesticks.

Kate rubbed her arms. 'Is it going to be any warmer in here by the time we eat?'

'You ask this every year, and the answer is always yes,' Amelie replied, then walked out of the room.

Kate followed her into the kitchen. 'Do you need a hand with anything?'

'No, darling. Everything's under control,' Amelie said.

'When are we eating?' Rob asked Amelie. 'I'm starving already.'

Amelie flicked her eyes to the clock. 'We will eat at one pm, just like we always do. I'll go and get changed, then we can open some presents before we eat. *If* you can bear to wait that long.' She gave Rob a pointed look, then walked out of the kitchen.

Kate lowered her voice. 'Don't annoy her today. You know how important Christmas is to her.'

'I'll bite my tongue,' Rob said. 'I can tell she's on edge. I'm guessing she's missing Nanna and Papa.'

'She is, and she's missing Marie.' Kate lowered her voice. 'They actually got on with when she came over last month, and I bet she wishes she was here today. Let's do whatever we can to make sure she has a good Christmas.'

'I'll be on my best behaviour.' Rob swiped a chunk of raw carrot out of the saucepan on the stove. 'This should keep me going for a minute.'

Kate left the kitchen and walked into the living room, which was warm and cosy, thanks to the roaring fire. She dragged each one of the three large, fabric stockings out from under the tree and put them by the coffee table, while Rob connected his phone to the speakers and found a Christmas playlist.

When Amelie swept into the living room, her hair and makeup were immaculate, and she wore a black lace dress that sat below her knee, her waist pinched in with a wide black belt. Her black peep-toe stiletto heels clicked across the floor.

'Looking gorgeous as usual, Mama.' Kate smiled at her.

'Oh, this old thing?' Amelie pretended to look coy. She spun around, making the full skirt flare out. 'Thank you, my darling. If you can't make an effort on Christmas Day, when can you?'

'You look beautiful, Mama.' Rob stood up and gave her a hug. 'Do you want to open some presents?'

'Of course,' Amelie said, sitting down on the sofa. 'You two go first.'

'No, you go first, Mama.' Kate passed her mum's stocking over to her. 'That little one on the top is from me.'

Amelie pulled out a neatly wrapped box and carefully took the paper off. Inside, was a small, navy blue cardboard box with the word Correll's etched into it in gold writing. She opened the box and pulled out a pair of teardrop-shaped emerald earrings. 'Oh Kate, these are stunning!'

Kate blushed and, as she watched Amelie slip the earrings into her ears and show them off to her and Rob, her heart felt like it was going to burst with pride. 'Do you like them, Mama?'

'Darling, they are beautiful.' Amelie stood up and admired them in the mirror above the fireplace. 'This is clearly what you're meant to do.' She sat back down on the sofa next to Kate. 'Thank you for these. I will treasure them. I'm so proud of you for following your heart.'

Kate smiled. 'You have no idea how good it feels to hear you say that.'

'I just wish I'd said it sooner,' Amelie said softly.

'It doesn't matter now. Christmas is a time for moving on and forgiving.' Kate thought about her dad and Mia, and smiled, then looked at Amelie's stocking. 'Open another one.'

Amelie pulled out a haphazardly wrapped bottle and looked at it, puzzled. She peeled off the paper and smiled. 'Thank you, Rob! I've just run out of this.' It was her favourite L'Occitane body lotion. 'You two need to open some presents now,' she said firmly.

'Age before beauty,' Rob said to Kate, smirking.

Kate ignored her brother, and reached into her stocking, pulling out a large, squashy parcel, which contained a canvas tool wrap. 'Oh wow, Mama, this is beautiful. Thank you.'

This was the final confirmation that Kate needed that her mum really did approve of her career choice. She pulled Amelie in for a tight hug, being careful not to squash her neatly styled hair.

Amelie nodded. 'Good. I'm glad you like it.'

'Your turn now, *beauty*,' Kate said sarcastically.

Rob pulled a present out of his stocking, tore off the paper, and opened a familiar navy blue box. He pulled out a silver bangle with a set of numbers engraved into it. 'Wow! You made this?' He turned it over in his hands.

'It's got your birth date and the coordinates of where you were born engraved into it,' Kate said. She had been inspired by the bangle that Alex wore.

'It's awesome. I love it.' He held out a box to her. 'Your turn.'

Inside was a similar selection of L'Occitane products, but in Kate's favourite scent, Cherry Blossom. 'Perfect, thanks, dude.' She raised her hand in the air and Rob high-fived her, the noise echoing around the room.

After they'd opened their presents, they all pitched in to get the dinner ready and into the dining room, which had been warmed by the blazing fire.

Surrounded by ceramic dishes and plates full of food, Amelie raised her glass. 'To us, and to our loved ones.' She nodded to the photo of her parents, smiling at them from the sideboard.

'Merry Christmas, Mama.' Kate raised her glass to her mother. 'Merry Christmas, darling brother.' She grinned at Rob who clinked his glass against hers.

'I know it's a little quieter this year,' Amelie said as she took a sip of her wine. 'We'll make up for it at my party in a few weeks.'

Kate gave Rob a wary glance as they started to eat. Amelie threw a party for their friends and family every year in January. There was always too much food, way too much alcohol, and usually some kind of drama.

Amelie looked at Kate's glass of lemonade. 'Don't you want a glass of wine, darling?'

'No, thank you,' Kate said. 'I'm cutting down on my drinking.'

'Cutting down on your drinking? That's the only thing you're good at.' Rob smirked.

Amelie ignored him. 'I suggested that you should cut down, I didn't say you had to give it up.' She put her cutlery down and lowered her voice. 'You're not pregnant, are you?'

Rob leant forwards, his elbows on the table. 'I'm not ready to be an uncle yet.'

'No, I'm not pregnant.' Kate took a deep breath. 'Alex's dad was killed by a drunk driver when he was young.' When she said it quickly, it didn't hurt as much, but she still felt her chest tighten as she imagined a young Alex, knowing he'd survived but his dad hadn't. 'It's made me rethink how much I drink.'

'My goodness. That poor man.' Amelie put a hand on her chest. 'How tragic. I struggled so much with losing Papa and I was in my thirties. To go through that as a child must have been so hard.'

'I can't imagine it, Mama,' Kate said. 'But he's so strong. He's always looking out for everyone around him, me included. He was so closed off at first, but he's really opened up to me.'

'People who've experienced trauma are often very cautious,' Amelie replied. 'They're constantly assessing every situation, weighing up the risks. He must have decided you're worth the risk.'

Kate smiled. 'I've come to the same conclusion about him.'

Chapter Twenty

Deceмber 2012, Canterbury, Kent, England

Kate stood in front of the mirror in her bedroom as the sun set on Boxing Day, holding her breath as she added a flick of black eyeliner to her eyes. She was wearing another one of Leon's creations, this time a scarlet shift dress. In her bare feet, she walked down the stairs, her heels in one hand and her overnight bag gripped tightly in the other. She walked into the living room, where Amelie and Rob were playing cards.

'OK, I'm going to see Alex, how do I look?' She twirled around, her skirt flaring out.

'Beautiful,' Amelie said.

'I agree,' Rob added. 'Have a great time.'

'Thank you.' Kate smiled and smoothed her skirt down. 'See you guys later.'

Christmas with her family was so important to her, and the fact that she was leaving them, to see Alex, was a bigger deal that she wanted to admit. While Alex had said he couldn't offer her the relationship he wanted to, she was certain that she was in love with him, and now she had no idea if they were in the same book, let alone on the same page. She pulled on her coat, then walked out of the house, her face immediately battered by the icy wind.

She drove through seemingly endless country lanes, past darkened fields, hemmed in by towering hedges. Above her in the cloudless sky, the stars sparkled, guiding her to her destination.

Twenty minutes later, Kate arrived at the hotel, and walked through the hallway. In the bar, the lights were dim, and the tables were empty. She'd texted Alex to let him know that she was on her way and she'd only been in the bar for a minute, when he walked in, his face lighting up as he saw her.

He took her coat and planted a kiss on her lips. 'Wow! You look beautiful. That dress is stunning.'

'Isn't it gorgeous? You look gorgeous as usual.' He wore a pair of slim fitting dark washed jeans, brown boots, and a cream, cable knitted jumper, which she instantly decided was coming home with her. It looked cosy, and would no doubt be scented with his aftershave.

'Thanks. Let's get you a drink.' He went behind the counter of the bar and turned on the spotlights above them. 'Spiced rum and Coke?'

'Perfect, thanks,' Kate said, sitting on one of the bar stools, watching the way his hands deftly moved from the glass rack to the bottles. Once he'd made their drinks, he set them on the counter and came back around to the other side of the bar, sitting next to her.

Kate picked up her glass. 'Santé.'

'Santé,' Alex said, picking up his own glass and clinking it against hers. 'Joyeux Noël.'

'Et toi,' Kate replied with a coy smile. 'How was yesterday?'

'It was full on, but brilliant.' Alex took a sip of his drink. 'My aunt and uncle came over with my cousins, Chris and Scott. Stefan and Mel were both here too. Christmas is always a bit hard, but with everyone here, it feels special, kind of magical. How about you? From your messages, it sounds like you've had an eventful few days.'

'That's an understatement,' Kate said. 'I only spent a few hours with my dad, but somehow I let go of six years of hurt. I'm so glad he wants to be part of my life again.' She smiled at Alex. 'You made me realise that appreciating my dad was more important than holding a grudge.'

'I'm glad. It sounds like he wants to be part of your life again too. What happened with Mia?' he asked.

'We both apologised to each other,' Kate replied. 'I turned up at her house just as she was leaving to come to mine. Turns out she didn't love how we left things either. We talked it over, and we fixed things. I feel like we understand each other a little better now.' She took her phone out of the pocket of her dress. 'Then I helped Pete assemble Lilly's princess castle.' She showed him the photo. 'Check this out.'

He nodded approvingly. 'Impressive work. Next time we're looking to renovate this place I'll give you a call. What was Christmas Day like?'

'It was great. I love Christmas Day in our house. We always get dressed up, and we eat in the dining room. It felt kind of quiet this year as it was just me and my mum and brother. My aunt usually comes over, and sometimes we have friends, but this year it was just us.'

'It meant you got to talk more though, I bet,' Alex said. 'How did your brother's first term at uni go? Did he tell you much?'

'Uh no. Whatever he got up to, he's keeping it to himself. That's probably a good thing though.' She laughed.

'It probably is. Do you want to take these drinks upstairs?' He asked. 'I need to give you your Christmas present.'

'Of course.' She stood up. 'Are we the only ones here? It's really quiet.'

'Mum's out on a date with Stefan,' he said, his expression neutral.

'How do you feel about that?' she asked as they walked down the corridor.

'I thought about what you said, and I want her to be happy,' he said. 'Stefan is perfect for her. He's so caring, and even though he was off duty yesterday, he insisted on making us an absolute feast.'

'Hmm, who does that sound like? Always going the extra mile for others?' Kate teased as he let them into his room.

'Some people are worth going the extra mile for.' He put her bag on the foot of the bed and slid his arms around her waist. 'How long do I have you for?'

'All night,' she whispered, her face almost level with his in her heels. 'I have to work tomorrow, though.'

'Shame.' He nibbled at her neck.

She raised an eyebrow. 'Are you're telling me *you're* not working tomorrow?'

'Of course I am,' he said, 'but I'm working *here,* and it would have been more fun with you. Mel's taken a bit of a shine to you too.'

'I noticed.' She raised an eyebrow. 'Looks like you've got competition.'

'You were mine first,' he said, his eyes darkening.

'Are you claiming me?' she asked, her eyes falling to his lips.

'Well, I don't want to share you with anyone...' He kissed her. 'I'm all yours. If that's what you want.'

'It is what I want,' she murmured as she pulled away from him. 'I *said* I wasn't ready for a relationship, but I can't stop thinking about what that might be like. I know you're not ready for that, and that's OK...'

'What if I was though?' He interrupted her. 'What if everything had fallen into place, and I was in a position where I could say let's go on a date, and I wouldn't have to rush off halfway through, or where I could stay over at your house without leaving right after breakfast?'

'Then I would leap into your arms and say that I want that,' she said, her heart about to burst.

This was what she'd been waiting for him to say. There was no way she'd tell him that she was in love with him though, not until she heard him say it first.

'Go for it,' he replied, smiling.

She took a step back, swishing her skirt back, then flew at him. He scooped her off her feet and kissed her. 'Like this,' he whispered.

'Yes, just like that. You're the best Christmas present ever!'

He kissed her, before pulling away. 'Hold on. I didn't need to get you an actual present? That's a shame, because I can't take it back.' He gestured to a large pot on the coffee table with a dark green cactus in it. 'Do you like it?'

'I love it!' she said. 'Thank you so much. I can't believe you remembered that I collect them.'

'I remember all the details, Kate.' He raised his eyebrow.

'It's perfect.' She picked up her bag and opened it, pulling out a square box, wrapped in navy blue, corrugated paper, and handed it to Alex. 'Here's yours. I hope you like it.'

He unwrapped the paper, pulling out a velvet box, and she watched his face light up as he opened it, revealing a pair of silver cufflinks shaped like vinyl records.

'These are so good! I can't believe you made these.' His eyes lit up as he turned them over in his hand, running his finger over the engraved grooves.

She looked at him cautiously, biting her lip. 'Do you really like them?'

'They're brilliant.' He kissed her cheek. 'I love them, and I'd like to show you just how grateful I am.'

'And how would you like to do that?' she asked.

'It won't be with words,' he said, scooping her up in his arms and carrying her over to his bed.

She sank into the crisp white sheets, taking him with her.

Chapter Twenty-One

December 2012, Canterbury, Kent, England

The sun started to disappear behind the trees on New Year's Eve as Kate walked with Alex through the woods at the back of the hotel. 'It's so peaceful out here, Alex.'

Alex smiled at her. 'I know. Whenever I have something on my mind, I come out here. It helps me work through it.'

'Are you excited about your mum's birthday party tonight?' she asked. 'Or are you nervous?'

'Nervous,' he said. 'I know Mum will love it, but it's going to be a huge test for the hotel to see whether we can host events.'

She squeezed his hand tightly. 'You guys have worked so hard. I can't wait to see the bar.'

'It looks very cool. I'll show you when we get back.' He led her to the top of a hill, where he slid his arm around her as they admired the view across the fields. 'Ben and I used to come up here with our sledges when it was snowy. You can see all the way across the city from here when it's not so foggy.'

She turned to face him. 'How do you feel about seeing him tomorrow?'

'Even more nervous,' he said. 'It's been so long since he's been back here, and I know it'll be hard for all of us.'

'It's a New Year,' she replied, putting her arms around his waist. 'It's a time for new beginnings, and hopefully a new start for you and your brother.'

'You're right. Maybe next year will be better than this one. I'm glad you'll be with me tonight, and tomorrow.'

'It means a lot that you asked me.' She swallowed hard, trying to hide how nervous she felt. 'I know that trusting people is hard for you.'

'It is,' he said, 'but I know I can trust you. Honesty is the most important thing to me, and ever since we first met, you've been up front with me about how you feel and what you want from me. That's why I love you.'

Her breath caught in her throat. 'Hold on, what did you just say?'

'I love you, Kate,' he said, his voice vibrating through her body. 'I've loved you for a long time. I just didn't want to tell you until I could offer you all of me.'

'I love you too. I realised I loved you before Christmas, but I wasn't going to say it first,' she admitted.

He smiled. 'You could have told me. I would have told you right back. I didn't want to tell *you* in case I freaked you out after you said you weren't ready for a relationship.'

She laughed. 'Looks like we're both good at keeping secrets.'

'How about we just be open with each other?' He brushed her hair out of her face. 'You can tell me anything.'

'Same.' She leant forward and kissed him. 'I love you. Now I've said it, I don't want to *stop* saying it.'

'I love you too. Tell me as many times as you like. I'll always say it back.' He kissed her again as the sun sunk below the trees behind them.

❧❧❧ ❧❧❧

Kate sat on Alex's bed, wrapped in a thick white bath towel as she carefully applied her makeup. 'How are we doing for time?'

'It's a little tight,' Alex said. 'I gave us half an hour to get ready, but...' He smirked at her. 'You had other ideas.'

'You definitely should have allowed extra time,' she giggled, then smeared her mascara.

'You're not wrong,' he said. 'I didn't realise how many layers you'd got on. 'It was like pass the parcel.'

'Well, you got the prize in the middle,' she quipped, carefully removing the mascara from her eyelid.

He buttoned up his shirt and put on his bow tie, and her mouth fell open as he slipped on his black tuxedo jacket.

'Wow.' She slid off the bed and wrapped her arms around him. 'Do we have to go downstairs?'

'Yes, but don't worry, we'll have time to ourselves later.' He unhooked her towel, letting it drop to the floor. 'Love the outfit,' he said, running his eyes over her naked body.

'That's cute, but I don't think your mum will approve. If anyone should be in their birthday suit tonight, it's her.' She raised her eyebrow.

'Way to kill the mood.' He wrinkled his nose and checked his watch. 'We need to get a move on. She'll be here soon.'

'She really has no idea about tonight?' she asked as she put her underwear on.

'I've done all I can to make sure she doesn't. I've sworn enough people to secrecy.' He shrugged.

'I can't stop thinking about meeting her,' she said. 'She's your mum. It's her sixtieth birthday tonight, and I feel like a gate crasher.'

'You're not a gate crasher, you're my girlfriend,' he said firmly.

'I like the way that sounds.' She raised her eyebrow. 'Say it again.'

He laughed. 'You're my girlfriend.' He kissed her cheek. 'And I can't wait for you to meet everyone.'

'Me neither.' This was true, she couldn't wait, but she was also incredibly nervous. She lifted the dress cover from Leon's latest creation, a sequin covered shift dress. She carefully slid it on. As usual, it fit like a glove.

'You look beautiful,' he said.

'It's not too much?' She looked at her reflection in the mirror, her doubtful face staring back at her.

'It's New Year's Eve!' he said. 'You've seen the bar. It's covered in glitter and tissue paper. You'll fit right in. Come on, we need to go downstairs.'

Downstairs in the bar, silver and gold decorations hung everywhere, and fairy lights were draped across the bar. At the back of the bar,

Kate could see the guys from Future Proof sound checking. Her eyes lit up in anticipation, remembering the last time she'd seen them. In front of them, some of the tables and chairs had been cleared to make a dancefloor, and on the ceiling, a disco ball glittered.

'What do we do?' Kate asked.

'I don't know. I'm not in charge tonight,' Alex whispered. He turned to Mel. 'Mel, what do we need to do?'

'Welcome the guests,' Mel said and nodded to several trays of Champagne flutes on the bar. 'Can you hand out drinks? We've got about ten minutes to get everyone in place.'

Kate and Alex picked up a tray each and started handing out glasses to the guests. The bar soon filled up, the noises of their laughter floating into the high ceilings.

Kate returned her empty tray to the bar and looked up as a stocky red-haired man walked up to her. 'Kate? I'm Sam, the hotel manager. Alex asked me to come and introduce myself to you.'

'Hi, Sam,' Kate said, smiling at him. 'This place looks amazing, and it's packed in here.'

'Thank you.' He smiled back at her. 'Alex has probably told you already, but I've not had much experience with events. Tonight's going to be a bit of a baptism by fire. Your mate Sophia has been really helpful. She's got grand plans for this place.'

Kate smiled. 'Sophia's always ready to pitch in and help out. She's brilliant and she knows what she's talking about.'

Sam looked up as Mel shouted to him from the bar, then smiled at Kate. 'The birthday girl's arrived.' He walked over to the light switches and turned them off. 'Places everyone.'

The door opened, and a tall woman with dark hair walked in. Sam turned the lights on and the crowd greeted Alex's mum, all shouting "Surprise!"

As she watched Alex hug his mum, Kate felt a tightness in her chest, one that wasn't related to the sequin covered dress. Why had she agreed to meet his mum tonight? What if she embarrassed herself or Alex in front of her? She ran her sweaty palms over her dress, as her eyes met Alex's.

'Kate, this is my mum, Sarah,' Alex said, interrupting Kate's doom spiralling.

'Happy birthday,' Kate said nervously. 'It's great to meet you.'

Sarah had the same piercing blue eyes as her son, and they sparkled as she smiled at Kate. 'Thank you, love. Wonderful to meet you too. That's a stunning dress.'

'Thank you,' Kate said as Sarah let her go. She hadn't expected her to have such a strong Cornish accent. It was a contrast to Alex's clipped tones. 'I hope you have a great time tonight.'

Sarah beamed at her and Alex, the fairy lights reflecting in her eyes. 'I'm sure I will. I just can't believe you lot have done all this for me.' She turned to Alex. 'How on earth did you manage to keep this quiet?'

Alex shrugged. 'Quiet is my middle name.' He smiled at Sarah. 'I'll go and get you a drink.'

As he walked away, Sarah turned to Kate. 'I was wondering when I would get to meet the elusive Kate. Alex has done a good job of hiding you away, but he talks about you a lot.'

'I talk about him a lot,' Kate said, smiling. 'He's amazing. You know that he literally rescued me? You must be so proud of him.'

'I am,' Sarah replied. 'He told me about what happened at Correll's. I wasn't surprised. He's the first to help someone in need, but he doesn't ever put himself first. You've helped him to step away from this place and focus on his own happiness.'

'His happiness is really important to me.' Kate bit her lip. 'Do you mind him stepping away? I know you've not been open for long.'

'Yes but this was my dream, my vision.' Sarah paused. 'I just wasn't able to do it on my own, and Alex helped me. I never meant to put so much pressure on him. It's been a really hard year for him, but you've made him see that he doesn't need to be here all the time.'

'What are you two talking about?' Alex asked, handing glasses of Champagne to Kate and Sarah.

'Oh, nothing, darling, just girl stuff,' Sarah said, winking at Kate, then turning back to Alex. 'Thank you for organising this. It really is a dream come true.'

'I hope you enjoy it.' Alex smiled as a tall, slender man joined them. 'Stefan, this is my girlfriend, Kate.'

'Wonderful to meet you, Kate,' Stefan said, with a thick French accent. He turned to Sarah. 'Your sisters are asking for a tour.'

'Please excuse me,' Sarah said. 'Duty calls. It was lovely to meet you, Kate.'

As they walked away, Alex slid his arm around Kate. 'How did it go? I was watching you from the bar. I can tell she likes you.'

'I hope so. I really like her. She's very... open.' Kate said, raising an eyebrow.

'You mean the complete opposite of me?' Alex laughed. 'She wears her heart on her sleeve. She's definitely not a mystery.'

'Why does she have a Cornish accent?' Kate's brow furrowed. 'And why don't you have one?'

'My mum and her sisters grew up in Cornwall,' Alex said, 'but Mum went to university here, and she never went back, so I was born and grew up here.' He nodded to a large group of people standing at the bar. 'Do you want to meet my cousins?'

'Sure,' Kate replied, a nervous flutter in her stomach. 'I'd love to.'

She had the feeling that he didn't introduce many people to his family, that they were something that he kept for himself, and she felt privileged to be admitted into his inner circle. The gravity of this moment was not lost on her. She took Alex's hand and he led her over to the bar.

'Guys,' Alex said. 'This is my girlfriend, Kate. Kate, these are my cousins, Chris, Scott, and Jake, and Jake's girlfriend, Cora.'

'Hi.' Kate felt overwhelmed as they all looked at her. 'It's good to meet you.'

'Oh, wonderful to meet you,' Cora said. 'Alex has been very secretive about you, but he does like hiding things.'

Alex smiled. 'Only the most important things. Anyway, you can't talk. Have you told your parents about Jake yet?'

Cora shook her head, then looked at Kate. 'My parents and Jake's parents hate each other. It's complicated.' She sighed. 'Now I'm at university, it's even harder because we're miles away from each other.'

'We make it work,' Jake said, sliding his arm around Cora's shoulder. 'I'm not even allowed in her house, or should I say, her *estate*.'

'We're like Romeo and Juliet,' Cora replied drily. 'Let's hope it doesn't end in tragedy.'

'I hope not!' Kate exclaimed. 'Your parents really don't know that you're together?'

'Her parents don't,' Jake said. 'Mine do, and my mum loves her, but my dad doesn't. As Cora said. It's complicated.'

Kate glanced at the mermaid tattoo on his arm, and the cloud of red hair swirling around her head, clearly a representation of Cora, who had a mane of copper curls. She couldn't imagine what it must be like to have to hide your relationship from your parents.

'Are you ready for tonight?' Alex asked Chris.

'You know it,' Chris said. 'It's been a while.'

'Chris and Scott live in Leeds,' Alex explained to Kate. 'So we haven't seen each other for a while, but Chris is DJing with me tonight.'

'I can't wait to hear this,' Kate said, smiling at them both.

'Me too.' Scott turned to Alex. 'I hear you've got something really big in the works next year.'

Alex shot Scott a glance. 'It's not confirmed yet.'

Kate looked between Scott and Alex, intrigued. What had Scott meant? Alex's cheeks had coloured, and he was still looking at Scott, a look that suggested he'd overstepped the mark.

Behind them, the band started playing, and Alex led Kate to the dancefloor, holding her tightly as the disco ball sparkled above them.

'Your cousins are great,' Kate said to Alex, as she slid her arms around his neck. 'I was so nervous about meeting them.'

'Why?' Alex asked. 'You're amazing, and you always seem to just fit in. I admire that about you. I don't find it as easy.'

'I don't either, actually,' she said. 'Maybe I make it look that way, but inside I'm a bag of nerves, and sometimes I say the wrong thing. You always know just what to say. I admire that about you.'

'Oh, trust me, I get nervous too.' He unhooked her arms from around her neck, kissing one of her hands, and twirling her around. He pulled her back in again, locking eyes with her. 'I've never been nervous with you though. I think I've always known you were right for me.'

'Seriously? I could barely *sleep* after our first date,' she said. 'It wasn't just the kiss, it was more. I think it's because you're a mystery that you feel familiar to me. You like your privacy, and so do I. I've never had to explain that. You just... got it. You got me.'

'You got me too,' he replied. 'You never asked me to tell you more than I was comfortable sharing. And now, I want to share you with everyone I know and love, because they'll love you just as much as I do.'

Her eyes misted with tears. No one had ever spoken about her like that before. 'I never expected to meet someone like you, Alex. I'd convinced myself that I didn't want a relationship, and I put all these walls up, but you knocked them down, and you made me so happy.'

'You did the same to me,' he said. 'I don't want walls anymore. I'd rather have you.'

'I'd rather have you too,' she replied, wiping her eyes.

She rested her head on his chest as they danced. He held her close, and she knew that she would never forget this moment.

The song finished and George addressed the guests. 'We're going to take a short break and hand over to some familiar faces.'

'Is that your cue?' she asked Alex.

'I'm afraid so.' He let go of her, then kissed her hand. 'Let's get you another drink.'

He led her to the bar, where his cousins were. With an elderflower cocktail in hand, she sat down on one of the bar stools, watching Alex and Chris stride across the room towards the band. Alex got to work straight away, setting up his decks with Chris's help. She still hadn't had her private performance from Alex, but she had listened to every one of his remixes that she could get her hands on, and she was excited to see him play them live.

'Hey, love, are you having a good time?' Cora asked.

'I am,' Kate replied. 'I was so nervous about meeting everyone, but you guys are so lovely.'

'I was the same when Jake introduced me to everyone a couple of years ago, but his family are cool, and so much more chilled out than mine.' She shook her head. 'I love my parents, but they're all about appearances, and I'm the kind of person who is always wearing, doing and saying the wrong thing.'

'That sounds like me.' Kate laughed. 'I've managed not to embarrass myself so far tonight, but I can't relax yet. He wasn't even like this with Ava, and they lived together.'

'Ava?' Kate frowned. 'Who's Ava?'

'Ignore me.' Cora shook her head. 'I shouldn't have said anything. What were we saying about embarrassing ourselves?'

'Uh, babe, I don't really think Kate wants to listen to you talk about Alex's ex-girlfriend.' Jake slid his arm around Cora's waist, and smiled at Kate. 'She has no filter, this one.'

'I was trying to say that she's a good match for Alex, that's all.' Cora looked apologetically at Kate. 'I'm sorry. Jake's right, I have no filter.' She laughed nervously.

'Don't worry, it's fine.' Kate looked over at Alex. Why hadn't he told her about Ava? He hadn't mentioned any ex-girlfriends, and definitely not one that he'd lived with. She put it to the back of her mind as the music started. 'Come and dance with me?' she asked Cora cautiously.

This wasn't her family, and she felt slightly self-conscious, but Cora's eyes lit up and she grabbed Kate's hand, leading her to the dancefloor.

As the next song finished, Kate walked up to Alex. He slid off his headphones and smiled at her. 'Can I make a request?' she asked.

'Sure.' Handing his headphones to Chris, Alex leant over to her and she whispered to him.

He smiled. 'Good choice.'

A minute later, her song, "Last Night a DJ Saved My Life" was playing, and he was twirling her around on the dancefloor, making her sequins sparkle under the disco ball. The song was so fitting and it reminded her of the night he came to her rescue at Corrells.

As the song finished, she let go of him. 'It isn't a private performance, but I'm still loving it,' she said.

'Oh, trust me, you'll get one. I always keep my promises,' he replied, and kissed her hand. 'I'll come find you later.'

She joined Cora, Jake, and Scott on the dancefloor as Alex returned to the decks.

After Alex and Chris finished their set, Future Proof came back for a second set.

Kate squeezed onto the packed floor with Alex. 'Remember the night we first kissed? I'll never forget that. No one's ever kissed me like that.'

'I hope no one else gets the chance to,' he said, as he held her gaze.

Around them, the countdown to midnight began loudly, and when the clock hit midnight, Alex pulled Kate close, kissing her. She zoned out from the glasses clinking and the cheering, focusing only on him.

'Happy New Year,' he said when he finally let her go.

'Happy New Year.' She kissed his cheek. 'Thank you for sharing all of this with me. I know how important your family are to you, and tonight's been amazing.'

'You're important to me.' He paused. 'I've been hurt before, and I won't pretend I'm not scared, but you're worth the risk.'

'You have no idea how much that means to me,' she said. 'Just so you know, you're worth the risk too.'

As she kissed him again, she thought about Ava. Was she who had hurt him? And why hadn't he told her? Her future with him relied on him being able to tell her about her past.

Chapter Twenty-Two

January 2013, Canterbury, Kent, England

In the hotel bar the following afternoon, Alex showed off his bottle flipping skills, making Kate laugh. They'd had a long lunch with his family, who had all left to go back to Cornwall, and Leeds, and now they were waiting for his brother to arrive.

His brow furrowed as the door to the bar opened, and she turned around, following his gaze. 'They're here.'

She slid off her bar stool, and looked into his eyes, which today were dark and stormy. 'You've got this,' she whispered.

Alex's brother, Ben, walked towards them. He and Alex were exactly alike, from their dark hair to their ice blue eyes. Ben wore an expensive looking cashmere coat, but she could see that, underneath, he wore the same tight black jeans as Alex. He put down the large leather holdall he was carrying.

'Hey, man, how are you doing?' Alex stepped forward, and he and Ben exchanged an awkward hug.

'I'm good.' Ben gave Alex a tight smile and wrapped an arm around the woman standing next to him.

'H, Corinne.' Alex kissed her cheek, then gestured to Kate. 'Guys, this is my girlfriend, Kate.'

Ben smiled politely and offered her his hand. 'Good to meet you. This is Corinne, and this is our son, Oliver.'

Kate's throat felt dry. She was nervous and she could sense Alex's nerves. 'It's so good to meet you all.'

Ben had the same taut, unreadable expression as Alex, but Corinne gave Kate an easy smile. Her bright green eyes sparkled and her smooth dark hair was pulled up into a ponytail. Around her neck, a tiny peridot heart on a gold chain sparkled. Kate caught sight of Oliver's tiny face, and his tightly shut eyes, and wondered what Alex's babies would look like. Cute, if George was anything to go by .

'Kate, so nice to meet you,' Corinne said, before turning to Alex. 'I'm sure you're dying to show us around, Alex, but we've been in the car for what feels like a week, and I need to freshen up and feed Oliver.'

'Of course.' Alex slipped behind the bar and pulled a key from one of the hooks on the wall, handing it to Ben. 'Here's your room key. I'll show you where it is. Mum's in her office. We can stop there first.'

'Thanks,' Ben said. 'I can't believe this used to be our house. You've done an amazing job, Alex. We would have loved to have come last night but Oliver's a little too young for a party.'

'He is, and you're here now,' Alex replied. 'Mum's going to be so happy to see you.' He turned to Kate. 'I'll just show Ben and Corinne to their room. I'll be right back.'

When Alex returned to the bar, Sarah was with him.

'Do you guys want a drink?' Alex asked Kate and Sarah.

'An elderflower lemonade would be great,' Sarah said.

'I'll get it.' Mel appeared behind Alex. 'Your focus today is Ben. I'll sort the drinks out. Let me guess, black coffee?'

'Yes please, Mel,' Alex said. 'Thanks for looking out for me.'

'All part of the job,' Mel replied, before turning to Kate. 'Rum and Coke?'

Kate shook her head. 'I'll have an elderflower lemonade too, thanks.'

'Go and sit down.' Mel nodded to an empty table. 'I'll bring them over.'

Ben and Corinne returned a while later, joining the three of them at the large table.

'Mum, while he's awake, do you want a cuddle?' Ben asked. Oliver's eyes were now open, and he seemed to be taking in the room around him.

'Oh, darling, I'd love to.' Sarah held out her arms and Ben carefully handed Oliver to her. Her eyes sparkled with tears as she looked at him. 'He's beautiful, you two. Absolutely adorable. How are you both?'

'A little sleep deprived, but otherwise, great,' Ben said. 'How are you doing?'

'I'm just fine. Stronger than ever,' Sarah replied, beaming. She turned to Corinne. 'What about you, love?'

'Same as Ben. Surviving on caffeine and power naps.' Corinne laughed.

'I remember it well. Would you like something to eat?' Sarah nodded to the menus on the table. You must be hungry after your drive.'

'Thanks, Mum, that would be great,' Ben picked up a menu and handed it to Corinne, before picking up another one for himself.

'Thank you, Sarah. Today was our first big drive with Oliver, and I think we're all still recovering from it,' Corinne said, with a laugh, before looking at the menu. 'We haven't been out to eat for a long time.'

'Well you're here now, so you can relax,' Sarah replied. 'We're here to help, anything you need, just ask.'

'Thank you.' Corinne smiled at Sarah.

'We'll keep that in mind when Oliver wakes up at three am,' Ben said to Sarah with a smirk. Oliver chose that moment to let out a loud gurgle and they all laughed.

Alex looked around the table and shut his menu. 'I'll take your orders to Mel if you like. She looks a bit busy at the moment.'

'Thanks, darling. Why don't you take Ben, and then you can show him around?' Sarah suggested.

Ben smiled. 'I'd like that. I can't believe how much work you've done in the last year. It doesn't even look like our house anymore.'

Kate wondered if that was a good or a bad thing. Would Ben's bad memories disappear with the old house? She watched Ben and Alex walk off together and prayed that tonight they would reconnect. She met Corinne's eyes and smiled at her.

'You look as worried as I feel,' Corinne said. 'I hope they actually talk to each other. Ben isn't a huge fan of words, or feelings, and Alex is a mystery. I've known him for about six years, and I've still not figured him out.'

'I think Kate's making some progress.' Sarah smiled.

'He and I are alike.' Kate felt her cheeks flush, as Corinne and Sarah looked at her. 'We take our time to open up.'

'I love that he's found someone he can be himself with,' Corinne said, 'and I hope that he and Ben can open up to each other. After Oliver was born, Ben started seeing a therapist to help him work through the grief of losing his dad, and when you had your stroke, he went back to her. He's getting better at talking about how he feels.'

Sarah bit her lip. 'It breaks my heart to think of him struggling with all of that, and not feeling like he could say anything. I love coming to visit you in Cornwall, but I wanted him to be able to come back here too.'

'So did he, but he just wasn't able to. In a way I think it's helped that the house is now a hotel. He isn't coming back to the *same* place.' Corinne paused. 'Hold on, they're coming back over.'

Ben and Alex sat back down at the table, and a few minutes later, Stefan came over with their food. Oliver had fallen asleep in Sarah's arms, and she held onto him while Ben and Corinne ate, deftly using one hand to eat her risotto. Kate smiled, remembering her own clumsy attempts to eat her pancakes with Lilly on her lap at Mia's.

'What are your plans while you're here?' Sarah asked Ben after they'd eaten.

Ben smiled at Alex. 'We're going to meet Pete and Dan in the pub tomorrow afternoon.'

'And I'm going to have a walk around the city,' Corinne said. 'I haven't been here in years.'

'I could show you around the city,' Kate offered. 'If that works for you and Oliver? I don't know what your routine is.'

Corinne's eyes lit up. 'I'd love that! As for a routine... we're still figuring that out.' At that moment, Oliver woke up, letting out a tiny cry. She held out her arms to Sarah. 'Shall I take him?'

Sarah stood up, rocking him gently. 'Give me a second. Let me see if he'll let me comfort him.'

Oliver cried again, then his eyes shut as Sarah swayed back and forth.

'You've got the magic touch.' Corinne smiled at Sarah, then turned to Kate. 'I'd love a tour of the city, but I don't want to disrupt your plans.'

'I don't have any,' Kate said. 'I've got tomorrow off, so I'm all yours. Sarah, did you want to come?'

Sarah shook her head. 'No, love, I need a rest after last night. Come back for dinner, though, won't you? Stefan and I are going to make something special for you all.'

'I'd love to, thank you, that sounds great.' Kate smiled.

'We'd love to have dinner with you again,' Corinne said. 'I don't know if Oliver will be quite as peaceful as he has been tonight, though.' Oliver woke up again, and cried loudly. 'I spoke too soon.'

Ben stood up, carefully taking Oliver from Sarah and draping him over his shoulder. He rocked him, gently whispering to him, but the crying continued. 'I think he wants you,' he said to Corinne.

'Come here, sweetie,' Corinne stood up and took Oliver. 'I think we'd better call it a night. Thank you so much for having us to stay. The hotel is absolutely beautiful.'

'You're very welcome, darling,' Sarah said. 'I'll see you in the morning. Breakfast will be in the restaurant, and if you need anything, come and knock on my door.'

Ben stood up too. 'Thanks, Mum, for everything. We'll see you in the morning.'

After they had left the room, Sarah turned to Alex. 'Please tell me you talked to each other.'

Alex nodded. 'We talked, Mum. We talked about a lot of things, and I'm genuinely excited about tomorrow.' He turned to Kate. 'Thank you for offering to show Corinne around. I was worried about her being left out while Ben and I caught up with Pete and Dan.'

Kate smiled. 'No problem. She seems lovely. Are you sure you don't want to join us, Sarah? Or if you wanted some time alone with her, I'll butt right out, I know I just jumped in earlier.'

'You're fine,' Sarah said. 'You like to help, love, and I like that about you.'

Alex raised his eyebrow. 'She fits right in, doesn't she?'

Kate swallowed hard. It wasn't just Alex that saw her for who she was, but Sarah too. 'You two are the sweetest.'

'He's right. You fit right in.' Sarah stood up. 'I'm going to bed; I'm still exhausted from last night.'

'Sleep well, Mum,' Alex said.

Kate smiled at Sarah. 'Thank you for dinner tonight, it's been great.'

Sarah smiled back at her. 'Very welcome, love. See you tomorrow.'

As Sarah walked out of the bar, Alex took a sip of his drink. 'Tonight went well, huh?'

Kate nodded. 'I'm so glad you and Ben have reconnected. I know you've probably still got a way to go, but it's progress, right?'

'It's definitely progress,' Alex said. 'He told me that he felt so guilty for not coming back sooner, but Corinne had literally just had Oliver when Mum had her stroke. He came to London right away, and I persuaded him that I had it all under control so he wasn't leaving Corinne on her own with a new baby, but I made him feel like he wasn't needed, and I hurt him without realising. Once we talked that out, he seemed to relax a little. I'm hoping we can all reconnect while they're here.'

She leant over and kissed him. 'I remember what you said to me a while back. Families are complicated.'

He nodded. 'They are, and you understand that. I don't feel like I have to hide anything or pretend with you. My family is complicated. They've been through a lot.'

'I'll never fully get it,' she said. 'I haven't been through the same things, but I'm doing my best to understand.'

'You're incredible.' He drained his glass. 'Come on, let's get out of here.' He stood up and offered her his hand.

Smiling, she took it, and let him lead her back to his bedroom.

The following day, Corinne drove Kate into the city, with Oliver fast asleep in the back of the car.

'What would you like to do this morning?' Kate asked. 'What are you into? Art? History? Shops?'

'Can we go to the Cathedral? I've only ever seen it from a distance,' Corinne said, her eyes fixed on the crawling traffic.

'Of course,' Kate replied. 'Anything else?'

'A bookshop?' Corinne turned into the car park, and scanned it for an empty space.

'There are some great bookshops.' Kate smiled. This was her area of expertise.

Battling the freezing winds, they settled Oliver in his pram and made their way into the city centre.

'I'm so sorry about the cobbles,' Kate said as they walked down the Burgate.

'Don't worry,' Corinne replied. 'They might even rock Oliver off to sleep.'

Kate paused outside the ancient Tudor building that housed her favourite bookshop, bent down and helped Corinne lift the pram into the shop. 'If you like to read, you'll love this bookshop.'

'What do you read?' Corinne asked as they browsed the shelves. 'I love a romance. Ellie Rochefort is my favourite.'

'Really?' Kate turned to face her. 'My mum is her editor.'

Corinne's eyes widened. 'No way!'

Kate nodded. 'Yep. We have all her books. I've got an advance copy of her latest one. I can lend it to you if you like?'

'I'd love that,' Corinne said. 'Thanks, Kate.'

After they'd walked the length of the bookshop and back, Kate led Corinne to the Buttermarket, where they looked at the statue of Jesus on the Christgate.

'Wow,' Corinne said, 'this is beautiful.'

'This is the entrance to the Cathedral.' Kate pulled out a small card. 'I work just around the corner, so I have a pass to get us in for free.' She showed it to the man in the ticket booth, and they walked through the gate.

'Thanks, Kate.' Corinne smiled. 'You're so lucky to be able to come here whenever you like. I'm not really religious, but I do love religious buildings. They have such a calming atmosphere, don't they?'

'They do,' Kate said. 'I'm not religious either, but I like to light a candle and look at the stone carvings. It makes me feel at peace, somehow.'

Corinne parked Oliver's pram inside the door of the Cathedral, before wrapping a fabric carrier around her waist, and putting Oliver in carefully.

Silently, they walked along the aisle. Kate had been there hundreds of times before, but still marvelled at the high arched ceilings, meticulously carved hundreds of years ago.

'Those are stunning,' Corinne whispered, nodding to the brightly coloured stained glass windows ahead of her.

'They were actually created in the 1950's by a Hungarian artist, and they're really similar to some of the Disney artwork of the time, as a lot of the Disney artists of the 1950's were Hungarian,' Kate whispered back.

Corinne studied them closely. 'They look so much more modern than the others, and I can definitely see a Disney resemblance.'

Kate guided Corinne up the stone steps that led to the top of the Cathedral. 'I usually light a candle here. Would you like me to light one for you as you've got your hands full?'

'I'd love that. Thank you,' Corinne replied.

Kate carefully lit two candles and set them down with the others. She and Corinne paused thoughtfully, and Oliver's eyes widened as he looked at the flickering tea lights lined up in front of them.

They descended the stairs, back to the Cathedral floor, and Kate pushed open the heavy wooden door, which led them into the cloisters.

'There are over eight hundred coats of arms on the ceiling here,' Kate said as they looked up at the brightly coloured shields above them.

'I'll trust you on that one,' Corinne replied. 'I'd have a serious neck ache if I tried to count them.'

They walked back into the Cathedral, settled Oliver in his pram, then left through the arched stone entrance.

Corinne smiled at Kate. 'Thank you for showing me around, and for the informative tour. You could be a guide there.'

Kate laughed. 'I've listened in to enough tours, and I have the kind of brain that remembers random information. I love the contrast of the busy city, and the peace of the Cathdral. When I first started working in the city, I used to come in here at lunchtime, just to sit in silence.'

'What do you do?' Corinne asked.

'I'm a jewellery designer. The shop I work in is just down here,' Kate said.

Corinne's eyes lit up. 'Oh that's so cool!. Can we go and take a look?'

'Of course.' Kate nodded, and a minute later they'd arrived outside Correll's. 'Here it is.' She pushed open the door and the bell jangled as she walked in. 'Hi, Emmett.'

Emmett looked up from his position behind the counter. 'Hello, Kate darling! What are you doing here today? You're supposed to be on leave. And who's this?' His eyes were on Oliver, not Corinne.

'This is Corinne, Alex's sister-in-law, and this is her baby, Oliver,' Kate said. 'Corinne, this is my lovely boss, Emmett. I was just giving Corinne a tour of the city.'

'Oh, wonderful,' Emmett said to Corinne. 'And what do you think?'

'I love the Cathedral, and the bookshop we went to was incredible.' Corinne looked into one of the display cases, then back at Kate. 'Can I see some of your work?'

'Hold on.' Emmett bent down, unlocked the display case and pulled out a small white velvet pad, handing Corinne a small gold ring, set with rubies. 'This one is Kate's.' He ran his fingers over the pad. 'And these two here.' He gestured to a couple of other rings, both set with tiny diamonds.

Corinne studied the ring, then looked at the velvet pad. 'Oh, wow, they're all stunning.'

'Thank you,' Kate said, smiling. 'I learnt from the best.' She nodded to Emmett.

'What? Me?' Emmett put a hand to his chest. 'More like that Scottish giant. He's really helped you hone your talent.'

Kate laughed. 'He means David, the other jewellery designer,' she said to Corinne. 'I'd take you to the studio but I don't want you taking your chances with those stairs.' She pointed at them.

'Yikes, they look scary.' Corinne wrinkled her nose.

'They are, trust me,' Kate said. 'I've seen them from all angles.'

Corinne looked puzzled, and Kate smiled at her. 'Come on, I'll tell you about it over lunch.' She led Corinne down the road to Blossoms, where they took a table in the window. Kate took Oliver, nestling him against her chest, so that Corinne could drink her latte.

'Your jewellery is beautiful, Kate,' Corinne said after the waitress had taken their order. 'I can't believe you made those rings.'

Kate smiled. 'Thank you. Jewellery is my passion. I notice every-one's jewellery.' She nodded to the tiny heart around Corinne's neck. 'I love your necklace. It's a peridot, isn't it?'

'That's right.' Corinne ran her fingers over it. 'It was a gift from Ben after I'd had Oliver. Ben, Oliver, and I were all born in the same month, so we all share the same birthstone.'

'That's going to be a very busy month from now on,' Kate said. Oliver stretched and she froze, hoping he wouldn't start crying. She breathed a sigh of relief as he settled back to sucking his dummy.

'It is. We weren't quite ready for Oliver,' Corinne replied. 'I'd only just started my maternity leave when he arrived. I thought I'd have some time to relax, but no.'

'What do you do?' Kate asked.

'I'm a beauty therapist. I work for a salon in Truro. You'll have to come down for a treatment some time.' Corinne paused. 'I could show *you* around.'

'I'd like that.' Kate smiled. 'I love Cornwall.'

The waitress put their sandwiches on the table. Kate thanked her, at the same time as Corinne did and they both smiled at each other.

'I'll hold onto Oliver so you can have your lunch,' Kate offered. 'I've got good at eating with one hand.' She picked up her sandwich with her free hand and took a bite. Having practiced with Luca, she felt more confident about juggling a baby and her lunch.

'Are you sure?' Corinne asked, biting her lip.

'Of course. Let me give you a break.' Kate shifted Oliver in her arms. He was content for now, but she had a feeling that they were on borrowed time. 'I spoke to Alex last night. He and Ben seem to have opened up to each other a little.'

Corinne nodded. 'They do. When Sarah had her stroke, it was a real shock for him, and he rushed off to London, but he felt helpless because Alex wouldn't let him do anything to help. He came back feeling like he'd failed both Sarah and Alex, but Alex set him straight last night.'

'I'm so glad they talked. How does Ben feel about being back in the house?' Kate asked. 'It must be a shock to see it looking so different.'

'He loves what Alex and Sarah have done, and I think he prefers it as a hotel as it doesn't look like the place he remembers.' Corinne took a bite of her sandwich.

Kate swallowed her mouthful. 'That's a good thing, right? He can make some new memories there.'

'That's the plan,' Corinne said. 'I've told him that he needs to be open and honest with Alex and his mum for it to work. I'm amazed you've managed to get Alex to open up. How did you do that?'

'I let him come to me,' Kate said. 'He needed time, so I gave him time.'

'You're very smart.' Corinne nodded approvingly. 'I did the same thing with Ben. I gave him the space to realise that he couldn't live without me. Now, here we are.'

Kate laughed. 'I like your style.'

While they drank another cup of tea, Corinne fed Oliver, then Kate led Corinne back down the ancient streets to the secluded Greyfriars gardens.

After collecting Alex and Ben from the pub, Kate and Corinne returned to the hotel. Stefan and Sarah had prepared a French feast, with crusty homemade bread, French onion soup, and a huge cassoulet. As Kate ate the tarte aux pommes that Stefan served for dessert, she watched Alex and Ben. Sat next to each other, they were talking non-stop, sharing stories of their childhood and laughing.

'It's the best birthday present ever,' Sarah whispered to Kate. 'Seeing those two talking again, just like they were when they were kids.'

'I'm so happy for all of you,' Kate whispered back.

Once the plates were cleared away, Oliver wriggled in Kate's arms, and she stood up, rocking him, copying Corinne's movements from the previous evening.

Alex smiled at her, then looked at Ben. 'Could I hold him?'

'Of course, man.' Ben smiled at Alex. 'I was waiting for you to ask for a cuddle.'

Kate carefully handed Oliver to Alex. Oliver looked intently at his uncle, then back at Ben. Kate smiled, her heart skipping a beat as Alex rocked Oliver gently, cradling his tiny head. Oliver settled into Alex's arms and his eyes closed. Cautiously, Alex sat back down, holding Oliver against his chest, and Kate zoned out, imagining Alex holding *their* baby. Where had that come from? It was way too soon. Yet, as she looked at Alex, whispering to his nephew, it didn't feel that way.

'Kate?'

Kate startled, realising that Corinne was talking to her. 'Sorry, I was miles away,'

'We're going to head upstairs now,' Corinne said. 'Thanks so much for today. We'll see you guys in the morning.'

'Oh you're welcome. I had a great time. See you tomorrow.' Kate smiled.

After Corinne and Ben had left, Kate helped Alex, Stefan and Sarah clean up the restaurant, then went back to Alex's room, smiling as he closed the door behind him.

'What a day, huh?' He took his shoes off and sprawled out on the bed.

She took her heels off and lay down next to him. 'Did you guys have a good time at the pub?'

'We did,' Alex said. 'I've not seen Ben smile as much in a long time. I think the therapy has helped him so much. I'm glad he was brave enough to do it. It's not easy to admit that you need help. As you know.'

She smiled. 'It's always better when you do though. Do you feel like you're closer to him now?' She lay her hand on his chest, feeling his heartbeat underneath her fingertips.

He stroked her hair. 'I do. I feel closer to him now than I have in years. 'We've said all the things that were on our minds, so now we can both move on.'

'That's amazing. I've been thinking about you both all day,' she said.

'I was thinking about you. Did you have a good time with Corinne?' he asked.

She nodded. 'I did. She loved the Cathedral, and I took her to the bookshop and my favourite café. We had a blast.'

'I thought you would. She's so easy to get on with and you looked pretty cosy with Oliver too.' He paused. 'I could see you with a baby.'

'Really?' her eyebrows shot up. 'So much for taking it slowly.'

'Don't look so shocked. I didn't say my baby.' He raised his eyebrow, as if waiting for her response.

She laughed and gave him a playful shove. 'Hilarious. Your baby would be ridiculously cute, though.'

'Maybe.' His eyes met hers. 'They'd be even cuter if they were yours too.'

Her heart skipped a beat, and she swallowed hard. 'Well, who knows what fate has in store for us, Alex?'

'I can't wait to find out,' he said.

Chapter Twenty-Three

January 2013, Canterbury, Kent, England

In Alex's bedroom a week later, Kate watched him pace the floor nervously. He was about to meet her whole family. She'd never seen him anxious before and she wasn't sure what to do. 'Alex, I promise, everything's going to be just fine. My mum will adore you.'

Alex walked over to his wardrobe, pulling out his jacket and slipping it on. He looked at his watch. 'I guess we should go, right?'

'You look so hot.' She slid her fingers into the lapels of his jacket and kissed him. When she pulled away breathlessly, she asked, 'How about now? Are you ready?'

'Ready as I'll ever be,' he said.

She followed him out of the room, and down the stairs. The hotel bar was busy as they walked through it, and as she stepped out of the front door, the bitter wind blew her hair across her face.

Alex unlocked the car and she hurried over to it, as fast as her heels would take her. She sank into the seat and put her seatbelt on, then flicked a glance at Alex. As ever, he seemed deep in thought, yet he said very little.

'Hello, darlings,' Amelie said as she opened the front door to them.

'Evening, Mama.' Kate kissed her on the cheek. 'Looking stunning as usual.' She walked into the hall, the click of her heels echoing around the grand space.

Amelie shut the front door behind Alex. 'You must be Alex. It's so wonderful to meet you.' She took his hand and clasped it between hers. 'I've heard many good things.'

'Don't believe them,' Alex said, his face poker straight.

Amelie laughed. 'Oh, Kate, he's a hoot. You're just in time. I know I said I didn't need any help... but I've no idea what I'm doing when it comes to non-alcoholic cocktails, so I'll let you two take over.' She led them into the kitchen.

Kate looked at the kitchen table, laden with plates and dishes wrapped in cling film. 'Wow, you've been busy.'

'I did have some help.' Amelie gestured to the back garden. 'My sous chef is just chopping some more wood. I can't have my guests freezing.'

'Do you mean Rob? I'm surprised you let him loose with an axe,' Kate quipped.

The back door opened. 'Hello, Kate.' James gave her a wide smile as he walked in, his arms full of neatly chopped logs.

'Hi James,' Kate said, stunned. 'So good to see you.'

'Same,' James replied, then looked at Alex. 'You must be Alex. Good to meet you. 'I'll just put these logs in the basket.'

The second he'd left the room, Kate turned to Amelie. 'Wow, Mama he's here!' she whispered.

'New year, new me.' Amelie raised her eyebrow. 'And I've never been happier.'

'I like the new you, Mama.' Kate glanced at the empty jugs on the counter. 'Where do we start?'

Amelie opened the fridge. 'There's all kinds of fruit juice in there, some lemons, oranges, and some fresh herbs, so do whatever you like with it. I'm going to get the fire lit in the dining room.'

Kate started taking the fruit juice out of the fridge. 'Leave us to it

She was in the middle of chopping lemons into neat slices, when Rob drifted into the kitchen, and her heart sank. *Please let him say something nice*, she thought to herself.

Rob made a beeline for Alex, who was stirring a jug of virgin pina colada. 'Alex, right? I'm Rob, Kate's brother. She's great isn't she? I mean, I've had eighteen years with her and I'm still a fan.' He smirked at her. 'Most of the time.'

Alex burst out laughing. 'That's a glowing review.'

Kate rolled her eyes at Rob. 'Thanks for that.'

'Very welcome.' Rob lifted the foil from one of the plates, sneaking a sausage roll and stuffing it into his mouth.

'Your bangle's cool. Did Kate make it?' Alex asked Rob.

Swallowing his mouthful, Rob nodded. 'Yes, it's got my birth date and coordinates on it.' He turned it over so Alex could see.

'I was inspired by your bracelet,' Kate said to Alex.

Alex rolled up his sleeve, showing Rob his own bangle. 'This is my dad's birth date and location, not mine. Maybe one day you can pass yours down to your kids.'

Rob nodded. 'I like the idea of passing it down to the next generation. I hope we can do the same with this house.'

'Your mum's worked so hard to keep it going,' Alex said. 'I know a little bit about what that's like.'

'Right,' Rob replied. 'I'd love to see the hotel. Kate's told me about it, it sounds amazing.'

Alex smiled. 'I'll take you up there for a drink sometime,'

'I'd like that.' Rob smiled back at him. He looked at the debris on the counter in front of Kate and Alex. 'Do you guys need a hand?'

'We're good, thanks,' Kate replied.

'Sure. I'll see you both later,' he said and walked out of the room.

Kate let out a long exhale. 'I'm glad he's gone. I was so scared about what he was going to say. He can be a bit of a gremlin sometimes.'

Alex shrugged. 'He's a younger brother. It's what they do best. He's great though.'

The doorbell rang and Kate went to answer it, her face lighting up as she saw Hannah on the doorstep. 'Hey! My long lost sister is back!'

'Hey, bud!' Hannah gave Kate a hug.

'Hey!' Kate said. 'I'm so glad you're here. You won't believe who Mama's invited – James!'

'No way!' Hannah's eyes lit up. 'Sure, I'm excited to see him again, but where's Mr. Gorgeous? That's who I've come to see.'

'He's right behind you.' Kate giggled as Alex appeared in the hallway.

A blush spread across Hannah's olive-skinned cheeks.

'Alex. So sorry. So nice to meet you.' Hannah smiled sheepishly at him.

'Mr. Gorgeous huh?' He nodded. 'I like it. You must be Hannah.'

'That's me. Excuse me while I take my shoes off and my foot out of my mouth.' Hannah shook her head.

'I'm just going to grab your present,' Kate said to Hannah. 'I'm sure Alex will make you a mocktail if you ask nicely.'

'Sure. I'll try not to embarrass myself any further,' Hannah replied, her cheeks still bright red.

'How does a pina colada sound?' Alex asked and led Hannah into the kitchen.

Kate grabbed Hannah's neatly wrapped present from her wardrobe and went back down to the kitchen, where Hannah and Alex were sitting at the table with their mocktails. 'Here you go.' She handed Hannah the present then sat down beside Alex. 'Happy belated Christmas.'

'Thanks! Here's yours!' Hannah passed Kate her present.

Kate tore off the paper and smiled. 'Oh, wow! Sloths this year? Love it.' She showed Alex. 'We always get each other comedy pyjamas for Christmas.'

Hannah took off the green ribbon and unwrapped the paper. 'Nice. Frogs with crowns. Thanks, love.' She gave Kate a hug.

'Is Mia coming?' Hannah asked. 'She loves your mum's parties.'

'No, she's working tonight,' Kate replied. 'But guess what? She's pregnant!'

'No way! How's she doing?' Hannah asked.

'She had a rough start, but she's feeling better now,' Kate said. She wouldn't share Mia's slightly worrying news about her excess fluid, but Mia and Hannah got on well, and Mia had told Kate that she could tell Hannah about the baby.

'That's awesome!' Hannah smiled. 'What else have I missed out on?'

'Hannah!' Rob walked back into the kitchen, making a beeline for Hannah and giving her a high five. 'How are you doing?'

'I'm good. How are you getting on at Loughborough?' Hannah asked.

'I love it,' Rob said. 'How's teaching?'

'It's...interesting,' Hannah replied. 'I'm still finding my feet.

'I bet.' Rob filled a plate from the buffet, then turned to Alex. 'If these two are boring you, you can come and join me for a game of Call of Duty.'

Alex looked at Kate. 'You're not boring at all, but I'm going to let you guys catch up.' He kissed Kate on the cheek, then took his own plate and followed Rob out of the room.

Kate flicked a glance at Rob, then back at Alex. 'Sure.' She tried to seem nonchalant, but secretly she was terrified about what Rob might say to Alex. 'Have fun.'

Kate was mid-conversation with Hannah when Amelie walked unsteadily into the kitchen with a glass of wine in her hand.

'Mama, have you had anything to eat yet?' Kate asked.

'No, darling, I'll grab something in a minute,' Amelie said before picking up a pile of napkins and leaving the room.

'She won't though, will she?' Hannah replied, laughing.

'Probably not.' Kate got up and quickly put a plate of food together for her mum. 'I'd better intervene.'

'I'll come with you.' Hannnah picked up her glass.

As Kate walked into the living room her jaw dropped. Her dad was there, talking to Alex and Rob.

'Why is your dad here?' Hannah hissed.

'I don't know.' Kate handed the plate to Hannah. 'Can you give this to Mama? I'll be right back.'

She walked over to her dad, baffled. Her parents hadn't been in the same house for years. 'Hi, Dad, how are you? I didn't expect to see you here.'

'Your mum invited me,' he said, ' and Rob's just introduced me to Alex.'

'Great! So glad you and Alex have met. Excuse me for a minute.' Kate hurried over to the sofa and sat down next to her mum. 'Mama, why didn't you tell me that you and Dad were talking again?'

Amelie finished her mouthful before she spoke. 'We started talking again after your graduation. He contacted me to check in as he could tell you and I weren't talking. I figured seeing as you and Rob had made your peace with him, he should be here. Is that alright? You look shocked.'

'It was just a bit of a surprise,' Kate said. 'I couldn't imagine seeing him here again, but I'm so pleased you guys are talking again.'

'I invited him, but I had no idea if he would actually come,' Amelie whispered. 'I didn't want to tell you and Rob that he was coming, and then him not turn up.'

'What about James?' Kate asked. 'Does he mind that Dad's here?'

'We're all adults, Kate.' Amelie rolled her eyes. 'We've all moved on. I wasn't the only one who had an affair.'

'Keep your voice down.' Kate looked around the room. 'Where's Hannah?'

'She went to answer the door. She said I had to sit here and eat.' Amelie giggled. 'I don't have time for that! I'm the hostess. I need to be looking after everyone!'

'I'll go and find Hannah. Do not have anything else to drink, alright?' Taking Amelie's glass, Kate walked into the hall. She followed the sound of voices into the kitchen, where Leon and Hannah were sitting at the table. Leon had a huge plate of food and was talking at a hundred miles an hour, while Hannah nodded, probably unable to get a word in edgeways.

'Hey, Leon, you made it.' Kate sat down next to him. 'How are you doing?'

'Very good,' Leon said. 'Hannah's just filled me in. Seems like tonight's going to plan, doesn't it?' He started laughing.

'Don't.' Kate shook her head. 'Mama is so drunk, and my *dad* is here. I have literally no idea how this is going to play out. I just hope that he and Rob aren't embarrassing me, or themselves in front of Alex.'

At that moment, Rob and Alex walked into the kitchen. Leon flew out of his chair to greet Rob with an overenthusiastic hug, before greeting Alex. 'You must be Alex. I'm Leon.'

'The designer!' Alex offered Leon his hand. 'You're a talented man.'

Leon blushed. 'I don't know about that.'

'Leon's going to fashion college tomorrow.' Kate smiled at him. 'I'm so excited for you, dude.'

'Thanks. I'm gonna miss you guys.' Leon looked around the room. 'And this house.'

'Maybe not the blue room, though.' Kate smirked, before turning to Alex. 'He slept in there.'

Alex's eyes widened. 'You did? But it's full of stuff. And it's creepy.'

'It wasn't full of stuff then. I was told not to sleep in there and I ignored that advice,' Leon said with a shaky laugh.

Kate glanced at Alex. 'It's not so bad in there if you give it a bit of time to warm up.'

Leon shook his head. 'Not a chance. I looked in there last time I was here, and that was bad enough. You can keep the piano and the Narnia wardrobe in there, I don't want any of it.'

Rob opened the fridge and handed Leon a bottle of beer. 'Alex, what can I get you to drink?'

'Just a Coke, thanks,' Alex replied. 'Leon, are you joining us for a game of poker? Call of Duty isn't really my forte, but cards are.'

'Of course.' Leon's face lit up. 'See you later, ladies.'

Hannah turned to Kate after Rob, Alex, and Leon left the room, drinks in hand. 'It's a big deal that Alex is here tonight, isn't it?'

'It is,' Kate said, 'but he's a big deal to me. He told me that he loved me on New Year's Eve.'

Hannah squealed with delight. 'This is so exciting. I love this for you. He's gorgeous and he seems so caring. Does he have a brother?' She raised her eyebrow.

'Yes, but he's *married*,' Kate replied. 'I've never felt like this before. I love him and I don't care who knows it.'

'Is this the same Kate who spent last summer getting drunk and copping off with her mates?' Hannah paused. 'Callum, Tom, no one was safe.'

Kate rolled her eyes. 'Very funny.'

'When you told me about that night at the Bastille gig, I was like, here she goes again, another summer fling,' Hannah said.

'Oh it was a hot summer fling, but then...' Kate stopped talking, noticing Alex standing in the doorway.

'Your mum needs a glass of water and some painkillers,' he said stiffly. 'Can you point me in the right direction?'

'Uh, sure.' Kate flew out of her seat, her heart pounding as she wondered how long he'd been there. Her fingers trembled as she pulled the medicine drawer open and got out some tablets, giving them to him. 'Thank you...' She tried to catch his gaze, but he offered her a fleeting glance, before looking away.

'Let me grab you some water,' Hannah said, filling a glass, and handing it to Alex, who left the room without another word.

'Oh, fuck.' Kate collapsed into her seat again and put her head on the table.

'I'm so sorry.' Hannah winced. 'I feel awful. Can I go and speak to him and explain?'

'Explain what?' Kate sat up. 'He *heard* me say that he was a fling. I was just about to say that it got serious, but he didn't hear *that* part!'

'What can I do to help?' Hannah asked.

'Nothing. This is my mess and I need to sort it out.' Kate stood up and walked into the living room.

Amelie was sitting on the sofa, sipping at the glass of water, with James beside her. She looked up when Kate came in, giving her a weary smile. 'Hello, darling. Are you alright?'

Kate glared at her. 'No, I'm not. Where did Alex go?'

'I don't know. He brought me this and then he disappeared.' Amelie shrugged.

Kate walked out into the hall, noticing that Alex's coat and shoes were missing. She pulled open the front door and saw him walking to his car. 'Wait,' she shouted, running after him. 'You can't just leave!'

He stopped and turned around, his stormy eyes illuminated by the floodlights over the drive. 'I needed some space.'

'You were just going to go? Without even saying anything to me?' Kate put her hands on her hips.

He shook his head. 'So this *is* a fling to you, is it?'

'No.' Her throat felt like it was going to close up. 'You walked in before I'd finished. I was going to say that it got serious.'

'I didn't hear that,' he said. 'I *was* one of those guys though, wasn't I? You were drunk when we first kissed, and you told me that you thought I'd just be a fling. I didn't realise I was one of many.'

'That was before I got to know you,' she replied angrily. 'Sure, I have a past, but *you* are my future, and that's what Hannah and I were talking about.' She thought about her conversation with Cora. 'I'm not the only one with a past, Alex. What happened between you and Ava? I told you about my past, but you're still keeping secrets.'

He frowned. 'How do you know about Ava?'

'I don't know about Ava.' She swallowed hard. 'I don't know, because you didn't tell me.'

'I can't do this right now,' he said, shaking his head.

'Then maybe you *should* go,' she hissed, her body pulsating with anger.

He nodded and walked to his car, driving off into the night.

She sat on the front step, watching the stars above her in the dark sky. Hearing the front door open, she turned around to see Leon and

Hannah coming out of the front door. They sat down either side of her, both sliding an arm around her shoulders.

'What happened?' Hannah asked.

Kate let out a long exhale. 'Alex did overhear you, and what you said has obviously hit a nerve with him. He's now questioning our relationship, so I asked him to leave.'

Leon raised his eyebrow at Kate. 'Was that what you wanted?'

'It was the best thing to do,' Kate said. 'I asked him to go before I said something I would regret.'

'Wow, you've learnt to put your claws away.' Leon nodded approvingly. 'I'm impressed. Look, he really likes you. Tonight's just been a lot. These parties always are.'

'I hope you're right.' She rested her head on his shoulder. 'I'm going to miss you so much.'

'I'm only a couple of hours away,' he said softly.

'And I'll keep an eye on him.' Hannah assured her.

As Hannah and Leon started talking, Kate drifted off, thinking about Alex, and wishing this evening had gone differently.

Chapter Twenty-Four

February 2013, Canterbury, Kent, England

The following morning, Kate woke up feeling awful. Her eyes hurt from crying and her bed felt empty without Alex in it. She could still picture the angry storm swirling in his eyes as he spoke to her. She rubbed her eyes and picked up her phone. There was a message from Alex. The lyrics were from "Flaws" by Bastille, and it was definitely a sign, but what did it mean? Did he think she was flawed? Was he admitting that he had flaws? She got up, showered, dressed and as there was no sound coming from Rob or Amelie's rooms, she crept quietly downstairs.

She made herself a cup of tea and a piece of toast, and watched the tiny flurries of snow fall on the lawn outside the window as she ate. It was beautiful, but it didn't do much to calm her restless mind.

Amelie walked into the kitchen, bringing Kate out of her thoughts and back into the room. 'Darling, where's Alex? Did he have to work today?'

'Nope.' Kate shook her head. 'We had a row and he left last night.'

'Oh, no! What happened?' Amelie's hand flew to her chest.

Kate took a deep breath and explained what had happened as she drank the last of her tea.

'But you've changed,' Amelie said. 'And you're allowed a past.' She filled the kettle and switched it on.

'That's exactly what I said!' Kate exclaimed. 'And when he walked out last night, it hurt, just like when Dad walked out on us.'

It had hurt more, though, because Alex was hers.

'Remember, it wasn't quite like that, darling.' Amelie made herself up a cup of tea, then sat down next to Kate. 'I need to apologise to you. I drank too much last night, and I embarassed myself, and you. I'm sorry.'

'It's OK. You didn't do anything wildly offensive. And you didn't do it deliberately,' Kate assured her.

'I barely sat down all day yesterday, and I didn't even realise I hadn't eaten anything until I'd had three glasses of wine.' Amelie shook her head. 'James had to carry me to bed last night.'

Kate giggled. 'I wish I could have seen that. When did everyone leave?'

She had taken Hannah and Leon to the library, and they'd hidden there for a while, where she had cried, and wondered if she should have persuaded Alex to stay. Once Hannah and Leon had left, she'd snuck upstairs, and somehow fallen into a deep sleep.

'It was at least midnight.' Amelie frowned. 'To be honest, I have no idea.' She took a sip of her tea. 'This place is such a mess, and I swear it's making my headache worse.'

'I'll help you clear up,' Kate offered. 'It'll take both of our minds off last night.'

She stood up and took her plate and cup to the dishwasher, stacking them neatly, then cleared the counter of empty glasses and plates.'

'Thank you, darling,' Amelie said. 'I appreciate you, and I'm going to take a leaf out of your book and cut down on my drinking.'

'You won't regret it,' Kate replied. 'I love waking up with no hangover.'

Rob ambled into the kitchen, his hair sticking up in all directions. 'Morning, Mama. Morning, Kate. You guys alright?'

Kate sighed. 'Sort of,'

'Less than sort of,' Amelie said. 'Dealing with an evil hangover, and a trashed house.'

He took a mug out of the cupboard and spooned some coffee granules into it, then fillled up the kettle and turned it on. 'Anyone else want one?'

Kate shook her head. 'No thanks.'

Amelie lifted her mug. 'I'm good.'

Rob nodded and stuffed a couple of slices of toast into the toaster. 'I'll have this, and then I'll help you clear up.' He frowned. 'Where are James and Alex?'

'James is still asleep,' Amelie said.

'Alex left last night. He couldn't stay.' Kate wasn't prepared to go over it with Rob.

Rob nodded and finished making his coffee, then buttered his toast. When he sat down next to her, Kate felt grateful for his presence. As he cracked jokes and teased Amelie about her hangover, Kate started to feel less like she might burst into tears, and more able to think clearly. She hadn't lied to Alex. He was the one who had concealed information from her. And if he couldn't deal with her past, she didn't want him to be part of her future. Or at least that was what her angry little heart was telling her.

She had just finished cleaning the kitchen when her phone started ringing and she grabbed it from the counter, hoping it was Alex. It wasn't.

'Bonjour, darling, how are you?' Marie said. 'How was last night?'

Kate bit her lip. She didn't want to go into it again. 'Oh, you know, the usual. Great food, lots of drinks. How are you?'

She didn't want to admit the truth to her aunt.

'I'm wonderful, darling. We had the best Christmas in Normandy, but I did miss you lot.' She paused. 'Are you still interested in coming over in April?'

'Uh, yes. I thought you guys had forgotten about that,' Kate said.

'No, we haven't. Lucien was getting advice about how that would work, and what paperwork he would need to complete. Can I send you an email with all of the information we need?' Marie asked.

'Of course,' Kate replied. 'So, is it confirmed yet or not?'

'Not yet,' Marie said. 'Let me hand you over to Lucien and he can explain.'

There was a pause, and then Lucien spoke. 'Bonjour, Kate. As your aunt has said, I need some details from you, and you will need to apply for a work visa. There is no guarantee that it will be granted, but those are the steps that we must take. Are you happy to do this?'

'I am, yes,' Kate responded. 'Marie has my email address. Let me know what you need from me, and I'll get right on it.'

'Wonderful. I do hope that we see each other in April,' he said. 'Have you discussed this with your boss yet?'

'No,' she replied. 'I was waiting for more information.'

'If you are applying for a work visa, you will need to let him know. I realise that it might come to nothing, and I apologise if it does, but we need to ensure that he is aware that you may be coming to work for me.'

'I'll talk to him tomorrow,' she assured him.

'Wonderful. I shall be in touch. I will pass you back to your aunt,' he said.

'Thank you, or merci!' She smiled.

'Hello, darling,' Marie chirped. 'All sorted with Lucien? I'll send you over an email later on. Give my sister my love. I bet she'll need it today. Tu me manques.'

'Moi aussi,' Kate said and hung up. She looked at Alex's message again, and still felt unable to decide how to respond to it. She sighed and typed a response, sending it before she thought better of it.

The following morning, Kate drove into the city, and walked to Corrells as the icy wind whipped her hair around her face. Last night she had barely slept, a complicated mixture of emotions keeping her awake. This year would bring all kinds of changes, and the first of these would be her job. She stopped outside Corrells and a pang of sadness stabbed at her chest. She didn't want to leave, but this was Rebecca's job, not hers. And she would soon be returning. Whether or not the job in France happened, her time at Corrells would soon come to an end. She had deliberately arrived early today so that she could talk to Emett before Lisa and David arrived.

She pushed open the door and took a deep breath as she walked over to Emmett's desk. 'Emmett, before we open today, can I have a word?'

'Of course.' He smiled. 'What can I help you with?'

She sat down in the chair opposite his desk. 'I've only got four months left here, and I wanted to talk about what happens next. I've had an offer to spend the summer in Nice, at L'Étoile. My aunt knows Lucien, the owner.'

'L'Étoile?' He raised an eyebrow. 'I know it. It is a beautiful studio. Very upmarket.' He nodded approvingly. 'I wanted to talk to you too. I met with Rebecca yesterday and she has decided that she is not coming back.'

Her jaw dropped. 'Really?'

'Yes. She has decided to devote her time to her son, which I cannot fault her for. I was going to offer you her job, but it seems I am too late.' He cocked his head to the side. 'What are you thinking?'

'I'm wondering if there is a way I can do both. The contract at L'Étoile is short term, only from April to August, but that would mean I would miss wedding season here.' She chewed her lip. 'I can't do both, can I?'

Emmett tapped his pen on the desk. 'We *could* make it work. If we had enough pre-orders, and if you stayed until the end of April, it might work. This experience in Nice would be good for you, and selfishly, it would be good for us, as you would learn new skills.'

'So you wouldn't mind if I went?' She couldn't stop the smile from spreading across her face.

'As long as you come back.' He smiled. 'I think we have a plan, and I think it'll work. Have you applied for a work visa yet?'

She shook her head. 'No, I haven't. Lucien sent me an email last night and I need to go through it properly to work out what I need to do.'

'Ah.' He winced. 'Then we put the plan on hold for now until that comes through. I won't say anything to David or Lisa until you've got the visa. Keep me posted.'

'I will,' she said, and the door opened.

He tapped his nose, and smiled at her, then Lisa. 'Morning, Lisa. Isn't it cold today?'

Kate stood up. 'Thank you.' She whispered, then greeted Lisa, before going carefully up the stairs to her studio.

The kitchen was empty when Kate got home, so she got her notebook and her laptop out and sat at the kitchen table to apply for her visa. She'd just sent the application off when Amelie walked in.

'Evening, darling. How was your day?'

'Good.' Kate looked up. 'I've just applied for my work visa.'

'Ah, *bien !*' Amelie said in a heavy French accent. It's a wonderful opportunity for you. I hope it comes through.'

Kate smiled. This was a new Amelie, one who was encouraging her to spread her wings. 'I know. I feel really excited about it.'

She also wondered if she was good enough to work there, but she squashed that thought to the back of her mind.

'I'm so pleased for you.' Amelie paused. 'I might be speaking out of turn here, but promise me, if and when you mend your relationship with Alex, don't give up this opportunity for him.'

'I won't,' Kate said. 'Whatever happens between us, I'm going.'

She'd never turned her back on her dreams for anyone, and she wasn't going to start now.

After dinner, and having not had a reply from Alex, she felt restless. His message yesterday had given nothing away. She pulled the curtains and looked out of the window. The gentle smatter of snow that had fallen yesterday had all but gone. If she drove to the hotel, would he want to see her? Would she interrupt him when he was trying to work again? He'd said he was stepping back from his role at the hotel, but she was certain it wouldn't be that easy.

The doorbell rang, jolting her out of her thoughts and she got up, walking into the hall and opening the front door.

'Hi.'

Her mouth fell open. 'Alex? She noticed he was holding a massive cactus in a pot.

'Can I come in?' His voice was gravelly and his eyes were red rimmed.

'Of course,' she said.

'This is for you.' He handed her the cactus as he walked into the hall. 'Can we talk?'

'Yes.' She shivered as the cold air in the hall penetrated her thin shirt. 'Come into the living room. It's freezing out here.'

She sat down on the sofa and put the cactus on the table, noticing a tiny little piece of card stuck into the pot. Plucking it out, she read it.

I'm sorry for being a prick. x
She smiled. 'I like it.'

'I'm so sorry about yesterday.' He swallowed hard, holding her gaze. 'I overreacted.'

'I'm sorry too. I shouldn't have told you to go, but I was afraid that if you stayed I'd say something I would regret. I was afraid I already had.' She twirled the piece of card in her hand. 'I was about to come up to the hotel.'

'I thought you might. I didn't want you driving up there in this weather,' he said. 'Ever since we've been together I've had this hang up about *why* you're with me, and when I heard you say to Hannah that I was a fling, I just...' He paused. 'It made sense to me.'

'Would I have met your family and introduced you to mine if you were just a fling?' She gazed into his stormy blue eyes. 'Would I have told you that I loved you if this was just a fling?'

She had never seen this side of him before. He had always seemed so confident. Invincible. There was definitely a chink in his armour, and she had no idea why.

'I wasn't thinking straight.' He let out a long exhale. 'I thought I'd dealt with what happened with Ava, but obviously not. That's my issue, and not yours.'

'Do you want to talk about it?' she asked.

'Not really. She was someone I loved, and saw a future with, but she left me, and broke my heart. I couldn't believe I'd got it so wrong. I was afraid I'd made the same mistake with you.' He shook his head. 'When I say it out loud, it sounds ridiculous, but...'

'But it's a weird time of year, and emotions are heightened, and you were in an unfamiliar house, with people you didn't know, and you overheard a conversation that triggered something that you thought you'd buried,' she said.

'Exactly that.' He nodded. 'You understand me even when I don't understand myself.'

She smiled. 'I love you, Alex. I have done for a long time. And I've never lied to you. I've always been upfront with you. You know why I didn't want a relationship, when we first started dating, and you know why I changed my mind. I wanted more from you, more than one kiss, more than one night, and I still do. Yes, I used to get drunk and I *did* kiss a couple of my friends, but that was then, and this is now. Can you deal with that?'

'Of course I can,' he said. 'You *have* always been honest with me, and I was the one who wasn't honest with you.'

'The cactus is the perfect peace offering, by the way,' she said. 'I love it. Remember what you said to me about how we just needed to keep talking to each other. Let's do that. This can work, but only if we keep talking.'

He nodded. 'More talking. Less storming out.'

She moved closer. 'And more kissing.'

Chapter Twenty-Five

February 2013, Canterbury, Kent, England

On Valentine's Day, Kate walked hand in hand with Alex through the city after dinner at her favourite Thai restaurant, past the storefronts with their gaudy red heart decorations. She and Lisa had helped Emmett decorate Correll's and handed out handmade chocolate hearts from Papillon to their customers. She'd never been a fan of Valentine's Day, but, with Alex, it was different. Rather than showy, expensive gestures, they'd eaten pad Thai, drank jasmine tea, and shared stories of disastrous dates. It had been the perfect Valentine's Day.

Since their argument at her house, they'd both been more open with each other, and she felt that they were now more deeply connected. She'd seen a very different side to Alex that night, a vulnerable side that she had no idea existed. He still hadn't gone into any detail about Ava, and she hadn't pressed him. When he wanted to talk, she knew that he would.

Tonight, she had to make the most of every minute, as the following week he was going on a training course to London, and she'd have to spend a whole week without his stormy blue eyes, and his firm, but gentle touch.

His hand gripped her thigh as they drove back to the hotel. 'I know you said I didn't need to get you a gift, but I do have something waiting for you at the hotel,' he said, his eyes on the road.

'Maybe I have something for you too,' she replied, feeling a thrill of excitement as she imagined his response to her gift and her brand new satin underwear.

He raised an eyebrow. 'I'm intrigued.'

When they got back to the hotel, Kate asked Alex to go inside first, while she went to her car, and got out a large, square parcel. She walked through the hotel, waving to Mel as she went through the bar.

She knocked on Alex's door, and before he opened it, she hid the parcel behind her back.

'You look suspicious,' he said.

'Me?' She looked at him and fluttered her eyelashes. 'I don't think so.'

He let her in, and she handed him the parcel. 'You can probably guess what this is. The lyrics sum up how I feel about you.'

He frowned and unwrapped the brown paper, sliding out a vinyl record, Candi Staton's *You Got the Love*. His eyes widened. 'Where did you find this?'

She smiled. 'I might have had to do a little searching online.'

'I love it,' he replied, 'but I can't believe this.'

He stood up, and walked over to the decks, sliding the paper cover off the record and putting it onto one of the turntables. The vocals floated through the air as he walked over to his wardrobe. He pulled a large, rectangular parcel out of the wardrobe, and sat down next to her, handing it to her. 'I think this is one up from the song lyric texts,' he said as she pulled off the red paper.

'Oh, Alex, I love it,' Kate squealed. It was a sheet of music, in an ornate cream frame. It wasn't just any sheet of music, though. It was also Candi Staton's *You Got the Love*.

He laughed. 'We got each other the same song?'

'We're on the same page. Literally.' She looked down at the frame. 'This is so thoughtful, thank you.'

'Thank you.' He held out his hand. 'Come and dance with me.'

She stood up and walked over to him, sliding her arms around his neck. 'This is the best Valentine's Day ever.'

His lips grazed her neck. 'It's not over yet,' he replied, as his lips grazed her neck.

When Kate walked into Mimosa on Friday night for post-Valentine's Day drinks, she couldn't keep the smile off her face as she joined Mia and Lucy at their table. 'Evening, ladies.'

'Evening!' Lucy picked up the bottle of wine in front of her and an empty glass. 'I figured you'd join me, so I got a bottle.'

'Obviously, I'm on the soft drinks.' Mia held up her glass of Coke.

'Obviously. Thanks, love,' Kate said, taking the glass from Lucy, clinking it against Lucy and Mia's. 'Did you guys have a good Valentine's Day?'

'We had a takeaway and watched a film,' Lucy said. 'It was low key, but it was just nice being together.'

'Sounds lush. Pete, Lilly and I made heart shaped pizzas, and pink mocktails.' Mia smiled. 'It was so cute. I've been trying to spend time with her, as we only have two months left before we become a foursome.'

'It's only two months?' Kate exclaimed, biting her lip. Just as Mia was going to have her baby, Kate might be boarding a plane. If her visa ever turned up. Until it did, her plans were on hold. She wiped her sweaty palms on her dress and cleared her throat. She wanted to go, but the idea of leaving everyone she loved - even for a few months - made her feel sick with nerves.

'Guys, I've got something I need to tell you,' she said. 'It's not confirmed yet, but I've had a job offer.'

'At Correll's?' Mia asked. 'Is Rebecca not coming back?'

'She's not, but that's not quite it.' Kate wasn't even surprised that Mia had figured out that much. She was always two steps ahead of her. 'I've had an offer for a short-term contract to work in Nice from April to August.'

'Nice? With your chaotic cougar aunt?' Mia blurted out. 'Really?'

'She's forty-two,' Kate said, rolling her eyes. 'She's not a cougar, her boyfriend is *older* than her, remember? It's actually his studio that I'd be working in.'

'That's amazing!' Lucy said. 'What a great opportunity, isn't it Mia?' She nudged Mia.

'It is...' Mia trailed off. 'I'm very happy for you. I'm just being selfish. You'll be going away right when the baby arrives, and I'm scared you won't come back.'

'Of course I'll come back!' Kate said, squeezing Mia's hand. 'Emmett has offered me Rebecca's job, and he's happy for me to go to Nice.'

Mia nodded and took a sip of her drink. 'What about Alex? How does he feel about it?'

Kate winced. 'I haven't told him yet, or anyone at Corrells, because all of this depends on me getting a work visa, which I've not even got. And I didn't even apply for it until last month, the day after Alex and I had a row at Mama's party. I'd just convinced him that actually I *do* love him and I do want to be with him, I didn't want to then say "oh by the way I'm going to France".

'I guess that makes sense.' Mia bit her lip. 'When are you going to tell him? I don't like knowing this if he doesn't.'

'He's on a training course this week,' Kate said. 'When I see him next, I will definitely tell him. So can you just keep it to yourself for now? I mean not even Pete. I don't want him to find out from anyone else but me.'

Mia put her hand on Kate's arm. ' He won't. I'm sorry for butting in *again*. You know Alex better than I do, and I can see that you're making sure you've got the time and space to discuss this.'

'It's OK. I know you're just trying to look out for us.' Kate understood Mia's perspective. Mia was close to Kate and Alex, so she had both of their interests at heart.

Rather than feeling annoyed with her, Kate could actually see things from her point of view, something she hadn't always done.

⁂

The next week flew past in a blur as Kate battled through the stack of custom orders that had flooded in after her viral engagement ring. She'd missed Alex, but his morning texts were making her a pretty unique playlist. She thought of him as she drove home from work on Saturday evening, her car being battered by cold, icy rain. He was out with Pete and his cousins tonight, and she shivered at the idea of anyone fighting their way through the city streets in this weather.

When she got back home, the dogs barked, and the lights were on, but there was no sign of Amelie. She called out, but there was no answer. She walked into the kitchen, and her eyes fell on a note on the worktop.

Am at James's tonight, I'll be back tomorrow afternoon,
Love you,
M x

Next to the note, was a large envelope with her name on it. Picking it up, she noticed the airmail stamp on it. She swallowed hard, knowing that it would be from Lucien. She wasn't ready to think about going to France right now. Instead of opening it, she stuffed it into her bag and made her way to the study, switching on the lights as she went. The study was cold, but she turned on the radiator before settling herself at the desk and pulling out her sketchbook. She'd been given an order for a toi et moi ring, and she hadn't been able to finish her sketch before she left. There was no way she was staying late on her own again.

An hour later, she had a number of sketches, and a plan for that ring. A smile crept across her face and relief washed over her. Despite Rebecca's compliments on her work, she still felt like she had big shoes to fill. Remembering the envelope in her bag, she pulled it out and opened it, her heart pounding as she read the contents. It was her contract from Lucien, and a note saying that her visa should be sent soon. She chewed her lip. Now she definitely needed to tell Alex.

The sound of the dogs barking made her jump, and she put the contract into her sketchbook, flipping it shut and hurried to the front door.

'Alex?' She gasped. His face was streaked with blood, and he had a gauze pad pressed to his eyebrow. 'I'm sorry. I didn't know where else to go.'

Her breath caught in her throat. 'Come in.' She helped him take his coat off, and led him to the kitchen, guiding him into a chair. 'I'm going to sort that cut out on your forehead, Alex, then you need to tell me what happened to you.'

When he nodded, she got the first aid kit out, carefully cleaning the cut on his forehead with an antiseptic wipe, before applying a dressing, then she sat down next to him.

He cleared his throat. 'I was in the bar. One of my engineers rang me. I slid out of the side door to talk to him. I'd just hung up when I felt someone behind me. It was some guy stealing my wallet. I tried to stop him, but he hit me, and I fell. I dropped my phone, and he took that too. I chased after him, but he got away.'

'Oh, Alex, I'm so sorry,' she said, a lump forming in her throat. 'We need to call the police.'

'It won't make any difference,' he replied. 'They won't find whoever it was.'

'You were *assaulted*, Alex. You need to report this,' she insisted.

He nodded. 'I'll do it tomorrow.'

She went back over what he'd just told her. 'We need to cancel your cards.'

'I already did that,' he replied. 'My work phone was in my car. I'd diverted it to my personal phone so I didn't have to take two phones out with me tonight. There wasn't much else in my wallet. I never carry a lot of cash. Whoever robbed me is welcome to the receipts and bits of paper in there.'

'How about your phone, have you reported that stolen?' she asked.

'I have.' He winced as he sat back in the chair.

'I'm sorry. You're injured and I'm firing questions at you.'

'Don't be sorry. You're being practical, he said.

I'm trying.' She ran her eyes over him. 'Are you hurt anywhere else?'

'I landed on my left side, so my ribs are a little sore.' He gave her a wry smile. 'You know what that feels like.'

'I do,' she said. 'It bloody hurts. Didn't anyone come to help you?'

He shook his head. 'By the time I lost him, I was almost back at my car. My face was bleeding, so I cleared it up as best as I could with the first aid kit and came to you.'

'What about the guys? They won't know where you are. Do you want my phone?' She took it out of her pocket and handed it to him.

She stood up, wanting to give him some privacy and filled the kettle. Tea would help. Tea always helped. She made two mugs of sugary tea, and sat back down at the table as he hung up.

'They thought I'd been called into work,' he said, rolling his eyes. 'I could be lying in a gutter right now and they'd be none the wiser.'

'Or maybe they're used to you rushing off to help other people,' she suggested. 'Who did you call?'

'Chris. They're all still in the bar. He and Scott were playing pool.'

'Here.' She passed him a mug. 'It's not a black coffee, it's a milky, sugary tea. You've had a shock and it'll help.'

'Thank you.' He took a sip of the tea. 'This is good.' He closed his eyes, taking another sip.

She noticed that he was shivering. 'I'm going to run you a bath. Then we'll go to bed and figure everything else out tomorrow. How does that sound?'

'Sounds good,' he said. 'I'm sorry to drag you into this. I just... I needed to see you. You make everything better, even when it's really shit.'

'That's what I'm here for.' She smiled, and took a sip of her tea. 'I'm gonna run the bath. I'll be right back.

She hurtled up the stairs, and into the bathroom, turning the taps on in the bath, and sloshing some of the fancy French bubble bath into it. Once it had filled up, she went back downstairs.

Alex was still clutching his mug tightly.

'The bath's ready. Are you OK?'

'I will be,' he said, standing up.

She let him go up the stairs first, then ushered him into the bathroom, helping him pull off his wet clothes.

'Are you joining me?' he asked as he climbed into the bath.

'I don't want to hurt you,' she said.

'I get that, but I could do with some company.' This time his smile reached his eyes.

'In that case...' She smiled back at him, then took off her clothes and got into the bath.

A while later, Alex climbed out of the bath and wrapped himself in a towel.

Kate ran her eyes over him.

He shook his head. 'Seriously? You're still eyeing me up, even when I'm bruised and cut up?'

She shrugged. 'I can't switch it off. You're still gorgeous.'

She got out of the bath, and wrapped herself in a towel. Her chest tightened as she thought about him in the alley, alone. He was a part of her life now, and she couldn't imagine it without him.

His eyes met hers. 'Thank you for... everything. I know it's a lot.'

'It's not a lot, Alex. I'm always here for you.' She gently kissed him. 'I love you.'

'I love you too,' he replied, kissing her back.

When Kate woke the next morning, it was still dark. She'd slept badly the previous night, imagining all of the things that could have happened to Alex. What if Alex had hit his head when he fell? What if the guy who robbed him had had a gun or a knife? This was why it was scary to get close to people. It meant you could lose them.

She pulled on her bathrobe and tiptoed down the stairs, having learnt as a teenager which ones creaked and which ones didn't. She made tea for herself and coffee for Alex, sure he wouldn't sleep for much longer. When she crept back into the bedroom, he was just waking up. In the dim morning light, his swollen eye was visible. 'Morning,' she said. 'How are you feeling?'

He coughed, then winced. 'Sore. Did you sleep?'

She shrugged. 'Sort of. I was worried about you. Here.' She handed him the mug.

'Thank you.' He took a sip from it, then set it down on the bedside table, and rubbed his face He frowned. 'Oh, shit. My dad's bracelet. It's not here. Did you take it off last night?'

She shook her head. 'No. I didn't see it. We'll check the kitchen and your car. It might have fallen off there.'

'I can't believe I've lost it.' He sighed.

'We'll find it. We can go into the city and retrace your steps,' she said.

He shook his head. 'I can't. I have to be at work in an hour. I said I'd cover Sam's shift behind the bar.'

'I don't think you're going to want to do that...' She paused, wondering how to tell him that his face was way too bruised to be stood behind a bar.

'It's bad, isn't it?' he asked. 'I don't know if I want to look.'

'Then don't,' she said. 'You can stay here today while I do your shift at the bar.'

'I can't let you do that. I'll be fine.' He moved to get out of bed, wincing.

'You can, and you will. Think about everything you've done for me. Let me do this.' She dressed quickly in black jeans and a t-shirt. 'What time are they expecting you?'

'Not for another hour,' he said. 'Are you sure about this?'

'Yes.' She nodded. 'I'm sure.'

She found a hoodie and sweatpants in Rob's wardrobe for Alex to wear, then made them both some toast, keeping her eye on the clock.

'I'll be back soon,' she said, finishing the last of her second cup of tea. 'What do I say to your mum?'

'I'd rather she didn't know what happened. I don't want her to worry,' he said.

She looked at the dressing above his eye. 'That's going to take some time to heal. I think she needs to hear the truth.'

'You're probably right. I can't hide here forever.' He sighed.

'You could, but then she'd worry even more,' she said.

'Good point. I trust you to give her the details she needs to know, and omit anything that might worry her.' He took a sip of his tea.

I trust you. She replayed his words in her head, knowing that his trust was hard won.

She leant over and kissed him. 'I love you. I'll do my best to be honest, but also not scare your mum, and I'll be back soon. Mama will be back at some point this afternoon, but I'll call her and tell her that you'll be here. Do you want the TV on?'

He shook his head. 'I think I'm gonna go back to bed. I didn't sleep at all.'

'Get some rest. I'll see you soon.' She blew him a kiss, and grabbed her car keys and bag, then pulled on her coat.

She debated how much to tell Sarah as she drove up to the hotel, and once she arrived, she had perfected her story.

Sarah let Kate into the bar, with a concerned look on her face. 'What's going on? I was expecting Alex. He didn't come back here last night. Is he at your place?'

'He is. He came to my place last night after he'd been out with the guys. There was a little incident at the bar, and his wallet was stolen. He didn't want to worry you.'

She hoped that this was enough, but also not too much.

'Is he OK?' Sarah asked.

'He's fine. He's a little bruised, and he has a cut above his eye, but he's OK,' she said, hoping her tone was reassuring. 'I'm so sorry, I know this is horrible news.'

Sarah sat down on one of the bar stools as the colour drained from her face. 'Why didn't he come back here?'

'He didn't want you to see him,' Kate said gently. 'I'm amazed he came to my house, to be honest. He keeps his cards close to his chest.'

'Not with you.' Sarah smiled at her. 'He trusts you. He even talks to me about you. That's how I knew it was serious.'

Serious, Kate thought to herself. It was serious, and she had to tell him that she was going to France for the summer. She swallowed hard, her heart pounding as the thoughts swirled through her head. How would he react? How could she tell him now? It could wait. It could definitely wait a few days.

'I think we both realised it was serious long before we were prepared to admit it,' Kate said, smiling as she thought about Alex. 'We're very alike in some ways.'

'You are.' Sarah smiled. 'You're good for each other. I'm so grateful that you're here. It means a lot to me.'

'You and Alex mean a lot to me,' Kate said, swallowing the lump in her throat. 'I can't take away the pain he's in, but I can be here so he can rest.'

Sarah's eyes shone with tears and she nodded. 'It's very kind of you.' She blinked several times and looked over at the glass washer. 'Let's get these glass racks filled back up then you can serve with Mel while I do a quick stock check.'

The door to the bar opened and Mel walked in. 'Hello, Kate! I wasn't expecting to see you! Has Alex skipped out of his shift?' Her face dropped as she took in Sarah's pale expression. 'What's happened?'

When Kate returned to her house later on, Amelie was home and playing Scrabble with Alex in the kitchen. Kate paused by the door, watching the two of them together. He fitted right in here. The house had tested him, with a power cut and a chaotic party, but he'd come back.

'Hey, guys,' Kate said, putting down her bags, and sitting down next to Alex. 'How are you feeling?'

'I'm alright.' His smile didn't reach his eyes. 'Nurse Amelie has kept me going with tea and painkillers.'

'He's much easier to deal with than you are, darling.' Amelie said, 'but he still hasn't called the police.' She raised an eyebrow. 'Maybe you can persuade him?'

Alex held up his hands. 'I will, I promise,' he said to Amelie, who nodded to him before she walked out of the room.

'How did you get on at the bar?' Alex asked. 'And what did Mum say?'

'Your mum and Mel were worried about you, but they know that you're fine,' Kate said. 'I didn't go into details. And I loved working behind the bar. It was brilliant! Mel is hilarious.'

'She's great.' He bit his lip. 'I wish I could have been there today. It was supposed to be my last shift there.'n

'How do you feel about stepping away from the hotel?' she asked.

'Kind of sad,' he said. 'I've invested so much of my time and energy into it. I keep wondering if my dad would be proud of me.'

'I know he would be really proud of you,' she replied.

'Thank you.' He leant over and kissed her cheek. 'Even if he was, and was here, I don't know if he would tell me. He was pretty quiet, and he didn't really talk about his feelings. As you know, Mum does all the talking.'

'Just like us.' She smiled. 'You're quiet and mysterious, and I talk way too much.'

'It's all about balance,' he said diplomatically.

'Exactly.' She stood up and got the holdall that she'd left by the door. 'I figured you'd need some of your stuff, so your mum let me into your room. I've got some clothes and your laptop.'

'Thank you so much,' he said, opening it and smiling at the contents. 'That's so sweet of you.'

'You're welcome. I got to look in the secret wardrobe. I'm disap-pointed. There were no superhero costumes in there,' she quipped.

He laughed. 'Maybe that's not where I keep them.'

'Intriguing.' She kissed him again, delighted to see the sparkle back in his eyes.

Chapter Twenty-Six

March 2013, Canterbury, Kent, England

As she drove home from work the following evening, Kate felt frustrated. She'd put a poster of Alex's bracelet up in the shop window, and walked the city streets on her lunch break, but hadn't found it. Alex had called the police the previous day, but they had no idea who'd robbed him, or where his wallet, phone and bracelet were. Worst of all, she had to tell him about the job in Nice. Her work visa had arrived in the post this morning just as she was leaving for work, so it was official. She was going to France. In three weeks.

She pulled onto her her drive, and got out of the car.

The dogs barked as she opened the door and she stroked them. It was strangely quiet. She took off her shoes, frowning.

'Alex?' she called.

There was no reply. She ran up the stairs, and into her room. Alex was folding clothes into his bag, his eyes dark and stormy under his furrowed brow.

'Hey,' she said, her heart pounding. 'Are you alright?'

'Is there anything that you want to tell me?' he asked, shutting the bag.

She opened her mouth to speak, but he interrupted her.

'Your mum let me work in the study today, which was really kind of her,' he said, his tone clipped. 'You'd left your sketchbook on the desk, so I moved it, and something fell out of it.'

The contract, she thought to herself. In the chaos of Saturday night, she'd forgotten all about it, even when she went to turn the lights off and lock the door, she hadn't thought to pick up her sketchbook.

'Kate, why do you have a contract for a job in France?' His eyes were cold.

Her mouth went dry. 'I was literally coming home to tell you about it tonight.'

'So it's real? It's actually happening? You're just moving to France?' He narrowed his eyes. 'I thought we talked about how important honesty was. About being open with each other.'

She followed him down the stairs, pleading with him as he pulled open the front door. 'Please don't go. Let me explain.'

'You're moving to France. What is there to explain?' His eyes darkened. 'I can't talk to you right now.'

He turned away from her and closed the door behind him.

She stumbled into the living room, her limbs suddenly heavy, and collapsed on the sofa. A hundred thoughts flashed through her mind. Why hadn't she told him sooner? Why hadn't she moved the contract? She thought about that night when Alex had turned up covered in blood, and how she'd abandoned the contract on the desk, not able to think straight, imagining what could have happened to him. Those thoughts had stayed with her since then, and she'd been unable to switch them off.

The front door opened and she looked up, hoping it was Alex, but Amelie walked in. 'What happened? Where's Alex?'

Kate took a deep breath as Amelie came and sat down next to her. 'He's gone.'

After Kate explained what had happened between her and Alex, Amelie took Kate's hand in hers. 'I'm so sorry, darling. You and Alex, you're so similar. You both keep people at a distance, and you both hide things. I always wondered if it would be something that came between you.'

'I hadn't ever looked at it that way. You mean, this was always inevitable?' Kate asked.

'I don't know,' Amelie said. 'I thought you had started to open up to each other.'

'We had. I need to speak to him, but he was so angry when he left. I don't know how I can fix this.' Kate looked around the room, suddenly feeling restless, and swiped at her eyes. 'I don't want to sit here dwelling on it, though. I need to move. I'll take the dogs out for a walk.'

'Do you want some company?' Amelie asked.

'I'd like that,' Kate said and followed Amelie into the kitchen, where they pulled on their wellies and coats.

Kate drove to Mia's the following evening, having barely slept the night before. There had been no song choice from Alex. No message with cryptic lyrics for her to figure out. His replacement phone would have been at the hotel when he got back there yesterday. He would have her number, but she didn't have his. She could call him at work, or call the hotel, but she couldn't face doing either of those things.

She knocked on Mia's door, feeling tearful as Mia opened it. 'Can I come in?'

'Sure. What's going on? You look awful,' Mia ushered Kate into the house and closed the door.

Kate followed her into the living room and sank into the sofa. 'I need to tell you something.' She took a deep breath and filled Mia in.

'Oh, Kate. I knew this would happen. I didn't want to be right about this,' Mia said sadly.

'I should have told him.' Kate looked at Mia, biting her lip. 'I've never felt this way about anyone, Mia. I love him so much. I feel like we're meant to be together and this hurts so much.'

Mia slid an arm around Kate, her belly pressing against Kate's side. 'I know you weren't trying to hurt him, but sometimes you need to think about other people.'

'Wow.' Kate shook her head. 'Thanks for that.' She pulled away from Mia. 'I *was* thinking about him. That's why I hadn't told him.'

'Is it?' Mia asked, her voice raised. 'You hide stuff, Kate, rather than dealing with it. You hid from your row with your mum, you hid from me and Lucy, and you hid this from Alex. How did you expect him to react? How would you have reacted?'

'I would have been furious. I never meant to hurt him.' Kate swallowed the lump in her throat. 'I'd planned to tell him, but I thought it wasn't right to do that just after he'd been mugged.' Tears sprang from her eyes, and she wiped her face roughly on her sleeve.

Mia looked at Kate and her face softened. 'I'm sorry, Kate. You need a friend right now.'

'You're bringing up our past and that's not fair. You told me you'd forgiven me, and clearly you haven't,' Kate said, her voice shaky. 'You're holding a grudge against me, and I don't know why.'

Mia looked down at the floor. 'I'm sorry. Maybe it's because I know you're going away again. I'm going to have this baby, and you won't be here, just like last time.' A tear fell from her face onto the floor.

'I'm sorry, Mia. I really am.' Kate moved closer to Mia. 'I know you think I'm being selfish, but I'm going to France because of Alex. I know that if I'd told him sooner, he would have supported me. I thought that being without him for a few months didn't matter because we would be together for a long time, maybe even forever. It's the first time I've felt like that about anyone, and now it's ruined.'

'Not necessarily,' Mia said. 'You have the opportunity to make it right. You've learnt that walking away from things doesn't...' she trailed off as she winced and stood up, taking a few deep breaths.

'Are you alright?' Kate's brow wrinkled and then she flew to her feet as a pool of water appeared on the floor around Mia's feet.

'Oh, shit. Is that what I think it is?' Kate asked, her eyes wide with fear.

'That would be my waters, yes,' Mia said, breathing heavily. The colour drained from her face.

'Hold on,' Kate replied, running into the kitchen and grabbing the mop and bucket. She cleared up the water and helped Mia upstairs, fetching her a towel while Mia got some dry clothes out. 'I'll call an ambulance. You ring Pete.'

Mia nodded, breathing heavily, and pulled her phone out of her pocket.

Kate dialled 999 with shaky fingers while Mia spoke to Pete. They both hung up and turned to each other.

'The ambulance is on its way,' Kate said.

'Pete's going to meet us at the hospital. Luckily, he was on his break.' Mia shook her head. 'I've been having contractions all day.' She paused, wincing. 'I thought it was Braxton Hicks. They're kind of like fake contractions.'

'Mia,' Kate said quietly. 'How early are you? Is the baby...'

'I'm thirty-eight weeks, so I'm only two weeks early. We should be fine.' Mia's voice was calm, confident, but Kate could see the fear in her eyes.

Kate held out her hand to Mia. 'What can I do?'

Mia smiled at her and took her hand, squeezing it tightly. 'Time my contractions, hold my hand and... will you come with me in the ambulance?' She let go of Kate and sat down on the bed.

'Of course I will,' Kate replied, her eyes filling with tears.

Mia nodded, then closed her eyes and grabbed Kate's hand, crying out in pain.

'Oh, love, that was a big one. You're doing so well.' Kate noted the time on her phone. 'What do we need to do now?'

'Can you get the hospital bag out of the wardrobe please?' Mia asked.

Kate grabbed a large blue bag out of the wardrobe and followed Mia's directions, adding in underwear and spare clothes to the already immaculately packed bag. She helped Mia back downstairs to the living room, where they sat on the sofa to wait for the ambulance.

'Mia, are we OK?' Kate asked. 'I feel so bad for getting angry with you.'

'I got angry with you first.' Mia looked at Kate with teary eyes. 'Sometimes I feel jealous or left out with you and Lucy. You guys can meet for a drink whenever you like or just go off to Brighton for the weekend, and I can't. You were right, we aren't the same.' She paused as another contraction washed over her.

'I had no idea you felt that way. Why didn't you tell me?' Kate asked.

'I didn't think you would understand,' Mia said. 'You don't know what it's like to have a baby while your friends are all off at university. I had Lilly while you were on a pub crawl dressed as Spiderman. We live in different worlds, and, when you and Alex got serious, I kind of hoped that you'd settle down together and we'd have that in common.'

Kate nodded. 'You thought it would bring us closer. Now I've ruined it, that's kind of off the table.'

'Maybe it's not ruined.' Mia took a deep breath. 'I don't think you were completely to blame here. He could have let you explain. He's clearly not told you what happened between him and Ava and that's what made him storm off.'

'What do you mean?' Kate asked.

Mia paused. 'I think you need to talk to him.'

'He won't return my calls, Mia. I'm done with the mystery. If you know something, tell me.'

'She left him.' Mia closed her eyes and gripped Kate's hand tightly again as she rode out another contraction. 'Shit. That was a strong one.'

Kate looked down at her phone. 'They're getting closer.'

Mia took a deep breath. 'Ava's Italian, and she took a job in Italy without telling Alex. He came home from work one day and her stuff was packed. She just told him that she was going. No discussion. Nothing. Then he found out that she had also been seeing someone else.'

'So me not telling him about Nice would have felt a lot like that,' Kate said slowly.

'It's not the same thing, but it probably felt like it to him,' Mia replied. 'Give him time. I know how much he loves you.'

As Kate squeezed Mia's hand, their eyes met, and she knew that whatever happened with Alex, she and Mia had each other. She saw a flash of blue lights outside, and went to the window, where she could see an ambulance had parked on the drive. She opened the front door and let in two green-suited paramedics who checked Mia over.

'We need to get her to the hospital now,' one of them said to Kate.

'No problem, her bag's packed and we're ready to go.' Kate grabbed Mia's house keys and followed Mia and the paramedics to the ambulance. As they sped towards the hospital, Mia called Pete's mum, who was looking after Lilly.

By the time they arrived at the hospital, Pete was waiting at the entrance, still in his blue scrubs and with tears in his eyes. The paramedics helped Mia out of the ambulance and into a wheelchair.

Kate walked over to Pete, gave him a hug, and handed him the hospital bag. 'Good luck, dude.'

'Thanks for getting her here,' he said.

'You did a good job.'

'Thanks, mate.' She smiled at him and turned to Mia. 'Do you want me to stay?'

'No, you're alright.' Mia smiled through teary eyes. 'You'd never be able to look at me the same way. '

Kate laughed through her tears, before kissing Mia on the forehead. 'Love you.'

'Love you too,' Mia said. 'See you on the other side.'

It was only after Pete and Mia went inside and the darkness had settled around her outside the hospital, that Kate realised that she was alone. Sighing, she pulled her coat tightly around her, and slid her phone out of her pocket. She called a taxi, which took her back to Mia's house. She collected her car and drove home with her heart still pounding furiously. She thought about Mia, praying that she and the baby would be alright.

Chapter Twenty-Seven

March 2013 Canterbury, Kent, England

At six am Kate's alarm went off and she groaned, pulling herself out of bed. She picked up her phone, hoping to see a message from Alex. There was nothing from him, but there was a message from Mia.

> Baby Patterson has arrived! No name yet. We're both fine. Thank you for looking after me last night. You did such a good job! I'm hoping they'll discharge us today. M x

Tears sprang to Kate's eyes as she typed a response.

> Love you all so much and cannot wait to meet him!!! K x

Kate had a hot shower, slapped some makeup onto her tired face, and blasted her hair dry, then walked into the kitchen, where Amelie was making a cup of tea.

'Morning, Mama,' she said, pulling a mug out of the cupboard.

'Morning, darling.' Amelie winced at Kate's face. 'Late one, was it? I didn't even hear you come in.'

'Just don't. Mia and I had a row, and then she went into labour.' Kate took a jar of instant coffee out of the cupboard and added a hefty spoonful to her mug.

Amelie's hands flew to her face. 'Oh my God! She's early! Are they alright?'

'She's had the baby and they're all fine,' Kate said. 'She's hoping to be let out today.'

Amelie let out a long exhale. 'Thank God.' She poured some hot water into Kate's mug, before picking up her own, leaning against the worktop. 'Why did you and Mia fall out?'

Kate added some milk to her coffee, taking it over to the table and sitting down. Amelie sat next to her, and Kate filled her in, watching as her face fell.

'That's a lot.' Amelie took a sip of her tea. 'How do you feel now?'

'I feel awful,' Kate said, gulping down her coffee. 'I feel like everything that's happened this year has all just resurfaced. I ruined my relationship with Will. I've ruined my relationship with Alex.'

'No. Amelie shook her head. 'I'm going to set you straight. You didn't ruin your relationship with Will. He did that with his unrealistic expectations of you. And of course you should have told Alex about Nice, but it sounds like his reaction was driven by his breakup with Ava, and he should have told you about that. It's time you stop blaming yourself for all of this.'

Kate looked up at Amelie. 'You're right. I felt like it was all my fault, but there are always two sides to every story, right?'

'Always,' Amelie said. 'Be kind to yourself. You've been through a lot in the last few weeks.'

Kate blinked away her tears. 'I just feel so bad for being angry with Mia, although maybe it was a good thing as we actually got everything out in the open. I never realised that she felt left out.'

'I know what it's like to be nursing a baby when all of your friends are out partying, Kate,' Amelie said. 'It sounds like Mia's realised she can't expect you to follow her path.'

Kate took another sip of her coffee. 'She said just that. Last night was rough, but she's the only one brave enough to have the hard conversations with me, and we always come out of it stronger.'

'You have to know someone very well to have the hard conversations with them,' Amelie said. 'I know it's difficult sometimes, and it will mean you'll fall out, but it means she is a true friend.'

'Thanks, Mama, you are so wise.' Kate smiled. 'Like a glamorous Yoda.'

Amelie laughed and took another sip of her coffee. 'Is that a compliment?'

'Oh, definitely.' Kate drained the rest of her coffee and stood up, planting a kiss on Amelie's forehead. 'I've got to go to work. See you later.'

Emmett studied Kate closely as he briefed her on a custom order later that day. 'You've not been yourself today. I've not heard any singing. Is something going on?'

Kate paused. She didn't want to tell Emmett about what had happened between her and Alex, but she couldn't keep it to herself anymore. She took a deep breath before filling him and David in on what had happened with Alex and Mia.

'I'm so sorry, mate.' David's brow furrowed with concern. 'Should you be here? I don't want you injuring yourself. These chisels take no prisoners.'

Kate shook her head. 'No, I need to keep busy. I'll be fine.'

'You've had a lot to deal with,' Emmett said, his tone firm. 'You need to look after yourself. If you need to take some time away from here, you come and let me know, alright?'

'I will. Thank you. You're so kind.' Kate felt close to tears, but she bit them back. She wasn't going to cry here.

'Not at all. You've been through a lot.' Emmett gave her a sympathetic smile. 'I'm here if you need me.

Kate nodded, and he smiled at her before he left the room.

'I second that, David said. 'Whatever you need, let me know.'

'Thank you,' Kate replied. 'Can you find me a really complicated order? I need distracting.'

After she finished work, Kate breathed in the heady, sweet scent in Papillon as she collected the box that she'd ordered, putting it into her shopping bag with the blanket and muslins she'd picked up from the baby boutique in the city. She walked back to the car, a fizz of excitement rushing through her body. In just a few minutes, she would get to meet Mia's new baby. They'd been discharged from the hospital earlier, and she couldn't wait to see them.

'Hello, love. How are you?' Pete asked as he opened the front door to Kate, and stepped aside to allow her in.

'I'm fine. How are you doing?' She set her bag down and put her arms around Pete, and he pulled her into a hug.

'I'm just fine, thanks,' Pete replied as he let her go. 'I know it's not me you're here to see, though.'

'How are they? And how on earth did Mia manage to get discharged already?' Kate asked, taking off her shoes and clutching her bag tightly.

'He's totally fine and so's Mia. He's thirty-eight weeks, so he's just past premature.' Pete lowered his voice. 'I think the nurses were slightly scared of Mia, to be honest, so when she said she was fine and wanted to go home, they let her.'

'She's a handful, isn't she?' Kate said. 'Where is she?'

Pete pointed her towards the stairs. 'She and the baby are in our bedroom.'

She went up the stairs and pushed open the bedroom door, smiling as she saw Mia in her bed in a pair of stripy pyjamas, her hair tied up in a messy bun and a tiny baby nestled on her chest.

'Hello, love!' Mia beamed at Kate through tired eyes and patted the duvet next to her. 'Come and join us.'

Kate put the bag on the bed but hovered cautiously. 'Are you sure? Are we good?'

Mia nodded. 'We're good. I waded in where my opinion was not asked for. I know your life is different from mine, and I'm not going to expect you to follow in my footsteps. Come and sit down.'

Kate sat down on the bed and smiled at Mia. 'I'm so relieved, I've been so worried about you. And about us.'

'We always ride out the storms, Kate,' Mia said.

'We do.' Kate smiled. 'You look surprisingly good for someone who gave birth a few days ago. Are you sure you're alright? I thought you'd be in there longer.'

'Why?' Mia replied. 'He's a little on the small side, but he's perfectly formed and I had the quickest labour. We were lucky the ambulance came when it did. Our friendship nearly went to a whole different level.'

Kate laughed. 'I would have held your hand the whole way, I promise you!' She opened the bag and pulled out the box of chocolate, putting it on the bed between them. 'That's for you.' She rummaged in the bag again and pulled out a neatly wrapped tissue paper parcel with a white ribbon bow. 'And that's for the baby.'

'Thanks, love. That's so sweet of you.' Mia held out the baby to Kate. 'I'll swap you.'

'Really?' Kate cautiously took the baby from Mia. 'Oh, Mia, he's gorgeous.'

She looked down at his tiny fingers and his tightly shut eyes, the fine dark brown hair on his head. He was perfect. A warm, happy feeling flooded her as she held him. He was safe. Mia was safe. She could relax.

'I might be biased, but I totally agree.' Mia opened the tissue paper, pulling out the blanket and muslins.

Kate glanced up at her. 'I didn't know what size he would be, so I didn't get any clothes.'

'These are perfect. Thank you.' Mia leant over and kissed Kate's cheek. 'We have a name! Henry, this is your Auntie Kate. She loves smelly nappies and cuddles.'

Kate smiled at him. 'Hi, Henry. It's wonderful to meet you. We nearly met the other night.'

'That was a night we'll never forget, wasn't it?' Mia laughed, shaking her head. She studied Kate's face. 'Are you alright? I'll be honest, you don't look great.'

Kate paused before she spoke. 'I don't want to complain about my lack of sleep in front of you. I can't stop thinking about Alex and I'm nervous about going to France.'

Mia nodded. 'Have you spoken to him?'

'No, and I can't go to France until I do,' Kate said, looking down at Henry. 'Have you or Pete seen him?'

Mia nodded. 'Pete met him for a drink last week. He asked about you, and seemed pretty interested in knowing how you are, but didn't tell Pete anything about how he was.'

'Sounds like Alex,' Kate said, then looked back down at Henry. 'He really is gorgeous, Mia. I love you so much, and I might not always be here, but I'm always here for you. I hope you know that.'

'I love you too,' Mia replied. 'I know you won't always be here, and even if I'm not with you, I'm with you every step of the way.'

The following morning, Kate got on a train to London. Alex still hadn't returned her calls, and she felt sick every time she thought about going to the hotel to see him. She pushed all thoughts of him from her mind as the train arrived at London Victoria. This weekend was all about Hannah and her birthday. As she swiped her ticket and walked onto the station concourse, she saw Hannah waving her arms furiously at her. 'Hey, bud! You made it!' She put her arms around Kate.

'Happy birthday, love!' Kate pulled away from Hannah and handed her a small box. 'Open it later,' she said, kissing her cheek.

'Thanks!,' Hannah put the box in her bag. 'We're heading back to my flat, and then my housemates will tell us what they have in store for us today.'

'You don't know?' Kate's eyebrows shot up. 'You hate surprises.'

Hannah shrugged. 'I trust them.'

When they got back to Hannah's flat, Hannah introduced Kate to Matty and Scarlet, her housemates. Matty was tall and slim, with messy brown curls, tied up in a bun on the top of his head, and Scarlet was curvy, with a bright red bob, matching her name perfectly.

'Hi, Kate,' Scarlet said, stepping forward and giving her a hug. 'We've heard a lot about you.'

'Oh, no.' Kate winced. 'Don't believe it. It's not true.'

Scarlet let out a husky laugh. 'Oh, don't worry, it was all good. Apparently you're the life and soul of the party, which is good because the party starts in an hour with bottomless brunch.'

Kate's eyes lit up. 'Now you're talking.'

'We have no idea what we're doing today, so, are we dressed appropriately?' Hannah asked Matty and Scarlet.

Matty glanced at Kate's outfit of black jeans, a tight shirt, and the infamous gold studded boots. 'Kate is,' he said. 'Hannah, you might want to swap the trainers for some other shoes.'

Hannah looked puzzled, but slipped on a pair of ankle boots, while Kate put her bag in Hannah's room and applied a coat of red lipstick before they left the flat.

After endless pancakes and several mimosas, Kate's head was spinning. She clung to Hannah as they laughed at Matty's jokes in the quirkily decorated bar.

'What's next on the agenda?' Hannah asked, looking at Matty and Scarlet.

Matty produced some tickets from his pocket. 'How about a matinee performance of West Side Story?' He smiled at Hannah. 'I know you've never seen it.'

'Really? I love it!' Hannah shrieked. 'Thank you!' She threw her arms around him and kissed his cheek.

'Phew,' he said, as he let her go. 'I know surprises aren't your thing, but I figured you'd like this one.'

'But we need to pay you back for the tickets.' Hannah looked worried.

'We're going to cover your ticket.' He kissed Hannah's cheek. 'It's your birthday. You don't need to worry about anything.'

'You're amazing,' she replied. 'Thank you.' She looked at Kate and Scarlet. 'Thank you guys too.'

'You're so welcome,' Kate replied, smiling. Matty had asked her to chip in while Hannah was changing her shoes.

'I second that,' Scarlet slurred and finished her drink.

Matty rolled his eyes. 'Seeing as Kate and Scarlet are already half cut we need to get going.' He stood up and held his hand out to Hannah, pulling her to her feet. 'Come on guys.'

As they walked to the theatre, Kate lowered her voice so that Matty and Scarlet, who were ahead of them, didn't hear her as she spoke to Hannah. 'What's the deal with you and Matty, then? I'm picking up on a vibe between you.'

'We're kind of seeing each other,' Hannah whispered. 'He's amazing in bed... but it's nothing serious. We live together, so we don't want a proper relationship.'

'Nice,' Kate whispered, giving Hannah a discreet high five. 'He's hot, clever, and funny.'

'I know,' Hannah whispered back as they arrived at the theatre. 'He's a triple threat.'

After the theatre, Matty led them to a bar where some of Hannah's other friends turned up. Kate's earlier tipsiness had worn off, and she and Hannah sampled the extensive mocktail menu, while the others ordered huge jugs of cocktails. As the evening turned to night, a giant chocolate cake arrived at their table with giant sparkler candles in it. They all sang to Hannah, and she blew out her candles, keeping one arm around Matty and the other around Kate.

Hannah and Matty led everyone across the city to the Printworks, a dark, sweaty club, where they danced underneath sweeping strobe lights. The DJs were playing a mixture of drum and bass and garage, and, as Kate looked up at the DJ booth, she thought about Alex. Was he sad? Angry? Over her? She couldn't decide what was worse, and her heart sank when she looked again at the DJ booth. *This* was worse. He was here! Right on the stage, playing alongside another DJ. She froze, like a deer in headlights, unable to decide if she should run or stay.

Her heart pounded furiously, and she fought the urge to run up to the stage. The sensible thing to do, would be to get out of here before he saw her. Pushing her way through the crowd, she pulled open the door, and walked down the brightly lit corridor to the bathroom. As she looked at her reflection in the bathroom mirror, cheeks flushed, eyes wild, she wondered if he'd seen her. After splashing some water on her face, she felt calmer. She took a deep breath and pulled the door open, walking back out into the corridor and straight into Alex, who was holding a bottle of water.

'Kate?' His mouth fell open. 'What are you doing here?'

'I'm here with Hannah and her friends,' she breathed. 'I didn't expect to see you here... on the stage.' She suddenly remembered his conversation with Scott about something being "in the works." Now it made sense.

'I...' His eyes raked over her body, stopping at her shoes. 'You're wearing those boots.'

She nodded. 'They remind me of the night we first kissed.'

'It was a good kiss.' His eyes moved to her lips.

A rush of adrenaline pulsed through her body, and she pulled him towards her, her lips meeting his. He hesitated for a second before his hand tangled in her hair. This kiss was worlds apart from their first one, which had been tentative, then passionate. This one was urgent and desperate, like two drowning people clinging to each other. When she pulled away from him, she was breathless. Her heart was beating so hard she could almost hear it. She had so many questions to ask him, but she was still reeling from his kiss. She looked into his eyes, trying to figure out what he was thinking.

As she opened her mouth, the door at the end of the corridor opened, and a man wearing a black bomber jacket came out of it, and, spotting Alex, he walked up to him. 'Alex, mate, you're up.'

Alex looked at him and nodded. 'I'll be right there.' The man gave Alex a thumbs up and disappeared back through the door. Alex turned back to Kate. 'I have to go, I'm sorry.'

'Sure. I should go too,' Kate replied, her heart sinking.

He nodded, then held her gaze for a second. It was too painful to see him walking away from her, so she turned away from him and walked back through the door to the dance floor, scanning the crowd for Hannah and her friends. Catching Hannah's eyes, she made her way over to her.

'Alex is one of the DJs tonight.' Hannah pointed up to the stage. 'How weird is that? Is this OK?'

'It's fine,' Kate said, still feeling the ghost of his touch on her body. When his set finished, she raced out into the corridor to see if she could see him again, but he had already gone.

It was two am when Kate collapsed into bed next to Hannah, exhausted. 'Have you had a good birthday, mate?'

'It's been the best.' Hannah smiled. 'Thank you for coming up. It's been amazing having you here. I know it's probably cost you a small fortune.'

'You're worth it, and I've loved every part of it.' Kate took a deep breath. 'I need to tell you something. I kissed Alex tonight.'

'What?' Hannah shrieked. 'How? When? Where?'

'He was just coming off stage to get a drink as I came out of the bathroom,' Kate replied. 'We bumped into each other, and we just went at each other like animals. It was intense.'

'What happened?' Hannah asked. 'Did he apologise for storming off?'

'No.' Kate let out a long exhale. 'I literally have no idea what's going to happen next, but surely, if it was over, he wouldn't have kissed me, would he? And definitely not like that.'

'I agree,' Hannah nodded. 'If you're really over someone, you definitely don't kiss them and it's not like he was drunk and you weren't either, right?'

'Nope,' Kate said. 'I decided to slow down after the cocktails at brunch.'

'I noticed, and tomorrow you won't feel like shit, unlike Matty and Scarlet, who are going to feel so bad.' Hannah smiled at Kate. 'What do you think of Matty?'

'I like him. He's not what I pictured you going for. I thought you were saving yourself for Indiana Jones? Hannah's obsession with whip cracking Indy intrigued Kate.

Hannah let out a murmur of pleasure. 'I've never found a hero I like better than Indiana Jones. Rugged, intelligent, quick-witted. He loves history, he can drive a car, fly a plane, I mean what can't he do?'

'You know he's fictional, right?' Kate asked, laughing. 'Matty's great, though, and if you're both on the same page, then I'm happy for you. As long as he treats you right, I approve.'

'He organised everything today,' Hannah said. 'He's very sweet, but as I said, I don't think it's anything serious.'

'Because you don't want it to be? Or because you think it can't be?' Kate asked.

'Good question,' Hannah said. 'I'm not sure right now.'

Kate yawned. 'You don't have to be. Take your time and figure out what you want.'

'Since when did you get so wise?' Hannah smiled at Kate. 'That's good advice.'

'Thanks. I need to sleep now. I need to recharge my wise little brain.' Kate closed her eyes. 'Night, dude, love you.'

'Love you too.' Hannah switched off the light.

The last thing Kate thought about before she drifted off to sleep was that kiss, and the way Alex had looked at her. It couldn't be over between then could it? But if it wasn't, why hadn't he called her?

Chapter Twenty-Eight

Kate walked down the King's Mile on Monday morning in a good mood. She'd arrived back in Canterbury the previous afternoon after a late breakfast with Matty, Scarlet, and Hannah, who had loved the silver compass necklace that Kate had made for her. Despite Matty and Scarlet's hangovers they'd spent the entire meal talking at full volume, and by the time Kate got home, her head was pounding. After a long sleep, she was ready to take on her week. As she walked towards the shop, she thought about her kiss with Alex, and smiled to herself.

When she arrived at the shop, she noticed a large sign outside that read "WET PAINT" and Emmett stood talking to a man wearing paint splattered overalls.

'Morning, Kate. What do you think?' Emmett gestured to the newly painted window frames.

Kate admired them. 'Looks great.'

'Hello, love, I'm Greg,' the man in the overalls said. 'Nice to meet you.'

'Greg's found something that I think you'll want to see' Emmett said.

'When I arrived this morning to do your windows, I saw your poster.' Greg put his hand in his pocket. 'I've had this in my van for a while. I found it when I was doing the windows at Mimosa. I keep meaning to take it to the police station.'

Kate's mouth fell open, and her heart began to race as she stared at the silver bracelet in his palm. 'Thank you so much.' She pictured Alex's face the morning he'd realised he'd lost it, and a rush of nervous energy flooded her. 'You've no idea how happy this will make Alex.'

'No worries, love. I'm glad it's going back to its owner,' Greg said.

Kate smiled at Emmett and Greg and went up the stairs to the studio. Gently, she washed the bracelet in soapy water, removing the dirt from it. With a soft cloth and some polish, she worked on it until it shone.

After she left the shop that evening, Kate drove up to the hotel, parked her car, and gripped her car keys tightly as she walked down the familiar drive. When she pushed open the door of the hotel and walked into the bar, it was full. Every single table was full, and there was a crowd of people at the counter. She froze, wondering whether to stay and give him the bracelet or leave it with Mel and go. As she debated with herself, her eyes locked onto Alex's through the crowd. After handing a drink to a customer, he came around to the front of the bar towards her.

'Hey,' he said. 'This is a surprise.'

'I'm sorry to just turn up here, but this couldn't wait.' She looked around the packed bar. 'Can we talk?'

'Let's go to the office,' he said and Kate followed him past the bar, where he nodded at Mel as they walked out into the corridor. He unlocked the office door and walked in, then leaned against the desk.

She put her hand into her pocket, pulling out the velvet bag, handing it to him. 'This was handed in today at Corrells. The painter found it when he did Mimosa's window frames.

He opened the bag and slid out the bracelet, the storm in his eyes dissipating. 'Thank you. You know how much this means to me,' he said quietly, his gaze still on the gleaming bangle. He slipped it onto his wrist, then looked up at her. 'I haven't stopped thinking about you since Saturday night.'

She nodded. 'Me neither.' Cautiously, she moved closer to him. 'I've wanted to talk to you for so long, and now I'm here, I need to say this.'

He nodded. 'Go ahead. I'm listening.'

She continued. 'I should have told you earlier about the job in Nice, but I didn't, and I'm sorry. I'm going to be there for a few months, but...'

'Wait, what do you mean a few months?' He stood up. 'It's not a permanent job?'

'No.' She shook her head. 'No, it's just for the summer, then I'm coming back in August. I'm taking over permanently from Rebecca.'

'Really?' He swallowed hard. 'You're coming back.'

'Yes,' she said, her face inches from his. 'I was planning to tell you the weekend you were robbed, but then you found out before I had the chance to. I can't take that back, but it hurts that you didn't even give me the chance to explain myself.'

She thought about what Mia had told her about Ava but held her tongue.

His eyes burnt into hers. 'Kate, I need to apologise to you. My ex left me for another job, and another man, in another country, and when I saw the contract, I felt like it was happening all over again.'

'Why didn't you tell me? she asked, her hands still stuffed into her pockets, afraid she would wrap them around him if she took them out.

'It was still too hard to talk about,' he admitted.

She sucked in a breath. 'You told me that honesty was so important to you, but you've withheld this massive thing from me. It feels like a double standard.'

'You're right,' he said. 'I should have told you, and I didn't, and it massively blew up in my face. I'm sorry, Kate. I let my past come between us.'

Her mind flashed back to their kiss in the club corridor, and a shiver of anticipation tingled in her chest. 'So, where does that leave us? I can't stop thinking about you, and not speaking to you has been so painful. If this is over, tell me it's over. I can't go to France not knowing where I stand with you.'

'It's not over for me.' He glanced up at her. 'What about you?'

'It's definitely not over for me.' She gazed into his ocean blue eyes, seeing something in them that gave her hope. 'Where do we go from here?'

'We've both kept secrets from each other, and hurt each other,' he said, 'but I want this to work. You have this amazing opportunity ahead of you and I don't want to get in the way of it. Make the most of every single moment of it, and when you come back, if you still want this, we can try again.'

'Is that what you want?' she asked, her heart pounding.

'More than anything, but only if you're on the same page,' he said, holding her gaze.

'I am.' She stood on her tiptoes and kissed him, cupping his face in her hands. When she pulled away from him, she rested her forehead against his. 'It would be so much easier to leave you if we'd had a dramatic, angry fight.'

A smile pulled at the corner of his lips. 'We can do that if you like. If it makes things easier.'

She shook her head. 'You are too good to me. I'm gonna miss you so much.'

'I'm going to miss you too, but you can call me or message me any time you want to,' he said.

'I can't. I don't have your number. I've been wanting to call you, but I didn't want to call you at work, and I didn't want to call the hotel either,' she admitted.

'Oh.' He looked thoughtful. 'I just assumed you didn't want to talk to me.'

'I did, I just didn't want to risk having to speak to Mel, or Sam, or your mum, and having to explain why I didn't have your new phone number.' Now she said it out loud, it felt ridiculous.

He took his phone out of his pocket, and unlocked it. 'You can definitely have my new number, and you can use it any time you like.'

She got her phone out and swapped numbers with him. 'Can you just send me something really mean. I'm taking something really insulting, so that I can keep looking at it every time I miss you.'

He laughed. 'I'll see what I can do.'

She smiled. 'I should go.' As she turned to leave the room, he caught her hand. 'I love you.'

'I love you too.' She kissed him again, and afraid she would burst into tears, pulled away from him, and walked quickly out of the hotel.

Two days later, Kate walked into the studio at Corrells. It was her last day there for four months, and while she was excited to go to Nice, she would miss everyone she'd spent the last six months getting to know. She climbed the stairs, and squealed as she saw her bench, which was covered in balloons and presents.

Lisa and Emmett appeared in the studio and huddled around her bench.

David gave her a broad smile. 'We got you a few not-leaving gifts.'

'I love that.' Kate beamed. 'Not-leaving, because I'm coming back.'

'Open them!' Lisa said.

Kate took off the wrapping paper, revealing a beach towel, a pair of flip flops, and a sun hat. 'I love them, thank you so much!' She picked up the flip flops, and looked at David. 'Don't worry, I won't wear these in the studio. Sensible footwear only.'

He laughed. 'Glad to hear it.'

She put the straw sunhat on. 'How do I look?'

'It suits you,' Emmmett said. 'Spare us a thought when you're sunning yourself on the beach, won't you?'

'I'm going there to work!' she insisted, 'but there might be a *little* down time.' She put on her apron. 'Now, it's my last day, so I need to get on.' She was afraid she'd get too emotional if she said anything else.

She and David worked in companiable silence for the rest of the day. She finished the last of her orders, then tidied up her tools and her bench, hanging her apron on the hook on the wall.

When five pm arrived, she walked to Mimosa with Emmett, David, and Lisa. With a cocktail in her hand, Kate stood up and cleared her throat.

'Thank you all for making me feel so welcome here. I'm not saying goodbye, it's à bientôt, right?' She laughed, tears welling in her eyes.

'I bet you'll send us all photos from the beach, though, while we're battling the wind and rain here,' David said, rolling his eyes.

'I still expect a daily catch up,' Lisa added. 'We'll just do it via text instead.'

'Oh, oui, bien sûr!' Kate replied.

'Hello, stranger!' A familiar voice made Kate turn away from Lisa. It was Lucy, with Mia and Leon.

'Oh, my goodness! Where did you come from?' Kate stood up and threw her arms around Leon.

'Lisa and I arranged it so that you got to say goodbye to everyone at once,' Leon said.

Kate beamed at him. 'You came back, just for me?'

Leon smiled at her. 'Of course I did. I had to give you this.' He handed her a dress cover. 'Something for your travels.'

Kate carefully unzipped it, revealing a pink skater dress, printed with sunglasses and bikinis. 'I love it! Thank you so much.' As she let him go, she moved on to Mia. 'I can't believe you're here! You've only just had Henry.'

'I know, but you're my best friend and you deserve a proper send-off.' Mia sat down next to Lisa. 'Plus, I've been hogging him over the last few days, so I've let Pete have some time with him.'

David smiled at her. 'We're going to head off,' he said, gesturing to Emmett. 'Have an amazing time, and I'll see you in September.' He pulled Kate in for a bear hug so tight she struggled to draw a breath.

When he let her go, Emmett smiled at her. 'It's been a pleasure, Kate. Keep us posted, and we'll see you in August.'

'Thank you for letting me go, and letting me come back,' Kate said. 'I'll miss you so much.'

'I'll miss you too,' Emmett replied. 'Take every opportunity that comes your way while you're there.'

'I will,' she assured him.

He and David left, and Kate returned to the sofa with her friends.

'How are you doing, Kate?' Lucy asked. 'Are you excited about tomorrow?'

'Yes,' Kate said, before taking a deep breath. 'It'll be amazing. I know it will, but I've been fighting this feeling that I'm not good enough for a while, and, right now, it's pretty loud.'

'Lucien wouldn't have offered you the job if he didn't think you could do it.' Lucy put an arm around her. 'You're going to smash it. I know you are.'

'Thanks, love.' Kate smiled. 'I've not seen you in ages. How are you? How's Rachel?'

Lucy bit her lip. 'Trying to schedule time together is getting harder with my assignments and her shifts, but we're doing our best. I love her, and I know she loves me, so we'll make it work.'

Kate leant her head on Lucy's shoulder. 'I know it's tough right now but think about how cool it's going to be in September when you've finished your course and Rachel's graduated too.'

'That's what I'm holding onto.' Lucy smiled. 'I'm going to miss your little pearls of wisdom.'

'I can still deliver them via text message,' Kate assured her. 'And I'll only be gone for four months. You won't even notice I'm gone.'

'Oh, I think we will,' Mia said. 'I'm missing you already.'

'Stop,' Kate said, biting back tears. 'I'm going to miss you so much.'

She took a sip of her cocktail and reflected on how lucky she was to have so many people around her that she loved. And somewhere, not too far away from the city, in a luxury, countryside hotel was a man that loved her enough to let her go, and be there for her when she came back.

Chapter Twenty-Nine

Kate smiled as the warm air hit her when she left the plane, following the crowd of travellers to the shuttle bus that would take them to the airport terminal. Sometime later, reunited with her suitcases and adjusting to the difference in temperature, even in the airport, she made her way to the Arrivals lounge, where she saw Marie, waving furiously at her.

'Hello, darling!' Marie ran over to Kate, wrapping her arms around her. 'I'm so excited that you're here!'

'Me too!' Kate said. She had a whole new job, and four months of living in Marie's cute hilltop villa to look forward to.

Marie took one of her suitcases and gestured to the exit. 'I've parked in the pick-up point, so we need to be quick.'

Kate picked up her other bags and followed Marie to her car. They drove through the city, along the palm-tree-lined promenade, and Kate looked at the choppy sea. The beaches were quiet today; the crowds of the summer were still a way off yet.

Before long, they were turning off the main road and up the hill, along the winding lane that led to Marie's villa. Palm trees lined the gravel drive, and a pair of rusted iron gates guarded the entrance to the white stone house. Marie unlocked the heavy wooden door, ushering Kate inside, where their sandals clacked across the tiled floors of the hallway. The white walls were covered in paintings. Potted plants in various shapes and sizes sat along the walls, leading the way to the living room.

'Just put your bags down anywhere, Kate.' Marie kicked off her shoes. 'Would you like a drink?'

'Yes, thank you, that would be great.' Kate took off her sandals and put her suitcase and backpack on the floor in the hall, before following Marie into the kitchen.

'I made us some lemonade,' Marie said, handing her a glass. 'We'd usually have a glass of wine, but I know you've cut down on your drinking and I want to prove that I can too.'

Kate laughed and took the glass. 'Thank you. You don't need to prove anything to me. You're perfect just as you are.'

'Thank you, darling.' Marie took a sip of her lemonade. 'I'm so excited that you're finally here. Lucien can't wait to meet you.'

'I can't wait to meet him,' Kate said. 'He must be something special. You've got that glowy, loved up look on your face.'

'He's a sweetheart,' Marie replied. 'Come on, we'll take these outside.'

Kate followed Marie through the French doors and onto the patio outside. It wasn't really a garden, more of a terrace, with a turquoise-tiled swimming pool, neat pots of plants, and a stunning view. The cloudless sky stretched for miles above them and the houses, which looked like tiny dots in the distance, ran all the way down the hill to the beach.

'God, I've missed this view,' Kate said, sitting down at the table on the patio. 'It's just gorgeous.'

'It's a tiny slice of heaven up here.' Marie sat down next to her. 'I know you're going to be busy working while you're here, but I bet you want to do some fun stuff, too, don't you? Shall we go to Monaco again?'

Kate laughed. 'Can I watch you lose all your money in the casino again?'

Marie shook her head. 'That will not be happening. How's everything back in cold, rainy Canterbury? What have I missed?'

'I honestly don't know where to start.' Kate took a sip of her lemonade before she caught Marie up on the last few weeks.

'Wow,' Marie said. 'That is a lot. How are you doing, darling? Are you alright?'

'I think so. It's been a wild few months.' Kate thought about her fight with Mia, and Alex storming out of her house. 'I've weathered a few storms, but now I've got four months of sunshine ahead of me.'

'You have,' Marie said, 'and I'm here if you want to talk about anything.'

'Thank you, I appreciate that.' Kate smiled. 'It's good to be here.'

She was already missing Alex, but she wouldn't admit that. As promised, he'd sent her a message, but it wasn't mean or unkind. It was sweet and funny, and made her want him more.

'Are you hungry, or did you want to go and get settled in before dinner?' Marie asked.

Kate finished her lemonade. 'I'll go and unpack in a minute, unless you need a hand?'

Marie shook her head. 'I'm good. Your room's all ready for you. Make yourself at home.'

Kate climbed up the stairs with her bags, admiring the tiny alcoves in the stone that held chunky, white pillar candles. She pushed open the door to the guest room and put her cases down on the tiled floor. Just like in the rest of the villa, the stone walls were painted a bright white. One of Amelie's paintings was on the wall above the bed, a portrait of a woman with hair like rays of the sun streaming out above her. Unpacking her suitcases and filling the wardrobe and chest of drawers with her clothes made her feel at home, just as it always did, and she felt a shiver of excitement as she looked out of the window at the winding hill road which led down to the city. It was another home away from home, just as Brighton had been.

As she walked back down the stairs, the front door opened, and a man walked in, looking up, and noticing Kate on the stairs.

'Ah, you must be Kate,' he said, as she walked over to him. 'I'm Lucien.' He kissed her on each cheek, shaking her hand at the same time.

Kate returned the kisses. 'Great to meet you, Lucien, and thank you for offering me this job. I can't wait to get started.'

'You are keen!' he said. 'I like it. What's your French like?'

'Pas mal,' she replied, as they walked into the kitchen. 'It'll get better the longer I'm here. It sort of comes back to me.'

'It is the same for me when I go to England,' he said, his eyes lighting up as he saw Marie. 'Chérie!' He kissed her cheeks. 'It smells wonderful in here.'

'Perfect timing, as always,' Marie replied, returning his kisses. 'Dinner's ready.'

The following morning, Marie drove Kate into the city and walked with her to Lucien's studio. L' Étoile was elegant and judging by the array of eye-wateringly expensive jewellery, his customers were wealthy and discerning. In the South of France, money was no object, it seemed.

Lucien showed her around her new workplace. Instead of a tiny studio at the top of a spiral staircase, this was a large, bright room, with tiled floors and scrubbed pine benches. He showed her the transparent plastic boxes which displayed the precious stones. As she looked around, she had a sinking feeling in the pit of her stomach. Was she out of her depth?

Lucien led her to the benches at the back of the room, and he gestured to a man with thick glasses sitting at one of them. 'Kate, this is Thibault. You will be working with him.'

'Bonjour, Thibault,' Kate said, smiling at him.

Thibault stood, running a hand through his floppy blond hair, and kissed her cheeks. 'Kate, wonderful to meet you.' He looked at Lucien. 'What would you like me to show Kate?'

'Everything,' Lucien said, raising an eyebrow. 'Why don't we start with the new collection?'

'Bien sûr,' Thibault replied. 'Kate, come with me.' He stood up. 'Let me show you what we are working on.'

Lucien followed as they walked down into the shop, where Thibault pulled out a couple of the white velvet pads, talking Kate through their latest range. After this, they returned to the studio, where Kate started to sketch some of her own designs. Her earlier nerves disappeared as Lucien and Thibault nodded approvingly.

Marie appeared at the large glass doors of the studio at six pm to meet Kate and Lucien. They walked along the seafront to a restaurant where the staff clearly knew Lucien well. He was given the best table, which had a view of the promenade, and the fairy lights that twinkled between the palm trees.

'Kate, how was your first day, darling?' Marie asked as they ate.

'The shop is a lot fancier than Correll's,' Kate said, then turned to Lucien. 'You and Thibault have taught me so much already.'

'Ah, well, we have more to show you.' Lucien replied. 'That was only the first day.' He turned to Marie. 'She has her eye on my collection of untreated sapphires. I am excited to see what she will create with them. And how was your day, chérie?'

'Frustrating. We're supposed to open next month and we're at least a month behind schedule. But what can I do?' She took a sip of her wine.

After dinner, Kate took some photos as they walked back along the promenade. The moon's reflection on the sea, the fairy lights strung between the streetlamps, everything was so beautiful. It was an entirely different landscape to the ancient city streets of Canterbury, yet she somehow felt just as at home here.

'We must have an ice cream,' Marie said, jolting Kate out of her revelry. 'Shall we go to Fenocchio?'

'Uh, yes!' Kate said, slipping her arm into Marie's.

Fenocchio's was her favourite ice cream shop in Nice. There were two locations, one near the Cathedral, and one just behind the flower market. With almost a hundred flavours, there was always something new to try, and as well as the usual vanilla and chocolate, there were more unique flavours, lavender, basil, and tomato.

When they reached the scarlet awning, Kate and Marie joined the queue, while Lucien found a table.

Kate opted for the orange blossom ice cream, while her aunt and Lucien had chocolate and pistachio.

She joined Lucien at the table, where she ate her ice cream, and people watched as she tried to follow the fast paced conversation in French that Marie and Lucien were having.

When she got back to the villa, she said goodnight to Marie and Lucien and made her way up the staircase into her room. She had pulled the curtains before she went out, and it was now cool, dark and cosy. She sat on her bed, and sent some photos to Mia. Mia replied with a photo of her and Henry, nestled in her bed together.

> I hope you're having the best time. That ice cream looks so good! Henry sends his love. Mx

Kate smiled and sent a reply

> The ice cream was SO GOOD! You'd love it. Please give both of your babies a kiss from me! Kx

She typed another message, second guessing herself as she did.

> Bonsoir from sunny Nice. The first day has been awesome, and it ended with good food, good wine, and the best ice cream. How are you? I wish you'd sent me something mean so that I didn't miss you. PS what's your favourite ice cream flavour? X

She put the phone on her bed and chewed her lip nervously. Would he respond? He'd told her that he loved her, but she still hadn't forgotten their row, or how close they'd come to tearing their relationship apart.

> Your first day sounds incroyable. I'm glad it's all worked out. I've been thinking of you. I couldn't think of anything mean to say to you, and I miss you. PS mint chocolate chip. You can take me out for an ice cream date when you come back. Ax

That was it. That was all she needed to feel reassured. He still loved her. He still wanted her. And the time apart would only make them want each other more, wouldn't it?

On Saturday morning, at the bakery in the old town, Kate ordered croissants and coffee for her and Marie. They sat down on one of the benches that lined the promenade and opened the paper bags, flaky crumbs of pastry escaping onto their laps.

Through a mouthful of croissant, Marie spoke to Kate. 'We'll pop into the bar after this. It looks a lot different to how you saw it last summer.'

'At least there's no chance of you roping me into working there today,' Kate said with a smirk. A lot of her summers at university had been spent behind the bar with Marie.

'No, but even if it was open, I wouldn't.' Marie took a sip of her coffee. 'You're here to work with Lucien. He made it very clear that I was not to interfere.'

Kate laughed. 'I like him. He's a good mentor. I've learnt a lot already.'

'I'm so glad,' Marie said. 'When I showed your work to Lucien and he said he wanted you to work for him, I selfishly saw it as an opportunity for us to reconnect.'

'That's not selfish,' Kate replied. 'You live in another country, and I don't see you very often. It's a great opportunity for us to reconnect, and I'm so looking forward to spending the summer here.'

Marie nodded. 'I won't steal you from Lucien, and I won't make you work at the bar. I can't ask anyone to work at the bar, because it's not even open!'

'Let's go take a look,' Kate said, finishing her coffee. 'I want to know what you're dealing with.'

'OK, if you're sure.' Marie brushed the crumbs from her dress, and crumpled the paper bag from her croissant. 'Come with me.'

Kate followed Marie through the back streets of the old town to the bar. The ancient, solid wooden door was open, and Kate walked into the dimly lit space. The dark, brick walls made the bar seem smaller than it was, and, in here, it felt cool and dark, a contrast to the bright sunshine outside. The wooden soles of Kate's heels clicked across the floorboards, which were covered in centuries worth of dents and scuffs.

Marc, Marie's bar manager, was standing behind the bar. He came out to greet Marie, kissing her on both cheeks, before turning to Kate, his strong hands gripping her shoulders as he kissed her. 'Ah, bonjour Kate, tu es revenu,' he said, his dark eyes meeting hers.

'Yes, I'm back,' Kate replied. 'I'm working for Lucien for a few months.'

'Tres bien,' he said. 'How was your first week?'

'Amazing,' Kate replied. 'How are things going here?'

Marc let out a long exhale, before running a hand through his dark, almost black hair. 'It is difficult, but we will get there.' He turned to Marie, gesturing to the pile of paperwork on the bar and asking her questions in rapid-fire French that Kate struggled to understand.

'We're just agreeing on the plans for this week,' Marie said to Kate once Marc disappeared behind the counter. 'As you can see, there's still a lot of work to do.'

Kate nodded as she swept her gaze across the room. Behind the bar, the old counter had gone, along with the spirit and liquor bottles. Above their heads, the glass racks had been removed, leaving the stone of the ceiling exposed. 'When are you planning on re-opening?'

Marc and Marie exchanged glances. Marie sighed heavily. 'When we started to replace some of the wiring, we found a whole heap of problems, and it set us right back. We'll be lucky if we open in June.'

'I'll keep my fingers crossed.' Kate looked at the wires dangling out of the wall next to the bar. 'I'm guessing there's more electrical work to be done.'

'Yes, my electrician is coming back next week. He's been amazing, considering what he's had to deal with. He's very willing.' Marie grinned.

Kate smiled back. Clearly, charming electricians was a family trait. 'Is there anything I can help with?'

'Perhaps you could help me go through all of this paperwork?' Marie asked. 'I'm having a hard time of keeping track of everything.'

'Sure.' Kate picked up some of the letters and started to read them. 'I find reading French so much easier than speaking it. You guys speak so fast.'

Marie smiled. 'You get used to it.'

By lunchtime, Kate had helped Marie sort through all the paper-work, and make a schedule for the next few weeks. Marie knew who to contact, and when, and when each contractor should be on site.

Kate's stomach rumbled, and she glanced out of the door. 'Shall we get some socca? It's been way too long.'

Marie put down the notebook she was holding. 'Good idea, let's go.'

Stepping out into the bright sunlight, Kate put on her sunglasses and walked alongside Marie through the narrow streets to Cours Saleya, the market area in Vieux Nice, the old town. Marie greeted the friendly elderly man at the socca stall as he cut them slices, before folding a large paper napkin around each one.

Kate took her slice from Marie. 'Merci.' She she took a bite. 'Oh, wow. I've missed this.'

The hot chickpea flour pancakes were unique to that area, and they reminded her of summers with her aunt.

After they'd eaten, Marie handed Kate one of her canvas shopping bags and they walked through the market. Stall after stall of fresh fruit, vegetables and flowers covered the paved streets. Marie flitted from between the stalls, talking to the vendors, sampling a slice of melon or cheese, a ripe fig, or a freshly baked biscuit.

'Thank you so much for your help today,' Marie said as they walked back to the car. 'I feel a bit more in control of things with the bar now.'

'Ah, you're welcome,' Kate replied. 'It must be so hard trying to work all of this out.'

'It is. That's why I asked for help.' Marie smiled at Kate. 'I get lost in the details.'

'Sometimes I don't pay enough attention to the details.' Kate thought about Alex, who noticed every detail.

She helped Marie load the grocery bags into the car, and, as they drove back to the villa, she closed her eyes and thought about him and the conversation they'd had in his office. The way he'd looked at her, the way he'd held her. She missed him more than she'd let on to anyone, but he was in her dreams, in her mind while she worked, and the last thing she saw before she closed her eyes at night.

Chapter Thirty

June 2013, Nice, Provence-Alpes Côte d'Azur, France

The opening night of the bar arrived, and Kate sat on her bed putting her makeup on. Her phone buzzed, and she picked it up, her breath catching in her throat. It had been three months since she'd last seen Alex, but the notification was from his YouTube channel, and her heart skipped a beat as she clicked on the video, her fingers shaking.

She watched as the camera zoomed in and sucked in a breath. He was wearing a black shirt, covered in fine silver stitches, which, as she studied them, she realised were constellations. The silver bracelet slid back and forth on his wrist as his fingers moved between the dials and the turntables, and as she looked even closer, she noticed he was wearing the cufflinks she'd made for him. When the soaring strings faded, she recognised George's vocals immediately although she had never heard the song before.

The lyrics were beautiful, and spoke of two hearts, one fractured, one guarded, and how they drove two lovers apart until one fixed the other. Her eyes filled with tears and when the song ended she immediately went to find the original song on Future Proof's website. It was being released next week. Right under George's name was Alex's, credited as a song writer. She gasped. There was no doubt that he'd written it about them.

Her fingers shaking, Kate typed out a message.

> That song, YOUR song was the most beauti-
> ful thing I've ever heard. Miss you. Kx

As soon as she'd sent the message, she put her phone down, touched up her eyes, and applied a coat of lipstick. Tonight was about Marie, so she put Alex to the back of her mind. Laughter came from the living room as she walked down the stairs. Amelie had flown over that morning for the opening night, and had spent the day helping in the bar, only coming back with Kate and Marie for an outfit change before they joined the party.

'You two look like twins.' Kate shook her head at Marie and Amelie, who were both wearing long, printed dresses, with their hair piled on top of their heads.

'Are you ready then, Kate?' Marie asked. 'You look gorgeous by the way.'

'Thank you.' Kate smiled, looking down at the dress that Leon had made her. 'So do you. And you, Mama. So glad you could come out.'

'Me too. I've missed you,' Amelie said, squeezing Kate tightly. She looked at Marie. 'And you, of course.'

'Of course.' Marie raised her eyebrow, then looked at her watch. 'If we're all ready, then let's get going. It's party time!'

When they arrived at the bar, Marie assigned everyone tasks. She lined up glass flutes on the expensive granite counters next to the ice buckets with bottles of Champagne, while Amelie filled the racks with glasses. Kate set out the newly upholstered chairs and stools under the tables, before joining Marie and Marc behind the bar. Above her head, large copper lampshades shone a soft, warm light over the bar.

Lucien arrived, looking sharp in a blue linen shirt and dark jeans, and made a beeline for Marie. He kissed her cheek tenderly, before turning to Amelie. 'Ah, this must be your sister.' He kissed Amelie on each cheek. 'Enchanté.'

'Moi aussi.' Amelie kissed Lucien. 'I've heard many good things about you.'

'Pah.' Lucien waved his hand. 'She is the good one,' he said, nodding to Marie. 'Look what she has done with this place.' He picked up a glass of Champagne, handing it to Marie, then handed one to Kate and Amelie. 'We shall celebrate your wonderful sister.' He raised his glass. 'Bonne chance, my love.'

Kate, Marie, and Amelie raised their glasses and Kate spluttered as she took a sip, the bubbles hitting the back of her throat. Once they'd finished their drinks, Kate sprang into action behind the bar with Marc as the place filled with customers. Marie stood at the door, handing out glasses of Champagne, with Amelie by her side.

As the sky outside darkened, Marie took over the bar, and Marc pushed the tables and chairs to the back of the room before turning up the music. He held out his hand to Kate. 'Would you like to dance?' he asked.

'Bien sûr!' Kate replied, taking his hand and following him out to the floor.

As he slid his arm around her waist, her heart didn't pound. And as he told her how beautiful she looked, she didn't get the urge to kiss him, and she knew why. He wasn't Alex. Her chest felt heavy as she thought of him, but she tried to forget about him, holding onto Marc as he expertly twirled her around.

It was almost morning when the taxi dropped Marie, Lucien, Amelie, and Kate back at the villa. The opening night had been a huge success, and as Kate walked up to the villa, her ears were still ringing from the noise, and her throat was sore from talking over it. She left everyone else downstairs and, after a noisy round of hugs and kisses, went to her room.

Flopping down on her bed, she pulled her phone out of her bag, remembering the message she'd sent earlier. There was a reply, and a smile spread across her face as she read it.

> It was for you. An apology was never going to be enough. I miss you too. A x

Kate let out a little squeal of joy. Every day in Nice had been incredible, and there was no way she would have sacrificed this opportunity for Alex, or for anyone else, but she couldn't help missing him and wondering whether they could have repaired their relationship if she had stayed. Two months wasn't very long, but it seemed like an eternity.

The following evening, when Kate returned to the villa, she went out onto the sunny patio to call Mia.

'Happy Birthday, love! Have you had a brilliant day?' she asked.

'The best,' Mia said, her smiling face filling the screen of Kate's phone. 'Thank you for the necklace. It's beautiful. I'm guessing these are our birthstones, right?'

'They are! I'm glad you like it,' Kate replied as Mia showed off the thin silver chain dotted with gemstones.

'I love it.' Mia cleared her throat. 'There's something else that I need to tell you about,' she said, her voice going up an octave.

Kate was intrigued. 'You're not pregnant again are you?'

Mia snorted. 'Uh, no. Pete proposed!' She waved a hand in front of the screen, showing off a pear-shaped, diamond engagement ring.

Kate's heart filled to the brim and she nearly dropped the phone. 'Congratulations! That's amazing news! Tell me everything.'

Mia's voice got higher as she spoke. 'We went to the beach today, and while I was playing with Lilly, he wrote "Will you marry me?" in the sand. He got the ring from your shop. David made it for him.'

Kate squealed. 'Oh, Mia, that's so sweet. He's such a romantic.'

'He's a romantic for sure,' Mia said. 'We've decided we want to get married pretty soon.'

'How soon is soon? Like this year?' Kate asked.

Her head was spinning. Mia was engaged? Tears pricked at her eyes, and she wished she could give Mia a hug.

'Next month.' Mia sped up as she continued. 'We're going to have a small ceremony and a big party afterwards. I know it's a big ask, but could you come back for the weekend?'

'Wow, that's incredible! I mean yes, of course. I'll be there. Count me in. I'm just bummed I won't be there to help you plan it.' A pang of homesickness hit Kate.

'There won't be a whole lot of planning, because...' Mia trailed off. 'Well, we just want something simple. I want you and Lucy with me, though. Will you be my bridesmaid?'

Kate squealed again. 'I would be honoured! I'll do whatever you need me to do, just let me know.' She paused, biting back the lump in her throat. 'Put Pete on the phone.'

'Sure. Hold on.' Mia disappeared from the screen.

Pete's face appeared. 'Hello, long lost sister. How's it going?'

'Congratulations, mate!' Kate grinned. 'So happy for you.'

'Thank you,' Pete said. 'You're gonna come back, right?'

'Of course I am.' Kate narrowed her eyes at the worried expression on Pete's face. 'You look nervous. What's going on?'

Mia reappeared. 'We're having the wedding at Alex's hotel. We want a small, intimate reception and Alex wants to trial a wedding, so we're his guinea pigs. Are you alright with that? I mean you guys are cool, right?'

Kate's mind was racing. The thought of Alex in a suit... he looked so hot in a suit, and she could already imagine herself as the bride walking down the aisle towards him. 'We're cool, and it sounds like a brilliant idea. I'm totally on board.'

'Good. I'll keep you posted. I'm loving your updates, by the way. That beach looks heavenly,' Mia said, raising her eyebrows. 'See you next month. Love you.'

'Love you too,' Kate replied. 'So happy for you guys!'

When she hung up, Kate thought about how much had changed since she had left. Mia was engaged. Lucy had started a new job and moved across Kent with Rachel. Leon was living in London, and Lisa would probably join him. She closed her eyes, thinking about Alex. Would they be able to start over? Or would they hurt each other again?

Chapter Thirty-One

July 2013, Canterbury, Kent, England

A month later, Pete collected Kate from the airport and drove her back to his and Mia's cottage, where Mia flung the door open, and threw herself at Kate. 'Come here! I've missed you so much!'

'I've missed you too,' Kate mumbled, her face squashed in Mia's chest. She escaped from Mia's clutches and followed her into the living room. 'You're getting married tomorrow!'

Mia shrieked in response. 'I know!'

Pete followed Kate in, putting her suitcase on the floor, before turning to Mia. 'Are you sure you're alright with me going to the hotel tonight?'

'Yes,' Mia insisted. Go and help Alex set up. I can manage here.'

He looked down at Lilly, who had wrapped herself around his leg. 'I just feel bad for leaving you on your own with these two.'

'I'm not on my own,' Mia said firmly, picking Lilly up. I've got Kate, and Lucy will be here soon. If I need you, I'll call you.'

'I can be here in ten minutes if you need me.' He bent down to kiss Lilly. 'Have a good time with Mummy and Auntie Kate and Auntie Lucy.' He put his arms around Mia and kissed her cheek. 'The next time I see you, you'll be walking down the aisle.'

'I know.' Mia nodded, her eyes full of tears. 'Love you.'

'Love you too. Have fun guys.' Pete waved to them and shut the door.

Mia sat down on the sofa next to Kate. 'Wow, you look amazing. The South of France clearly suits you.'

'Thanks, love,' Kate replied. 'It does suit me, but I'm so happy to see you. And I've not come empty-handed.' She opened her bag and took out a colouring book, opening it. 'Lilly, this book has some words in French, see? That's a cat, or chat, and that's a dog. In French that's chien.'

'Thant you, Auntie Tate,' Lilly said, sitting down on the floor with it.

Kate handed her a box of crayons before turning to Mia. 'I've got something for you as well, but I'll give it to you later.' She flicked her eyes at Lilly.

'I get you,' Mia said. She was interrupted by a cry from the Moses basket. 'Looks like someone's awake.' She carefully lifted Henry from the basket and settled him into her arms.

.'Hold on, I got something for him too.' Kate pulled a small, brightly coloured butterfly soft toy out of her bag. 'How's this? It's suitable from birth. I checked.'

'Thank you. That's really sweet.' Mia gave the toy to Henry, who held it, and started chewing one of the wings. 'Yep, he likes it.' The doorbell rang, and she laughed. 'It's chaos here.' She looked at Kate. 'Can you take him for a second?'

'Of course.' Kate took Henry from Mia, while she went to answer the door.

'Bonjour!' Lucy said as she walked into the living room, sitting down next to Kate on the sofa. 'You two look cosy.'

'We are,' Kate replied, 'He's changed so much since I last saw him.'

'Same.' Lucy glanced at Henry. 'And I only saw him last month.'

Kate looked up, noticing Mia by the door, watching them with amusement. 'I'll make us a cup of tea. You guys keep an eye on the kids.'

'How's life in la belle France then?' Lucy asked. 'Your photos are giving me serious job envy. I'm so jealous of you being able to just casually go and get an ice cream after dinner.'

'You could do that too,' Kate said. 'They have ice cream parlours in Broadstairs.'

'They do, but it's not the same as wandering down the palm tree lined promenade is it?' Lucy grinned. 'You've caught the sun. Your freckles are to cute,'

Kate laughed. 'They've all sprung up out of nowhere. Can you believe that Mia is getting *married* tomorrow?'

'I know,' Lucy whispered. 'That's wild. I *love* weddings, and I can't wait to see her and Pete get married, I'm going to bawl my eyes out.'

'Me too,' Kate said. 'I can't wait.'

'How do you feel about seeing Alex tomorrow?' Lucy asked.

'I doubt I'll sleep tonight,' Kate admitted. 'It's been so long since I've seen him. He might have forgotten about me. You might have to stop me from throwing myself at him.'

Lucy giggled. 'I'll do my best.'

'Thanks. I mean technically you're my plus one as neither of have partners. How's Rachel getting on India?' Kate asked.

Rachel had gone out there not long after Kate had left for Nice, on a work placement.

'Um, good I think.' Lucy bit her lip. 'I don't hear from her very often, and I don't know whether that's a good thing or not. I worry about her, but she's a doctor, and she isn't great at admitting when things are hard, so I have no idea how it's actually going.'

Kate frowned. 'Are you guys OK?'

Lucy nodded. 'I think so. Long distance relationships are just tricky.'

Once Lilly and Henry were asleep, Mia disappeared, then returned with two dress covers, laying them on the armchair opposite Kate.

'I realise that if these don't fit, we're in trouble, but do you guys want to try on your dresses?'

'Of course.' Kate flew out of her seat and unzipped one of the dress covers.

'Do you like them?' Mia asked.

'Yes, they're gorgeous,' Kate said, running her fingers over the soft, pale blue fabric. 'Can we see yours now?'

Mia shook her head. 'No. Not until the morning. No one's seen my dress, not even my mum.'

'Oh man.' Lucy's face fell. 'Not even a little peek?'

'Nope.' Mia folded her arms. 'No way. Now put your dresses on.'

'She's so bossy,' Lucy huffed, unzipping her dress cover.

The dress fitted Kate perfectly, and she glanced at her reflection in the mirror, admiring the way that the pale blue silk brought out her tan. 'I like it. How about you, Luce?'

'Love it,' Lucy said. 'Great choice, Mia.'

Kate slipped off her dress and hung it back up. 'Now the kids are in bed, I can give you guys your gifts.' She opened her bag and took out two small boxes, handing one to Lucy and one to Mia.

'You went to the biscuit pic and mix shop!' Mia and Lucy said at the same time.

'I did!' Kate replied. 'I'd love to take you guys there one day. It's right on the seafront, and the smell in there is divine.'

'Sounds heavenly.' Mia opened her box. 'Once we've had these, we're having an early night. I know I'm not going to sleep, but I at least need to try.'

'Same,' Kate said, pinching a biscuit from Mia's box.

The following afternoon, Kate held Lilly's hand tightly, while Mia slid her arm into her dad's and Lucy held Henry in her arms. They were in the garden of the hotel, waiting for the go ahead to walk down the aisle.

Around them, strings of bunting hung in the neatly trimmed hedges, and in front of them, wooden slatted chairs were arranged in neat rows, with an aisle in the middle. Kate watched as the seats filled up with Mia and Pete's friends and family. She caught Corinne's eye as she sat down next to Ben, and they exchanged a smile.

'It's time,' Elodie, the photographer, said to Kate, as Pete, Dan, and Alex appeared at the end of the aisle.

Kate struggled to catch her breath. The navy blue of Alex's suit made his hair seem darker, his eyes bluer, and his gaze more intense as he looked out across the seated guests. Her eyes met his and his usual serious expression disappeared, replaced with a tentative smile. She zoned out, picturing him there as she walked towards him in a wedding dress, taking his hand, kissing him.

'Kate? Are you listening? It's time to go! Come on,' Lucy said, nudging Kate.

'I'm so sorry, I drifted off for a second,' Kate replied.

'Can't imagine why,' Lucy whispered, following Kate's gaze. 'Go on, I'm right behind you.'

Kate held Lilly's hand tightly in hers as they walked down the aisle together, the guests smiling at them all the way.

As she reached the end of the aisle, her eyes met Alex's again and she smiled at him, while her heart pounded furiously in her chest. She would have given anything to be able to throw her arms around him. Instead, she nodded politely and took her place on the other side of the aisle. Kate felt her chest swell with happiness as Mia walked towards them with her veil blowing gently in the wind, and her hand clasped tightly in her dad's.

Kate was unable to keep her eyes off Alex as Pete and Mia recited their vows. Tears filled her eyes as they were declared husband and wife, and she noticed Alex discreetly wipe away a tear, making her heart swell. When Pete and Mia walked down the aisle together, Kate gripped Lucy's hand, smiling as Lucy squeezed back just as tightly.

'They did it,' Kate whispered.

'I know,' Lucy whispered back. 'I love them so much.'

Kate allowed herself another sneaky glance at Alex during the photographs. She wished she could have a minute with him alone, but they were separated again as Sam directed the guests into the restaurant. A seating plan, written in swirly gold calligraphy, stood on an easel by the entrance. Long rectangular tables formed neat rows with the wooden chairs from the ceremony tucked underneath them. A tiny jam jar of flowers sat at each place setting, with a thick, cream card name tag attached to the rim. She was sat at the long top table, at the opposite end to Alex. She hadn't been able to talk to him all day, and as she talked to Dan, she grew more envious of Lucy, who was laughing at whatever Alex was saying to her.

When the cups of tea and coffee arrived after the meal, Mia came over to Kate, clutching Henry tightly. 'I need the bathroom.'

'Thanks for letting me know.' Kate laughed. 'You know where it is, don't you?'

'Please get up. I need you to come with me,' Mia hissed.

'Fair enough.' Kate stood up, checking her dress for any escaped food. 'I didn't realise this was a team activity.'

'I bet when you agreed to be a bridesmaid you didn't realise this would be part of your duties, did you?' Mia asked as she let Kate into her and Pete's room.

Kate shrugged. 'It's nothing I've not seen before.'

After she'd helped Mia out of the bathroom, Kate got some crayons and a colouring book and sat on the bed with Lilly while Mia fed Henry.

There was a knock on the door and Mia groaned. 'Can you get it?'

If Pete was surprised to see Kate in his room, he didn't show it. 'Hey, Kate. Are you guys OK?'

'All good,' Mia said. 'Just having a pit stop.'

Kate walked to the door. 'If you two aren't downstairs in half an hour, I'm going to cut the cake myself.'

Pete laughed. 'We'll be down in a minute.'

Kate nodded, and pulled the door shut behind her as she left. As she got to the bottom of the stairs, she bumped straight into Alex. Her heart started pounding as her eyes met his.

'How are you?' he asked.

She took a deep breath. 'I'm good! How are you?'

There was so much she wanted to say, but she was unsure of where they stood. Did she kiss him? Were they friends, or were they more?

'Good.' He smiled, but he seemed nervous. 'I've been meaning to talk to you all day.'

'Oh, same.' She nodded, twirling the bracelet around her wrist to keep her hands busy. 'You look good, by the way. That suit is super hot. I mean, it must be hot out there, in the suit, but it looks good on you too.' She laughed. 'I'm rambling, sorry.'

'Why don't we go somewhere more private?' Alex asked.

'Alex? Can you come and check out the lighting setup?' George asked, appearing behind Alex in the hall.

Alex looked at Kate, and she could see in his eyes that he was torn between staying with her and helping George.

'Go,' Kate said quickly, making the decision for him. 'I'll see you later, Alex.'

They wouldn't be able to talk properly if he knew he was needed somewhere else anyway. She nodded to him, and, despite her high heels, she ran into the garden, sucking the summer air into her lungs, heart pounding. *Well done*, she thought to herself. You didn't throw yourself at him. She sat down in the grass and took off her heels, smiling as she saw Sarah walking over to her.

'Looking gorgeous, as usual,' Sarah said as she sat down next to Kate. 'How are you? How's France?'

'I'm loving it,' Kate replied. She assumed that Alex wouldn't have told Sarah what had happened between him and Kate, and didn't want to reveal anything to her that she didn't already know. 'The weather is gorgeous, the studio is incredible, and my aunt is so much fun. I cant believe I only have a month left. It's gone so quickly. How are you?'

'Very good.' Sarah smiled. 'The warmer weather has sped up my recovery, but Alex still watches me like a hawk. I had a week down in Cornwall with Ben and Corinne last month, and that was wonderful. Oliver has grown so much.'

Kate was just about to reply when Amelie walked over to her. She'd forgotten that her mum and James had been invited to the evening reception, as she'd been so distracted by Alex.

'Hello, darling!'

Kate stood up and gave her mum a hug. 'Hey! I didn't see you arrive.'

'We sneaked in,' Amelie said. 'I was hoping to see the bride and groom, but they're busy.'

'Mama, this is Alex's mum, Sarah,' Kate said as Sarah stood up to greet her. 'Sarah, this is my mum, Amelie.'

'You two look so alike!' Sarah said. 'Welcome to Woodlands, Amelie. It's good to meet you.'

'Lovely to meet you, Sarah. If I were to get married again, I'd want to get married here. It's so beautiful,' Amelie gushed.

'Thank you,' Sarah said. I don't know if we would even be doing weddings if Kate hadn't introduced us to Sophia.' She smiled warmly at Kate. 'I'm very grateful to you darling, and Sophia, of course.'

'Kate loves to help,' Amelie replied. 'But then, so does Alex...' she trailed off. 'He's very caring, isn't he? He's always looking out for people.'

'He is. I've managed to persuade him to take a step back now we have Sam here, but he always finds another job to do.' Sarah checked her watch. 'I'm sorry, but it's almost cake cutting time, so I'd better go. I'll see you later, Kate, and Amelie, I'm happy to show you around anytime.'

'Thank you, Sarah,' Amelie said. 'I'd like that.'

As Sarah walked away, Amelie turned to Kate. 'Well that's food for thought, isn't it?' She raised her eyebrow. 'How are you, darling? Doesn't Mia look beautiful? What was the ceremony like? Did you cry?'

'That's a a lot of questions,' Kate said. 'I'm fine. Mia is gorgeous, the ceremony was perfect, and yes I did cry. Anything else you want to know?'

'Have you spoken to Alex?' Amelie asked.

'We got interrupted,' Kate whispered, 'but I'm not leaving until I speak to him.'

'Decisive. I like it.' Amelie raised her eyebrow. 'I saw him when I arrived. He looks smoking hot today, doesn't he?'

Kate shook her head and glanced at Amelie's glass. 'How many of them have you had? Yes, he is smoking hot but I still don't know whether that ship has sailed or not.'

'I reckon he'd let you on board.' Amelie snorted with laughter.

Kate shook her head and stood up. 'Let's go see this cake being cut, shall we?'

Kate sat with Lucy at the bar after Mia and Pete had cut their cake, which was a tower of Victoria sponges topped with summer berries. When Sam and Stefan appeared with slices of the cake on tiny plates, Kate and Lucy had helped themselves and, having found seats at the bar, clinked their glasses together.

Kate picked up her fork, taking a bite of her cake and letting out a moan of pleasure. 'This is heavenly.' She looked up, her eyes meeting Alex's from across the room, and she blushed.

'Lucy,' she whispered. 'If I don't get some time alone with him tonight, I think I'm going to explode.'

Lucy took a sip of her drink. 'I get you. He looks ridiculously good in that suit. Have you spoken to him at all today?'

'Sort of,' Kate said through a mouthful. 'We got interrupted.'

'Oooh, to be continued. I like it.' Lucy took a mouthful of her cake. 'I agree. Heavenly.'

Kate had just finished her cake when Corinne walked over to them. 'Hello, stranger, how are you?'

'Très bien.' Kate grinned at her. 'Et toi?'

'Moi aussi.' Corinne replied with a heavy French accent, making Kate laugh.

'This is Lucy, one of Mia's friends,' Kate said to Corinne. 'Lucy, this is Ben's wife, Corinne.'

'Lovely to meet you.' Lucy put down her empty plate, and wiped her mouth with a napkin.

'Same. I feel kind of bad being here, I haven't even met Mia before.' Corinne looked at Kate. 'You're one of the only people I know here.'

'Don't feel bad, think of it as a chance to get to know everyone,' Kate said. 'They're all super friendly, and you can hang with if you like?'

'Thank you. Are you having a good time in France?' Corinne asked.

Kate wasn't sure what Alex had told Ben, but she assumed from Corinne's friendly greeting that it wasn't the whole truth.

'It's been great,' Kate said. 'Lucien' studio is a little more upmarket than Corrells so I've been working with some expensive stones, and having the beach on my doorstep is amazing. I can go for a swim at lunchtime if I want, or go for a walk when I finish work.'

Corinne smiled. 'Sounds dreamy. Will you want to come back?'

'Of course!' Kate put her plate down. 'My life is here. France is just a fun working holiday.'

'It sounds like it. Are you missing Alex?'

Kate bit her lip. Alex hadn't told Corinne or Ben the truth, which she felt immensely grateful for. 'I am, yes, but I'm back next month.'

'Amazing! You'll havet to come to Cornwall,' Corinne said.

Before Kate could reply, the lights dimmed, and George appeared on the makeshift stage at the back of the bar.

'We've never done a wedding, but for these guys, we couldn't say no.' Cheers rang out across the bar. 'For their first dance as husband and wife, please welcome Mr. and Mrs. Patterson.'

Pete led Mia to the dancefloor and twirled her around, the sparkles in her dress catching the lights above them.

Kate rested her head on Lucy's shoulder. 'Aren't they gorgeous?'

'The most,' Lucy agreed. 'I've spent the whole day wanting to burst into tears.'

When the song finished, George called for the rest of the guests to join Pete and Mia on the dancefloor.

Ben took Corinne's hand, and she blew Kate a kiss as she walked away.

'Guess it's just you and me, then. Want a dance?' Kate asked Lucy.

Lucy smiled. 'Of course I do.'

As Kate danced with Lucy, she started to relax for the first time that day. Mia was married. Her duties as bridesmaid were over, and she was surrounded by her friends and family, in a stunning hotel. There was just one thing missing. Alex.

A while later, Kate put her arm around Mia, who had a sleepy Henry tucked into her shoulder.

'How are you doing, Mrs Patterson?' Kate asked. 'I'm so happy for you guys.'

'Thank you.' Mia smiled, her eyes shining with tears. 'Today's felt like a dream and I don't want to wake up.'

'You don't have to,' Kate said. 'This dream is real. You're married, with two beautiful kids.' She smiled at Henry, who was somehow fast asleep, despite the noise and the lights.

'Im very lucky,' Mia replied. 'And lucky to have you two.'

Lucy kissed her cheek. 'We love you too. And we'll share you with Pete as long as he knows you were ours first.'

Pete appeared behind her. 'I'm well aware of that, but tonight, she's all mine.'

Mia took his hand. 'I am, but remember, my parents are currently in our room looking after Lilly. And we still have to hope we can get Henry settled in the travel cot.' She laughed. 'Why did we decide to do this with two kids under three?'

'Because I didn't want to wait any longer to call you my wife,' he said.

Kate pressed her hands to to her chest. 'You two are too sweet. I'm gonna cry again.'

Lucy's eyes filled with tears. 'Too late! Get out of here, you two!'

'Breakfast is from eight til ten,' Kate said. 'Is it safe to come knock on your door if you haven't surfaced by then?'

Mia laughed. 'We have two kids, Kate. We'll be up by six am. It's you two who won't be up on time.'

'Good point.' Lucy laughed. 'We'll carry on the party for you.'

Mia blew them both a kiss, then left the room, hand in hand with Pete.

Kate held out her hand to Lucy. 'One more dance?'

'Of course.' Lucy took her hand and they walked back to the dance-floor.

'Guys, this is our last song tonight. If you know it, sing along. If you don't, just come and dance,' George said and picked up his guitar.

Goosebumps spread over Kate's body as "Shattered Hearts," the song that Alex had written, started playing.

'Smoke show at ten o'clock,' Lucy whispered to Kate.

Walking towards them in the darkness was Alex. His suit jacket had come off, the tie had disappeared, and the first couple of buttons of his shirt were undone. His shirt sleeves were rolled up, and the silver bracelet gleamed in the light as he silently held his hand out to Kate. A shiver of anticipation ran through her body as she gave him her hand. She breathed in, afraid to move, afraid he would let go of her, even as they walked on the dance floor. He pressed his body against hers as the band played on behind them.

'Alex,' she said, 'this song is...I've never heard anything like it. I love it.'

'I meant what I said. It was for you.'

She dared to meet his gaze, knowing that the look in his eyes would tell her what the next play was. They were dark, the pupils dilated, the icy blue gone. She leant forwards, almost the same height as him in her heels. His lips brushed against her cheek and over to her lips. It was a ghost of a kiss, one that held so many memories, yet seemed untraceable.

When the song finished, she didn't want to let him go. There was so much that she wanted to say, but a crowded dancefloor wasn't the right place to talk.

'Come to my room?' he whispered in her ear.

She glanced up at him and nodded. 'When?'

'Give me half an hour.' He kissed her cheek, then walked away from her.

Kate walked, dazed over to Lucy as the dancefloor emptied.

'Kate!' Lucy's eyebrows had disappeared into her fringe. 'You're gonna kiss him like that and just let him *walk away from you?*'

'He asked me to go to his room,' Kate said. 'I've spent the whole day wanting *this* moment and now it's here, I dont know what to do!'

'Go to his room!' Lucy hissed.

'Come with me, I need to get ready.' Kate linked her arm with Lucy's and ushered her out of the bar.

When she reached the room that she and Lucy were sharing, she unlocked the door and kicked off her shoes.

'OK, what do you need?' Lucy asked.

'Hair, make-up, everything!' Kate said, hurtling into the bathroom and cleaning her teeth. Checking her reflection, she went back into the bedroom and grabbed her make-up bag. She sat down at the dressing table and applied a fresh coat of mascara, then a slick of lipstick.

Lucy brushed Kate's hair, then ran her styling wand through it, creating loose curls that flowed over her shoulders.

Once Lucy was finished with her hair, Kate packed her make-up away. 'You don't mind me bailing on you?' she asked Lucy.

Lucy shook her head. 'No, of course not. I'll be asleep in about three minutes.'

Kate put her heels back on. 'Wish me luck.'

'You don't need luck. Fate's on your side.' Lucy kissed her cheek, then smacked her ass. 'Go get him, tiger!'

'Great pep talk!' Kate laughed. 'Short and to to the point, I like it.' She opened the door of their room. 'See you later.'

She closed the door behind her and took a deep breath. Did he still want her? Did he still love her? Was he going to break her heart? She had no idea, but she walked along the corridor to his room, and stopped outside, knocking on the door.

Alex opened the door, and her heart leapt into her throat. Tiny droplets of water clung to his bare chest. A towel was wrapped around his waist, and his dark hair was damp and tousled.

She stood still, unable to move or speak.

'Kate?' A smile pulled at the corner of his lips. 'Are you coming in?'

'Yes.' It was the only word she could get out, and it was the only thing she wanted to say to whatever he asked her.

She stepped into his room and he closed the door behind her.

'You're early,' he said. 'I was just taking a shower.'

'Looks like I'm right on time.' She ran her eyes over him, then moved closer, putting her arms around his neck. 'Now that I'm here, what are you going to do with me?'

'Whatever you want me to do,' he said, then kissed her with a ferocity that made her knees weak, before pulling away from her, his eyes searching hers.

'We should probably talk,' she murmured as his lips moved to her neck.

'Do you want to talk?' he asked.

'No. I just want you.' She paused. 'I need you.'

He nodded. 'I need you too. We can talk tomorrow.'

He bent down and scooped her up, carrying her to the bed.

Chapter Thirty-Two

July 2013, Canterbury, Kent, England

The sun streamed through Alex's window the next morning, waking Kate up. She was still nestled under Alex's arm, and he kissed her forehead, pulling her closer to him. She looked up into his eyes. 'Last night was incredible, but before I leave, we have to talk.'

'I know,' Alex said, and kissed her cheek, before propping himself up on one elbow. 'Before we do, I need to know, are you definitely coming back next month?'

'She nodded. 'I am. Nice is beautiful, and I love my job there, but this is my home.' She took a deep breath. 'And this is where you are.'

A smile spread across his face. 'That's all I needed to hear. I'm really sorry about...everything. I wasn't open with you, and I held my own hurt against you. I won't do that again.'

'You were trying to protect yourself.' She smoothed a hand over his chest, feeling his heart beating underneath her fingers.

'I want to protect you too.' He picked up her hand and kissed it. 'I want to protect *us*.'

'I like the sound of that,' she said softly. 'We need to leave the ghosts of our past where they belong. In the past.'

'So poetic.' He smiled. 'When do you go back to France?'

'Tonight,' she said, 'so this is goodbye until next month.'

'Next month?' He brushed her hair away from her face. 'That feels like forever.'

'You could come to Nice?' she suggested. 'Sun, sea, and the best ice-cream you'll ever eat.'

'Maybe,' he said. 'If it's as good as it looks in your photos, I'd love it.'

'It's even better,' she replied. 'When was the last time you took a holiday?'

His brow creased. 'I can't remember.'

'Then you definitely need a holiday.' She smiled.

He looked thoughtful. 'I guess I could...'

'You should!' she exclaimed.

'Leave it with me.' He glanced at his watch. 'Aren't we supposed to be meeting everyone for breakfast?'

'Oh shit.' She picked up her phone. 'Agh, it's nearly nine am.'

'Then we better get up.' He climbed out of the bed, and she admired his naked body, bathed in a golden glow from the sun streaming through the window.

She got up too, pulled on her dress, and picked up her heels. 'I'll see you downstairs.' Blowing him a kiss, she let herself out of his room.

After a quick shower and a change of clothes, Kate made her way downstairs, aware that her hair was slightly wild and her cheeks were still flushed. There was a long table set up in the restaurant, and most of the seats were full, but there was one free next to Lucy, which Kate slid into.

'You made it,' Lucy whispered. 'I didn't think you would.'

Kate smiled. 'It was a very quick shower, *without* Alex.' She waved at Mia and Pete who were at the other end of the long table. 'He's not here yet?'

'No. I figured you were both together.' Lucy nudged Kate. 'Here he is.'

Alex walked in and scanned the room, smiling as his eyes landed on Kate. He sat down next to Dan and poured himself a coffee.

Kate held his gaze for a second, then turned her attention to the vast spread of pastries, fruit and toast. 'Luce, you need to try one of these croissants, they are so good.' She picked one up and tore it apart, then slathered it in jam.

'I've already had one and I'm considering a second,' Lucy said, eyeing up the plate of croissants.

After breakfast, Mia and Pete's families left, then Mia sat down next to Kate and Lucy.

'Hey, guys. We're off on our honeymoon.' She smiled. 'When we're all back in this country, we need to meet up.'

Kate nodded. 'We're going to have *so* much to catch up on!'

'Did you speak to Alex yesterday?' Mia asked. 'If you don't want to tell me, you don't have to, but I saw you dancing with each other, and...' She paused. 'I love you both, and I just want you to be happy - whatever that looks like.'

'We talked,' Kate said. 'That's all I want to say for now.'

'And I respect that,' Mia replied.

Kate hugged her, then Pete, then she and Lucy waved them off as they left to travel to the Lake District for their honeymoon.

Alex had disappeared, so Kate went back to her room with Lucy and packed her bag.

'Are you ready, love?' Kate asked. 'I'm going back to my house before I go to the airport. You want to come?'

'No, I better go and see my parents,' Lucy said. 'Can you drop me over there?'

'Sure,' Kate replied, picking up her bag.

As they walked through the bar, Kate's eyes locked on Alex's, and her breath caught in her throat as she thought about last night.

'Kate,' Lucy whispered. 'If you want to talk to Alex, I'll wait for you in the car.'

'Thank you,' Kate whispered back, slipping her the car keys. 'I'll be there in a minute.' She walked over to the bar, where Alex was stacking glasses in the racks above his his head. 'Hey.'

'Hey.' Alex smiled at her. 'I should say au revoir, right?'

'No.' She shook her head. 'It's not goodbye, it's see you later, or à bientôt.'

He came round to the front of the counter. 'That sounds way better.'

She kissed his cheek. 'Last night was amazing. I can't wait for more.'

'Me neither, but I hope your last weeks in France are everything you want them to be.' He tipped her chin up so she was looking into his eyes and kissed her. 'I love you, Kate.'

'I love you, too.' She smiled. 'Now say something mean so that I don't miss you.'

'What happened to your hair this morning? It looks like you rolled out of bed and just hoped for the best,' he said, smirking.

'Brilliant.' She laughed. 'And whose bed did I roll out of?'

'Mine, and when I get into it tonight, I'll be imagining that you're still there.' He kissed her cheek. 'Can I take you to the airport?'

She shook her head. 'No, that would be way too painful. I hate airport goodbyes. I'll let you know when I'm back in Nice.' She picked up her bag, blew him a kiss and walked out of the bar, feeling a thousand times happier than the last time she had walked out of there.

When Kate returned home, Amelie was stretched out on a sun lounger in the garden, floppy hat and sunglasses on, sipping a drink. James was holding a pair of shears and carefully cutting one of the hedges. Amelie sat up as Kate walked into the garden. 'Morning, darling. Come and have a lounger.'

'Are you forcing him to do this? Kate asked, gesturing to James.

Amelie rolled her eyes. 'No, darling, he came straight out here this morning to get started on it.' She shrugged.

'Fair enough.' Kate pulled up one of the wooden sun loungers, topped with striped white and yellow cushions. James and his shears moved further along the garden.

'How was it this morning? Lots of sore heads?' Amelie giggled.

'Not really,' Kate replied. 'We had a lush breakfast, and the newly-weds have gone on their honeymoon.' She lowered her voice. 'Were you serious yesterday about marrying James?'

'I could be,' Amelie said. 'But I think we'll start off slowly. I'd like him to move in here with me. We're always flitting between one house and the other. How do you feel about it?'

'I love it,' Kate replied, sitting up. 'You guys are so cute together, and I'll be happier knowing you aren't here on your own. I'm so happy for you both.'

'I knew you'd approve.' Amelie nodded, a huge smile creeping across her face.

'What about Rob?' Kate lay back down on her sun lounger and slid her sunglasses on.

'He's all for it.' Amelie smiled, adjusting her floppy hat. 'I realised how much I relied on him when he was here, and that wasn't fair. Both of you deserve your own lives.' She looked intently at Kate. 'How do you feel about coming home?'

'So excited.' A shiver of joy ran down Kate's spine at the thought of coming back. 'I want to look for my own place when I come back. It's about time, especially if you two lovebirds are going to be holed up here.'

Amelie looked thoughtful. 'You could always rent James's cottage. I'll mention it to him later on.' She raised an eyebrow at Kate. 'I saw you dancing with Alex. Did you two clear the air?'

'We talked,' Kate replied. For once, she wasn't going into details.

'Good.' Amelie nodded. 'He was so nervous about seeing you again, darling.'

'How would you know that he was nervous?' Kate narrowed her eyes.

Amelie's face scrunched up under her sunglasses. 'Ah. He didn't tell you? Whoops.' She winced. 'He came over about a week after you'd gone.'

'Why?' Kate asked, puzzled.

'He was concerned about me being here on my own, with no form of security system, so he installed one.' Amelie gestured to the discreet silver cameras on the wall.

Kate beamed. 'He's the best, isn't he?'

This was one of the many reasons she loved him. He wasn't just looking out for her, he was looking out for her family too, and her heart ached for him, even though she hadn't even left yet.

Kate glanced from the cameras to the window frames, which were considerably shinier than when she'd left. 'Mama, are they new windows?'

Amelie nodded. 'I finally braved the blue room and the white-sheet-covered things, with Alex's help. He helped me redecorate it, and he took one of the paintings to one of his clients, who's an art dealer. Turns out it was pretty valuable. So valuable, we have new windows.'

Kate blinked back tears. 'I can't believe he did that.'

'He told me that the blue room was where he realised that he loved you, so it had a special place in his heart.' Amelie smiled. 'I don't want to pry, but I'm guessing it's not over between you two?'

'It's not,' Kate said, 'but I don't know what it is right now, and I'm OK with that.'

'Then I'm happy. You don't have to tell me anything, but the smile on your face says it all.' Amelie paused. 'When I saw the two of you dancing last night I had a feeling that everything was going to be just fine.'

'I have the same feeling.' Kate smiled.

Later that night, Kate arrived back in Nice. The moon streaked across the sea in the darkness as Lucien drove her back to the villa, where she fell into her bed. The following morning, she joined Marie and Lucien on the patio overlooking the sea for an alfresco breakfast of fresh croissants.

'Tell me everything,' Marie said. 'I need details, photos, everything.' She took a sip of her coffee.

Kate filled Marie in on the wedding, then pulled out her phone, showing her the photos she'd taken, finishing with one of her and Alex on the dancefloor together.

Marie put her hand on Kate's arm. 'I'm guessing that's Alex. It couldn't possibly be anyone else.'

Lucien looked at the smile on Kate's face. 'That is the look of love, mais non?'

'Ah oui, c'est vrai,' Kate replied. 'We had the most incredible evening together.' A smile crept across her face.

'And you still came back here?' Marie asked, raising her eyebrow.

'Bien sûr!' Kate said. 'I've still got a job to do here. And he understands that, which is one of the reasons I love him.'

'You're a strong woman,' Marie replied, the rings on her fingers clinking on her coffee cup. 'Hearing how you've left things with him makes me think about one of my favourite phrases. What is meant for you will not pass you by.'

'I think he's meant for me, Marie.' Kate smiled. 'Actually, I'm sure he is.'

Chapter Thirty-Three

August 2013, Nice, Provence-Alpes Maritime, France

Kate's last day at L' Étoile was marked with a leisurely lunch in a restaurant with a view of the sea. Thibault and Lucien conversed in French and English, with Kate following along, switching between the two languages effortlessly now. After they'd eaten, Kate returned to the villa and sunbathed for the afternoon in an empty house.

Marie had instructed her to come to the bar at eight pm. They'd held enough events over the summer for Kate to know that Marie was likely to throw her an unforgettable going away party, and she closed her eyes, letting the rays of the sun sweep over her. She had one more week left in France and she planned to spend it travelling across the Côte d'Azur by train. In just a week, she would be swapping her view of the beach for one of the cathedral spires in Canterbury.

Over the last four months, she had learnt so much from Lucien and Thibault, skills she was ready to take to her new, permanent job at Correll's. James had agreed to let her rent his cottage, and she imagined setting up her own little home. She thought about Alex and smiled to herself. He was always worth waiting for, and she was excited about what lay in store for them both.

At eight pm, Kate's taxi dropped her on the seafront and she walked to the bar, the breeze blowing her hair out behind her like a sail. When she arrived, the doors were open and there was a crowd of people outside drinking, smoking, and talking to each other. She recognised some of the vendors from the market and exchanged kisses with them. Music was coming from inside the bar, dreamy, beachy house music, and she pushed her way through the crowd of people into the humming space.

Marie gave her a tight hug. 'Now the party can really start.'

'Wow, this place is packed.' Kate looked around the room. 'You did all of this for me?'

'You've worked so hard this summer. And not just for Lucien, but for me as well. Tonight is just a little thank you.' Marie nodded towards the back of the bar. 'I've got you a leaving gift.'

Kate frowned, looking at the DJ decks, then gasped. Although the bar was dimly lit, she knew instantly who was standing behind them.

As his hands moved across the dials, a flash of silver caught her eye. She walked over to him, her legs feeling like jelly, as he slid off his headphones.

'Alex?' she exclaimed. 'You're here!' She slipped behind the decks and put her arms around him.

He kissed her cheek. 'I'm here. You said I should come so...'

She hadn't thought that he actually would though. And she hadn't mentioned it again over the last couple of weeks in the many messages and phone calls they'd exchanged.

'You always keep your promises.' She smiled. 'How did you know about the party, and how did you get here though?'

'I spoke to your mum after the wedding,' he said. 'She put me in touch with Marie, and she told me about tonight. I know you've got a week left here, and I wondered if you wanted to spend it with me?'

'I would love that!' she replied excitedly. 'I can't wait to show you around.'

'I've never been here before, so you'll have to show me *everything.*' He raised his eyebrow.

'I can definitely do that.' She looked across the bar at the packed dancefloor. 'I should probably go and say hello to some people. Is that alright?'

He nodded. 'Of course. It's your party, and I'm not going anywhere. Go mingle. Do your thing. I've got a surprise for you later.'

'Intriguing. I'll see you later.' She walked over to the bar, and cocked an eyebrow as Marc handed her a glass. 'What's this?'

'Kir Royale. Champagne and cassis,' he said. 'Try it.'

She took a sip. 'Oh, this is good. Why haven't I had this before?'

Marc shrugged. 'Je ne sais pas. It is good, no?'

'Delicious. Thank you.' She took her drink and worked her way through the crowd, kissing and hugging customers from L 'Étoile, some of the workmen who had put the bar back together, and Marie's electrician, before returning to the bar and taking a stool next to Lucien.

'Are you enjoying the party?' Lucien asked, before nodding at Alex. 'And did you like your gift?'

'Of course.' Kate smiled. 'Best present ever! I'm so happy he's here.'

'I can see,' Lucien said. 'You know your aunt, she has a lot of wild ideas, but her heart is very much in the right place.'

'I'm glad you two found each other. You suit each other,' Kate replied.

'Thank you. She is a wonderful, strong woman. Like you.' He looked at her intently. 'I know you have your job to return to, but if you ever find yourself in France again, there would be a job for you.'

She was touched by the offer, even though she couldn't accept it . 'That's so kind of you. I love it here, and I will always come back to visit, but I belong in Canterbury.'

'I understand you completely. I could not leave this place.' His eyes crinkled as he spoke. 'I am fortunate that Marie feels the same way.'

'How do I feel?' Marie asked, appearing beside them and leaning on Lucien's shoulder.

'You love this place as much as I do. This is your home,' Lucien said.

'I couldn't live anywhere else.' Marie turned to Kate. 'I've loved having you here, darling, and I'll make more of an effort to come back to see you.'

'You should,' Kate said. 'You and Mama are getting on much better now. It won't be anywhere near as awkward as it used to be.'

Marie burst out laughing. 'We were so horrible to each other. Just like when we were kids. Oh dear.' She wiped her eyes. 'I love her more than anything, you know that?'

'I know.' Kate slid her empty glass to Marc as he walked past. 'She loves you just as much.'

'Let's get on that dancefloor, darling. Come on.' Marie held out her hand, leading her into the middle of the dance floor.

At ten pm, Marc rang a bell and everyone started leaving, showering Kate with kisses as they went. Everyone pitched in to clear up the empty bar, and Kate turned to Marie, puzzled as she pulled a set of keys out of her pocket. 'What's going on?'

'You'll see,' Marie said. 'Come on Marc, time to go.'

Marc kissed Kate on both cheeks. 'À bientôt, my friend. It has been an absolute pleasure.'

'Same,' Kate replied. 'À bientôt.'

Marc walked out of the bar, a cigarette ready in his hand.

'We'll see you later on,' Marie said. 'All you need to do is lock up.' She slipped her arm into Lucien's and they walked out of the door.

Kate turned around, still puzzled. In the darkness, she could see Alex, with his head buried in his record boxes. She walked over to the decks. 'Alex, what's going on?'

'I promised you a private performance didn't I?' He stood up, holding a handful of records. 'I always keep my promises. You know that.'

She smiled. 'It's a long way to come for a promise.'

'You're worth it,' he said. 'I'll always keep my promises.'

'So will I.' She sank into his arms as he kissed her.

In the darkened bar, Alex played Kate song after song. The last track he played was one of his own remixes, a slowed-down, bass-heavy version of Future Proof's "Shattered Hearts". He led her onto the empty dance floor, where they held each other until the end of the song.

Acknowledgements

There's a huge amount of people to thank for bringing this book to life. To my incredible editor Melanie Scott, I am so glad we 'met'. You not only steered the story to shore, when it was lost at sea, but you love it (and Alex) as much as I do, so thank you.

My wonderful critique partners, you are the best! Gen, you are the queen of body language and comma splices. I promise to always add in a rough, gravelly voice just for you. Cherry, you are the kindest, most chilled out person and you've helped me to become a better, bolder writer. Hannah, your guidance, and knowledge has been invaluable, and in you, I've learnt that my 'unique' little brain is not so unique at all. Thank you to Stefanie, and Kate for being the proofreaders I didn't know I needed. I love you AND your awesome books.

Thanks to my amazing beta readers, whose hilarious and sweet comments kept me going through the hardest parts. Special mentions to Ash, Monika, Juli, and Katie, for going above and beyond.

I'm so grateful to every member of the "Smuttering," a group of female writers, who have taught me more about writing, life, and myself than I could have ever imagined. The writing community is incredibly supportive, and I'm cheering for every one of you!

Massive thanks go to my amazing parents, who have always told me I could do whatever I put my mind to, and to my unofficial sister Claire, who always has my back.

Lastly, but most importantly, thank you to my awesome husband (my very own dark and mysterious DJ), who has allowed me the time and headspace to make my dreams come true. You and our son both inspire me to be a better person.

About the author

Laura Elise Bishop is a romance novelist from South East England, where she lives with her husband and son. She was the kid in the corner with a book for most of her childhood and she's been writing ever since.

Her favourite place is the beach and her hobbies are sea swimming, baking, embroidery and watching romantic comedies.

Also by

The Ivy House is the first part of the Wilder Hearts Series.

If you enjoyed this, you might like the other books in this series, which are available now

Incomplete Strangers (Book Two)

On the surface, Molly seems to have the perfect life. She's got a dream job, great friends and a sister who adores her. Deep down, she's afraid, and lonely. Taking care of everyone else ensures she doesn't have to think too closely about what's missing from her life and the secret she's keeping - that the smile that she exchanges with a handsome stranger on the train is the best part of her day.

After landing his dream job, Chris is adjusting to moving back to the city he grew up in, and a long commute. He's always been the one that people turn to, but when he finds the fast pace of his job and city life hard, he struggles to open up. He finds solace in the smile of the beautiful blonde woman on his train, but he can't seem to work up the courage to talk to her.

After a traumatic incident, Molly's return to the commute is disrupted when the train is plunged into darkness. It isn't the armrest she grips in fear though; it's the arm of the handsome stranger next to her.

An Alpine Proposal (Book Three)

Caro Brown's life is chaotic. As an ex-West End actress with a famous family, dealing with paparazzi, fake friends and endless parties is par for the course. All that glitters isn't gold though. Her friends are never there for her, her dates are selling stories, and she can't stop thinking about the man she stormed out on a year ago.

Jeremy Hawksworth has spent the last year trying to put his life back together after his relationship with Caro went down in flames. While she parties with the Mayfair set, he keeps himself out of the limelight, throwing himself into his work.

When Caro loses her beloved grandfather, she's shocked to discover he left her his Alpine chalet in his will. However, it comes with a caveat, one that forces her to rethink her lifestyle. When her path crosses with Jeremy again, it sets of a chain of events that makes him question everything he's ever known.

Buried Treasure (Book Four)

Cora Trevellyn is on a high from her first book tour when the woman who unknowingly slept with her husband turns up at her door. Leaving him, Cora flees London for Cornwall, to find solace in the town she grew up in. It's not plain sailing though. The only man she has ever truly loved is there, and there's stormy waters between them.

Jake Curnow is speechless when the red haired siren he has never stopped loving walks into his pub. Their relationship had always been secret, because of a mysterious centuries long feud between their families, but Cora is determined to find out what caused it, and she's taking Jake along for the ride.

When their feelings for each other resurface, is their love for each other strong enough to withstand the storm ahead of them? Or will it sink like the treasure they're seeking?

www.ingramcontent.com/pod-product-compliance
Lightning Source LLC
Chambersburg PA
CBHW071555030726
47593CB00001BA/170